Highest Praise for
JOHN LUTZ

1/15

Mister X

"*Mister X* has everything: a dangerous killer, a pulse-pounding mystery, a shocking solution, and an ending that will resonate with the reader long after the final sentence is read."
—*BookReporter.com*

"A page-turner to the nail-biting end . . . twisty, creepy whodunit."
—*Publishers Weekly* (starred review)

Urge to Kill

"A solid and compelling winner . . . sharp characterization, compelling dialogue and graphic depictions of evil. . . . Lutz knows how to keep the pages turning."
—*BookReporter.com*

Night Kills

"Lutz's skill will keep you glued to this thick thriller."
—*St. Louis Post-Dispatch*

"Superb suspense . . . the kind of book that makes you check to see if all the doors and windows are locked."
—*Affaire de Coeur*

In for the Kill

"Brilliant . . . a very scary and suspenseful read."
—*Booklist*

"Shamus and Edgar award–winner Lutz gives us further proof of his enormous talent. . . . An enthralling page-turner."
—*Publishers Weekly*

ALSO BY JOHN LUTZ

Mister X

Urge to Kill

Night Kills

In for the Kill

Chill of Night

Fear the Night

Darker Than Night

Night Victims

The Night Watcher

The Night Caller

Final Seconds (with David August)

The Ex

featuring Frank Quinn

Available from Kensington Publishing Corp. and
Pinnacle Books

FEAR THE NIGHT

JOHN LUTZ

PINNACLE BOOKS
Kensington Publishing Corp.
www.kensingtonbooks.com

PINNACLE BOOKS are published by

Kensington Publishing Corp.
119 West 40th Street
New York, NY 10018

All Kensington Titles, Imprints, and Distributed Lines are
available at special quantity discounts for bulk purchases for
sales promotions, premiums, fund-raising, and educational
or institutional use. Special book excerpts or customized
printings can also be created to fit specific needs. For details,
write or phone the office of the Kensington special sales
manager: Kensington Publishing Corp., 119 West 40th Street,
New York, NY 10018, attn: Special Sales Department, Phone:
1-800-221-2647.

PINNACLE and the P logo are Reg. U.S. Pat. & TM Off.

ISBN-13: 978-0-7860-2622-7
ISBN-10: 0-7860-2622-7

First Pinnacle Books Printing: November 2005
Fourth Printing: July 2011

10 9 8 7 6 5 4

Printed in the United States of America

For Michaela Hamilton, Doug Mendini,
and so many others at Kensington

I must become a borrower of the night
For a dark hour or twain.

—Shakespeare

Macbeth. Act III. Sc.2. L. 404.

1

He flung open the service door and was on the roof and in the cool, dark vastness of the night. In the building beneath his feet people fought and loved and hated and dreamed, while he lived the dream that was real. He was the one who decided. Below and around him the Theater District glowed, as did the stars above. He was sure that if he tried he could reach up, clutch one of the stars, and plunge it burning into his pocket. The end and the beginning of a dream . . .

On the night he died, Marty Akim was selling.

Marty sold anything that would fetch a price, but he specialized in nineteen-dollar watches that he bought for ten dollars.

Warm evenings in New York would find him lounging outside his souvenir shop, Bargain Empire, just off West Forty-fifth Street in the theater district. Inside the crowded shop were lettered T-shirts, cheap umbrellas, plastic Statues of Liberty, Broadway show posters, glass snow globes that played New York tunes while dandrufflike flakes, swirled by shaking, settled among tiny replicas of the buildings Chrysler, Empire State, and Citigroup, towering inches over Rockefeller Center and Grand Central Station. There were plenty of cut-rate laptop computers, digital cameras, cell phones, recorders, and suitcases, many with brand names that seemed familiar at a glance.

Outside the shop, next to a rack of rayon jackets featuring colorful New York scenes, and a table with stacks of sports logo caps and pullovers, was the display of wristwatches. Alongside them, his seamed and friendly face bunched in a perpetual smile, sat Marty in his padded metal folding chair. Marty caught the eye, with his loosened silk tie and his pristine white shirt with its sleeves rolled up, his slicked-back graying hair, and his amiable keen blue eyes. Sitting there gracefully and casually, his legs crossed, a cigarette either wedged between yellowed fingers or tucked loosely in the corner of his mouth, he looked like a once-handsome, aging lounge singer taking a break between sets. A man with tales to tell and eager to tell them for the price of a return smile.

But interesting and approachable as Marty seemed, it was the watches that drew customers, all the glimmer and glitter of gold and silver electroplate and plastic gemstones, colorful watch faces with bright green numerals and hands that looked as if they'd surely glow in the dark. There was something about all that bright, measurable time so closely massed, the tempo of Times Square, the chatter and shuffle and hum and shouts and roar of traffic and pedestrians, all of them moving to some raucous, frantic music punctuated by blaring horns. In the middle of all this happy turmoil was this ordered display of shining metal and geometric precision, and Marty, waiting.

Customers would come and he would talk to them, not pressuring them, not at first. Where were they from? What shows had they seen? Were they having fun? Sure, he could recommend a restaurant or direct them to the nearest subway stop. All the while they'd be sneaking peeks at the watches, the Rodexes, Hambiltons, Bulovis, and Mowados. (The cheap, illegal knockoffs bearing correctly spelled brand names were kept out of sight beneath the false bottom of a showcase inside the shop, sold only to customers who'd been referred to Marty and could be trusted.) Often Marty's customers were a couple, a man and woman, and the woman would invariably find something that interested her, squint at it, pick it up, then hold it to her ear, like with this couple.

"They're all quartz movement, ma'am." Marty smiling wider and whiter, beginning to work his magic on the two of them. "Factory seconds of quality brands—I'll leave you to guess which brands—some of them with flaws you'd need a microscope to see. But ordinarily they're expensive and the people who buy them expect perfection. Perfect they're not, but then neither are you and me, and I know these watches are closer to heaven than I'll ever get."

"They're reasonably priced," said the woman. She was about forty, short, with a chunky build and dyed red hair. The man was older, lanky, with rough hands and a lot of hair sprouting from his nostrils. He had sad eyes and a wheezy way of breathing.

"I notice the lady's not wearing a watch," Marty said to the man, trying to draw him into conversation.

"I left it in the hotel safe," the woman said. "Bob warned me I might get robbed if I wore my good jewelry out on the streets."

"Bob's wise to advise caution," Marty said, nodding sagely to Bob, both of them seasoned by wide experience. "What New York women do is wear their cheaper but still high-quality jewelry when they go out at night."

"Makes sense," said the woman.

"And they dress stylishly but discreetly, like you're dressed.

Attractive women need to be careful. Bob knows what I mean." Marty wished Bob would mention her name. That would make things easier.

He'd get the woman's name, he decided. And he'd sell her a watch. He could sell air to these two.

It was a challenge Marty enjoyed, selling watches on a fine warm night like tonight, practicing the basics of his trade. He stood up so he could point to a Rodex. "That one would suit Marie just fine," he said to Bob, "with its dainty band."

"He better not give it to anybody named Marie," the woman said.

Marty looked confused. "I thought I heard Bob call you—"

"Forget this crap and let's get going," Bob said to the woman. Bob catching on.

"I dunno, Bob. Some of these—"

"We're gonna be late." Bob edged away, as if he might pull his companion along with some kind of magnetism.

Marty was still smiling. "I understand your cynicism, Bob."

"It's not cynicism, it's reality."

"Most of the time, I'm sure."

Bob ignored him. "C'mon, Ellie."

"If you're not interested, that's okay." Marty still with the smile. *Fuck the both of you.*

"Nice patter but no sale," Bob said. He gripped Ellie's elbow and guided her away from the watch display, almost getting tangled with a couple of teenagers in gangsta pants swishing past. Ellie glanced back at Marty and grinned and shrugged: *What're you gonna do?* She didn't mind being taken, if she was having fun and would come away with something.

Bob had been like a brick wall. Marty figured he must be some kind of salesman himself, big farmer type, maybe sold tractors in Iowa or some place where there were crops. He put the couple out of his mind and neatened up his display where Ellie had inadvertently rearranged some of the watches.

There was this *crack!* that didn't belong. Louder than the din of the street, like a crisp clap of thunder that bounced and echoed down the avenue.

Marty would have wondered what made the sound, but that was when he had his heart attack.

At least that's what Marty thought it was at first. A sudden sharp pain in his chest, a hard time breathing. Not heartburn. Too painful. So painful he could hardly move. It even hurt when he absently lifted his hand to massage the lump of pain in his chest.

He felt wetness. Looked down. His hand was red. So was his tie and the front of his bright white shirt he'd bought just yesterday on sale at Filene's Basement. His fingers danced over his chest, probed.

Huh? He'd been shot.

Shot! Oh, Christ!

Bob the farmer had shot him. That was all Marty could think of. He looked around. Bob and Ellie were nowhere to be seen. People had stopped streaming past the shop and were standing staring at him. He felt light-headed. And breathing was even more of an effort.

He sat down cross-legged on the sidewalk in front of his watch display.

Blood all over the concrete.

My blood . . .

Marty was recovering from his shock enough to be terrified.

A doctor visiting from Toronto with a woman not his wife was walking past and saw what was happening.

He hurried to help Marty but it was too late.

Time had stopped for Marty.

2

A spring shower that was almost mist was falling the next evening when Assistant Chief Lou Melbourne wrestled his bulk out of a cab in front of Vincent Repetto's residence on Bank Street in the Village.

Repetto, who'd gone to a living room window to see if it was still raining, noticed Melbourne crossing the street. The two men were about the same age—midfifties—but almost exact opposites. Melbourne was short and very much overweight, balding, with a pug face and clothes that were always a size too small. He had on a blue jacket that didn't look water resistant, and he walked fast for an obese man and with an economy of motion.

Repetto was several inches over six feet, lean and with long arms and big hands. The progeny of a Dutch mother and an Italian father, he still had most of his dark hair, but it was fast turning a gunmetal gray. His eyebrows, graying but not as fast, were permanently arched in a way that gave him an expression of alert and aggressive curiosity. *I will get to the truth,* said his arched gaze. His clothes tended to black and gray and were well tailored, but tonight he was wearing faded jeans and a white pullover with NYPD on its chest.

Melbourne, crossing the street diagonally, saw him watching through the decorative iron bars on the window and raised a hand in a wave. Repetto nodded to him, then left the window to open the door. Two months ago, Melbourne had presented Repetto with an engraved silver platter at one of his many retirement parties. Repetto appreciated it. A man couldn't have too many silver platters.

"Lou, you should have an umbrella," Repetto said, as Melbourne took the concrete steps to the stoop, then hesitated.

"They bring bad luck."

"Like making it rain?"

Melbourne grinned. "Like making it rain harder because you have an umbrella." After wiping the soles of his shoes on the doormat, he shook hands with Repetto. "How you been in your brief retirement, Vin?"

"I haven't quite figured that out yet." Repetto used the handshake to pull Melbourne in out of the rain, then waited while Melbourne worked out of his jacket. Repetto draped the jacket on the antique brass coatrack and ushered Melbourne into the living room.

Repetto and his wife, Lora, lived in a narrow redbrick house that had been built over a hundred years ago. Lora, who was an interior decorator, had chosen almost all the decor and furnishings. The upper floor was her office and sometime storeroom. Living quarters were downstairs.

The living room, where Repetto invited Melbourne to sit on a soft Queen Anne sofa, was furnished eclectically, mixing traditional with Victorian and Early American. On the wall behind the sofa stood a tall nineteenth-century walnut secretary. A Sheraton library table with stacks of books was along another wall, a Cape Cod window seat nearby where

Lora sometimes sat sipping tea and looking out at Bank Street. The house was on a quiet, brick-paved block in the West Village, a desirable piece of real estate.

Repetto had married into money. Lora's mother and father had died young in a boating accident and left her well off. She wasn't your usual cop's wife, but then Repetto wasn't your usual cop. He'd risen through the ranks by virtue of his own hard work and ingenuity. When he retired after catching a stray bullet in the lung during a hostage situation that went sour, then being kicked up to captain, he was considered the shrewdest—and toughest—homicide detective in the NYPD. His specialty was serial killers.

When Melbourne was seated, Repetto asked him if he wanted a drink. "Some good eighteen-year-old scotch?"

Melbourne smiled and shook his head no. "I'm on duty, sort of."

Uh-oh. Repetto settled down in a brown leather wing chair facing his old friend and superior officer.

Still smiling, Melbourne glanced around. "I don't see any ashtrays. And I don't smell tobacco. I guess for health reasons you gave up those Cuban cigars you used to smoke. The bad lung and all."

"The lung's pretty much healed. I still get winded too easy, though."

"But still no cigars."

"I allow myself one every few days. The doctors said it's okay as long as I don't inhale."

"Sure they did."

"Other than that, I don't smoke. For Lora."

"She make you lighten up?"

Repetto didn't bother to answer.

"So it's true what they say about life after you retire and you're home with the wife."

"What do they say?"

"She takes over the company."

"Yeah, that's true. She's been a cop's wife over twenty years, Lou. If she doesn't want me to smell up the house with cigar smoke, I won't. She deserves to be spoiled."

"She doesn't want you dying of lung cancer."

"That, too."

Melbourne focused his flesh-padded gray eyes on Repetto. "How'd you and Lora manage it, staying married all this time, you doing the kinda work we do?"

Repetto had to give it some thought. "I don't know for sure. Maybe somewhere along the line we learned how to stay out of each other's way."

"That's an unsatisfactory answer," Melbourne said with a touch of bitterness. Twice-divorced Melbourne.

"Lora's at a meeting with a client," Repetto said. "You wanna come back to my den and we can smoke some cigars?"

Melbourne cocked his head to the side. "You won't get in any trouble?"

Repetto laughed and stood up. "I haven't had a smoke in two days. Haul your ass outta that sofa and come with me." He didn't tell Melbourne the den was the only place he smoked in the house, and he had to make sure there was plenty of ventilation.

Repetto's den was large, carpeted in deep red with thick red drapes, a quiet room, considering it was at street level. There were commendations on the walls, a mounted trout Repetto had caught in Vermont, and several signed and framed publicity photos of Broadway stars.

Repetto walked over to his desk and opened a small mahogany humidor near the green-shaded lamp. He gave Melbourne a Venezuelan cigar and a cutter, then chose a domestic brand for himself. Before lighting the cigar, he went over and opened a window, letting in some dampness and cool night air. Within a few seconds he could feel cross ventilation from the already cracked window on the adjacent wall stir the hairs on his bare forearms.

When he returned to sit in his black leather desk chair, Melbourne had already seated himself in one of the upholstered chairs angled toward the desk and lighted his cigar.

Repetto settled down behind his oversize cherry-wood desk. "You mentioned you were on duty."

"Sort of. Here to ask you about something."

Repetto smiled. "Am I a suspect?"

"I don't believe you lead an exciting enough life now to get in any trouble." Melbourne puffed on his cigar. "This is great. Cuban?"

"Aren't those illegal?"

"A rhetorical question, I'm sure." Melbourne might have winked. He knew Repetto favored and could obtain Cuban cigars. He took another draw and seemed to roll the smoke around in his mouth before exhaling. "What exactly *do* you do these days?"

"Lora and I go to the theater, dine out with friends, plan on doing some traveling. Things we never had time to do when I was on the job."

"Sounds nice, actually. You always had it good for a cop."

Repetto was getting the idea Melbourne was hesitant to bring up whatever he'd come to discuss. "Get to it, Lou."

"I'm asking you back to the NYPD, or at least to work for us."

Repetto didn't hesitate. "Nope. Lora wouldn't stand for it."

"You'd please her before me?"

"I don't sleep with you."

"You wanna hear the deal?"

"No."

"Okay, here it is. Last night a guy named Martin Akim was shot to death outside his shop in the theater district."

"Marty Akim? Watches?"

"The very Marty."

"Holdup?"

"No. Shot from a distance. Relatively small-caliber bullet, misshapen by bone and the wall it hit after tumbling through Akim. People heard the shot, but the way sound echoes around all those tall buildings and concrete and glass, nobody knows where it came from. Far away, though, not close by."

"Stray shot, maybe." *Like the one that caught me in the lung.*

"We don't think so."

"A sniper?"

"Yeah. Here's the thing. Akim wasn't the first victim. He was the third in the last six weeks. The first was a sales rep from Cincinnati, in town on business. The second a prostitute down in the Village."

Repetto leaned back in his chair and drew on his cigar, then exhaled and watched the smoke drift toward the ceiling and make a slow turn toward the open window.

"A serial killer. Your specialty, Vin."

"Was."

"Not that you need the money, but we'd like to put you back on the payroll while you track down this sicko."

Repetto sat forward and looked directly at Melbourne, then removed the cigar from his mouth. "I wasn't the only competent homicide detective in the department."

"You were sure as hell the best."

"And now somebody else is. I'm sorry, Lou, the answer's no."

Melbourne stood up. He walked slowly over and looked at Repetto's commendations, then stood staring at the mounted trout. "You catch this thing?"

"Yeah. Only kinda thing I'm gonna catch from now on."

"This killer's been in contact with us. He's bursting with ego and thinks he's smarter than we are."

"Don't they all think that?"

"Some of them *are* smarter."

"A few. The ones we never heard of."

"Vin—"

"Talk to me and not to the fish, okay?"

Melbourne turned to face him. "I didn't come here on my own. I was asked." He looked at his cigar now and not at Repetto. "He asked me. Told me, actually."

"He?"

"The killer. He musta seen all the publicity about you when you stepped down. How you were like a combination bloodhound and avenging angel when it came to tracking serial killers. He wants you on the case. He said you were the only one of us who was a worthy adversary."

Repetto stared dumbfounded at Melbourne, then laughed. "Cease the bullshit, Lou. The answer's still no."

"You think I'm kidding?"

"I don't care if you are. I don't dance just because some maniac plays a tune. And I know you don't either."

Melbourne removed the cigar from his mouth. "This one's different, Vin. If you'd heard him on the phone . . ."

"The answer's still no. I mean it. I'm not some pro athlete that can be talked into thinking he might have a little more gas in his tank. I'm retired."

"You might get winded a little easier and be a little grayer, but you're not suited for retirement. You're gonna go crazy without the job." Melbourne pointed with the cigar. "You're gonna rot."

"I'm rotting happily. I told you my situation. I'm not gonna double-cross Lora to work on one more case. Put Delmore on it."

"The killer laughed at Delmore. Called him up and laughed at him. He wants you, Vin. Only you."

" 'Only You.' Isn't that a song?"

"Your song. Yours and the killer's."

Repetto knew what Melbourne meant. When Repetto was thirteen years old in Philadelphia his mother had been murdered by a serial killer. It was what had made an older Repetto join the police force, then become a homicide detective. His mother had divorced his dad, a Philadelphia cop, and had custody of him, so Repetto was the one who'd found her in her bedroom when he came home from school. She was lying nude on the bed with her legs spread incredibly wide. There was the blood on the wall, his mother's blood, the bloody numeral 6 indicating she was the killer's sixth victim, the blood pooled beneath her body, the blood on her pale flesh and between her thighs.

With his father gone, Repetto was the man of the house. He should have protected his mother. Somehow. Should have been there. Somehow. Even at thirteen he knew it wasn't logical, but guilt still wrapped itself around his heart. Somehow, he was partly to blame for his mother's death. He couldn't get the image of all that blood, *her* blood, out of his mind.

He remembered the word it had brought to his lips. Not *Mother* or *Mommy* or an expression of rage. Simply, *Blood*.

Almost a year passed before he again spoke that or any other word. His father had died in a robbery shoot-out only a month after the death of his mother. For the young Repetto it was like being struck by speeding trains coming and going, and being left to die alone.

Two of his aunts took him in and brought him back to being human again, raised him with kindness and love, saved him. Mar and Mol, short for Marilyn and Molly. Mol had died ten years ago. Mar was still alive, and would be in town for Repetto and Lora's daughter Amelia's twenty-first birthday next week.

Mar and Mol, the blood . . . So long ago and still so vivid.

Repetto swallowed. He thought he'd gotten past this kind of reaction, the thing that had made him stalk serial killers in a way that was legendary in the NYPD. The reason why Melbourne was sitting across from him now:

"Jesus, Lou!" Repetto said. "So this guy doesn't get what he wants. He'll get over his disappointment."

"He's not gonna quit, Vin. Not this one."

"I didn't say he was gonna quit. Delmore can shut him down."

Melbourne seemed about to say something more, then plunked his cigar back in his mouth as if it might prevent him from speaking imprudently.

"Sure you don't want a drink, Lou?"

Melbourne stood up. "No, thanks. This excellent Cuban cigar's more'n enough." He moved close to the desk and looked down at Repetto. "Listen, you're probably right. You deserve a rest. Have a good retirement. Food, shows, booze, travel. Enjoy, old friend. I mean that." He offered his hand.

Repetto shook with him, standing up to show him out. He propped his cigar in an ashtray and walked around the desk.

"Still raining," Repetto said, when he opened the door to the street. "Take an umbrella. You can keep it as long as you want."

"No, thanks. Listen, I sincerely gotta advise you, if you don't want a troubled conscience, better avoid reading the papers or watching TV news. This sicko's deeply dedicated to his calling."

"Forget the umbrella offer," Repetto said.

"Kidding," Melbourne said with a smile. "Don't rot." At the base of the steps, the rain already spotting his jacket, he looked back and up at Repetto. "Really. Don't rot."

"That didn't sound at all sincere," Repetto said.

He stood at the open door, watching Melbourne until he'd crossed the street and lowered himself into his car.

Then he remembered the open den door, sniffed the air, and went back to extinguish his cigar propped in the ashtray.

3

"You said no?" Lora asked, after Repetto told her about Melbourne's visit.

"Sure I did."

She leaned forward and kissed him lightly on the lips, then, after sniffing his breath, looked up at him with mock seriousness. Well, not completely mock. "Cigar?"

"Half of one. With Melbourne. Being a good host."

"Ah." She walked over to the window and stared outside. Repetto studied her. The beige dress she was wearing complemented her long, honey-blond hair. Lora was trim not from exercise, other than her daily walks, but from genetic good fortune.

He thought she might say something else about Melbourne's visit, but when she turned around to face him she smiled. It was what had first attracted Repetto, that smile. It changed her cool, blue-eyed impassive features into a warm and engaging signal to the world: I'm approachable and up for adventure. Repetto had learned it wasn't a sexual invitation, but occasionally men took it for such. Lora was used to that response and knew how to fend them off without making enemies.

"It's still raining," she said. "How 'bout I make us some tea?"

"Fine." The Melbourne matter was closed. If a maniac was murdering people one after another and might soon be terrorizing the city, that wasn't Repetto's problem. He was off the force for good. And it felt good.

Lora must have guessed what he was thinking. "Thanks."

"For what?"

"Meaning what you said to Melbourne."

She went into the kitchen to brew the tea. Repetto walked over and stared through the rain-distorted window out at the street. New York. The city he'd spent his life protecting. His city. A young couple who'd moved in last month exited the building across the street, laughing. The woman, a skinny brunette, ducked her head at the first raindrop, while her bulky, bearded husband squinted up at the sky and opened an umbrella. Watching them, Repetto remembered when he and Lora had moved here almost twenty years ago. It was odd, how the street didn't change but the people did, generations playing out their lives on the same stage.

It occurred to him that Lora, who was six years younger than Repetto and not carrying a partially collapsed lung, would almost certainly outlive him. Would she remain here? Wouldn't she be lonely in this house that was too large for one person? Might she be afraid without him, a single woman living at street level in Manhattan? Their daughter and only child, Amelia, who was in law school and lived on the Upper West Side, might move in with her. Though probably not. Amelia was fiercely independent. Maybe Amelia would marry. Repetto and Lora had their ideas about whom they'd like as a son-in-law. Repetto smiled. *Hopeless to expect that kind of wish to come true. But Dal Bricker—*

The woman beneath the shelter of the umbrella glanced over and saw him, and Repetto raised a hand in an understated wave so she'd know he wasn't spying on the couple, simply happened to be at his window when they were going out.

He stood awhile longer looking out at the drizzle and lowering light. A lamp came on behind him, and he saw Lora's reflection on the windowpane and turned.

She'd placed a tray with a tea set on the heavy table by the sofa. Repetto watched as she poured cream in her cup, part of the set that was Bavarian china, antique but not particularly expensive. They'd bought it together ten years ago at a shop in SoHo. She added a lump of sugar and stirred. He walked over, added a dollop of cream to his tea, then sat down on the sofa and sipped. The tea wasn't quite hot enough to burn his tongue.

Lora remained standing. She'd put on her old blue cardigan sweater over her dress and looked an odd combination of sophisticate and homebody that Repetto found strangely appealing.

She sipped her tea appraisingly and smiled. "The critics like the new play at the Westside, *Left Bank*."

"Internet or newspaper critics?"

"Both. Not rave reviews, but uniformly good. It's about expatriates in Paris in the twenties, then later when they return to the U.S."

"Sounds political."

"It's not. George Kearn plays the old Hemingway." Kearn was one of their favorites. And the Westside Theatre, off Broadway but not far off, was also one of their favorites.

"Sounds okay," Repetto said. "You working tomorrow?"

"Meeting a client for breakfast, then a display house tour."

"Maybe I'll see if I can pick us up some tickets."

She took another sip of tea, then leaned down and kissed him on the forehead. Her lips were still warm from the tea. "I love you," she said simply.

He knew why she was saying it now. Because he'd refused Melbourne. He lifted her free hand and kissed it. He didn't tell her he loved her, too. It didn't seem quite the time, but he knew he should tell her more often and promised himself he'd do exactly that in his retirement.

He watched her walk to the window with her tea. She sat down at an angle on the window seat so she could look out through the glass at the rainy street. She appeared comfortable and contented. Repetto was sure that if she were a cat, she'd curl up in the window and go to sleep.

If she were a cat, he'd pamper her.

The next morning, after Lora had left to meet her client, Repetto walked to the Bonaire Diner on Fourteenth Street and had eggs and a grilled corn muffin for breakfast. He liked the Bonaire for more than its food. It was brightly decorated, with red-vinyl-upholstered booths and stools, and a dark counter made out of the kind of granite that sparked silver when the light hit it just right. A lot of the customers were from the neighborhood, or were people who worked nearby. Regulars. Business drones, artists, tradesmen, along with tourists, and mothers with their kids.

Carrie the waitress cleared away the dishes, then poured Repetto a second cup of coffee.

He settled in to scan the *Times*.

There was another favorable review of *Left Bank*. Nothing about a sniper shooting last night. Apparently Melbourne's serial killer was still between murders.

Why am I even thinking about this?

He turned to the sports section and read about the latest

Yankees acquisition, an expensive free agent pitcher who was almost a guarantee that the team would make the play-offs. Repetto read on about the pitcher and felt himself relax. When he was on the job, he'd always found solace in this part of the paper. The only murderers' row in the sports section was the '27 Yankees.

The breakfast rush was falling off, so there was space at the counter and empty booths. Repetto took his time with the paper, then left Carrie the usual tip and paid the cashier on the way out.

It was a great morning. The sky was clear and the air had been cleansed by last night's rain. Repetto decided to stroll around for a while before returning to the house. Then he'd . . .

What?

What would he do?

How would he occupy his time?

He felt suddenly alone. Lost and without purpose. He noticed that his mouth was dry and he felt slightly unsteady.

Some kind of retirement panic, he told himself. Not to worry. There was plenty to do that was unconnected to police work. He grinned to reassure himself. Other people retired and found ways to spend their time. So could he.

So *would* he.

Melbourne was about to leave his office when his assistant, Lieutenant Mike Mathers, knocked twice, then opened the door. There was excitement on his flushed, Irish face.

"For you on line two, sir. It's him."

Melbourne didn't have to ask who. He sat back down behind his desk, taking as much time as he dared before picking up the receiver. Not that it would help; this killer was aware that the police were tracing his call and knew exactly how long it was safe to stay on the line.

When it was time, Melbourne lifted the receiver and identified himself.

"You know who this is?" came the answering voice. Neutral, sexless, perhaps filtered through something that might disguise it.

"I know. What do you want this fine morning?"

"What did he say?"

"He?"

"Don't play tricks to try keeping me on the line. That might cost somebody their life, and that would be on your conscience."

"He said no."

A laugh, as cold and neutral as the voice. "He'll change his mind. I know him. Know about him. Captain Vincent Repetto. Hero and legend. Know him as well as I know myself."

"I'd say there's a lot of difference between you two."

"Only the twists and turns of fate."

"Hardly. I know Vin Repetto."

"But you don't know me."

"So tell me about yourself."

"I'll tell you what I want, *who* I want, and that's Captain Vincent Repetto. The only worthy opponent in your entire incompetent bureaucracy."

"He's no longer part of the bureaucracy."

"He can be again."

"I told you, I asked him. He said no."

"Then ask him again. Be persuasive. Give him the third degree. I'll accept no one other than Repetto."

"The choice isn't yours to make."

"But it is, and I've made it."

"Listen—"

"Better think of some way to give me what I demand, and soon. I'm patient, but I won't wait forever."

Click. *Buzzzzzzzzzz.*

Melbourne replaced the receiver and looked at his watch. He knew the killer had cut the connection soon enough.

Mathers stuck his head back in the office. "The call was from a cell phone, sir."

"Sure," Melbourne said, knowing that if the phone were ever found, it would turn out to be stolen and wiped clean of prints. "We record the call okay?"

"You betcha."

Instead of leaving his office, Melbourne sat behind his desk for a long time, thinking of ways to be persuasive.

4

At ten the next morning, Repetto was seated at his desk cleaning his father's old .38 police special revolver, when the doorbell rang.

Lora was upstairs selecting paint samples to show a client. Usually she didn't hear the doorbell there. Repetto put down the container of bluing he was holding and wiped his hand on the rag the gun had been wrapped in, then made his way to the front door and peered through the peephole.

A tall woman with long red hair stood on the concrete stoop. Repetto opened the door to get a less distorted look at her.

Since it was a sunny April morning, she wasn't wearing a coat. She had a good figure beneath a brown blazer with a matching skirt. Her face was angular, her eyes green and pink-rimmed beneath strands of hair the breeze had laid across her face. She appeared to have been crying, but he suspected her eyes were always like that, in the manner of some red-heads. Her makeup was sparse but it was there, pale lipstick, paler green eye shadow. Repetto guessed her age at about forty.

She smiled. Straight teeth, nice smile. She said, "Only an ex-homicide detective could size up a woman like that."

Repetto grinned, embarrassed. "Sorry. I didn't mean to stare. It wasn't . . ."

"Lascivious?"

"No. I mean, yes, it wasn't."

"So what did you decide about me?" She cocked her head to one side as she asked the question, almost the way Lora did.

"We haven't met," Repetto said. "You're educated—that word lascivious—and well enough off financially but not wealthy."

She raised her eyebrows. There wouldn't have been much to them were it not for eyebrow pencil.

"Your clothes," Repetto explained. "A good cop can judge clothes like a fashion expert, at least when it comes to price. Yours are in good taste, and medium-priced except for your shoes. They're expensive."

"You can't be too kind to your feet," the woman said.

"You've got a job, maybe a profession, that pays you well enough. You're unmarried." He saw her glance at her ringless left hand. "You're well adjusted and reasonably happy, ambitious, and you want something."

She smiled. "What makes you think I want something?"

"You've managed to stir my interest and keep me talking while *you're* sizing *me* up."

"You can learn a lot about people from what they think about you," she said.

"If they're honest."

"A former NYPD detective would be honest."

"Different kind of honest," Repetto said.

She seemed to think that over but didn't say anything.

"You don't strike me as the type who's selling something, so what do you want?" he asked.

"My name's Zoe Brady," she said.

"I wondered when we'd get around to that. You obviously know things about me, including my name, I'm sure."

"You're Vincent Repetto. The legendary Repetto. Tough cop and true. Smart and every kind of honest."

"Now I know you want something."

"I'm a profiler in the NYPD," Zoe said.

"And I know what you want." Repetto stepped outside and closed the door behind him; it wouldn't do for Lora to hear any of this. "Lou Melbourne sent you."

"He okayed it. Coming here was my idea."

"Whoever came up with the idea, it wasn't a good one. I'm not going to change my mind about the sniper."

"The thing is," Zoe said, "he's not going to change his mind about you. I've worked to get inside this guy's head, and I've got some small idea of how he reasons—or thinks he reasons. He's not going to give up on something he wants, and he wants you to engage in a contest with him."

"He isn't going to get what he wants."

"Well, we want it too. Because we know how dangerous the sniper is. And we understand why he wants you as his nemesis. You're legendary, and in his mind, he soon will be." She stared earnestly at Repetto. "Have you at least given the matter any thought since Captain Melbourne talked with you?"

"I have," he said. "I haven't changed my mind. The game this sicko wants is one I'm finished playing." He smiled at her. There was something he liked about her despite her mission, despite the fact she wasn't really a cop. If only he didn't have to get professionally involved with her. He'd never been crazy about profilers. In his experience they were more often wrong than right. And when they were right, it was about the obvious—male, certain age bracket, poor or unemployed, tough childhood . . . "I'm sorry, Zoe, but I'm not subject to threats from a psychotic killer. Next time the sniper contacts you, tell him I said no, I don't want to play."

She shrugged. "Okay, I tried and failed. The AC was right about you. You're a hard man."

"Was I just insulted?"

She backed down the steps gracefully and grinned up at him. "Not by me. I like hard and proud. That way I know where I stand."

"You'll tell Melbourne what I said?"

"I'll tell him." She nodded to Repetto, then started to stride down the sidewalk. After a few steps, she stopped and turned. "I'll also tell him that the way I size you up, I don't think you're likely to change your mind."

"You've got me profiled."

"Sure. You're a cinch."

Repetto smiled at her, nodded good-bye, then opened the door and went back inside to his wife and his new life and his father's gun.

5

Jim Lu had a talent given by his ancestors. Even as a child in Dom Ning he could sketch likenesses of anything, but especially of people. He had never attended school beyond his basic education in China, and never had the benefit of an art class. But what he saw, he could draw. He could look into it, understand it, see what made it what it was; then he could recreate it.

He and a dozen others made their livings as sketch artists, working mostly in Times Square after the theater curtains dropped and people spilled out into the streets to walk to subway stops or their hotels or futilely wave for taxis. For twenty dollars Jim Lu or his fellow sketch artists would provide a charcoal likeness of any person who would pose for ten minutes. For an additional fifteen dollars they would provide a sturdy cardboard frame. This was illegal, of course, but when the police chased them they would simply open shop on some other busy corner, often just across the street. There was much for the police to tend to in the theater district when it was jammed with people, and simple sketch artists moved them only to cursory efforts.

This woman—Betty Ern was her name, and Jim Lu had elicited from her that she was from Iowa—was quite easy to capture in charcoal. She had thick black hair and dark eyes, and a receding chin that Jim Lu would give definition. He knew how to flatter his subjects, removing a few years here, adding cheekbone or eye width there, and still they would look like themselves.

He sat on his wooden folding chair before his easel, his back to the traffic, facing pedestrians streaming past beyond those who'd decided to pose or simply to observe. Jim Lu began with the left eye, as he always did, working carefully and slowly. Once he had Betty's left eye perfectly, her brow and the side of her nose, he would work faster, enlarging, keying off the eye. Every living thing he drew, he began with its left eye. He thought sometimes that the soul must live there.

Betty Ern seemed a nice enough lady. Every twenty seconds or so she'd become embarrassed by his quick, appraising glances, and a smile would sneak onto her face. Her husband or boyfriend, a large man in a gray suit, stood off to the side and watched, trying not to seem too impatient to be going.

Jim Lu ignored the man, ignored the traffic teeming noisily behind him on Broadway, ignored the mass of humanity flowing along the sidewalk before him. Gray Suit edged toward the curb so he could see what Jim Lu was doing, then grinned at Betty.

"Not much there yet," he said, "but what there is sure looks like you."

Jim Lu smiled and nodded at the compliment he'd barely heard in his deep concentration.

Yet a part of his mind thought of Michelle, as it had more

and more often lately. Michelle who so liked to give and receive oral sex. When he was finished here—

A pain erupted in his back, then in his chest and arms. His head must have jerked backward because he was staring up through the haze of light at faint stars that became fainter . . .

Betty Ern heard the loud, echoing *crack!* and thought at first something had fallen from a building. But the artist, the little man with the neat dark beard and mustache, had slumped from his chair and crashed to the sidewalk with his easel. Betty stared numbly down at him, at the sketch paper on the pavement, at her single left eye staring back at her. Only her eye, but she knew it was her own.

She noticed specks of blood on it, around it.

Someone or something slapped her hard, high in the chest, just beneath her throat. She heard another of the loud, reverberating *cracks* and was aware that she'd fallen backward, aware of people surrounding her, arms supporting her upper body, screams off in the distance. *Where am I? What happened?* She tried to inhale but couldn't, and the pain and panic carried her to cold dark spaces. Her last coherent thought was of the loud, reverberating noise she'd heard, like the screen door slamming on the farm where she grew up. It was a sound she'd loved. As a girl she always slammed the door going out . . . coming home.

The next morning he read the front page of the *New York Post* and smiled. It hadn't taken the media long to decide what to call him: "The Night Sniper." That was fine. Nights were most convenient for him. And since the media were giving him the night, he accepted.

The Night Sniper. Crisp and descriptive.

It would make wonderful headlines.

* * *

Repetto sat staring at the *Times* in the Bonaire Diner when Carrie placed his eggs, toast, and coffee before him.

"Hell of a thing last night in Times Square," she said. "Must be a nut, this Night Sniper. World's full of nuts, don't you think?"

"Except for thee and me," Repetto said, moving the folded newspaper aside to make room for his plate.

"Two people shot to death, and three injured in a traffic accident when all the cars tried to get outta there, bunch of people damn near trampled to death when they realized they were being shot at." She topped off his coffee. "Musta been bedlam."

"New York," Repetto said sadly.

"Whatza difference?"

"People in Bedlam are certified insane."

As he began to eat, he stole glances at the paper. A sketch artist and a tourist from Iowa, both dead. A teenage girl in a limo killed when a cab collided with it near the shooting. More injuries from traffic accidents. A child almost trampled to death on the sidewalk.

Repetto felt an anger growing in him that supplanted his appetite.

It didn't help when his cell phone chirped.

He dug the phone from the pocket of his jacket folded on the seat beside him. "Repetto," he said, swallowing a bite of egg.

"It's Lou Melbourne here."

"It's breakfast here."

"I figured that's where you'd be. Don't you usually read the paper while you're abusing your arteries?"

"I was doing just that. Front page. Times Square last night."

"The Night Sniper phoned us last night after it happened, Vin. I gave him your answer. He didn't like it."

Repetto knew where Melbourne was going with the conversation. "It isn't my fault those two people were shot last night. It's entirely the fault of the asshole who squeezed the trigger."

"Sure. But does *he* see it that way?"

"He's insane," Repetto pointed out. "We don't know how he sees it, and it might not make sense to us if we did know."

"You're the expert with serial killers, Vin, but we both know they follow their own weird logic. It's why they kill. It's why they get caught."

Repetto sipped coffee. "I'm not personally responsible for any of that."

"We agree. But folks in the mayor's office are in a tizzy. So's the commissioner, and so's the chief of department, my boss."

"You don't sound in a tizzy."

"It's my job not to, but I'm all tizzied up inside. Two people shot to death; then the killer called and said you had a few days to think over my offer—his offer, really—then he'd kill two more. He said for me to tell you their deaths would be on your conscience."

"Anything else he tell you?"

"He said he had plenty of bullets."

Repetto said nothing. He sipped his coffee. He didn't like the way his heartbeat had picked up. The way his blood was racing. The cold rage in the core of him.

"I can hire you as an official consultant and give you two good detectives full-time until the Sniper is nailed," Melbourne said. "You won't be officially out of retirement, so you can still draw your pension and keep your promise to Lora."

"Isn't that a difference without a distinction?"

"That's the kind of bullshit we hear every day in court, Vin, and it floats there but not here. You do this thing for us, for the city, and you won't be bothered again. Travel, go to all the Broadway shows you want, eat well, drink well, rot the rest of your life away happy. That's fine. But we both know before God, you're the only one who can do this thing."

"Lou—"

"Okay, the one who can do it best."

"Lou—"

"Do this for me as an old friend. Ask Lora again. After last night, things have changed. She'll see that, I'm sure."

"Did the chief ask you to call me?"

"The mayor asked."

Repetto didn't know whether to believe him. Melbourne could be deceptive, relentless, and remarkably persuasive. That was why he'd been promoted over so many cops with more seniority. Why he'd be chief of department someday, and possibly even commissioner if he didn't stumble over his own ambition like so many before him. Melbourne wouldn't lie to Repetto directly, because he was too wily to have to lie, but he could massage the truth until it sighed and surrendered to him.

The bare facts were out there. The Night Sniper had killed twice because he didn't like Repetto's answer. If Repetto didn't change his answer, two more people would die, and soon. Maybe he'd kill more people anyway, but those two, like the two last night, would be Repetto's responsibility. That was the way the Night Sniper thought.

The way Repetto thought.

"I'll talk to Lora," he said.

"Thanks, Vin. You're gonna prevent a lotta blood being shed." Repetto had never heard Melbourne sound more sincere. "I'm gonna hang up now before you change your mind."

And Melbourne was gone.

Repetto killed his cell phone and sat for a moment staring at it. *Blood* . . .

He took his time with his coffee, reading the rest of the paper casually, until he got to page two of the front section and his name jumped out at him. Someone had leaked the reason why the Night Sniper had claimed his last two victims, and what he wanted. There it was in the *Times*, the paper of record.

He wanted Repetto.

6

Repetto wanted a piece of cake. He hadn't realized it had been so long since lunch, and he and Lora had cabbed to the Upper West Side where their daughter, Amelia, had an apartment that she subleased so cheap she didn't mind taking the subway five or six days a week down to NYU, where she was a senior in prelaw.

Amelia was a slender girl with her mother's fine features, luminous smile, and thick blond hair. She was proud of her golden hair and wore it combed back and in a long braid that hung to her waist. Today she was twenty-one, and celebrating with her family and best friends. Besides Repetto and Lora, there were Mar, older and grayer than when she and her partner Mel had healed and raised a teenage Repetto; Dal; and a girl named Peggy that Amelia knew from college. A small group, but close.

"We're going to sing," Dal said, after Lora had finished lighting the candles on a cake brought by Mar.

Amelia shot her great smile and shook her head, but the singing had already begun.

Repetto had a voice like a cracked foghorn, so he kept his

volume down. He didn't like the way Peggy was looking at
Dal, who seemed to be paying no attention to her. Good.
Maybe someday Dal and Amelia would see each other dif-
ferently. Less like brother and sister. So Repetto and Lora
hoped. But some things you couldn't force. Repetto told
himself to grow up at his late age. If Dal happened to prefer
somebody like Peggy, who was a beautiful young brunette,
then so be it. Some things were beyond a father's control.

"What are you thinking, Dad?"

Repetto realized "Happy Birthday" was over. "Thinking
you should make a wish."

Amelia did, closing her eyes briefly, then pursing her lips
and emitting two gusts of breath before all twenty-one candles were extinguished. Lora and Repetto exchanged a look,
knowing they were both making their own wish. Mar saw
them, grinned, and shook her head. Dal didn't notice. Peggy
appeared momentarily mystified.

"So what was the wish?" Dal asked.

"That she'd make it through law school," Peggy said, giving Amelia's long braid a playful tug.

While everyone was laughing, Mar made her way over to
Repetto. She was in her eighties now, whipcord lean and
wizened, but with carefully permed white hair and alert
brown eyes. She looked like one of those people who might
live forever. Repetto wished she could.

"You okay, Vin?" she asked. "You look sort of pensive."

"A lot to think about, I guess."

"Yeah, you always did think too much to be completely
happy."

"Is there such a thing as complete happiness?"

"Naw." She patted his arm and moved away.

Dal came up to Repetto as the cake was being cut and
drew him aside, until they were standing a few feet inside
the kitchen.

"I can't believe Mar came all the way from Philadelphia by train for this, at her age," Dal said. "She's a helluva lady."

"You'll never know."

"Michaels tells me I should test up for lieutenant," Dal said. "I'd be doing Street Narcotics Enforcement."

"Running a unit?"

"Before long."

"Not a bad career move."

"I want the shortest route to make detective, like you are."

"Were," Repetto corrected.

Dal grinned. "Word's around you're getting the call to go after the Night Sniper."

Repetto sighed. "The NYPD leaks like the *Titanic*. Got an underwater budget, too."

"You considering it?"

"We're opening gifts," Lora called from the living room.

"The beer's not in the fridge, you two," Amelia shouted. "It's out here in a cooler."

Repetto and Dal laughed. "She's got us figured," Dal said.

"Always has," Repetto said. "We'll finish this talk tomorrow morning."

Repetto hooked up with Dal Bricker the next morning where they often met, away from the apartment. Dal would leave the unmarked he was driving parked off Fourteenth Street, and they would stroll.

It was a clear morning, with the sun glancing warm off the buildings. The kind of morning Repetto liked most in New York. Night had been chased away. The sights and smells and sounds were as newly created. Anything might happen. City of promise.

"Lora told me about what Melbourne wants from you," Dal said. He was a taller, heavier figure in the corner of

Repetto's vision. Walking next to someone larger was an unfamiliar sensation for Repetto.

"I figured she would. No secrets. What do you think?"

"I think it's your call."

"What if it wasn't just my call, Dal? What if I asked for your advice?"

Bricker grinned as Repetto looked over at him: big, broad guy with curly black hair, looked like he should be a country-western star. *Why can't Amelia see a future with this man? Maybe they've been too close—more than friends, less than lovers—and can only think of themselves more as siblings than as a man and woman who might feel a mutual attraction.*

Sometimes it made Repetto ache when he thought how happy Dal and Amelia could be. Not that it mattered what he thought. It was just that people were so damned blind when it came to the future.

"I'm usually the one asking for advice," Dal said.

"Not this time," Repetto said.

Bricker took a deep, noisy breath. "What I think you should do is what Melbourne is asking."

"You've given it some thought?"

"Lots, since I talked with Lora. Bottom line is, I figure you've got an obligation. I didn't tell Lora that, but I've thought so from the start."

"Well," Repetto said, after a dozen more strides, "I asked you."

"Lora's gonna come around to your way of thinking anyway," Bricker said.

"*My way*? You think I *want* to tag on to this nutcase killer?"

"C'mon, Vin. You know damn well you do."

"Ordinarily I'd agree with you. But there comes a time in every marriage . . ."

"Yeah. Like I said, it's your call and yours only." But that wasn't the way Bricker was looking at Repetto. Damn kid always knew what was in his mind.

As if they were blood.

"I'll talk again with Lora."

"That'd be best."

But Repetto knew he wouldn't initiate the conversation. It would be better if she broached the subject, made the suggestion herself. He knew Lora, and Bricker knew both of them. There was no way Lora could hold Repetto to his word and watch him stay on the sidelines while the Night Sniper took more victims. That would, in a way, make her and Repetto responsible for the dead; they'd be the killer's once-removed accomplices.

Dal was right; it was Repetto's call. But Repetto was patient, confident of the decision Lora would soon make. She was a good woman, a brave woman with a nagging conscience.

"Got time to stop in at the deli?" Repetto asked. They'd gone around the block, and the unmarked Ford was visible beyond the corner deli. "I'm gonna pick up something for breakfast to take back to the apartment. You can join us."

Dal thought about it. "Sounds good, but I really got no time to stop. I'll get some fruit, maybe. Eat while I drive."

They walked to the deli's outside produce and flower stalls. Like the flowers, most of the fruit was flown in from sunnier climes where it thrived this time of year. Repetto preferred it in season, so he'd wait until Dal had chosen, then go inside with him to the register and buy something sweet and sinful in shrink-wrap to take back to the apartment.

"Peaches look best," Dal said.

He braced his thighs against the wooden stall, leaning forward and stretching out his right arm so he could reach a large, ripe peach in the last row.

Repetto saw the bullet slam into the back of Dal's head and heard its impact a moment before the rolling *crack!* of the rifle.

Bricker settled down on the peaches, his arm still extended, the fingers of his right hand straining forward. Repetto was aware of peaches forced over the edge of the stall, bouncing and rolling at his feet. Bricker's head tilted to the side, as if he were trying to get more comfortable on his pillow of peaches, and the blood came. And came and came.

Repetto backed away, unable to stop staring at Bricker, at the blood on the peaches, the blood now trickling from the stall onto the sidewalk.

"Christ!" he heard someone say. "Looka all the blood! Fuckin' flood!"

People were moving around Repetto. He could hear their soles shuffling on the pavement, see them like shadows at the corners of his vision. It was unreal. All so unreal.

". . . guy's clock has stopped . . . dead . . .dead . . ."

"Get back. Please, you get back from him!" Kim's voice. The deli's owner. Kim knew Repetto and had come outside despite the possibility of another shot.

"Don't matter, man. He's dead. Looka the fuckin' blood!"

Does there have to be so much blood?

"Watch where you step . . ."

"Get a cop!" a woman said.

Blood.

"Somebody inside's calling the police." Kim's voice. "Somebody's already calling."

"Get a cop!" the woman insisted, as if he hadn't spoken. "Get a cop."

Repetto stood motionless except for his chest heaving with his rapid breathing. His face was pale stone. The people around him might have thought he was in shock, but he wasn't. Not yet.

"I am a cop," he said.

* * *

Well before sunrise, he awoke hot and heavily perspiring, lying on his back beside Lora. Repetto guessed she hadn't been asleep, but had been crying since they'd gone to bed a few minutes past midnight.

For a moment he wondered why she was quietly sobbing; then the realization of yesterday collapsed in on him. He reached out gently with his left arm and pulled Lora to him, and she nestled her head against the base of his neck and continued to sob. Neither of them spoke. What had happened to Dal, to them, was black and ineffable.

After almost an hour, still welded together by grief, they fell asleep.

When the bedroom was slashed with morning light from the parted blinds, Repetto awoke as exhausted as he'd been last night. He carefully disentangled himself from Lora, who was still asleep. He thought about kissing her forehead, then decided against chancing that he might wake her. Instead he studied her as if she were a precious puzzle, loving her, knowing they needed each other now as never before. As quietly as possible, he climbed out of bed and went into the bathroom to shower.

With his left arm and hand he'd been gentle with Lora, but he became aware that the fingers of his right hand ached from having clutched the wadded sheet as he fell asleep, and perhaps as he slept.

When he was finished toweling dry, he stared at the man in the bathroom mirror.

Captain Vincent Albert Repetto stared back at him, the same as yesterday, yet unalterably changed.

7

Homicide Detective Meg Doyle steered the unmarked police car onto the exit ramp and watched for the turnoff for the service road. Beside her sat her partner, Bert (Birdy) Bellman. They'd left the city half an hour ago, after Meg had picked up Birdy at his house in Queens, and they'd had a quick breakfast of doughnuts and coffee as they drove. Cops eating doughnuts. Life imitating art, Meg thought. Blame it on Krispy Kreme.

They were up early and on the road because Dal Bricker's funeral was in New Jersey. His graveside service, anyway, for friends and family. He was already buried, after a full-dress NYPD funeral complete with dignitaries, bagpipes, and rifle salute. Today was the quieter, more private good-bye to Sergeant Dal Bricker. Immediately after the service, Meg and Birdy would be introduced to Repetto.

Meg was looking forward to meeting Repetto. He was something of a legend in the NYPD, and she wasn't surprised that the higher-ups would call on his expertise. That Repetto was also the Night Sniper's choice simply made it unanimous. Stories still drifted around the department about

Repetto, how he'd personally cornered the Midnight Leather Killer and traded shots with him before the suspect leaped to his death from forty stories up. About how two Mafia thugs had been sent around to intimidate Repetto and found themselves outmatched. Afterward, in their hospital beds, they'd been charged with assault, and their rights were read to them by Repetto.

Meg found the cemetery road and turned onto it. She was a diminutive woman of thirty-nine who would have risen higher in the NYPD by now if she'd been able to control her tongue. Not that she had a temper; it was more that her words were out and doing harm before she could stop them. Since her divorce from Chip she tended to say what she thought, what she knew, what was the truth—a dangerous habit and hard to break. Her figure was trim, her eyes a dark brown, her features elfin. Her dark, short-cropped hair grew in a cowlick that made it stand on end in front in a way reminiscent of a rooster comb. When she'd been a uniformed cop she'd kept her cap on as much as possible. Now aerosol hair spray battled her cowlick, not always successfully.

Birdy Bellman, on the other hand, was bald except for a few lank strands of hair plastered in a grid across his gleaming pate. His eyes were hooded and his face a series of vertical planes that made him always appear somber. He got tagged with the Birdy nickname because he often made silent pecking motions with his head when he was tense, which was almost always. Tense on the outside, anyway, while his brain was placidly and relentlessly working. Meg thought that if Birdy really *was* a bird he'd be a vulture. One that ate bad roadkill that had given him indigestion.

Some part of Birdy was always moving, fingers tapping, a foot bouncing in frantic rhythm, a hand clenching and unclenching, releasing the frustration and excess energy that plagued him. Sometimes Meg thought Birdy should see a shrink.

"There it is," he said beside her, drumming his fingers on his knee.

The car had reached the yawning iron gates to the cemetery. Meg slowed and made a left turn, noticing that the hinges on the gates were rusted over. The cemetery was an old one and encroached upon by commerce, the dead being crowded by the living.

Because they'd been doing duty, neither Meg nor Birdy had been able to attend yesterday's ceremony. Meg had never visited here. Glancing around, she thought it must have been a peaceful place before the highway was widened. The grounds were reasonably well kept, and tall poplar and maple trees lined the blacktop road that wound among pale tombstones and statuary.

Meg saw a knot of mourners up ahead and slowed the car, then parked it at the end of a line of vehicles strung out behind a shiny black Cadillac. She got out of the dusty unmarked Chevy and slipped into her lightweight black raincoat that was in keeping with the event. Birdy had worn his dark suit with a maroon tie that had some kind of spiral pattern. He looked halfway presentable. Birdy's wife had suffered a stroke two years ago and since then had been bedridden. Meg thought he'd done a pretty good job of dressing himself.

The service was under way, so Meg and Birdy edged up to the fifty or so mourners and stood politely and silently. Assistant Chief Melbourne, in his full-dress uniform, noticed them and nodded.

An extremely thin priest in dark vestments was standing beside the freshly filled grave and a simple tombstone bearing Dal Bricker's name. He was reading a eulogy that Meg was too far away to understand. Not far from him was a huge array of floral displays that had been used in yesterday's public ceremony. Not far from the flowers stood Vincent Repetto.

Meg stared at him, fascinated. He was a big man, over six

feet, with a boxer's weighty shoulders and long arms. His hands were huge and rough looking beneath white cuffs that showed below the sleeves of his well-tailored dark suit. She thought his eyes were blue but couldn't be sure. The wind ruffled his iron-gray hair and he looked incredibly sad.

A blond woman next to Repetto moved closer to him and gripped his arm as if for support. Probably his wife. Not far from her stood a young woman, late teens or early twenties, with incredibly long, braided blond hair; she bore a resemblance to the blond woman. Meg knew Repetto had a daughter. Did this woman look something like him, too?

Repetto must have sensed Meg staring at him, because he glanced up at her and the moment was electric. It wasn't so much sadness she saw in his face now. It was the kind of set, placid immobility she'd seen on the faces of truly dangerous men just before they acted. They were still and silent before they exploded. They were already committed, so there was nothing left other than action. It was only a matter of when.

Meg thought in that instant that the Night Sniper might have made a big mistake; then she looked away.

Halfway up a hill on the other side of the highway, the Night Sniper sat on the cool, hard ground beneath a maple tree. He was concealed in a small copse of trees, with a clear view of the cemetery and Dal Bricker's graveside service. At first he'd used his scope, which he'd brought with him in his backpack. Then he decided he was close enough to recognize people without it, and if he happened to be seen by someone while he was focused on the cemetery, it might attract suspicion. Cops almost always attended the funerals and memorial services of murder victims, the theory being that sometimes the killers were compelled to observe their handiwork and be among the mourners.

Not among them this time. Not quite.

The service appeared to be over now. The fifty or so mourners were turning away from the grave and milling around almost as if they were in a trance. They were repelled by death but didn't want to rush away and insult it, provoke it.

There was Repetto, and alongside him the woman who must be his wife, Lora, and possibly their daughter. They were talking to a woman in a hat with a flat black rim. She touched Repetto's upper arm gently and hugged Lora and the younger woman; then the three women left Repetto and walked together toward the parked cars. Captain Melbourne approached Repetto, along with a man and woman.

Cops in plainclothes. The Night Sniper could spot them even from this distance, and it was made easier because he knew who they were: Detectives Meg Doyle and Birdy Bellman. Research was the Sniper's specialty. He'd done his homework and knew about both of them. Doyle was a loose-tongued, sometimes insulting young woman made cynical by a recent divorce. Bellman was a middle-aged, frenetic little man who couldn't sit still very long in one place. The Night Sniper knew something about many of the NYPD homicide detectives. There were plenty of ways to learn, in this high-tech information age when everybody—even homicide detectives—claimed or were thrust into their fifteen minutes of fame. The NYPD liked to brag about its personnel, on the Internet at official and unofficial sites, and in small-print publications that chronicled the world of law enforcement. It was good public relations.

Now the Night Sniper would learn even more about Doyle and Bellman, as he had about Repetto. The intrepid Repetto had experienced great tragedy in his youth, then had fallen into kind hands. The loss, in a sense, had ended, the torn heart partially healed. The Night Sniper had experienced no such luck. Not in time to save him from the streets, and from the demons of the dark.

Luck was the difference. Luck was what defined and separated most people, no doubt including Doyle and Bellman. The Night Sniper would be even more familiar with them soon enough.

To fully experience and appreciate the game about to be played out on life's stage, the grand theater of death and vengeance that had only begun, it was best to know the players.

His fellow actors, who were about to play the roles of their lives.

8

Meg, Repetto, and Birdy stood loosely side by side. Repetto raised his old .38 Smith & Wesson revolver and fired six rapid shots at the target twenty yards down the range. They were at the outdoor shooting range at Rodman's Neck in the Bronx, on a peninsula jutting into Long Island Sound. Repetto had insisted they come here in the unmarked directly from the cemetery, after only a brief stop so he could get some things from his car before his wife and daughter drove it home. The other shooters at the range wore casual clothes. Meg and Birdy had removed their jackets, and Birdy had loosened his tie. Repetto remained fully clad in his dark suit, his tie knot neat and severely bound. Blasting away in his mourning clothes.

He reloaded.

Repetto's handsome but worn features were set and hard with grief and determination. Meg had been told Bricker was like a son to him. Looking at Repetto, Meg couldn't prevent a lump from welling up in her throat.

"You don't look so good, Captain," she said. "We can wait

till tomorrow if you want to discuss this, or even later today—"

"I'm okay," Repetto interrupted. "And time's important. Otherwise I'd be home with my wife and daughter serving cake to well-wishers."

In answer, Meg got off two careful shots at her target. It hadn't felt right; despite taking her time, she hadn't set herself.

Repetto lifted an old pair of oversize binoculars he'd brought from his car.

"Two in the middle," he said. "Not bad."

She felt immediately better.

Birdy used the point and shoot method, firing quickly and relying on instinctive aim. He'd learned it was the best method of shooting if you didn't have the steadiest hands. When he lowered his 9mm Glock, Repetto peered through the binoculars and said, "Uh-hm."

He let the binoculars fall on their leather neck strap and turned away from the range to look at Meg and Bellman. Meg felt Birdy shift his weight slightly beside her. Repetto's eyes, blue and with the cold spark of diamonds, had the same unsettling effect on him that they'd had on her. Here was a man in the thrall of a mission larger than his life. If the Night Sniper wanted a worthy opponent, he'd sure found one.

Meg holstered her gun. She hoped Repetto hadn't noticed her hand was trembling.

He said, "Two things. One is, despite the temporary rank, I'm on unofficial status, so call me Repetto." He wasn't quite ready to be on first-name-basis familiarity. "Two is we are going to nail this son of a bitch!"

Meg surprised herself by smiling slightly. Adrenaline, maybe. "I'll remember both of them."

"And I will," Birdy said beside her in his gravelly voice.

Meg saw that his index finger was nervously twitching where it was extended along the barrel of his Glock.

Repetto had apparently had enough shooting. He slipped his loaded revolver into its belt holster, then led the way back to where the car was parked. From the backseat floor he retrieved the scuffed, black leather briefcase he'd brought with him. He opened the briefcase and drew out two brown cardboard packets with their flaps tied with string wrapped around metal grommets. He laid them on the sun-warmed trunk lid of the car. "These are the murder files on all the Night Sniper victims, copies for both of you. When we leave here, take yours with you and study it."

"Study it some more, you mean," Meg said. "When Birdy and I knew we had this assignment, we went over all the material and talked about it."

Repetto smiled at her through the grief and cold purpose that possessed him. "Good. Come to any conclusions?"

"He likes to play," Birdy said, slipping back into his suit coat he'd carried slung over his arm. "They all do to some extent, but the game is a big part of this one's sickness."

"That's more or less what Zoe Brady says," Meg added.

Repetto was surprised. "The profiler's already talked to you?"

"Not personally. It's what she wrote in a summary of her findings. Also, he's a sadist."

"Aren't they all?" Birdy said, drumming his fingertips on the trunk.

Meg momentarily rested her hand on his to quiet the drumming fingers. They'd been partners long enough that she could do that and neither of them thought much of it. "For the most part, they are. But if our killer was driven primarily by sadism, he'd want to get up close and see the effects on his victims, instead of shooting them with a long-range rifle from far enough away that he can't see and feel their shock and fear."

Repetto looked at her. "But I thought you got from Zoe Brady's material that she thinks this guy's engine is sadism."

"She didn't exactly say that," Meg told him. "I surmised that's what she thinks."

He gave her a look that bored into her. Somebody on the range got off a long volley with something large-caliber, overwhelming the staccato reports of smaller firearms. "You put much stock in profiling?"

"Some, is all." Meg shrugged. A cloud moved away and she squinted against the sun. "Science, applied to a nutcase with a rifle, I don't know how accurate that can be."

"I'll take a good cop's hunch any day," Repetto said. He nodded toward Bellman. "What Birdy said makes sense, about the game playing, the challenge. It means a lot to our sniper." He reached again into his briefcase and removed a folded sheet of white paper. "This'll make Birdy's view of the Sniper seem even more accurate."

The paper was a copy of a typed note sent to Repetto, care of the NYPD. It said simply, *Now the Game begins.*

There was no letterhead and no signature.

"Plain, cheap white paper and envelope," Repetto said, before they could ask. "Sold in office supply stores and even drugstores. Same typewriter used on the envelope as on the note, probably a forty-year-old Royal manual. Mailed at the post office at Third and Fifty-fourth Street."

"Busy place," Birdy said.

"Latent Prints couldn't lift anything from the paper or envelope, and there's no thumbprint on the stamp. Not even DNA on the back of the stamp."

"Careful guy," Meg said.

"One who plans."

"Profilers call the planners organized serial killers," Birdy said.

"Fuck profilers." Repetto realized as soon as he'd spoken that he'd overreacted. "Well, not really. We need to factor in what they say."

"What Zoe Brady says," Meg told him.

"Right. Let's concentrate on our killer, not Zoe Brady."

Meg and Birdy glanced at each other.

"He doesn't use a sound suppresser," Meg said. "He's obviously an expert shot and must know something about firearms, so why doesn't he use a silencer?"

"Maybe he can't afford one," Birdy said.

"He'd steal one. I think he knows that here in New York sound bounces around the buildings, and it's impossible to know exactly where a shot came from. In each of the murders the sound of the sniper's rifle echoed off all the hard surfaces so witnesses not only had no idea of the shot's origin, some of them weren't even sure if only one shot was fired."

"He'd still be safer with a silencer," Birdy said.

"Maybe," Meg said. "But the rest of us would *feel* safer, and he doesn't want that. We wouldn't jump every time a car backfires or somebody drops something that makes a sudden sound like a gunshot. Our sniper likes the echoing crack of his rifle. It adds to the fear factor. He wants everyone to be on edge, afraid of him."

Repetto cocked his head as if listening to the rattle of gunfire from the range, then looked at Meg. "You're probably right that he's primarily interested in gamesmanship and evoking a general kind of fear, rather than in sadism."

"Only probably," Birdy pointed out. "And he might be interested in a general kind of sadism."

Repetto nodded. "We know about the game playing because of his contacts with the police, his insistence on me as an opponent, and the typed note. The rest of it's speculation, but it's worth keeping in mind." He focused again on Meg. "What you surmise about the reason he doesn't use a silencer fits in. Our man not only enjoys the fear factor, but it's a strategic plus. It's exactly the kind of thing I was hoping might come out of rereading the murder files."

Meg felt a flush of pleasure at his approval. *Why should I feel this way? I hardly know this guy. He's not my father.*

The shooter with the high-powered weapon opened up again. Meg thought she could smell gunpowder, though she knew they were too far away from the range unless the breeze was just right.

Repetto closed his briefcase and buckled a strap. "Let's get to work revisiting the crime scenes and talking to witnesses, see if something new clicks. We do the grunt work. The *we* is you two. I've still gotta study these files."

"So you're the official Captain Repetto sometimes," Meg said with a grin, trying a joke.

"All the time, actually," Repetto said, not smiling. "But usually we'll pretend otherwise."

Jesus! She felt her insides shrivel. *Make it better? Tell him I was kidding? No. Shut up. Don't make it worse. The man's virtual son was murdered days ago and he's in mourning. I shouldn't have played it light.*

Or maybe he was amused and joking back. Possible . . .

"The work'll keep us busy while we wait," Repetto said, opening a rear door of the unmarked and tossing the briefcase far enough inside that he'd have room to sit.

"Wait for what?" Birdy asked, as he and Meg moved to get into the car.

In a nanosecond he realized it had been a dumb question. They all knew what.

Vito Mestieri owned and worked long hours in Vito's Screwdriver, his small appliance and TV repair shop on the

Lower East Side. He'd gotten out of the army thirty years ago after Vietnam and inherited the shop from his father. Now Vito, slowed by age and hindered by rheumatic fingers, was considering selling the shop. He wished he had a son of his own to hand down the business to, but both his marriages had been bitter and childless.

He had friends, fellow Nam vets who met once a week to play poker and tell lies. But the Vietnam vets were gray and potbellied now, like Vito, and were slowly fading from the earth they way the World War Two guys had done. Vito knew that someday soon the *Times* obituary page would make a deal out of the last Nam vet dying. Maybe he'd be the one, but he doubted it. One thing was for sure: he wouldn't read it.

Vito flipped the sign in the door from OPEN to CLOSED and stepped outside. He unclipped the ring of keys from his belt and by feel found the one that fit the dead bolt lock on the door.

The lock gave a satisfying metallic click. No one had broken into the shop for over a year, since Vito had changed the lock and had the alarm system installed.

He clipped the ring back on his belt and stepped away from the locked door, and felt a sudden, sharp pain high on his side, near his armpit. At first he thought a bee or wasp had stung him. Then he took a few steps, experienced a different, deeper pain, and felt for the source of the first stinging sensation.

His hand came away bloody and he was back in Nam. He knew he'd been shot.

Had to get help!

The narrow side street was deserted except for some people up near the intersection. Vito raised a hand, tried to call out. The pain stilled his voice.

Back inside. Call 911!

He turned back toward the door and felt an overpowering weakness.

Then from the corner of his eye he saw a car turn the corner and start down the street in his direction.

Someone to drive me to a hospital!

He turned back away from the door and staggered out into the street, trying to scream for the car to stop, trying to wave his arms. Helpless, bubbling gasps were the only sounds he made, and his arms, which he thought he was waving, were hanging limp at his sides.

The car had been picking up speed. Now the driver saw Vito and stomped on the brake pedal. Yanked the steering wheel to swerve around Vito.

Rubber screamed as the car skidded sideways. Vito tried to get out of the way but fell. The car did a 180-degree turn and the back wheels rolled over him.

The driver, an eighteen-year-old Hispanic kid, was slumped on the curb weeping when the police arrived.

He felt somewhat better a few hours later, when he learned that when the car had rolled over Vito, he was already dead from a gunshot wound.

9

After being up most of the night, Repetto met with Meg and Birdy around ten the next morning at the Hobby Hole in the West Village. In the evening the place served dinner and drinks and was a lesbian jazz club. During the day it was breakfast and lunch and the clientele was more varied. All the time they served their specialty, warm biscuits with a sweetly flavored butter. It was within walking distance of Repetto's house and he ate there often, whatever the time or sexual orientation. He didn't give a damn; he was there for the biscuits.

Not this morning, though. He and Lora had eaten breakfast at home.

There was only one other customer, up near the front of the restaurant and out of earshot. A burned bacon scent hung in the air and would have made Repetto hungry if he hadn't already eaten.

"I'm just having coffee," he said.

"Us too," Meg said, speaking for Birdy. "We had doughnuts just a few hours ago."

Birdy tapped out a pattern with his fingertips on the table and nodded.

Meg hadn't been in here before. She tried not to look at what seemed to be a collection of photos of nude women but for cowboy boots and hats on the wall near the bar. They seemed to be spinning lariats. The server, a slim young woman somehow feminine in boots, baggy jeans, studded leather vest, and a butch haircut, poured three cups of coffee, left a small metal pitcher of cream, then withdrew.

When she was out of earshot, Repetto said, "Let's go over what we have on Vito Mestieri."

Meg sipped her coffee. Birdy seemed to have nothing to say, so she led. "Central fact is he's dead. Ballistics says the bullet's misshapen from bouncing around his rib cage, so they can't get a match on it."

"Not that it would match anyway," Birdy said. "Different gun for each victim. Our guy must have an arsenal."

"Gun nut," Meg said.

"Which is why we're gonna start checking out gun merchants and collectors," Repetto said.

"We're still trying to find out where the shooter fired from, but it looks pretty hopeless. He knows the sound of the shot will echo and be impossible to trace."

The baggy-jeaned server paused walking past their table and asked if anyone needed anything, looking at Meg.

Meg said maybe later.

Birdy winked at her.

Meg didn't like what must be going on in his mind. She couldn't believe he hadn't noticed the photos of the scantily clad cowpunchers. Or that he was gentleman enough not to mention them. The man seldom disappointed.

"Suppose he knows it enough to choose firing sites where he'll get the most echoing effect," Repetto said. "Let's put ourselves in his head and check out buildings and rooftops surrounded by a lot of hard surfaces."

"That's just about every building in New York," Birdy said dismally.

"Some more than others," Meg said, sticking up for Repetto as if he needed it. Birdy began nervously pumping a knee, making the table vibrate. Were they ganging up on him?

"Mestieri would be the first," he said.

Repetto and Meg looked at him.

"The first victim in the game," Birdy said. "Since the Night Sniper said the game was beginning."

"He's right," Repetto said. "The previous murders were prelude."

"Warming up," Birdy said, as if Meg needed explanation. "Like practice golf swings. Now it's for real."

"It was real for the people who got shot before Vito Mestieri," Meg said.

Birdy stopped with the knee and nodded. "Yeah, but to our shooter the earlier victims were just a way to get Repetto into the game. Even Bricker. Especially Bricker."

Meg gave him a cautioning look, considering Repetto's expression at the mention of Dal Bricker. Birdy shouldn't have gone there. He might catch hell now.

But the hardness in Repetto's expression had nothing to do with Birdy's insensitivity; it was about the Night Sniper.

"He made a mistake when he killed Dal," Repetto said in a soft, easy voice.

Which gave Meg more of a chill than if his rage had shown on his face.

They were back out on the street, walking toward the car, when Birdy grinned over at Meg and said, "Whoopee ti yi yo."

When they drove to their precinct basement office to check for any developments, and to pick up another city car so they could split up to check out gun dealers and collectors, they were surprised to find Assistant Chief Melbourne waiting for them.

Melbourne had arranged for the office, which was cramped and glum. The walls were pale green and the single window was narrow and at ground level, splattered with mud so it was difficult to see out and allowed only dim light in to relieve somewhat the relentless fluorescent glare of the cheap ceiling fixtures. The furniture and file cabinets were dented gray steel. A computer on the desk looked as if it had been upgraded over and over and was a technology basket case. Maps of all five boroughs, departmental notices with curling corners, a case chart, were pinned directly to the soft wallboard that covered concrete. The office was damp and smelled like a swamp. A patch of mold a few inches square grew in a corner of the ceiling. On one wall was a framed photo of former Police Commissioner Bernard Kerik in uniform, looking stolid and sincere and indestructible.

Melbourne was behind Repetto's desk, seated in Repetto's chair. Bulky as he was, he didn't fill the chair the way Repetto did.

"You wanna know what we know," Repetto said.

"That," Melbourne said, "and I want you to know about this."

Repetto saw that Melbourne was talking about a sheet of white typing paper on the desk.

"This is a copy," Melbourne said. "Lab's got the original and the envelope, but already they're saying nothing's coming out of them. Same cheap stationery, same postmark, same typewriter. That's about it."

At first Repetto thought the copy paper was blank, but when he leaned closer he saw the brief message: *7-F.*

"That's it?" he asked.

Melbourne nodded. "An apartment number, would be my guess. Our sniper wants you trying to find where he shot from, because he knows all that'll happen is we'll get more frustrated. That's his game."

"There's that word again," Meg said. "Game."

"Here's something else," Melbourne said. He reached into a pocket and laid a small cassette on the desk. "Tape of the killer's phone calls. Voice sounds disguised. None of these calls were traced to any phone that meant anything."

"Male or female voice?"

"Can't say for sure, but probably male. These calls won't tell you much more than I told you about them."

Repetto picked up the cassette and carried it to a recorder on top of one of the file cabinets. "Does this relic work?"

"Sure," Melbourne said. "Sometimes the job calls for relics."

Repetto ignored him and inserted the cassette into the old recorder.

The voice was disguised, as Melbourne had said, and was most likely male. There was something in it that created a cold spot on the back of Meg's neck. Especially the last thing the killer said:

"I want Repetto and Repetto only. A man is judged by the quality of his enemies, and Repetto is to be my opponent. Repetto, Repetto, Repetto. I repeato, Repetto."

"Jesus!" Meg said. "He has a sense of humor."

"Most born killers do," Melbourne said. "They'd just as soon see somebody die as see them slip on a banana peel. Same thing to them."

"He seems to have switched from phone calls to notes now that Repetto's on the case," Birdy said.

Melbourne nodded. "His game, his rules."

"So far," Repetto said.

"Only so many apartment seven-Fs the killer could have fired from and hit Mestieri," Melbourne said, turning his attention again to the note. "Thing to do is check them out."

Repetto nodded, putting aside for the moment the canvassing of gun dealers and collectors.

"How many uniforms can you give us?" he asked Melbourne.

"Five. And they're already down on the Lower East Side doing their jobs. They need you to supervise them."

Repetto doubted it. The hunt for the Night Sniper wasn't the kind of case that prompted standing around jerking off when there was work to be done.

Melbourne gave a wheeze and heaved himself up out of Repetto's chair. "You want your desk?"

"Not now," Repetto said, on his way back out the door. "You fly it for a while."

Meg and Birdy followed, not glancing back at Melbourne.

Two apartment 7-Fs were found that provided clear shots to where Vito Mestieri had fallen with a sniper's bullet in him. One was owned by an eighty-year-old retired woman who needed an oxygen bottle to breathe and hadn't left the place in months. The other 7-F was in a steel and glass post-war monstrosity that had windows that didn't open.

Repetto, Meg, and Birdy had spent another futile day. If this was a game they were playing, the Sniper was winning.

At dinner that night at Mama Roma, a neighborhood Italian restaurant that was one of their favorites, Repetto watched Lora ignore her favorite pasta and stare idly into the wine she was swirling in her glass. She was taking Dal Bricker's death hard, as was Repetto. Dal, who had been like a son to them, and if dreams could come true, a son-in-law. For some reason Repetto thought Lora would emerge from her grief sooner than he would. He should have known better; she didn't have as much opportunity as he to act on her pain and hunger for revenge.

"Did you see your client about the condo near Gramercy Park?" he asked.

"Canceled the appointment," she said. "Somehow coordinating drapes and carpet doesn't seem so important now."

Repetto knew what she meant. "Dal?"

She stopped the swirling motion with her glass and looked at him. "Of course."

"We'll get his killer."

"That sounds like a line from an old B-movie."

"Maybe it does, but it's true."

She didn't insult him by pointing out what they both knew: apprehending the Night Sniper wouldn't bring back Dal. "Can you promise?"

"Yes."

"How?"

"I know I won't quit until we do get him." When she showed no reaction, he said, "How's Amelia taking Dal's death?"

"Not well. But she's losing herself in her studies. She's strong and can cope."

"Hard work as therapy." That was something Repetto believed in, so why not his daughter?

"Maybe she'll start seeing—"

"Someone else?" Repetto interrupted, almost angrily.

"She never did see Dal quite the way we would have liked."

"No," he admitted, "she didn't."

Lora artfully twirled a few strands of angel-hair pasta on her fork into a small tangle, put it in her mouth, and chewed. A sip of wine. "I had lunch today with Zoe Brady."

After Zoe's initial visit, Repetto was surprised when Lora had told him the two women had met, at a police banquet, and through an unexpected encounter in an antique shop when Lora was searching for a particular piece of furniture for a client. He was equally surprised they'd met for lunch.

They didn't exactly strike him as soul sisters.

"I called her," Lora said. "I wanted to talk to her about the Night Sniper."

"Why?"

"I need to know what's going on. I need . . . to do something. To help. For Dal."

"For you, you mean."

"That's true. Dal's gone."

"You're a decorator, Lora, not a cop. For that matter, Zoe's not a cop either."

"Zoe can help me understand. She can tell me about the man who killed Dal, the man my husband is trying to kill."

"Catch," Repetto corrected her. "It isn't my job to kill him."

"I wasn't talking about your job."

"I was *only* talking about my job." He took a large swallow of wine, dribbling some of it on his tie.

"Red wine," Lora said. "It'll stain."

"We changing the subject?" Repetto asked, dabbing at the stain with his napkin.

She smiled sadly. "Sure."

"I don't want to have to worry about you, Lora."

"This isn't 1890, and I'm not some wilting flower who's going to swoon under stress."

"I know that. It's the twenty-first century, and life is cheaper."

"Are you going to forbid me to help?"

He had to grin. "I wouldn't do that. It wouldn't work anyway. The thing is, I don't know any way you *can* help."

"Maybe there isn't one, but I can at least help myself. It makes me feel better to talk with Zoe."

"Not me," Repetto said. "I don't have as much faith as you do in profilers."

"Still, she's making the killer real to me."

"Somebody to disturb your sleep."

"Somebody I can hate."

Repetto understood how hate could supplant grief. He poured some more Chianti and took a sip, being more careful this time.

"I'll take the tie to the cleaners," Lora said. "We've got some other things that need to go."

They didn't talk about Dal or the Night Sniper the rest of the evening.

Everything but.

The next morning, after Repetto left the house, Lora was gathering clothes to take to the dry cleaner. She checked one of Repetto's suits to make sure the pockets were empty.

Deep in one of his suit coat's inside pockets, she found a ticket stub from a week ago, when they'd last attended a play.

No surprise; Repetto was forgetful.

As she set the ticket aside to be thrown away later, she saw that it was for an orchestra seat, six rows back and seven off the aisle.

Seat 7-F.

10

Ralph Evans moved aside and let his wife, Venus, enter the elevator first. They both stood against the elevator walls so the bellhop would have room with their luggage. They'd just checked into the Melrose Plaza Hotel on the edge of Times Square. Pattie and George Neverton, also from Columbus, Ohio, had checked in minutes before. The Evanses had known the Nevertons for almost twenty years. Venus had gone to high school with Pattie. The two girls had dated the same boys, made the same mistakes, fallen into the same resignation they'd decided was happiness.

Ralph, a buyer for Adcock's, an upscale men's clothing store chain, was in New York on business, but his appointments weren't scheduled till tomorrow. Plenty of time for talking with designer reps and feeling bolts of fabrics. Tonight the four Ohioans were going to have dinner at a good restaurant, then take in a show. That was why Ralph and Venus had invited their old friends the Nevertons to come along and play in fun city.

As soon as Ralph had tipped the bellhop and they were settled in their room, he called the Nevertons, who were also on the thirty-first floor. George and Pattie said they were right down the hall and would come over; they wanted to compare rooms, see if Ralph and Venus had a phone in the bathroom.

Venus, a plump former cheerleader, wandered over to the window and looked out at the city. "It's so big and busy. More so even than you said."

Ralph looked at her framed by the light, twenty pounds overweight (but so was he), still with the bright blue eyes and wild mop of blond hair. Somehow they came to be in their midforties, he a middle-aged cloth and clothing buyer, she a stereotypical housewife in Ohio. Both of them were stereotypes, Ralph thought. It wasn't so bad.

"Why are you smiling?" Venus asked.

"I still love you more than I can express."

She smiled back and started toward him, the fading light from the window catching a glint of tears in her eyes.

There was a knock on the door. Venus went to it and opened it.

"Hey, your room's bigger'n ours!" Pattie exclaimed in mock outrage, as soon as she and George were inside.

Ralph and Venus glanced at each other. Ralph knew what her look meant: we'll take up later where we left off.

"No phone in the bathroom, though," Ralph said, though he wasn't sure about that.

"Ah!" George said. "It's all fair then." He was a big man with sandy hair and horsey yellowed teeth that showed too much when he smiled.

Pattie had gone to the window and was looking out. "Where's that place where you can line up and get cheap play tickets, Ralph?"

"Just a few blocks away. TKTS."

"Why don't we walk over there and see what we can get for tonight?"

Ralph would have preferred going to a theater box office,

or calling Telecharge, but he knew Pattie and George were watching their pennies. "Tell you what, why don't Venus and I walk over while you two unpack? Then we can meet downstairs for a drink."

"That wouldn't be right," Pattie said. "We can all go."

"You two oughta unpack," Ralph said. He couldn't think of why they should unpack first; he simply wanted to be alone with Venus, so they could choose the play. Pattie would want to see something serious and sappy that would put them all in a somber mood, and he knew Venus would prefer a big musical. Then, tonight when they returned from the theater . . .

"*You* two unpack," Pattie said. "We'll go get the tickets."

"Ralph's the only one knows right where the place is," George reminded her.

"So let's flip a coin," Venus said.

Pattie was thinking it over, but Ralph already had a quarter out of his pocket.

"Heads we go," George said.

Wishing there were some way he could cheat, Ralph flipped the coin high so it would land on the bed. It bounced twice before settling on the taut spread.

Ah! Tails.

"Good," he said. "We'll go. That's how it should be. You're sort of our guests. You two unpack and we'll phone up to you from the lobby when we get back with the tickets."

The Nevertons agreed, Pattie reluctantly, and went back to their room.

When the door was shut, Venus kissed Ralph on the lips and stroked his chest. "Our lucky night," she said.

He smiled down at her and kissed her forehead. *Lucky life.*

They left the suitcases where the bellhop had placed them; then they left to get play tickets.

For a musical, Ralph hoped. They'd enjoy a good dinner,

then a loud, colorful musical with lots of dancing; then they'd have drinks with their best friends and talk about the show. Then it would be back to the hotel and to bed.

He followed Venus out and made sure the door was locked behind them.

Lucky life.

11

Zoe Brady watched the balding guy in the produce department as he fingered some arugula. He was in his late thirties, a little overweight, nice clothes and an expensive-looking ring that wasn't a wedding band on his left hand. He'd be fairly good looking without his glasses—if he ever was without them.

Maybe a keeper.

As he examined a pyramid of apples, he glanced her way. He was aware she'd been staring at him.

Zoe had picked up men before in her neighborhood grocery store. What better place to troll for men, to snare them unaware while they were thinking about food? Of course, they thought they'd picked up her. It was a game she knew and played very well.

She went to the zucchinis and touched one, then another, leaning forward so her skirt rose slightly in back. Give the guy a leg show. When she straightened up, she shook her head helplessly and approached him.

"I'm really sorry I have to ask," she said, "but do you know what arugula is? I think it's like a lettuce."

He smiled, a little shy, and not quite believing his luck. "Sure. It's right over there." He pointed. "The ruffly-looking stuff."

"Ruffly. That's just what it looks like. Are you a writer?"

He laughed. Nice teeth. "No, I'm an accountant."

"Oh. I thought, the way you knew about and described arugula, maybe you wrote advertising." She gave him her best hesitant smile. She could play shy, too. "Thanks."

"Thanks?"

"I mean, for knowing about the arrugla. I've got to buy this stuff to take to a dinner party where we're all supposed to bring something. I'm bringing salad, and the host asked specifically for arugula."

"She can keep it. It's kind of bitter."

"Really? Maybe she wants it because of her religion or something. Or for her health." Zoe doing naive now. "I don't know her well."

"I don't know you well, either," he said, "but I'd like to."

"You don't know me at all."

"True, but I want to change that." He reached into a wallet he carried inside his sport jacket instead of on his hip—sometimes a sign of wealth—and handed her his business card. It said he was Herb Closeman and confirmed that he was an accountant, for a firm Zoe had never heard of.

"Mr. Closeman—"

"It's Herb."

"Okay, Herb." She slid his card into a pocket. "It's funny," she said, "your name's Herb and we met when I asked you about a herb."

"Clearly it's fate."

"Clearly. I wouldn't want you to think—"

"I'm not even going to ask for your name and phone number," he said. "You have mine. Think about it, and if you're at all interested, call me."

She grinned and shrugged. "Well, that's a safe enough proposition."

"I'm a safe enough guy. Really."

She held out her hand and they shook. "I'm Zoe."

"A nice name for a nice woman." He seemed to catch himself; *nice* hadn't been strong enough. "And a beautiful woman."

"So now we know each other," Zoe said, "however slightly. But I have to buy my arugula and get out of here or I'll be late for that dinner party."

"Wouldn't want that," Closeman said. "Take a chance and call me, Zoe."

"Okay, Zoe," she said with a big grin.

Herb appeared confused for a moment, then grinned back.

She favored him with her brightest smile, chose a plastic container of arugala, and left the store.

On the way to her apartment, she tossed the stuff in a trash receptacle.

An hour later she sat, brushing her hair and getting ready to meet some friends at a restaurant for dinner and drinks. She was proud of her long red hair, so thick and slightly wavy, what some men might call luxurious. Some, in fact, had called it that. Herb Closeman was right, she thought, observing her reflection in the mirror. Beautiful wasn't too strong a word for her.

Neither was *smart*. And *ambitious* certainly applied.

She forgot about Closeman as she continued to brush, absently counting toward a hundred. Her mind drifted to Lora Repetto's discovery of the theater stub in the pocket of Repetto's suit. The seat number hadn't been a wild coincidence.

The Night Sniper must have been shadowing Repetto, studying him, and followed him into the theater, maybe even sat near him. Repetto had been in seat 7-F in the Bernhardt Theatre, and now there was no doubt as to the reference in the Night Sniper's message. This, Zoe thought as she brushed, was definitely creepy.

Taped unobtrusively on the bottom of the seat, where Repetto had sat a week ago to see *War Bond Babes,* a musical about New York debutantes during World War Two, police had found a small, folded note. Its typed message was simple and cryptic: *Detective Repetto, perhaps this will help you find rhyme and reason.*

The lab had matched the typeface with that of the Night Sniper's previous message. The typewriter used was the Night Sniper's. The meaning of the note had yet to be figured out.

The killer playing his game.

She closely examined her image in the mirror. There were crow's-feet at the corners of her blue-green eyes, if she looked closely enough. The beginnings of bags beneath her eyes.

Is it age or booze? Am I drinking too much lately?

She pushed such a notion from her mind and thought not of Herb Closeman but of Repetto. Maybe he intrigued her because he held a certain contempt for her. Men who disdained her for some reason attracted her. They frightened her, too, which was also an attraction.

Zoe had heard about Repetto, of course. Everybody in the NYPD had heard of him. She'd even been introduced to him once, at a police awards dinner about a year ago, and had struck up an acquaintance with his wife, Lora. Now, during her lunches with Lora, she tried to learn about Repetto while Lora tried to learn about the Night Sniper.

But like a cop's good wife, Lora didn't reveal much about her husband.

Zoe continued using the brush beyond a hundred, maybe because she was preoccupied thinking about Repetto.

Repetto had earned a rare respect from hard men. She'd expected him to be a macho type, and she supposed he was. But there was something else about him, after Dal Bricker's death, that touched her. The pain in him was like an aura. So palpable was Repetto's grief that Zoe felt she might extend a hand and touch it. A man who grieved for a friend so intensely, there must be a certain worth to him. And there was something more in him than pain and grief; there was a quiet rage, tightly sprung and dangerous, that she knew so well.

She'd seen it in some of the killers she interviewed in prison, the ones who, when pressed, would admit that if free they would kill again. They were way past any sort of identity crisis. They knew precisely who they were and what they must and would do. The dark power that drove them was a simple and accepted fact, and a commitment that lent them a terrible calculating strength.

Repetto wasn't a killer. At least not that kind of killer. Zoe had met enough killers to know that about him. He wasn't like the sick, delusional animals with pieces of themselves missing, who could freeze other humans with their utter contempt or disregard.

Repetto was simply a good man who had made up his mind to kill. There was a difference.

Zoe listened to the brush's stiff bristles sigh through her hair and told herself there was a difference.

Meg had dropped in at Kung Foo Go and was going to eat Chinese carryout in her West Side apartment. She didn't mind living alone or eating alone. It had been two years since her divorce from Chip and she still hated the bastard. *Who did he think he was? Swinging on me? Thinking he was going to beat me like the other pitiful women I see every week in my job?*

She remembered slipping Chip's second punch, after the

first had broken her nose, then grabbing his arm and jerking him off balance, bending the arm back and back, hearing him scream as his elbow slipped its socket.

Meg could still hear that scream sometimes at night. It made her feel better.

Since Chip, Meg was off men. Couldn't trust the bastards. It was built into them. Now distrust was built into her. She knew it and couldn't care less.

She was attractive in a tomboy, scruffy way, so she'd had to get used to rebuffing men who were drawn by her dark eyes, the way her short black hair curled and made her face seem even more elfin despite her now habitual deadpan expression. She knew she looked like a somber leprechaun, but apparently some men liked that.

Like this character, young and fresh-faced, handsome in a naive way, with curly blond hair and a loping way of walking that reminded her of a big friendly puppy. He'd been watching her at the carryout counter in Kung Foo Go, and here he was loping along behind her like some amiable stray hoping for a scrap of food.

Meg turned. "Do we know each other?"

The kid stopped and looked stunned. "No. I, uh, saw you back in the restaurant and I . . . I just wanted to talk to you." He tried a smile but it died in a hurry.

"So talk."

Hope flared in his wide, puppy eyes and his smile was back. "I—"

"Yeah, you," Meg said impatiently.

"I found you so pretty I wanted to talk to you." He raised a hand palm out. "Don't get the wrong idea."

"So what's the right idea?"

"I was—I am—lonely, and there was something about you that made me think you, uh, might wanna talk, is all."

"What's your name?" Meg asked.

"Daryl."

"Listen, Daryl, you're fucking with a cop here."

"Cop?" He backed up a step, stunned. "You?"

"Me. You know those big red peppers they put in Chinese food?"

"Yeah."

"You bother me again and I'm gonna shove one up your ass."

He looked small enough to dive into a crack in the sidewalk.

Meg turned and stalked away, keeping a tight grip on her carryout bag. She waited for the guy to yell at her, call her a bitch, or something worse. It was New York. That was the way it worked.

But the kid remained silent.

After half a block she turned around to glare at him, but he was gone. She calmed down some and walked on, listening to her heels tapping the pavement.

Nice young guy, really, Daryl. Playing out of his league. All he wanted was . . . what they all want, and she'd cut him off at the knees and left him bleeding on the sidewalk. Now she felt bad about it.

But not real bad.

After locking herself in her apartment, Meg placed the white carryout containers on the coffee table, then went into the kitchen and returned with a can of Pepsi, a fork, and a paper towel to use as a napkin. She worked her shoes off her tired feet, then sat on the sofa and used the remote to switch on *New York 1* news on TV.

She opened the white cartons and used her fork to take a bit of noodles, then sat back against the soft cushions and sipped from the soda can.

It had been a hell of a day, reviewing once again the Night Sniper murder files, interviewing witnesses who were tired of telling their stories, talking on the phone with other witnesses. None of it had gotten them anywhere yet, but it was good, solid police work and might still pay dividends. That was how it worked in the Job—thoroughness, doggedness, eventually paid off. Most of the time, anyway. Something would fit, or wouldn't fit, and the picture would emerge. Though Meg was exhausted, she was satisfied with the work she and her fellow detectives had done. Her work was the one thing in life that did afford her some measure of satisfaction, a reason to anticipate tomorrow and to climb out of bed in the morning. Right now, it was enough. It gave her purpose and identity. It made her different from the furniture.

She thought about the Night Sniper's note to Repetto: *Perhaps this will help you find rhyme and reason.*

The play in the theater where the note was found was *War Bond Babes.* Meg had read about it in the *Post.* Rhyme, reason, and debutantes . . . Was there any meaning there at all except in the mind of a deranged killer? Maybe the poor schmuck had married a debutante type and gotten what he should have expected.

Meg relaxed and let her subconscious worry at the puzzle. Probably she'd watch TV after supper and fall asleep on the sofa. Hers was a lonely life, and a defensive one. She was comfortable in her tiny apartment, chomping noodles, sipping soda, watching *Seinfeld* and *Law and Order* reruns, not unhappy, not exactly happy, passing time without incurring further injury.

It was a life.

12

The Night Sniper carried nothing incriminating other than what was locked away in his mind. This was the time when he scouted in preparation. There were so many possibilities that it wasn't much of a challenge.

He appeared unexceptional in his best khaki Eddie Bauer slacks he'd bought at a secondhand shop, his worn New Balance jogging shoes, his pale blue shirt and darker blue windbreaker. Then there were the baseball cap, the turned-up collar. Anyone who noticed such a forgettable figure at all would have a difficult time describing him to the police. With so many people in New York, it was easy to be unnoticeable.

His clothes might be common, but they were clean. He despised having fouled material next to his flesh. That worked out well. Their many washings gave the clothes a familiar aura and suggested he usually dressed in such a manner. But these clothes, and his other costume, never got to within ten feet of his real wardrobe.

Ah, here he was. At the Bermingale Arms.

The Night Sniper had learned something about the building. It was thirty-three stories, a combination of condos and rental units, with street-level shops facing the west side. No one even glanced in his direction as he went through the lobby and took the stairs instead of the elevator to the third floor.

He paused, waiting until a woman at one of the apartment doors finished balancing her many small grocery sacks while using her key. When she'd gone inside, he took the last few steps to the landing.

The third-floor hall was empty now. He could wait for the elevator here and no one would see him, as they might have in the lobby. If there was anyone in the elevator when it arrived, he simply wouldn't step inside, as if he were waiting for one going down.

But the elevator was unoccupied, as he thought it would be this time of day, and it made no other stop all the way to the thirty-second floor.

As the elevator slowed, he slipped the flesh-colored latex gloves he'd bought at a medical supply house onto his hands. The gloves were made for burn victims with scarred or deformed hands, and passed for flesh unless someone looked closely and noticed their smooth texture, and that there were no fingernails.

The Night Sniper was pleased to find the narrow hall empty as he walked along it to the door to the fire stairs. The heavy door wouldn't sound an alarm when he opened it, but it would close and lock behind him, leaving him to draw attention to himself or walk down more than thirty flights of stairs.

He removed a small roll of duct tape from his pocket, ripped off a rectangle, and placed it over the recess for the door's spring lock so it wouldn't latch behind him. Then he was on the fire stairs landing.

Not worrying about being seen now, he began climbing the stairs almost silently in his soft-soled joggers. He climbed fast, breathing evenly, keeping his feet to the sides of the wooden steps to minimize any squeaking.

It took him barely a minute to reach the top floor, then higher, to the service door to the roof. After using his duct tape again, in case the door was set up so a key was necessary for him to get back inside, he stepped out into the high breeze.

The view was terrific. Forty-fourth Street stretched beneath him away from the intersection almost directly below. He felt like the figure he remembered from one of the art books he'd leafed through years ago, Zeus (or was it God himself?) in the clouds, high above his subjects, muscular arm drawn back, about to hurl a thunderbolt toward the unsuspecting minions below. God was an older man, a father figure, bearded and wise and obviously with a terrible strength. He was about to mete out punishment. Justice.

Think about God later. About Justice.

The Night Sniper stooped low and settled in behind a billboard with a faded high-energy drink advertisement on it. It wasn't very visible from below, and there were no lights illuminating it. The pretty girl in an evening gown, holding up a glass in a toast and smiling out at the scene below, had endured every kind of weather and was almost too faint to discern. One of her shoulders was peeling, the heavy shreds of signboard paper flapping gently in the breeze.

The breeze was probably constant up here, right now blowing at about ten miles per hour but without gusts. It would affect his aim but prove no problem. He had a feel now for how the wind played among the tall buildings, and he could adjust for different velocities at various heights. It was a talent, a synthesis of the physical senses and internal mathematics. He was proud of his increasing abilities, his growth. What he was doing had become an art within a game that itself would become an art.

The sign was supported about two feet higher than the

parapet by a sturdy steel frame that was rusting badly. There were diagonal cross braces forming a kind of wide lattice-work. He knew he'd be able to crouch behind the steel braces and use one of them to help steady the rifle.

Staying low, he moved sideways along the bottom edge of the billboard, gazing through the steel framework, until he had a clear view of the spot he'd chosen in the street below. It was about fifty feet beyond the intersection, where a fire hydrant was located, and he'd noticed it was a natural place for people to try to hail taxis pulling away from the green light or turning the corner onto Forty-fourth Street. He smiled. He had the clear shot he'd imagined from ground level.

In his mind he aimed his imaginary rifle at a couple frantically waving at a cab. He stared unblinkingly through the night scope and centered the crosshairs, holding steady . . . steady on the woman in jeans and what looked from this height like a bright scarf or bandana around her neck.

There was a deep calm within him; right now he was as still as anything on earth. He waited for the moment, and when it came he squeezed the trigger and the woman fell.

Only she didn't fall. She climbed into the cab that had pulled up to the curb near her.

Her lucky night.

She'd never know.

13

Ralph Evans walked with Venus, guiding her gently by the elbow as they wove through the mass of pedestrians on the sidewalks of West Forty-fourth Street. Vehicular traffic was heavy but moving swiftly, horns blaring, cabs jouncing over the potholed street. At the corner was a swirl of sound and activity.

"All the people, all the cars," Venus said, keeping pace with Evans. "Kind of exciting."

"Not like Ohio," Evans said. "Wakes you up."

"Ohio has its charms."

"When you're there."

They walked along for a while, deftly avoiding collisions with people coming the other way, and stopped now and then to glance in a shop window.

"I like it here," Venus said, "noise, exhaust fumes, and all, but I won't be sorry to get back to Columbus."

"You're not in New York mode yet. You'll see, hon, the place'll grow on you. I didn't like the city either, first time the company sent me here . . . what, five years ago?"

"More like ten, Ralph. Time's rushing past like that traffic."

"I guess it is. Faster'n we know."

They stopped at an intersection to wait for a walk signal, then stepped down off the curb swiftly to avoid being trampled.

"Know what?" Venus said. "These high heels are killing me. How far is it to where we're gonna buy tickets?"

Evans slowed their pace. He realized he'd been walking too fast, forcing her to keep up. It got to be habit, after you visited this city enough. Five minutes and you were a New Yorker living by the New York minute. "It's a way yet. We can get a cab if you'd rather."

She paused to lift one foot and bent sideways, balancing herself, to adjust her shoe. It was a graceful pose he'd never tired of appreciating. "I think I'd rather."

As they continued walking, only more slowly, Evans glanced from time to time at the traffic. Now that they needed a cab, there were none in sight.

At the next intersection, he steered Venus away from the pedestrians packed at the corner waiting to cross when the light changed. He gazed down the line of parked cars.

"There's a space where we can stand. Let's move away from all these people to where we can hail a cab."

They stepped off the curb, then waited for a break in traffic. Evans led the way as they walked single file alongside the parked cars to where there was a clear spot near a fire hydrant, where Venus could stand behind him well away from the rushing cars and trucks.

A dusty cab roared past. Its driver ignored Evans's wave. Evans hadn't seen a passenger in the back of the cab. He felt a tingle of anger.

New York. Get used to it.

Another cab without a passenger sped past. This time the driver glanced over at Evans but didn't stop.

What is it, the roof light's on when they have a fare or a call, or is it off? Bastards probably don't bother with it anyway.

The light changed at the corner, and a cab in the far lane darted out ahead of the accelerating traffic and crossed in front of it at an angle, speeding toward Evans and his wife. The driver must have seen them waving for the other cab. This cab drew a few angry horn blasts as it veered toward the curb to pick them up, then coasted smoothly to a stop alongside where they were standing.

Evans opened the back door and stepped back for Venus to enter first.

She got into the cramped space, smelling leather and some kind of cologne or perfume from the previous passenger. The driver had classical music playing softly, a piano concerto, and it was warm in the cab.

Venus worked herself across the slick seat to give Ralph room.

He had one foot in the cab and was lowering himself to slide across the seat toward her, when she heard him grunt. Almost at the same time there was what sounded like a crack of thunder, but she couldn't tell where it had come from, the way it echoed. People on the sidewalks seemed to stop or break stride, and the cabdriver hunkered down on the other side of the clear panel that separated him from his passengers.

Ralph removed his shiny black shoe from the cab and she thought he was going to stand up straight so he could see what had made the noise. Instead he slumped down and fell forward so the upper part of his body was inside the cab, the lower half in the gutter. His head was in Venus's lap, turned so she could see his face. He looked puzzled and scared.

"Ralph . . . ?" she heard herself say. Something dark and heavy weighted his name and made it difficult to forge into sound.

"Ralph?"

He tried to answer, but when he opened his mouth blood gushed out.

Venus began screaming his name over and over.

The Night Sniper thought at first he might have missed, and his target would climb into the cab and be driven away.

Then the target seemed to change his mind about getting into the cab with the woman. He removed the one foot he'd put inside and started to straighten up; then he bent forward and almost dived back into the cab, leaving his lower body outside the vehicle. The Night Sniper could tell by the way the target's legs shuffled, as if he were dreaming of walking, then were still in an awkward, splayed position, that his bullet had found its mark.

The target was dead.

The Night Sniper had seen enough. He was satisfied. He backed away from the parapet and the steel framework supporting the billboard. It took him only a second to find the expelled brass casing and slip it into a pocket.

Moving with practiced precision and speed, he disassembled the rifle and fit stock and barrel into his backpack. He was still zipping the pack closed as he strode across the roof toward the service door.

He opened the door, then removed the rectangle of tape he'd used to block the spring lock.

The heavy door closed itself silently behind him, as he worked his arms through the pack's thick straps and wrestled its familiar bulk onto his back.

He made it to the lobby unseen, and few people glanced at him as he stepped out into the street. Those who did glance would wonder what such a person was doing in the lobby; then they would forget him almost instantly, reject him.

As he strode along the sidewalk, the people around him seemed slowed and erratic in their movements. Frightened.

Not wanting to be noticeable, he made himself slow to below their speed and assumed his unsteady, shuffling gait.

Sirens were wailing now, yodeling through the backed-up traffic. They didn't bother the Night Sniper. The vehicles sounding the sirens were making their way toward the commotion down the block, where blinking and dancing red and blue lights dashed formless, flickering shapes against the buildings.

Behind him.

14

Meg stood with Repetto and Birdy on West Forty-fourth Street, near the stain remaining on the sidewalk where Ralph Evans's body had lain after it was dragged from the cab. Traffic slowed as it passed and drivers glanced over at the scene.

They knew. It was obvious from their expressions. Less than an hour had passed since it had happened, and already what promised to be the latest Night Sniper murder was on the news. There were still several reporters and a cable TV camera crew milling around behind the police cordon. One of the journalists, an on-camera, handsome guy Meg recognized because of his cleft chin and million-dollar haircut, caught her eye, grinned, and beckoned her over, knowing she wouldn't fall for it.

Venus Evans's story had been straightforward and simple: her husband was getting into the cab when he grunted and then collapsed half in and half out of the vehicle. She was back at her hotel now, being comforted by her other traveling companions.

It was apparent that the Night Sniper had struck, so when

the shot was fired no one assumed Evans had suffered a heart attack or some other sudden illness. Instead of good Samaritans rushing to his aid, everyone remained hunkered down, fearing a second shot, or had disappeared into shops or doorways. Only Venus and the cabbie remained near Evans, Venus screaming for help while the cabbie pulled Evans from the taxi and laid him on the sidewalk. The cabbie was ex-military and knew immediately that Evans was dead.

"Doesn't look like there are as many people on the streets as there should be," Birdy said, glancing around.

Meg looked up and down the block and thought he was right. "Murder will do that, I guess." But the ambulance had left only fifteen minutes ago with Evans's body, and she knew the theater district, the city, would soon return to normal. Normal considering there was a serial killer at large, randomly taking lives.

Birdy buttoned his suit coat so the breeze wouldn't cause it to flap open and reveal his holstered 9mm. "He's like the Grim Reaper. I mean, he could harvest anyone at any time."

"Very biblical," Meg said.

"Where do you suppose the Grim Reaper concealed himself this time when he swung his scythe?" Repetto asked. He'd been figuring how the bullet must have entered Evans. It was difficult to judge the angle of the shot, since the cabbie had dragged the body from his taxi.

"What witnesses we have all give the same story," Birdy said. "There was the sound of the shot, echoing all over the place, and they ducked down or got to cover. When a few minutes passed, they poked their heads up and some of them heard Mrs. Evans screaming and saw Evans on the sidewalk with the cabbie standing over him."

Repetto had talked briefly to Venus Evans, who was in shock now that she'd come down from her hysteria. The Ohio couple who'd traveled to New York with the Evanses related how the four of them had come to the city, and told about the coin toss and that Ralph and Venus were on their way to TKTS to buy show tickets.

It all had the ring of truth, Repetto thought. The shooting happened on the shortest route from the hotel to TKTS. Venus, wearing high heels and unused to so much walking, had talked her husband into hailing a cab.

The cab hadn't moved from where it was when Evans had been shot. Repetto stepped closer to it, opened its back door as it must have been when Evans was killed, and looked up and around him.

Meg knew what he was thinking and said, "It's impossible even to guess where the bastard was when he squeezed the trigger."

"We don't even know if it was the same bastard," Repetto said.

Meg hadn't considered that possibility.

Repetto looked at her, smiling slightly so she wouldn't feel she was back in the academy. "We won't take anything for granted. We won't guess."

"We won't," Meg said.

"Nearest I can figure it—not a guess, a calculation—is with what we know from the direction of the shot, it could have come from any of those buildings."

Meg and Birdy looked down the block in the direction Repetto was pointing.

"I count nine buildings and something like three hundred windows."

Repetto nodded. "And nine rooftops."

"Gonna take legwork," Birdy remarked.

"For lots of legs," Meg said.

"I'll contact Melbourne," Repetto said, "and get him to assign some uniforms to help us try to find the origin of the shot."

Birdy was still staring down the block. "All those buildings, but the shot had to come from somewhere. If there's a shell casing, there's no reason it can't be found."

"Like Jimmy Hoffa," Meg said.

"Or the *Titanic*," Birdy said. "They found the *Titanic*."

Meg thought of pointing out to him that the *Titanic* was considerably larger than a shell casing, or any other clue the Night Sniper might have left behind, but she glanced at Repetto and figured it was wiser to let Birdy top her this time.

This time.

"Admirable," Repetto said, as they were climbing into the unmarked to call for more uniforms and begin the canvassing process.

Meg knew what he meant.

Melbourne got them half a dozen uniforms, and along with Repetto, Meg, and Birdy they worked the suspect buildings until ten that evening. They learned nothing from interviews or from entering and examining vacant apartments or offices with a view down the avenue. Just before they quit for the night, Repetto's cell phone chirped and he got word from the lab that the bullet removed from Ralph Evans was a 7mm, and its markings matched those of similar slugs removed from previous Night Sniper murders.

Repetto relayed the news before dismissing everyone. Nobody seemed surprised.

"I know this looks almost hopeless, but we have to try for the information while the crime's fresh. Tomorrow morning we'll take up where we left off. It'll be light out and we can examine the rooftops."

One of the uniforms rolled his eyes and looked like he was about to say something, then glanced at Repetto and remained silent.

When they dropped her off outside her apartment half an hour later, Meg wondered if she'd be able to climb out of bed tomorrow morning, or if she'd be as dead as Ralph Evans.

But she did make it out of bed, and three cups of strong coffee revitalized her enough to help in the continued canvassing and examination of the buildings along West Forty-fourth near where Evans was killed.

A little after ten, they got word that a uniform had maybe found something on the roof of a building a block away from the crime scene.

Repetto walked the short distance to the building. An ancient brass plaque to the left of the entrance said it was THE BERMINGALE ARMS. When he entered, he found it wasn't as grand as its name and probably never had been.

He crossed the barren tiled lobby and took the elevator to the top floor. At the end of the hall, he found the service door to the roof.

The door was already open, wedged at the bottom by a black leather-bound tablet Repetto recognized as a cop's notebook.

He also recognized the uniform who greeted him on the roof. Officer Nancy Weaver, who'd been a homicide detective second grade before she was demoted last year for sleeping with an uptown sergeant who'd been kicked off the NYPD for also sleeping with the wife of a drug dealer, giving the dealer wide latitude. Weaver hadn't been involved in the drug trade and remained a cop, but she was in uniform again. Repetto knew she was a good cop who slept around with other cops, which would have been okay, only she slept with cops without rank.

Weaver also recognized Repetto. She smiled and nodded to him. She was an attractive brunette with a certain look in her eye that drew the wrong kind of man. Over and over.

Repetto knew she'd been married to the right kind, a guy named Joe, who finally got tired of her shenanigans and ran away with a woman who'd been runner-up in a Miss Portugal competition. He heard it made Weaver mad if you spoke Portuguese around her. No problem.

The breeze was strong on the roof, causing a lock of dark hair that had escaped from beneath Weaver's cap to do a dance on her forehead. Repetto thought it must tickle, but she seemed unaware of it.

"What've you got?" he asked.

"The door," Weaver said. "I didn't have anything other'n my notepad to wedge it open."

Repetto's gaze went to the small wooden wedge lying nearby on the roof. It looked like it had been there for a long time. "What about that?"

"Didn't want to touch it."

Repetto nodded.

"But I don't think it was used so somebody could get back in off the roof," Weaver added. "The door's the kind that locks automatically if you let it close. It'd trap you out here. But look at the latch."

Repetto did, and saw a faint rectangle. He touched a corner of it gently with the back of a knuckle. "Sticky."

"That's what I thought. It looks to me like tape was put there to keep the door from clicking locked. That way it wouldn't be wedged open and maybe attract attention. Then, when whoever was up here left, they removed the tape. Could be they left a fingerprint."

"More likely a glove print."

Weaver smiled again and nodded. "Our guy's smart, isn't he?"

"Smart and evil go together all too often," Repetto said. "Anything else?"

"Yes, sir. I found where the shooter mighta sat or kneeled."

"Got an ejected shell casing?"

"Never that lucky," Weaver said over her shoulder, as she led Repetto toward where a billboard was mounted near the roof's edge. "He had a good view from there," she said. "Mighta fired through an opening in that rusty iron support gizmo. There's a clear shot to where Evans was killed, and look how the gravel's been disturbed."

Repetto looked. Weaver was right. The gravel that wasn't embedded in the blacktop roof appeared to have been recently shifted around, perhaps by someone finding a comfortable shooting position.

"Of course," Weaver added, "we can't be sure."

"True," Repetto said, "but it's something."

He went back to the service door and looked again where the door frame might have been taped so the spring latch couldn't protrude and do its job. "I'll get the techs to look at this," he said. "Nice work. Keep an eye on the scene and don't let anybody else up here."

"Yes, sir." Weaver was staring at him, her head cocked to one side, the wind whipping the errant lock of hair.

"You look good in uniform," Repetto said, "but you look even better in plainclothes. I'll see you get credit for finding this."

As he exited the roof, Weaver gave him her biggest smile.

By that afternoon they had the lab information. There were no discernible foot- or handprints on the disturbed roof surface or on any part of the billboard or its support frame. The service door's lock had been blocked at some point with a common brand of duct tape, but the only print on the doorjamb near the tape's adhesive residue was a partial finger, wearing a rubber or latex glove. The small wooden wedge yielded nothing other than that it was pine and didn't figure in the investigation.

There was no way to prove it, but Repetto was reasonably sure they'd found the killer's shooting position.

He got Meg and Birdy, and with three uniforms they concentrated their efforts on the building's tenants.

No one remembered seeing anything unusual. Most had heard the echoing sound of the shot, but they weren't sure what it was and weren't concerned. Obviously it had come from outside the building. They were polite but seemed impatient for the police to finish with them and leave.

When they were back on the sidewalk, Repetto said, "Nobody in the Bermingale Arms can see or hear."

"He came and went like a ghost," Birdy said.

Like the Grim Reaper, Meg thought.

15

Joel Vanya swung himself up onto the back of the trash hauler and watched the fog of his breath stream out into the crisp winter air. The compactor roared and whined on the truck's bed, the sound so many New Yorkers woke up to in the morning. Joel sometimes added to the din by banging metal trash cans, but they were becoming scarce, what with all the plastic containers and trash bags.

Recycling, Joel thought. *What a pain in the ass that is.*

He glanced around. This was a nice block, rich people still sleeping in, hours after he'd had to drag himself out of bed and into work. He wished he had some metal to bang now, maybe a pair of trash can lids he could use as cymbals. Wake up the rich snobs, let them know he had some control over their lives. Even things out. One thing Joel was sure of was that the world was rigged; once you were born down, or knocked down, everyone higher on the dung pile wanted to keep you down.

With a roar, the truck lurched forward, rolled about fifty

feet farther down the Lower West Side street, then hissed to a stop. Sal Vestamalo, the driver, dressed as warmly as Joel against the winter cold, opened the door and lowered himself to the street. A big man with a salt-and-pepper beard that seemed always to be crusted with frozen saliva or mucus, he swaggered around the front of the truck to start picking up the trash there, while Joel dropped back down to the street and headed for the mushroomed black trash bags piled at the curb behind the truck. It was a process they repeated, over and over, somewhere in the city almost every morning.

Joel had long ago decided this was a shit job even when the weather was good, but now he had seniority and no other marketable skills, so he couldn't afford to leave the Department of Sanitation. He was stuck working for the city. He didn't enjoy his work. The truth was, more and more, he didn't enjoy much of anything.

Joel Vanya was a small man and had been a small child in a tough neighborhood in Newark, New Jersey. His father had deserted Joel and his mother when Joel was ten. The mean drunk wasn't much of a loss. Joel's mother repeated that often as he was growing up. Joel agreed. His father had beaten his mother severely before leaving, and permanently injured Joel's right leg when he'd tried to interrupt the violence. In this weather, Joel's artificial kneecap hurt almost as badly as when his father had struck his knee with a beer bottle. Joel still walked with the same limp that had drawn bullies to him as a child.

Every day, Joel hurt inside and out.

He swung a heavy black plastic trash bag into the back of the truck, turned to pick up another, and almost slipped and fell when he stepped on a patch of ice.

"We got no time for you to dance, short shit!" Sal yelled. "You wanna move that fast, do it with a load of trash."

Joel didn't answer. He was used to swallowing his hate.

Sal was already back in the cab and gunning the engine

by the time Joel had returned with a cardboard box full of
trash and another black plastic bag.

The crusher was coming down as he tossed the box in,
then the bag. The steel lip of the compactor smashed the box
and ruptured the bag, then began scooping the trash back toward the front of the truck's hold, making room for more.

The truck lurched forward, then braked to a quick halt.
Sal up to his tricks again.

"Better jump on board!" Sal shouted back at Joel, locking
gazes with him in the rearview mirror.

Joel thought about flipping him the bird, but he didn't
want any trouble. He'd already complained to the boss, Frank
Dugan, about Sal harassing him and had gotten nowhere. In
fact, Sal had sold the idea that Joel was paranoid; then he'd
stepped up his campaign of terror.

The truck roared and jumped forward again just as Joel
clutched the grab bar and began swinging his body back on
board. He lost his grip and stumbled backward, knowing the
truck's sudden acceleration, then stop had been deliberate.
Sal would be laughing his ass off in the warm—or at least
warmer—cab.

Joel walked toward the grab bar, determined to be more
careful, and noticed a brown paper sack that had been in the
plastic bag ruptured by the compactor. The sack had torn
open. Something dark that it contained caught his eye.

He looked more closely as he prepared to get back up on
the truck. The dark object was the barrel and cylinder of a
blue steel revolver. With a glance up and down the deserted
street, Joel plucked the gun from the litter of trash and stuck
it in his belt beneath his jacket.

After the next stop, near the corner, he made sure Sal
couldn't see him in the rearview mirror and took the gun out
for a closer look. It had a checked wooden grip and a snub
barrel and looked to be in pretty good shape, the kind of gun
that was easy to conceal and perfect for committing a crime.

Most likely the owner had thrown it away for a reason, probably in someone else's curbside pile of trash. A gun with a history that might interest the cops.

If the cops ever got their hands on it.

The truck's motor roared, and the steel compactor screeched and bit down. Sal was yelling something unintelligible over the din.

Before slipping the gun back beneath his coat, Joel flipped the cylinder out and looked at it.

The gun was loaded.

Dugan the boss called Joel into the office when the truck had returned to the shed. Joel always felt inferior around Dugan, who was a tall, barrel-chested Irishman whose family had always worked for the city. Dugan had come to the sanitation department with certain advantages.

Twelve years ago, he'd started on one of the collection trucks, in a job much like Joel's present one, but he hadn't remained there long. From day one, Dugan had pull. Joel knew that was what it took to get ahead in a city job, pull. And that was what it took to get the assholes off you, once they settled on you as a target for their sick, cruel jokes.

Not only didn't Joel have pull, but Dugan and Sal had turned many of their fellow employees against Joel, spreading lies, making sure Joel was passed over for any promotion. Joel considered himself a realist and saw the situation as something he had to endure. In some matters there was no choice.

Just as he always did, big Frank Dugan glanced up at Joel over the frames of his glasses and made the smaller man wait while he finished what he was writing. He sat behind a wide, cluttered desk. On the wall behind him was a large cork bulletin board with schedules and notices pinned to it. Alongside the corkboard was a bank of battered filing cabinets that were the same gray metal as the desk. A space heater was glowing over in a corner. There was a pair of wet leather boots on the floor in front of it, smelling up the place.

Starting to sweat in his heavy coat, even though it was unbuttoned, Joel waited.

"I'm afraid I've got some bad news for you, Joel," Dugan said, when he finally put down his pen and looked up. His blue eyes were rheumy and his face flushed. He looked as if he'd been drinking before Joel arrived, not doing paperwork.

Then it suddenly struck Joel that when he had the revolver out, Sal might have caught a glimpse of it in the truck's outside mirror. A gun in New York, concealed on the person of a city employee, was a serious matter. It was especially serious now, because the gun was in Joel's black metal lunch pail, which was in Joel's right hand.

Joel began to perspire even more. He could feel beads of sweat running down his right side beneath his waffled winter underwear. This was just the kind of thing Dugan and Sal must pray for every night, a chance to rid themselves of Joel and at the same time humiliate him and make it impossible for him to find any kind of city job.

But it wasn't about the gun.

Dugan shrugged his bulky shoulders and said, "I got some bad news. We're going to have to lay you off, Joel. I'm sorry."

"Lay me off?" Joel was astounded. "With my seniority? You'd have to lay off a dozen men to get to me!"

Dugan nodded somberly. "The department's laying off twenty."

Joel could only stare at him. He'd been working for the Department of Sanitation for nine years. Getting flat-out fired for some lie cooked up against him was one thing, but the thought of a layoff had never occurred to him. His heart turned cold and dropped.

"It isn't the best of times for the city," Dugan said.

"I heard we were doing okay, with the new municipal bonds."

"Yeah, it sounds like a lotta money, but it's not." Dugan stood up, looming even larger in the small, warm office. "Not enough, anyway."

Joel nodded, swallowing loudly.

Dugan extended his hand. "I wish you luck, Joel."

Joel shook his boss's hand, feeling the powerful grip. *Christ! What's Doris going to say? And Dantè? How are we all going to get by?*

Dugan must have known what he was thinking. "You have union benefits, Joel. And there's always unemployment. I'd like to tell you it looks like you'll be called back soon, but in all honesty I can't."

Joel couldn't get the words out—not the ones he wanted to say, that this was a crock of shit, that Dugan was a phony, that he and Sal probably got together to shaft him, that this was goddamn unfair! Joel should get the gun out of his lunch pail and tell Dugan what he really thought. Tell Dugan he was gonna fuckin' die. Not that Joel would actually squeeze the trigger. But Dugan wouldn't know that.

What Joel said was, "Yeah . . . Yes. I understand."

Dugan nodded, then sat back down at his desk and picked up his pen. He began to write. Joel was no longer a city employee. Joel wasn't there.

Goddamn unfair!

Joel left the office. He felt empty inside. His life felt empty. Sal and Dugan had fucked him over, just as he'd been getting fucked over all his life. He should have expected it. In a way, he *had* expected it.

As he trudged toward the lot where his ten-year-old Ford was parked, the gun in his lunch pail was heavy. He recalled the gun's cold heft in his hand when he'd plucked it from the trash, how heavy it felt for its size. How deadly efficient it looked. How serious. How . . . important.

It was the only substantial thing in his world. It was his only source of comfort, though why it comforted him escaped him.

As he drove home he thought about the gun, what he might have done with it in Dugan's office, what he *should* have done. Guns made a difference, right when they appeared. They changed the game entirely. Power shifted. The magic changed hands.

Not that he really would have used the gun.

But it was something to think about as he negotiated the bumper-to-bumper New York traffic that he'd come to hate.

When his father walked into the apartment, twelve-year-old Dante Vanya saw the look on his face and knew something was wrong. Something *he'd* done? He couldn't be sure.

"School was okay today," Dante said.

His father nodded, as if he'd barely heard. "Where's your mother?"

"Walked down to the store. She needed something for whatever she's cooking on the stove."

For the first time, Joel noticed the pungent scents wafting from the kitchen. His nostrils actually twitched as he sniffed at the air.

"She's making some kinda stew," Dante said.

His father didn't answer. He simply trudged toward the bedroom he shared with Dante's mother. His shoulders were hunched and his head gave the impression of being bowed though really it wasn't. What he looked like, Dante thought, was somebody with about a thousand pounds of lead stacked on his shoulders.

After his father had disappeared down the hall to the apartment's small bedrooms, Dante stood up and pretended he was going to his room. It was the last door at the end of the hall, and it had one of the apartment's few windows that didn't look out on the brick air shaft.

He actually did go to his room, but first he paused in the hall and peered into his mother and father's bedroom.

The closet door was open and his father was standing on his toes with one arm raised. His back was to Dante. Dante saw that his father was placing his black metal lunch pail, which he usually set on the kitchen table when he returned home from work, on the top closet shelf. He was pushing the lunch pail back as if trying to make it as unnoticeable as possible, toward the rear of the shelf where shadows were dark and light didn't play.

An odd thing for him to do, Dante thought.

An odd way for his father to act.

He didn't know his father's unusual behavior had only begun.

16

The initial information on the Ralph Evans murder was mostly complete. Repetto could almost feel the case beginning to cool.

He knew that from the Sniper's point of view, that was how it was supposed to work. There would be nothing of substance for the police to grab hold of, no lead or clue of any sort. If they searched for a connection between killer and killed, they would find none until that fateful day of sudden, violent death. There would be no physical clues leading anywhere other than to a dead end. Normal activity on a busy New York street, then a thunderclap echoing among tall buildings, and almost simultaneous to the report of the rifle, someone would be dead. A clean kill. A clean getaway. Repetto didn't like any of it.

"Random murder," Birdy remarked. "The hardest kind to solve."

"They only seem random," Meg said.

They were in the basement office the local precinct house

had provided. It was a large enough room, with three green steel desks, a metal four-drawer file cabinet, and a table with an ancient but upgraded computer and printer on it. The printer was the kind that was also a copier and a fax machine and, for all Repetto knew, maybe ran out for coffee and gave massages. He had little idea of how to work the damned thing. There was a phone on each desk with buttons so people could listen in or talk on the same line. In the file cabinet drawers were the Night Sniper murder files, along with phone and cross directories, fresh folders, and whatever other office paraphernalia the detectives might need. On the wall behind the desk that Repetto used was a large city map with red-capped pins stuck where the Night Sniper murders had occurred. Like the murders themselves, the pins seemed to have been placed on the map randomly.

Repetto was at the desk now, leaning back in his chair with his fingers laced behind his neck. Meg was at her desk, where she'd been working the phone. Birdy, with his tie loosely knotted and his shirtsleeves rolled up, was perched on the corner of Meg's desk, absently pumping his right leg. He was staring past Repetto at the city map.

"No murders in any of the other boroughs so far," he said.

"True," Repetto said. "Manhattan seems to be his beat."

"It's ours too," Meg said, sounding proprietary. How dare a killer trespass in their territory? She knew she'd used the wrong tone. Very uncoplike. "One thing we can be sure of is he knows how to shoot," she added.

Repetto knew where she was going but said nothing, rocking slightly in his swivel chair and watching her. The chair made soft squeaking noises.

"Maybe ex-military," Birdy said. "A trained sniper."

Repetto continued watching Meg.

"Maybe an ex-cop," she said.

Repetto smiled slightly.

Birdy became still.

"Maybe," Repetto said, rocking forward in his chair so he was sitting up straight behind the desk. "Let's run a check on our SWAT snipers, present and past, and see if they all have alibis for one or more of the Night Sniper hits."

"Like chicken soup for a dead man," Meg said, "it can't hurt."

"I'll get some names," Birdy said, moving to sit at the computer.

"We won't forget ex-military," Repetto told them, "but that'll take a little longer."

"I can log in to army and marine records," Birdy said, already playing the computer keys, "soon as I'm done with the NYPD." His touch was fast and nimble. The keyboard seemed to provide an outlet for his nervous fingers.

Repetto and Meg exchanged a look. They were both more the street cop type and were glad Birdy was computer savvy.

"Where'd you learn to be so good with one of those?" Meg asked.

Birdy didn't look away from the screen. "My son."

A week later Repetto sat in Zoe Brady's office in One Police Plaza. She'd come out from behind her desk to make the meeting more informal, and sat in one of the matching brown leather armchairs. Repetto was seated in the other.

The office was small but well furnished, and had a window with its vertical blinds pulled so only slits of light showed through. Most of the room's illumination was from recessed lighting in the ceiling. There must have been a sachet around somewhere, or Zoe was wearing perfume, because there was a faint lilac scent in the office. Repetto found it kind of pleasant. Better than Melbourne's office, which always smelled of the cheap cigars he secretly smoked in defiance of city law.

Zoe had on a light beige dress and darker brown high-heeled shoes. Repetto heard nylon swish as she settled into the chair opposite him. He wondered idly for a moment if she was giving him a show as she crossed her shapely legs. She flicked a hand at her long red hair; he knew it was an unconscious gesture women made when interested in a man. Sometimes a conscious gesture. Whether she was flirting or it was simply his imagination, Repetto didn't care. He wasn't interested that way in Zoe Brady.

"I understand you and my wife have been doing the lunch thing," he said.

She stared at him. "Lunch thing?"

"Meeting for lunch."

"Yes. Do you mind?"

"No, except that I don't want her playing cop."

"Neither do I, to tell you the truth. But I'm learning Lora can be a very determined woman."

Repetto sat back, studying Zoe. "Are you using Lora?"

She didn't seem thrown by the question. "Only in the way I use everything. The Night Sniper case isn't the only thing we talk about."

"Are you using her to learn more about me?"

"Not unless you can get shoes or jewelry wholesale." She sighed loudly, maybe with mock exasperation, maybe simply because he was, in her mind, exhibiting typical male behavior. "Look, Repetto, your wife and I are simply acquaintances who occasionally meet for lunch. Sure, it seems to help Lora to talk to somebody about Dal Bricker's death, and the Night Sniper case, but if you think this is all about the case, or about you, I've gotta say you flatter yourself."

"I do that sometimes."

"I can't stop Lora from 'playing cop,' as you put it, but I promise I won't encourage her."

"Good enough," Repetto said. It had to be. He knew there was no way to persuade Lora to stop meddling in the case. And she *had* provided the theater seat number key to the Night Sniper's notes.

"So can we get down to business now?" Zoe asked.

Repetto thought it was a good idea.

"Our checks on the gun collectors and dealers in the area haven't panned out," he said.

"If the Sniper collects anything, he'd be doing it in secret, probably illegally," Zoe said, "even if he doesn't have to. He's a secretive type in more ways than one. Secrecy is in his blood. Are there ways to illegally obtain a sizable gun collection?"

"There are countless ways to obtain all sorts of guns illegally," Repetto said. "If he does have a large collection, he might be using the guns one by one to confuse us, then disposing of them."

"I doubt if he'd be getting rid of them."

"Why not? The guns could be used to tie him to the murders."

"He'd be too arrogant to dispose of his collection. He doesn't expect to be caught, or even suspected."

"You seem sure of that."

"I am. This guy is nothing if not arrogant. And he has the smarts to back up his high opinion of himself."

Repetto smiled. "You think he might be smarter than we are?"

"Only in stretches." She returned the smile. "And never more arrogant."

Repetto was tired of her verbal jousting and kept the conversation on business. "We eliminated most of the SWAT snipers as suspects," he said. "The military cooperated and we tracked down half a dozen former snipers who live in the New York area. Three are Vietnam age and not suspects."

"True," Zoe said. "Men over fifty usually aren't serial killers. But there are exceptions."

"The other two former military snipers are Middle East vets, and both have tight alibis for at least one of the Night

Sniper murders. We can get around to the exceptions over fifty later, if it's necessary."

She gave him a look, and Repetto knew he'd been short with her again. He wondered why that kind of impatience had crept into his tone. He started to apologize, but she interrupted:

"You said *most* of the SWAT snipers."

He found himself intrigued by the way she arched one eyebrow when she asked a question. It made her seem maybe more intelligent than she was. He nodded. "There are two former NYPD snipers, Sergeants Lou Mackey and Alex Reyals. In 1978 Mackey was shot in the side and had to have one of his kidneys removed. He's in his fifties now, but may be one of those exceptions. Reyals is thirty-seven. He left the NYPD with disability pay three years ago. I haven't been able to get a straight answer as to why."

"I know both of them. I interviewed Mackey once, and I was one of the consulting psychiatrists in the Reyals matter."

It was Repetto's turn to raise an eyebrow. "Reyals matter?"

"Four years ago a fleeing holdup man was crossing the Queensboro Bridge in a stolen car. It got in a minor accident that caused a bigger accident that closed the bridge in both directions. The holdup man, a teenager named Joe Mustang— his real name—took an elderly woman hostage, held a gun to her head, and tried to walk with her off the bridge."

"Not much chance of that," Repetto said, knowing how quickly the police would converge in that part of town.

"Alex Reyals was one of three SWAT snipers who scoped in on Mustang and Iris Beecher, the hostage. Iris was a squeeze of the trigger away from dying from a bullet fired by Mustang's gun, and the snipers had orders to fire if they got a clear shot at Mustang. If the aim of his gun momentarily strayed from Iris."

"And Reyals got the clear shot." Repetto remembered the incident now, though not all the details.

"He thought it was clear," Zoe said. "He was in a window, near the ramp to Second Avenue. Something caught Mustang's attention and he turned away from Iris for a moment, and the gun wasn't pointed at her head. Reyals took the shot, as he'd been instructed. The bullet didn't hit Mustang. It struck Iris in the ear and entered her brain. When she dropped, Mustang threw his hands up and surrendered without a struggle."

Repetto looked at Zoe. She'd told the story without emotion. He wondered what she thought of it. What she thought of Reyals. "Those guys almost always hit what they shoot at," he said. "What made Reyals miss?"

Zoe smiled sadly. "He doesn't know. That's his problem."

"He has a problem?"

"He doesn't think he should have missed. He thinks it's his fault Iris Beecher is dead. So does Iris Beecher's family. They let him know it. Then there were rumors that Reyals had been drinking when the call came in for him to go the bridge."

"*Had* he been drinking?"

Zoe shrugged. "He says no. What happened is, he missed his shot. If it had happened on the target range, he would have walked away from it not knowing why he missed and not needing to know."

"This was a different kind of shot."

"That's what Alex Reyals thinks. It's why his nerve went. He was pensioned off with a mental disability. Last I heard he was in private analysis." She sighed and ran her hands over her thighs. "It wasn't, you know."

"Wasn't what?"

"A different kind of shot. It was simply one he missed. Maybe his eyelid twitched, or a gust of breeze altered the course of the bullet, or Iris moved in front of his target. He simply aimed at something and missed. It happens all the time, but he can't think of it that way. He can't forgive himself."

"Maybe he shouldn't. A woman is dead."

Zoe stared at Repetto, her blue eyes amazingly steady. *What a poker player she must be.*

"You think it's a male thing," he said.

She smiled. "I know it is."

"What happened to Mustang?"

"He went to prison and was killed a year later, in a fight with another inmate."

"Justice," Repetto said.

"I knew you were thinking that. You might be interested to know that so was I. Because of him a good woman was killed and a good man is living in agony."

"The kind of agony that could make him a serial killer?"

Zoe stood up. She paced to the window and peeked out between two vertical blinds. Repetto still couldn't see what was out there.

When she turned around and faced him, she said, "It doesn't add up. Reyals hates himself more than he could hate other people."

"You don't know what else went on in his life."

"Some of it I do. From the hearing. From my interviews with him."

"Is this where you claim doctor-patient privilege?"

"Don't be such an asshole, Repetto. We've got a serial killer in this city. If there were anything in our sessions, or in Reyals's past, that might have the slightest bearing on that, I'd tell you in a second. There isn't. So I don't have to worry about doctor-client privilege."

"This means you'll tell me all about him?"

"Means I can't, because it has nothing to do with the Night Sniper. I can give you general information. Reyals grew up in rural Illinois where he hunted and became a crack shot. He went to college on a football scholarship but hurt his knee after his second year and dropped out, worked at a series of jobs, went back to school, and got his degree. He worked for a financial firm in Chicago, was transferred to New York, then got downsized. That's when he joined the NYPD. He had a great record until the incident on the bridge." She crossed the office and stood near Repetto. "You could find out all that in his personnel file."

"I already have." He stood up and, comparing his height to Zoe's, was surprised to find that she was taller than she appeared seated behind her desk or stalking around the office. "Did you like Reyals?" he asked.

"That didn't enter into it."

"Yeah, but did you like him?"

"Yes, I did. He struck me as a good and kind young man who had something terrible happen to him."

"Nothing happened *to* him. He did something to someone else. He acted and there was a consequence. He squeezed the trigger, and now he has to live with the result."

"For God's sake, he made a simple mistake! His skill and his luck deserted him when he needed them most. It could happen to anyone."

"No argument there. Can you tell me for sure that Alex Reyals isn't the Night Sniper?"

"I can't."

"Because you don't want to wind up with the same kind of agony Reyals is suffering."

She glared at him, then relaxed and gave him her thin, irritating smile. "You're right. Once I tell you he's not a suspect, whoever else he kills, if he *is* the Night Sniper, the murders are partly my responsibility."

Repetto nodded somberly and walked to the office door. "See?" he said, as he opened the door. "It isn't a male thing."

Zoe almost shot back an answer before the door closed

behind him, but she realized she didn't have a good one. At least not one she should utter. Not yet.

She knew Repetto was right, and she knew why he thought as he did. He felt he was partly responsible for what had happened to Dal Bricker, for someone else's death.

He and Alex Reyals had something in common.

17

Repetto was uneasy, as he often was after talking with Zoe. He wasn't sure why, and he shied away from trying to figure it out. He had other things on his mind.

He left her office and took a cab through the hazy morning to Penn Station, where he met Meg and Birdy at the Starbucks inside the terminal. Over coffee, he filled them in on his conversation with Zoe.

When he was finished, Birdy said, "Sounds to me like our profiler doesn't think either Reyals or Mackey are prime suspects."

"I'd like to think she's right," Birdy said, "considering they're ex-cops. And we all know there's really no such thing."

"She might be wrong." Repetto used both hands to play with his coffee mug. "Profilers are wrong a lot."

"Mackey doesn't sound likely," Meg said. "Mostly because of his age. It almost rules him out."

"Almost." Repetto looked out at commuters striding along the wide passageway from the tracks. Their ceaseless movement made a steady, rushing sound, but if you listened closely, you could hear the scuffing of hundreds of soles punctuated by the tapping of high heels. People in a hurry, turning the treadmill of the business world he'd never wanted to take part in.

"But I don't know why the profiler's cool on Reyals," Meg said. "He's the right sex, the right age, lives in Manhattan, and has a sniper's background. Also, some of his alibis for the times of the Sniper murders are thin."

"He lives alone," Birdy pointed out. "I used to live alone and not see or talk to anyone for days. I had no alibi for anything. Somebody coulda shot the pope, and I woulda had time to fly to Italy and back. That wouldn't make me a solid suspect."

Meg looked at him. "You don't like the pope?"

"I don't think we'd like each other."

"But you wouldn't shoot each other."

Birdy shook his head and stared into his coffee. "I guess not, unless he learned about some of my confessions."

Meg turned her attention back to Repetto. "I wouldn't be so fast to step over Reyals."

"I dunno," Birdy said beside her. "He's ex-NYPD."

"That doesn't put him above suspicion. A minute ago you were thinking the pope might take a shot at you."

"Here's what we'll do," Repetto said. "Since Meg likes Reyals at least a little for the Night Sniper, she gets to interview him. You get Mackey, Birdy. I know he's not likely as the doer, but serial killers don't always run true to type—except in Zoe Brady's mind."

"You're being kinda hard on her," Meg said. "She's got a good reputation for accuracy."

Repetto shrugged. Maybe Meg was right. And maybe he was being hard on Zoe Brady for another reason. What might really be irking Repetto was that Zoe seemed to understand that very private part of him where he harbored and nurtured his grief.

"You got addresses on these guys?" he asked his detectives. Mind on business.

They both nodded.

Repetto tossed down the rest of his coffee and stood up.

"What about you?" Birdy asked. "What are you gonna do?"

Repetto stared at him. "I get the pope."

Meg found Alex Reyals's apartment near Washington Square. The old brick building wasn't fancy, and the foyer had a cracked and stained tile floor. The walls might have had half an inch of enamel on them. At least the latest coat, a kind of putrid green, appeared fresh. A couple of mashed cigarette butts lay close together on the floor, and a faint scent of tobacco smoke hung in the air.

There was an intercom button above each of the tarnished brass mailboxes. Some of the names suggested many of the units were occupied by college students, men with not very clever nicknames, like *Boozemaster* in 4-C, and young women trying to hide their gender with simple first initials. There was always hope that a determined stalker would think *B. Tuttle* was a big hairy guy named Bart, instead of little Beth or Brenda. Meg saw that Alex Reyals lived in 3-E and gave his intercom button a hard press. It was difficult to know if the button moved in the dried mass of aged paint.

When she identified herself as the police, he buzzed her up immediately. *Expecting me?*

The building had no elevator, so she had to trudge up flights of narrow, creaking stairs. On each landing was a small, dirty window that made faint inroads against the gloom. The glued remnants of rubber treads clung stubbornly to each wooden step and provided unpredictable traction. A radio talk show that had been audible on the first floor faded to silence, and Meg heard her own breathing as she climbed.

Reyals was standing waiting for her with his door open.

He appeared younger than she imagined and looked more like one of the building's college students than a serial killer. Maybe *Boozemaster.* What she thought when she saw him was *average:* no hard edges or lines to his features, dark hair cut almost scalp short, military style. He was wearing loose-fitting faded jeans and a gray pocket T-shirt, brown moccasins.

He smiled pleasantly and held out his hand. "Alex Reyals."

"Detective Meg Doyle." She shook his hand briefly, noting he had a firm, dry grip, gentle but with contained strength. Noting also, now that she was closer, that his brown eyes were pools of agony.

He was taller than she'd first thought. At a distance, the bulk of his shoulders and perhaps thighs made him seem at a glance shorter than he actually was. It was the kind of build Meg had seen on powerful and athletic men. He stood back so she could enter, then followed her in and closed the door. When she turned, he was next to her. He motioned for her to sit on the sofa, his arm tight and corded with muscle.

The room's furnishings were a mix of old, new, and flea market. On one wall were shelves holding books, a stack of magazines, and what looked like an expensive sound system built around a CD player. A small TV and a lineup of ceramic vases sat on one of the upper shelves. Near a window was a spectacular wooden desk, modern and asymmetrical. There was a phone and answering machine on it, a small brass lamp, a folded *New York Times,* and a black notebook computer. Lighter, polished wood was inlaid in an angular design on the desk drawers, and the sturdy legs were capped with brass. This was some piece of furniture.

Meg lowered herself into a gray leather armchair instead of the sofa, not letting Reyals control the interview, and pretended to glance around for the first time.

"Nice room. Wonderful desk."

He smiled. "I'm glad you like it. I made it."

"*Made* it?"

"Upstairs in my shop. I rented that apartment and use it for my woodworking. It's on the top floor, directly above this one and pretty much soundproof."

"Why soundproof?"

"I hit my thumb with my hammer now and then, use terrible language."

"I suggest you take this interview seriously."

"Okay. My woodworking tools. Power tools. Some of them make noise and the neighbors might complain."

Meg was still disbelieving. "You make desks like that and sell them?"

"Not like that. And not all desks. The furniture I make is half functional and half art. Every once in a while I show it in galleries, and decorators buy it for choice clientele."

"Rich clientele?"

He grinned. "I do okay, though it was slow at first. I started doing it for artistic satisfaction. Then it became profitable. And it's good . . . relaxation."

She thought he'd almost said *therapy.*

He sat down on the sofa and gave her his smile again. It was one that stayed with you, that smile. She saw now that his hands were callused as well as powerful, the nails clipped short on blunt fingertips.

Meg warned herself not to be taken in by Alex Reyals, a charmer who might be a killer. She vaguely remembered some kind of deadly snake that mesmerized its victims by swaying gently and soothingly before striking. Charm was in the arsenal of so much that was deadly.

Reyals crossed his legs, laced his fingers over one knee, and assumed a waiting attitude. She could tell he was appraising her, and not as a cop. Oddly, she almost blushed.

"I'm here—"

"To talk to me about the Night Sniper murders," he finished for her.

"What makes you think it's not about all those unpaid parking tickets?"

"I don't have any unpaid tickets. I *do* have an NYPD background as a sniper, and you *are* NYPD."

"That's what I told you. How do you know for sure who I am? I never showed you any identification."

He grinned. "Hell, you don't have to. We're talking cop to cop here, Detective. When I saw you, I knew you were real."

Meg felt more complimented than was comfortable.

Reyals continued to appear completely relaxed, but for his eyes. "I assumed that sooner or later you or somebody like you would be here to talk to me, follow up on my conversation with the uniform who came around a few days ago. I don't object. It's logical that you're tracking down former military and law enforcement snipers in the area, checking and double-checking them. From what I've read in the papers and seen on TV news, the Night Sniper's a hell of a shot." His expression changed to one of sudden concern. "Can I get you something to drink, Meg? Coffee, water? . . . I know you won't accept booze while on duty. Hey, I've got soda, straight and diet."

"Nothing for me, thanks." *He called me Meg, and I let him get by with it. Too late to correct him now.* "I went over your statement and have a few questions."

"I would imagine. A couple of my alibis for the times of the shootings are pretty thin. I can't help that. When a man lives alone, he doesn't tend to have witnesses to his every action."

"You were married. . . ."

"My wife left me two years ago. You know why."

"No," Meg said, "I don't."

"After I shot that woman, I changed. My relationship with

my wife changed along with me. She finally had enough of my brooding and temper tantrums and left. I don't blame her."

"Temper tantrums?"

"Not directed at her, if that's what you're wondering. And it is."

Meg smiled and nodded.

"I'd be wondering, too. I don't hate anybody except maybe myself. I've got no reason anymore to shoot people from hiding. In fact, these days the thought of it makes me physically ill."

"Everything I've learned about the shooting on the bridge suggests it was accidental."

"I notice you didn't say it wasn't my fault."

"But it *wasn't* your fault. You didn't kill the woman deliberately."

"No, I didn't. It was more . . ."

"What?"

"Never mind. You're a cop, not a psychiatrist."

"Are you in analysis?"

"I was until about six months ago."

Meg scribbled on her notepad.

"Jesus!" Reyals said. "You're writing that down, getting me to hang myself. Sniper leaves analysis and turns into serial killer."

Meg didn't know if he was serious. "Mr. Reyals, you know how it works. I don't think anything at this point."

"I do know how it works, and it's bullshit. And call me Alex."

Meg was beginning to like this guy too much. "Alex, I've gotta say, some of your alibis aren't worth diddly. People who thought they saw you taking a walk near the time of a murder that happened on the other side of town. A waiter who thinks he served you spaghetti in an Italian restaurant when a different murder was being committed."

"I've got the charge card receipt for the spaghetti dinner."

"Which proves somebody used your card and signed your name."

"Forged my signature perfectly, too."

"Our experts aren't so sure that didn't happen." Meg didn't know that. A little lie sometimes greased the skids.

Reyals stood up and paced over to the CD player. For a second Meg thought he might switch it on. Then he turned and came back to the sofa, but he stood beside it instead of sitting down. The way the light hit his eyes, they had the same haunted sadness in them she sometimes glimpsed in Repetto's eyes. The two men were a lot alike, both in their own ways victims of bullets.

"You said I knew how it worked, Meg, and you're right. We both know you have no solid evidence that I might be the Night Sniper, but that doesn't matter. What you're really here for is to size me up, to see if you get a feeling about me. It's a kind of test."

Meg closed the cover of her notepad and sat back. "Yeah, I suppose it is."

"Do I pass, Meg?"

She stood up also. "You get an incomplete."

He shot her his beautiful tragic smile. "That's the best I could hope for. It means you might come back and we'll talk some more."

"That's not the game we're playing, Alex." *Isn't it?*

Still smiling, he said, "Well, I'm not going to go out and shoot somebody so I can see you again."

"That's reassuring." She gave him one of her cards. "Call if you think of something that might help."

He surprised her by reaching into his shirt pocket and producing one of his own cards. On it was his name, street address, phone number, and e-mail address, along with a red, artistic rendering of a handsaw. "And you call me if you think of something. Anything."

She couldn't help returning his smile. Responding. *How*

can he see into me? What does he know about me? She tucked his card in a pocket.

When she moved toward the door, he went ahead to show her out. She noticed for the first time that he gave off a curiously appealing scent, as if he'd just taken a fresh shower and dried off in a steaming room. Meg knew she had to get out of there without looking into his eyes.

Christ! I don't want this! I don't!

"Good luck nailing this guy," he said.

Without thinking, she looked.

She carried what she saw all the way downstairs and back to the car, where she sat behind the steering wheel and thought about what an idiot she might make of herself.

Meg didn't glance up at Alex Reyals's window as she drove away, afraid he might be watching. Afraid she might look back and this time turn into a pillar of mush.

She was sure he wasn't the Night Sniper, but it had nothing to do with evidence. It was how she felt about him.

Maybe it was how he wanted her to feel.

Charm was definitely part of his arsenal.

18

Dante sat on the edge of the sofa in the living room, smelling the onions his mother was cooking on the stove. He listened to the buzzing coming from the kitchen. That was how it sounded to him when his mother and father argued, how he wanted it to sound. He didn't want to hear the things they said to each other.

But sometimes, like tonight, the words worked their way through the buzzing:

". . . sold or pawned everything we owned!" His mother. Her hopeless voice, the one with fear in it. Dante recognized it because it was the same fear he felt. How a boat might feel breaking up on a vast and violent sea. Soon the protective shell would be gone and every fierce and terrible thing that lived in the wild ocean would have its way.

"Like you can't get a fuckin' job!" His father. Joel. Dante still worshipped Joel despite the things he'd said lately to his mother. His father was sick (he'd heard his mother say). *Para . . .* something.

"I don't *know* anything, Joel! Not anymore."

"And what I know how to do, the city won't let me do!" *The city.* That was what was keeping his father from going back to work. The city. "Different departments went ahead and hired the other guys that got axed. Guys with less seniority than I have. Me, I didn't just get axed, I also got knifed—in the back."

"Nobody's out to get you. It's in your head, Joel. You're paranoid and you need to get help."

Dante clamped his hands over his ears. He knew what was going to happen now. When his mother called his father paranoid, his father almost always went wild. That was when the real shouting began, when the neighbors might complain, when Dante heard fists striking flesh with a sound like he heard in the butcher shop; then the police would come.

It was happening again, now, and he didn't know if he could stand it. When his parents weren't fighting about money, about what the city had done to his father, they were fighting about him, how he was skipping school and his grades were terrible for a boy so smart. It was such a waste, they always—

"Joel! . . ."

His mother. There was a new horror in her voice.

Dante waited for it to begin.

But his father was silent for a long time.

"Joel! . . ."

Joel had been finished arguing, finished fighting, finished with her, with everything, with life in a world that was so devious and unfair, unfair. He didn't want to hit her. Not this time. He saw himself as if he were standing off to the side, watching, and he was somebody else at the same time, and that was how he understood. He understood it all, that there was no hope, it wasn't going to change, nothing was going to change unless he changed it by ending it. Let them win. He surrendered. Let them win.

He had no idea how he'd gotten in the bedroom, didn't remember going there, opening the closet door, and finding the gun behind the folded winter sweaters on the top shelf, the gun he'd found in someone's trash, and tell me that was an accident and see if I believe you, *the gun he'd wanted to use on Dugan and Sal but didn't and shouldn't have because it wasn't them, it was the city and the gun was no accident.* Try and tell me that was an accident.

Back in the kitchen.

"Joel! . . ."

The explosion in the kitchen was deafening.

Dante stood up from the sofa and dropped his arms to his sides, his hands clutched in fists. He was rooted to the carpet with shock, with the terrible certainty that something awful had happened and was rushing toward him.

And he had to go to meet it. Had to see it, to know what it was he feared. It was a dark kind of duty.

He made himself walk to the kitchen door, made himself open it.

The smell of the burning onions almost overcame him, making his eyes water. There was his mother lying curled on the kitchen floor. One of her eyes was gone, and the side of her head was missing. On the floor near her head was uncooked meat that had somehow dropped from the frying pan. That was what it was. That must be what it was.

His father said his name once, *Dante*, as if he loved him.

Dante saw the sadness and pain in his father's face, the kindness. He *did* love him. Saw the gun his father was aiming at him. The gun must be a toy, though it sure looked real. What would his father be doing with a gun, like people on TV or in the movies?

Then he looked again at his mother and knew the gun was real, and knew what had happened. What he feared.

"You'll be better off out of it," his father said. He began to cry, to sob, trying to hold the gun steady. "Evil everywhere! Everywhere in this city. Goddamn this city!"

Dante didn't know what he meant, what had happened to him, and why he'd done such a thing. Such a *wrong* thing.

His father wasn't evil.

Dante saw the gun's hammer draw back as his father's finger tightened on the trigger.

Saw the cylinder with the snub-nosed bullets like dull jewels slowly rotate.

Saw and heard the hammer drop.

The firm metallic *click!* struck panic in him. He saw his father staring down at the gun with a betrayed expression. It was no surprise that the gun would misfire, that it would trick and taunt him like everything else in his life.

Dante ran from the kitchen, through the living room, and toward the door to the hall. The hammer would be drawing back again and this time the gun would fire; he knew it. He was dead. He was dead. His father was close behind him. He was dead.

He was in the hall. There were the stairs. He could fly down the stairs. Escape.

The gun exploded again, a sound like the one that had killed his mother, only not as loud, not as close.

Dante didn't break stride. He did almost fly down the stairs, barely touching the banister, stumbling, almost tumbling—landing, steps, landing, steps, foyer, and outside into the cool city air. The dark city air that smelled like onions.

He wasn't going back. He couldn't. He knew he was never going back.

He found a dark doorway and lay in it exactly the way his mother had lain curled on the hard kitchen floor. The darkness wasn't so bad. It sheltered him. His mother and father were part of the darkness now.

Dante barely moved all night. Not when the roaches crawled on him, or when the men and women passed nearby, laughing and cursing.

In the morning, in the cold light, he knew he'd have to get to his feet and move and keep moving or someone would stop him, report him, make him go back to where he never wanted to go again, where, like every place else, there was nothing for him but loss.

By noon in the city it was easy to find a slightly used *New York Times* in the trash receptacles that stood like ragged sentries at busy intersections.

Dante was lucky. He not only found a paper, he found a wrapped, half-eaten hamburger someone had thrown away last night.

The morning was sunny but chilly. Dante had on a long-sleeved shirt, but he was still cold.

Trying not to shiver, he sat on a low stone wall, people and traffic streaming past him, and read in the paper what he knew had happened last night: The news item was brief, on a back page. A man in an apartment that had the same address as Dante's apparently shot and killed his wife and then himself. Neighbors said they were a troubled couple who often argued. The man had recently lost his job with the city.

They had a twelve-year-old son, the neighbors told police, who was missing.

19

In Repetto's mail was another note containing what was assumedly a theater seat number: *9-D*. Nothing more. Same typewriter, same envelope and paper stock and postmark. The Night Sniper.

When he showed them the note, Meg and Birdy looked at Repetto.

He shook his head no. "Lora and I are staying away from Broadway these days."

Which meant someone else, or maybe the Night Sniper himself, had sat in seat 9-D. Only maybe. It was always possible the Sniper was simply choosing seats at random, on his way out of the theater, and unobtrusively affixing the notes in passing.

"It would help if the bastard gave us the name of the theater," Meg said.

"It wouldn't be a game then," Birdy pointed out.

"One we've got no choice but to play," Repetto said.

They began working the phones.

Locating the theater took almost an hour.

Stuck to the bottom of seat 9-D in the Circle One Theater, where a musical comedy titled *Little Miss Muffet* was playing, they found the carefully folded and taped note: *Your move, Detective Repetto.*

"Gamesmanship again!" Meg said in disgust.

Repetto said, "Zoe Brady would tell you it's a male thing."

"She'd probably be right."

"Children," Birdy said.

They turned to look at him.

"This theater's playing *Little Miss Muffet,*" Birdy said. "It's a nursery rhyme, and the killer mentioned rhymes in his first note: *Rhyme and reason . . .*"

"And?" Meg said, cocking her head to the side, suspecting where he was going.

Birdy didn't disappoint her. "You suppose the Night Sniper's gonna shoot a kid?"

"It isn't likely," Zoe told Repetto later that afternoon, "that the Sniper will change his pattern and begin shooting children."

They were in her One Police Plaza office. It was dimmer than it had to be. The vertical blinds behind her desk were still only barely cracked, admitting light but not much of a view. It was as if she might turn around now and then in her chair and see the world outside in vertical cross sections, slices of life.

"We can't ignore the reference to rhymes," Repetto said, "and that the theater where the last note was found is playing *Little Miss Muffet*. And the Night Sniper probably sat in the seat where he taped the note."

"All true," Zoe said, brushing back a strand of her long red hair that was interfering with her vision. "But it doesn't add up to him killing kids. It does suggest that whatever's compelling him to kill is connected to an incident, or at least circumstances, in his childhood. But there's nothing new in that. Virtually all serial killers had wretched childhoods."

"That's hardly an excuse," Repetto said.

"No, it isn't. Most people who have wretched childhoods don't grow up to be serial killers. The difference between them and the ones who do kill is something that's still being studied."

"By people like you," Repetto said. "My job's to stop the ones who kill."

"Mine too," Zoe said. "I told you what I think. This killer seems more hung up on game playing than on children. It's probably simply coincidence that the theater where the Night Sniper decided to leave his note was playing a version of a nursery rhyme."

"You know what cops think of coincidence?"

"Sure. That's why I work for the city." She smiled at Repetto. He thought a little smugly. "If the next note turns up on a seat where *The Lion King*'s playing, maybe we've got a pattern."

Repetto left the office, his opinion of profilers unimproved.

Meg knew she could dismiss Alex Reyals from her mind until the investigation suggested otherwise. For some reason she simply couldn't imagine him as the killer, whatever the evidence. Anyway, the evidence pointing to him was indeed thin.

Still, it wouldn't hurt to talk to Reyals again. To make sure of a few things.

This time after buzzing her up, he wasn't standing with the door open, waiting for her. But as soon as she drew back a fist to knock, a voice called from above:

"I've been painting. C'mon up."

Reyals was leaning over the banister of the stairs leading to the landing above. He was holding a small, tapered paintbrush in one hand, a wadded towel in the other.

Remembering he'd said that he used the upstairs apartment as his workshop, she climbed the creaking wooden steps. She could smell something now—turpentine or thinner.

"Putting on finish?" she asked.

"No, actually painting," he explained. "One of my customers ordered an enameled piece."

As she stepped inside, she saw that the floor plan was exactly the same as the apartment below, but one of the walls had been removed. There were paint cans and various bottles on metal shelves, an electric mixer of the sort you saw in paint stores, a steel locker, a circular saw and another sort of table saw, and an entire wall that was Peg-Board on which were mounted various woodworking tools—chisels, hammers, jigsaws, several old-fashioned wood planes with glistening steel edges. Her gaze went to an ornate wooden rocking chair with a light oak finish. Its spindles were delicately turned, and there was a tapering grace to the chair's long runners. It really was a work of art, as well as furniture.

"That's beautiful," she said.

He smiled. "I'd invite you to sit down in it, but the finish is still tacky."

"Thanks for the warning." She sat instead on a small green leather sofa. She saw then what he'd been painting, a coffee table with a tiled top and knobbed legs. Each knob was a different color. Meg didn't like it as well as the chair. "Is doing this kind of thing relaxing?" she asked.

Reyals laid the paintbrush across a small, open can of red paint on the floor near the table. He tossed the towel aside and ran his hand over his dark stubble haircut. "Relaxing? Oh, you mean therapeutic? That's why I started it, and maybe part of the reason I've stayed with it." He smiled, and it hit her in the heart . "And of course, it's nice to sell some of my work now and then."

"I can see why your work sells. It's original and impressive."

"I have a feeling you mean that. Thanks."

She was momentarily at a loss for words, as she sometimes found herself when in his presence.

"Is this official?" he asked.

"Huh? Oh, my being here. Yes, official. Some more questions. Ones I forgot."

"Detective Meg, I don't think you forget anything."

"When's the last time you were at the theater?"

"Movies?"

"Plays."

He seemed disturbed by the question, or maybe she was imagining it. "Been years," he said. "I never was much of a playgoer. But if you like the theater and you're free tonight . . ."

"Do you own a typewriter?"

"Ah! I get it. This is about the Night Sniper notes."

Meg felt something cold crawl up her spine. The Night Sniper notes were one facet of the case that hadn't been released to the media.

"You okay?" he asked, concerned.

"Yeah, sure."

He gave her his smile again. "You're probably wondering how I know about the notes. I've still got lots of contacts in the NYPD, Meg. Once a cop, always a cop. And you might have noticed, the NYPD leaks like the *Titanic.*"

That was true. She had noticed.

Jesus! I'm trying to reassure myself.

"Don't worry," Alex said, "I don't leak." He walked across the room and moved a folding screen aside to reveal a rolltop desk with something beneath a plastic cover on it. He lifted the cover and stood aside. "My typewriter."

It was an old IBM Selectric, the kind with the replaceable lettered ball. Any police lab could identify one from the typeface immediately. Meg was relieved. The Night Sniper's typewriter was an ancient Royal manual.

"You actually came to see me, right, Meg?"

"Detective Meg—Doyle. And of course I came to see you. You're the only one who lives here, right?"

"Right. Please don't get pissed at me, Detective Meg."

"Doyle."

"Meg, we both know this is primarily a social call. I have alibis for the Night Sniper murders."

"You think they're tight ones? Remember, you used to be a cop."

"They're tight as could be expected. Like you said, I'm the only one who lives here. So there's nobody else to say for sure that, yes, I was home watching TV or reading a book or sanding a piece of furniture."

"What about copycat murders?" Meg asked. "Who's to say you didn't commit one, on one of those weak-alibi nights?"

He frowned at her. "This is all hypothetical, of course."

"Sure."

"It's possible that I could have committed one, or even more, of the Sniper murders. But I didn't, and you know it." He shot his smile at her again. "Tell me you know it, Meg."

"I don't regard you as a strong suspect," Meg admitted.

"But you do have a point about copycat murders. The sniper used a different rifle for each murder—that was in the papers, Meg. Have you guys figured out that one yet?"

"We thought he might be a dealer or a collector, only we've gone down the list and checked all of them out, and they look clean."

"Lots of people collect guns and don't let anyone know. Especially long guns. They're easier to buy outside the law because they're mostly used as collectibles or for hunting, not for holding up convenience stores."

"It could be somebody like that," Meg said. "There are all sorts of gun nuts."

He shook his head. "Not a nut, necessarily. Just a collector, a lover of precise mechanisms."

She looked around at all of his precision tools that he used so precisely. "By *nut* I didn't mean wacky, I meant he could be a gun enthusiast."

"Yeah, enthusiast is better."

He seemed mollified. Was he a gun nut? It wouldn't be a surprise—he'd been a SWAT sniper.

Meg knew she shouldn't be talking about the case this way with Alex. It was because he'd been a cop. That was why, once he got her talking, she couldn't seem to shut up. She told herself that was the reason.

She stood up from the sofa.

"Not going so soon, I hope," Alex said. He seemed genuinely disappointed.

"I got answers to my questions," she said.

"About the theater and typewriter?"

"More or less."

He moved closer to her, not much, but enough that his presence affected her just the way he planned. *Clever bastard. Seducer. Paint thinner never smelled so good.* "I'd like to see you again," he said, "on an unofficial basis."

"Not wise. Especially not while the Sniper case is hot."

Now he put on a sad expression. "You don't even want to see my rocking chair after it gets its final coat of finish?"

She did. Very much. But something told her it was time to leave. It was an instinct she'd learned to trust.

"Sorry, but I don't have time." She moved toward the door.

"You're the first person other than me who's been in here in months. Usually I don't show people my work before it's finished. I don't want their reaction to influence me." He reached out and touched her shoulder ever so lightly. "But for you I made an exception."

"Don't think of me as an exception," Meg said. "It doesn't make sense for either of us."

"Yet you came here."

"Yet I did." She went to the door and opened it. "Thanks for your cooperation, Mr. Reyals."

He was grinning.

"If you ever want to take in a play . . ." she heard him say as she went out.

Her heart was banging away like the percussion section of a symphony orchestra as she made her way back downstairs and outside. Seeing Alex had been a mistake, made her infection worse.

I screwed up, coming here, she told herself over and over, crossing the street toward her parked car.

What would Repetto think if he knew about this visit? He wouldn't buy that additional questions crap any more than Alex had.

I really screwed up!

20

Candy Trupiano cleared work in progress from her desk and switched off her office lights. It was past seven o'clock in the evening, and workaday New York had wound down. Towering buildings had dropped thousands of people to stream from lobbies and join the rush and roar of the homeward bound. The sun wouldn't set for more than an hour, but except for the pale fluorescent glow leaking in from the hall, the office was dark.

Everyone else at Hamilton Publications had gone home. Candy's was one of the few offices that didn't have a window. She didn't mind. Until a few months ago she'd been Army National Guard Corporal Candice Trupiano, Second Maintenance and Combat, stationed at Fort Campbell, Kentucky. Her unit hadn't left the country, but she'd served nonetheless and was proud of it. And apparently Hamilton Publications was proud of her. Not only had they saved her job while she was away, when she'd returned they awarded her with a sizable raise. This for a twenty-five-year-old associate editor. Old man Hamilton, who owned and ran the company, believed in her, and Candy was happy working hard in her windowless office in order to repay his faith and generosity.

She'd been a more than competent soldier, and the army had tried to convert her to a regular, but she was convinced she'd be a better editor. Besides, it was really what she wanted to do. She loved books and knew the marketplace, had a feel for what people wanted to read. She knew line editing, and she knew how to deal with writers, who could be a persnickety bunch.

Candy was a tall, lanky brunette, with bright blue eyes and a lean jaw. She was reasonably attractive in repose, and when she smiled she became incandescent. In the army she'd learned how to keep herself in top physical condition, and these were habits she didn't want to lose in civilian life. She worked out three times a week in a gym, and she jogged at least five evenings a week.

After leaving the office and subwaying uptown, she set out walking the three blocks from the stop to her apartment on West Seventy-second Street. Candy wouldn't have been able to afford the apartment except for her roommate, Annette, an American Airlines flight attendant who was away most of the time. It was an arrangement Candy could live with easily. Annette was working the international flights now and was somewhere in Europe, where she'd remain until later this month. Living with Annette was almost like living alone, only with a DVD collection Candy couldn't afford.

Candy was moving fast, taking long strides in her jogging shoes that didn't go well with her businesslike gray skirt and blazer. Her gray high heels were in her baggy black denim attaché case, along with the bulky manuscript for *The General's Lover*, which was on a fast-track production schedule. She was supposed to finish editing and get the novel back to the author by the end of the week. Not an easy task. It helped that she liked the novel a great deal, the World War Two story of a German general in Paris who fell in love with a French woman he knew was spying for the resistance.

Candy took the five concrete steps to her building entrance with an ease and grace that caused three teenage boys across the street to gawk at her. One of them shouted something she didn't understand. Just as well.

As she keyed the door to her second-floor apartment and pushed inside, she raised the arm carrying the attaché case and glanced at her watch. She should still have time to get in her run in the park before it became dark.

Whenever she got the opportunity, instead of running in the neighborhood, Candy walked the few blocks to Central Park and jogged along the path that followed the park's perimeter. The distance was 6.1 miles, exactly right for a runner of Candy's ability to stay in tune, if she ran it often enough. She was proud of her body, of her athletic ability. She'd entered the New York Marathon twice, finishing well back both times, but finishing.

She removed *The General's Lover* from the attaché case and placed the manuscript on her desk, where she'd work on it later that evening. Then she carried the case, along with her business shoes, into the bedroom.

As she changed into her sweats and training shoes, she glanced at the window. It seemed that the light was already failing, but that was because it was an overcast day.

Still . . .

For a few seconds she paused. The park could be dangerous after dark; there were people who saw female joggers as prey. Just last month a woman who lived in the next block, over on Seventy-third, was shoved to the ground and robbed at knifepoint near the jogging trail. She might have been killed or raped, if someone hadn't come along and scared away her assailant.

"Screw it!" Candy said, and continued dressing for her regular run.

She was young and strong and trained in hand-to-hand combat. There was no reason she should be afraid of the dark or anyone it might conceal. And she sure as hell had a perfect right to jog in the park—her park—whatever the hour.

When she was dressed to run, she tied back her long dark hair in a ponytail, then went into the kitchen and got a plastic bottle of water to sling in a holster at her waist. She went through the living room, then out into the hall, locking her apartment door behind her. Bending gracefully from the waist, she slid her apartment key into a small, Velcro-flapped pouch attached to her right shoelace. The pouch also contained a tightly folded twenty-dollar bill and a slip of paper with her name and address on it. She would have money in an emergency, and she could be identified, if anything happened to her. An oxygen deficiency or low blood sugar crisis might cause her to lose consciousness for a while.

It was wrong to be afraid, she thought, but right to be careful, as she jogged through lengthening shadows the three blocks to the park entrance.

Not far away, at Columbus Circle, Bobby Mays sat on a folded blanket with a chipped coffee cup before him. He hadn't eaten since wolfing down half a doughnut this morning, but that wasn't what was bothering him. He was plenty used to being hungry, and if he got hungry enough he could make his way to one of the shelters and take his chances on being assaulted or robbed in his sleep, in exchange for a genuine meal.

What Bobby needed was his medicine, his Xanax—that was what was working now. Working better than the rest of his meds, anyway. He glanced down at the few bills and change in the chipped cup. Not enough for his purposes. Not yet.

He didn't want to go to illegal drugs, and the last thing he wanted to become was an alky. But now and then he smoked a joint, or found what was left of a bottle and had to drink it. It turned off the pain machine for a brief period.

It would be dark soon. He examined the cup's contents more closely—three one-dollar bills, two dimes, and a couple of quarters. Not nearly enough to get his prescription filled.

Bobby was afraid that if he had the opportunity, he might forget about begging enough money to pay for the Xanax and steal some of it. From a hospital, pharmacy, doctor's office, anywhere. That would be a last resort, and just thinking about it bothered him, because in another life, in another city, he'd been a cop, and a good one.

He'd been a husband and father, too.

Maybe not such a good husband or father, because he'd been driving when the accident happened. He'd gotten his family killed. He killed his family. His family—

Margie dead beside him with her mouth and eyes so wide, little Midge swimming in blood without a—

Staring at him, but that was impossible.

Don't think about this! Don't go there! Stay away!

Impossible.

The oil dripping. The blood? He couldn't be sure. Dripping and ticking as if it were meting out time, only time had run out.

Not his time, though. That wasn't fair to anyone.

What the fuck's fair got to do with it? Fair's in another world, on another planet. Not where I am.

"You oughta think about it, Bobby. Work it out so you can understand."

My voice?

He rubbed his forearm across his eyes. *Gotta think about it.*

No!

He tried to shake his mind loose from that trap but couldn't quite do it. He was stuck there again, as he was so often, while being eaten away from the inside. Guilt was like acid. It was more like acid than acid. *Drip . . . drip . . . drip . . .*

A coin clinked in the cup and he automatically muttered a thank-you.

New York, not Philadelphia. What the fuck was I thinking about?

The man who'd spared the change didn't look back.

When people did look at Bobby—which, as any of the homeless would tell you, was rare, the homeless being invisible—they sometimes remarked on how young and handsome he was, and how presentable he'd be if he cleaned up, on what a shame it was, a young man like that. Ruined. No more. He knew by their eyes what they were thinking, that he was no longer human.

That was how it felt to Bobby to be homeless. He was other than human now. And it was what he deserved.

Bobby worked his way to a kneeling position on his blanket, then managed to stand, the bunched blanket in one hand, the chipped collection cup in the other. He didn't have enough money for the Xanax, or for a joint he could buy—thought he could buy—to help him through the coming night. He realized he didn't know where to go to buy the joint, though he remembered who he should see. He had a cop's memory for faces, just not times anymore, whole days.

Sometimes yesterdays simply didn't exist for Bobby. The head injury from the car accident, the headaches that came with memories, the guilt, the guilt. All of that was real and never went away for good.

"Jesus!" he said softly.

But he'd tried Jesus and hadn't found the answer. He thought there might not be an answer.

No yesterday for Bobby. No help for tonight. Enough money for a subway card, though. He could get it from one of the machines and ride the lines, steal some sleep, and hope none of the violent ones would steal what little he had, or kill him because he had so little and was a disappointment.

He took a few shuffling steps, then stopped.

There was something about the man on the other side of the street, another of the homeless, judging by his clothes— his ragged long coat too warm for the weather, his faded backpack that probably held all he owned—and his demeanor.

There's a word I haven't used in a long time. Demeanor . . . Demeanor!

That was what was wrong. The man on the opposite sidewalk looked like one of the homeless, one of Bobby's lost brotherhood, only he *didn't* look like one. Bobby had been a Philadelphia cop long enough to be brought up short when something didn't look quite right. And this guy—he was gone now, turned a corner—was walking too fast, with a stride too confident. As if he had some place to go.

None of the homeless had some place to go.

Well, the man was gone.

If he'd ever really been there.

Bobby was beginning to wonder. Some of the things that had happened to him lately made him wonder. It could be the man hadn't been real.

Forgetting the man, Bobby ambled slowly and painfully toward the subway stop up the street. People passing in the opposite direction glanced at him, through him, this shambling young man with the shock of unruly curly hair, the five-day-old beard, the dirt-stained face and lost eyes. Sometimes people whispered, making sympathetic or cruel remarks. Bobby continued on his way, not paying attention to them, not hearing them, not remembering if he had heard them. Bobby with yesterdays too slippery to grasp, losing his todays. Tomorrow was his birthday, but he wasn't at all aware of it. Bobby didn't know what month it was, much less what day.

He'd be thirty-one years old.

Repetto and Lora were in Mama Roma's, having salad and house Chablis while they waited for their pasta. The dinner crowd was at its peak, and every table was occupied. The aromas of the kitchen, dominated by garlic, were in the air.

Lora sipped her wine, then stared over the rim of her glass at Repetto. "You look pensive. What are you thinking?"

"How we used to eat here with Dal."

Lora finished her wine in one swallow. "That's what I was thinking. Zoe says she's learning more about him all the time."

Repetto knew that by *him*, Lora didn't mean Dal. He pushed away his irritation. He didn't come here to grieve Dal, or to think about the Night Sniper. "Either that or she's learning more about somebody she's invented who doesn't exist."

"You're not being fair to her."

Repetto reached for the wine bottle and replenished Lora's glass, as if urging her to drink more and forget more. Forget about Zoe. About Dal, at least for a short while.

"Zoe's a professional," Lora said.

"So are palm readers."

"According to the information I found, profilers are more often right than wrong."

"Yeah, the killer is usually within a certain age group, is male, athletic enough to do whatever it is he does, is the product of a lousy childhood, and the neighbors would describe him as a nice, quiet person. It doesn't take a professional to figure that much out, and usually the profiler has everything else wrong."

Lora pushed her wineglass away, miffed now. "Like I said—unfair."

Repetto drew a deep breath and let it out slowly before taking another sip of his own wine. "You're right. I'm being unfair." He smiled. "But I don't take back what I said about profilers in general. Zoe's better than the average, and you can tell her I said so, but I've seen too many investigations go down wrong roads because of profilers. I don't have much faith in any of them."

"Any investigation in particular that bothers you?" Lora asked. "That went down that wrong road because of a pro-filer?"

Repetto waited a few seconds before answering. "The Midnight Leather Killer."

"You caught him."

"Two months later than we should have. Because we acted on information a profiler gave us and wasted those months." The old anger was creeping into him, slowing his breathing and tightening his throat. "Three women were killed during that period."

"And you blame the profiler?"

"I blame myself, for listening to him."

"But you shouldn't."

Repetto didn't answer, staring past her out the restaurant's window at the street. There was no point in telling Lora that *shouldn't* didn't have much to do with it. She hadn't spent years dealing with the world of random heartbreak and evil that shadowed the orderly, civilized one. A cop walked in both worlds, had to survive and keep his sanity in both of them, and it could eventually become a high-wire balancing act without a net.

He made himself relax. It was unreasonable of him to think she should understand. You had to be there.

"It's going to be dark soon," he said, still staring out the window.

A young guy in a jacket like Dal used to wear passed the window. Even looked a little like Dal. Repetto felt a pang of grief that made him gulp. The conversation with Lora had touched a nerve. If Dal hadn't been killed, probably the three of them would be here together tonight.

Lora said, "Do you think there's a cop anywhere who doesn't feel guilty about something?"

Repetto poured them both more wine.

They both knew the answer to Lora's question. And they knew that guilt wasn't static. It was like a river with a powerful current that could drown you.

Or carry you to where you dreaded going.

21

Candy Trupiano ran smoothly, breathing evenly through her nose, her strides long and even. Her faint footprints on the path described a straight line. She ran with no wasted arm movement or side-to-side hip motion. Every muscle in use powered her forward.

She was tired, feeling the ache in her lungs, the burning sensation in her thighs, but she was in a groove where she could stay a long time. Where, if she had to, she could run forever.

Her heart told her that, and right now she wasn't listening to her brain. There was doubt in her brain, and apprehension, and none of either in her heart.

Candy felt a sharp pain in the fronts of her lower legs. First her left leg, then her right. Within a few more strides, the pain was like needles penetrating deep into her bones. Shin splints.

Damn!

Her stride faltered; then she slowed and stood bent forward at the waist, her hands cupping her knees.

She waited, catching her breath, impatient for the sharp pain in her shins to abate. This had happened before. Every runner sooner or later experienced the debilitating pain of shin splints. It had to do with diet, and improper training. Overworking. Candy knew she'd pressed herself too hard, trying to get home before dark.

That wasn't going to happen now. She straightened slowly and glanced around at the lowering sky and shadowed trees. Then she began to walk, slowly at first, testing her legs awkwardly as if she were a newborn colt.

The pain had let up. Within fifteen minutes she was walking almost at normal stride, gaining confidence in her stricken legs. Soon she'd be able to jog again, but at a much slower pace. She knew that she shouldn't press; waiting long enough was the trick here. If she began jogging too soon, the pain would return and be even worse. Why this had to happen tonight, when she was in something of a hurry, she wasn't sure. Maybe it was wearing those damned high heels at work all day. They compressed the calf muscles.

That had nothing to do with shin splints, she told herself.

Footsteps sounded behind her, and she moved to the side of the path.

A tall man wearing blue shorts and a gray sweatshirt padded past, glancing her way but saying nothing. He had on earphones, and a wire led to an MP3 player at his waist.

A few minutes later an older, incredibly thin woman with short gray hair smiled as she jogged past Candy. A small brown dog with a bushy tail ran effortlessly at her side, without a leash.

Then Candy was alone on the path.

Through the trees to her right she could glimpse traffic streaming past, and she knew she could easily leave the park. She could walk out through the trees and use the twenty-dollar bill in her shoe pouch for cab fare.

But shin splints or not, she hated to waste a workout. And she had only a mile or so to travel before she arrived again at the Seventy-second Street entrance to the park.

Candy Trupiano finished whatever she started. That was important to her. It was how she saw herself.

It was how she wanted to continue seeing herself.

Slowly, carefully, she began jogging again, increasing her speed in small measures.

There was pain in both legs, a slight ache that wouldn't go away, but she thought she could monitor and control it.

She'd make it to Seventy-second Street, because until she got there, she'd make Seventy-second Street the focus of her existence.

Candy was determined to live her life in such a way that there wasn't room for debilitating pain or uncertainty. She was convinced that if she finished what she began, good things were sure to follow.

The Night Sniper had no problem with the lock.

This was the second time he'd visited the vacant apartment. The first time, it took him a while to slip the latch on the knob lock with a piece of thin plastic. He'd used a knife to shave the door slightly so that now even a credit card could be inserted between door and frame and used to unlock the door. Fortunately, the dead bolt above the doorknob hadn't been thrown on his first visit. He'd jammed paper wadding into the keyhole with a penknife to make sure it wouldn't be locked tonight. The auxiliary inside locks, of course, were unfastened, including a flimsy brass chain lock, because the tiny efficiency apartment was vacant.

He'd searched the real estate classified ads for quite a while before coming across this apartment: *Ef, pk vw, vcnt, rsnble*. Without contacting the leasing agent, he'd gone to the address, found that the apartment was on the fifth floor in an expensive but older apartment building that was being renovated, and employed no doorman. Many of the units were vacant, and no one had seen him take an elevator to the fifth floor, locate the apartment, and make his way inside.

For a few minutes he'd stood at the window, staring out at the edge of Central Park. A jogger passed on the trail beyond the low stone wall that marked the park's perimeter. Another jogger. A Rollerblader. Then a woman walking a small child on a leash as if it were a dog.

How can people do that to children?

The apartment, he decided, was well suited to his needs.

Now here he was, dressed in chinos and a pale blue shirt, brown walking shoes. The uniform of the forgettable.

Not that it mattered. As before, no one had seen him as he made his way into the lobby, elevatored to the fifth floor, and entered the vacant apartment.

He went to the window. Darkness was falling, but a nearby streetlight threw faint illumination along the park's edge. The trail itself was barely visible and would be almost impossible to see with the naked eye within the next fifteen or twenty minutes.

The Night Sniper carried a tiny flashlight, but there was no need for it. The apartment was bright enough for him to see as he removed the custom-made Feinwerkbau target rifle from his backpack and assembled it. Even wearing the thin latex gloves, he could assemble the rifle by feel, and needed no light. He'd once done exactly that in total darkness to amuse himself.

He attached a magazine to the spare, deadly-looking rifle and made sure there was a round in the breech, then fitted the scope to the barrel. Placing the backpack against the wall where he'd be able to get to it quickly, he kneeled at the window that overlooked the park and raised it about six inches. Cooler evening air flowed into the warm apartment that had probably been closed up all day.

After adjusting his body so he could remain kneeling comfortably and steadily for a while, he raised the rifle and sighted in on the trail in the park across the street.

It was much darker now and there were fewer people on the path. Hardly anyone wanted to enter the park after nightfall, and who could blame them? There were dangerous people out there. Human predators.

Two young men bopped past on the path, wearing gangbanger pants that looked about to be left behind as they talked to each other and waved their arms. One of them was carrying something that looked like a closed umbrella, though there was no rain in the forecast. A man and woman walked past in the opposite direction, moving fast. Half a block down, they climbed over the low stone wall and were out of the park.

These were not the Night Sniper's targets. Not worthy of his gift of death.

There was another figure on the path. A man in dark slacks and a jacket, hands stuffed in pockets. Maybe looking for someone to mug.

The Night Sniper waited, unmoving. When he saw his target, he'd know it.

Ah! Here came another figure, jogging slowly through the shadows, almost at a walk. But this figure moved with a practiced, graceful motion. Interesting. Was this the one?

He leaned forward and peered through the rifle's infrared scope. A woman. She was young, slender, graceful, her long hair—a braid or ponytail—swaying with each step. Though she was laboring as if she might be in some sort of discomfort, there was a lithe elegance in her every shortened stride.

This was the one. The chosen.

He focused in on her, keeping the crosshairs trained on the thickest part of her figure, her torso. He knew the rifle would make noise, but it was doubtful that any other building occupants would suspect that what they heard was interior. And of course he counted on the echoing crack of the shot to add to the city's fear factor. He wanted people to jump at even slight abrupt sounds that might mean death. What was lightning without thunder?

Because of her graceful stride, the woman was moving faster than it first appeared. Darker shapes across the street, trees, would soon block his shot. If it was to be tonight, he had to make up his mind.

He allowed for the faint breeze, calculated his lead, then squeezed the trigger. Thunder cracked and echoed among the tall buildings.

Target down.

For a few seconds the Night Sniper studied the prone figure through the powerful night scope. There was no movement.

Time to leave.

He recovered the ejected brass casing from the floor and slipped it into a pocket. Then he quickly broke down the rifle and jammed it into his backpack. Carrying the pack in his right hand, he was in the hall, then the elevator and lobby, in less than a minute. Still without being seen.

There was no one in the lobby, but he didn't want to take the chance of changing clothes here or in the restroom, as he'd thought he might. Instead, he casually walked outside, noticing that none of the hurrying, obviously uneasy people on the sidewalks had apparently yet been made aware of the woman's body on the path.

That made things easier.

In the deep, dark doorway of a closed and boarded-up Chinese restaurant, the Night Sniper found the darkest point, then with practiced quickness and economy of motion removed his shirt and pants and stuffed them into the backpack, along with the disassembled rifle. He was wearing other clothes beneath them: baggy, filthy-looking pants and an oversize shirt with a torn collar and an unbuttoned cuff. One costume for another. He mussed his hair, put on his well-worn Yankees cap, then slipped his arms through his backpack's straps and made his way back to the street.

Now he was a shuffling, homeless soul making his way to the abandoned subway stop where he sought shelter. He looked not at all like the straight-arrow type who'd just exited the building down the street.

A block away, he lengthened his stride. There was no need to hurry, but he did anyway. Though not so much that he'd attract attention.

Bobby Mays was seated on his folded blanket, his chipped coffee cup before him, doing business a block off the park, when he heard the shot.

From his years as a Philadelphia cop, he knew it was a gunshot. Rifle fire.

Bobby shifted sideways so he could get on his hands and knees, then leaned against the building wall and started working his way to a standing position. He was stiff from sleeping in a doorway most of last night on his blanket, and he'd been panhandling where he was since early evening. His knee hurt where a punk on the prowl had kicked it out of meanness a week ago. His right shoulder ached where the pins had been put in after the accident. As long as his head didn't hurt the way it often did, he didn't mind the rest of the pain; it was something he'd learned to live with, and he knew that after he moved around for a while it would lessen.

He snatched up the cup as he stood, so he wouldn't have to bend over again, then glanced down at it—about five dollars. Not bad. He stuffed the money into the baggy side pocket of the ancient suit coat he'd found in curbside trash, then raised his face to the sky like an animal testing to pick up the scent. He was trying, as best he could, to determine at least the general direction of the echoing gunshot.

Curious, and with nothing else to do, he hitched up his

belt and began walking unsteadily in the direction of the re-port. People glanced at him and looked quickly away. No one blocked his path, or said excuse me as they stepped aside to let him pass. Bobby the invisible. Sometimes it seemed he was disappearing even from himself.

When he reached Central Park West, he could see blue and red flashing lights several blocks down the street, on the side where the park was. The emergency lights might have something to do with the shot he'd heard—might have heard. But there were emergencies all the time in the city. He began moving in that direction.

That's when he looked across the street, and there was the homeless man he'd seen at Columbus Circle. Bobby remem-bered him for the same reason he'd noticed him in the first place. The man was, at a glance, one of the homeless, like Bobby. But a closer look revealed something not quite right about him. He didn't fit. It was obvious to an ex-cop like Bobby, even if people only glanced at the ragged man and moved out of his way. No one wanted to disturb the man or attract his attention. People with nothing to lose could be dangerous.

Traffic was heavy, so Bobby didn't consider crossing the street toward the man. He studied him from where he stood. The man's clothes were ragged, stained, and ill-fitting, but they also seemed . . . clean? But mainly it was the way the man walked. Despite his humble clothing, his stride was purposeful and confident.

Not right, Bobby thought. Not right at all. The home-less—

Someone clinked a coin into the cup Bobby forgot he was carrying, startling him, and he lost sight of the man across the street.

Not that it mattered. Bobby continued walking toward the flashing lights a few blocks down the street.

When he reached the lights he saw that they belonged to

an ambulance and two police cars. Something had happened in the park, on the other side of the low stone wall. Bobby could see uniformed cops standing around, a couple of plainclothes detectives. They had yellow crime scene ribbon strung in a crude rectangle. Bobby couldn't see what was behind the low wall, what all the excitement was about.

He thought about moving closer and finding out what was happening, then decided it might be a bad idea. For all he knew, somebody had been mugged by a homeless man. One with beard stubble, wild hair, long dirty fingernails, ragged and soiled clothes, and no known address.

Who does that describe?

Bobby decided he'd seen enough. Instead of satisfying his cop's curiosity, he moved away and began walking back the way he'd come.

He'd gone only half a dozen steps before he forgot why he'd walked this direction in the first place.

A shot!

That's right; that was why. He'd heard gunfire. Somebody might have been shot.

Well, that was happening lately, people being shot. Like most New Yorkers, Bobby had been following the Night Sniper case. He heard people talk about the shootings, and he'd been reading about them. Bobby read the papers.

Slightly used papers, but he read them.

The problem was, he often had trouble recalling what he'd read.

This time the note police found taped to the theater seat read, *You would be wise to consider another profession.*

"Where was this one found?" Zoe asked.

She'd heard another note had been located. She was waiting for Repetto and his team in their dank precinct basement office, thinking there was no way to make the place more depressing, when they returned. Either she'd chosen not to sit or had risen when she heard them coming. Meg thought Zoe looked tired. Her eyes were puffy, and her long red hair was slightly tangled, as if she hadn't finished brushing it out.

"In an off-off-Broadway theater that used to be a produce warehouse," Repetto said. He tossed a copy of the Night Sniper's note on his desk for Zoe to read. The lab had the original. Nobody doubted that they'd learn nothing from it. "I'm getting tired of running around town just to find this asshole's notes."

"The theater still smelled like produce," Birdy said. "Potatoes, I think."

"That's interesting," Zoe said, slouched down in one of the chairs angled to face the desk.

"Potatoes?" Meg asked.

"No, that our guy would choose that kind of theater. What's playing there?"

"Something called *A Child of his Time*," Repetto said. "The premise is that Rudyard Kipling was secretly Josephine Baker's real father." He glanced at Birdy and Meg. "Josephine Baker was—"

"I know," Meg interrupted. "A famous African-American beauty who danced in Paris in the twenties and thirties."

"The infamous banana dance," Birdy said.

Everyone looked at him.

"She used to do a sexy dance wearing nothing but these bunches of bananas. The French liked it."

"Bananas . . . a produce warehouse," Meg said to Zoe. "Is that some way meaningful?"

"I doubt it," Zoe said. Her gaze wandered upward. Was that mold in the corner of the ceiling?

"It smelled like potatoes anyway," Birdy said. He sat down in the chair next to Zoe's and began to fidget.

"Maybe the Night Sniper has more than one reason for making us figure out where he's hidden his notes," Zoe said.

"I thought we'd settled on game playing," Repetto said. He sat down behind the desk, at eye level now with Zoe. "He'd rather aggravate us than simply mail the note instead of the clue."

"He might also want to keep us—us being the NYPD—busy searching theaters instead of searching for him."

Repetto thought that over and nodded. "It wouldn't be so stupid. A lot of good police work hasn't been done because personnel was walking up and down aisles, examining theater seats."

"Maybe there's a third reason," Zoe said. "Maybe the play titles have some kind of significance."

Repetto sat forward, picked up a pen, and wrote down the titles in the order in which their corresponding notes were found.

"The plays are all for or about children, or have children or a child in the titles," he said.

"Or as cast members," Meg said.

Repetto asked her how she knew that.

"I made it a point to read all but the last play. They're published and sold at bookstores, or the producers will turn them over if you ask in an official capacity."

"Wonderful!" Zoe said. As if Meg were her prize student.

Repetto knew he should have thought to get the scripts. "That's good work," he said.

Birdy stopped playing an invisible piano on his knees and nodded. "Kudos to my partner."

"Maybe coincidence, though," Repetto said. "There are children in a lot of plays."

"And our guy hasn't killed a child," Birdy pointed out.

"Yet," Meg said.

Zoe shook her head. "No, our sniper isn't a child killer. They're a breed apart." She looked at Repetto. "And you told me once what cops thought of coincidence."

Meg shrugged. "So what's it all mean?"

"That's for you guys to detect," Zoe said, standing up from her chair.

"It means something more than game playing's going on," Repetto said.

"Not necessarily," Zoe said. "But it might mean the game's more complicated and difficult than we first thought. And maybe we'll have to play harder."

When Zoe was gone, Repetto turned to Meg and Birdy. "She's right. We can start by trying to find out more about the Candy Trupiano shooting."

"It was pretty much the same as the others," Meg said. "Single shot fired from a distance. Admirable accuracy. And she was killed by an odd-size bullet."

"Nobody at the publishing company where she worked thinks the victim had any enemies," Birdy said, "only friends. You know how it goes. People get killed and achieve saint-hood for a while before anybody says nasty things about them."

"Such a cynic," Meg said, but it annoyed her, and kind of scared her, to think he might have something there.

"We'll hit the neighborhood again where she was shot," Repetto said. "Also around where she lived. Talk to her neighbors, or the doormen or shopkeepers who might have been in position to witness the shooting."

"Word is she jogged regularly in the park," Meg said. "Maybe some of the other joggers knew her."

"I dunno," Birdy said. "People don't tend to strike up conversations when they're out of breath."

"At least the ones who are still jogging might have the balls to speak up if they do know anything helpful."

"She has a good point," Repetto said.

"The city's getting more shook," Birdy said. "People scared of sudden loud noises. The mayor's catching hell from talk show hosts and TV-news dickheads."

"He'll get over it," Meg said.

"Police are catching hell, too," Birdy said. "And people got a right to be scared."

Repetto knew that whether they had a right or not, they *were* scared.

Candy Trupiano had been shot at 8:17 PM. The earliest the Night Sniper had claimed a victim, the media had pointed out.

Beginning that night, after 8:30 every night, there would be noticeably fewer people on the streets of Manhattan.

22

Alex Reyals came to the door this time wearing faded jeans, a black T-shirt, and in his stocking feet. He needed a shave, so his dark beard seemed almost as long as his buzz-cut hair. He smelled not unpleasantly of turpentine and raw wood.

"Been upstairs in your workshop?" she asked.

He smiled. "Yeah, but it's nothing that can't wait." He moved back so she could enter.

The apartment was neat and clean today, squared up in a way that reminded Meg of military quarters. Definitely the place could use the application of some simple decorating basics. Meg thought Repetto's wife, Lora, should see this. Lora understood interior decorating and would know a man lived here alone and devoid of color sense.

On the other hand, Alex must have *some* sense of color and design. He was more than a simple craftsman and furniture maker; he was an artist. She glanced again at the example of his work in the apartment, the massive, multilayered desk.

"It's mahogany," he said, noticing where she was looking. "Inlaid with teak."

"It looks futuristic," she said, of the desk's sharply angled planes, "and yet it doesn't."

"It's the present," Alex said. "Stuck right in the middle of now."

"Waxed slippery and full of angles?"

"Aren't you perceptive?"

"My job."

"Sit down," he invited, motioning toward the sofa. "Want some coffee?"

"Kind of late for coffee."

"I drink it all day long."

She declined the coffee, but she sat. "Speaking of my job, I'm interested in where you were two nights ago."

He rubbed his unshaven chin. Meg could hear the friction. "I was here."

"Alone?"

He looked at her in a way that was unsettling. "Ah! Two nights ago. I know what you're up to, Detective Meg."

"Doyle."

"Two nights ago was when that woman was shot in the park. The editor . . ."

"Candy Trupiano," Meg reminded him.

"Yeah. I had the Candy part. Listen, do I need an alibi? If I'd known you were coming I would have made something up."

"You don't seem to be taking this seriously."

"It's wearing a little thin, trying to keep track of my life in case I might be questioned about the who, where, what, when, why."

"You should know how it is. We're both stuck with the routine. You said you were here two nights ago. Were you alone?"

"Yes. Unfortunately, I didn't choose that night to have a party."

His joking manner was beginning to aggravate Meg. "Feel like talking about why you left the NYPD?"

That caused a dark cloud to pass over. She was instantly sorry she'd brought up the subject when she saw the look of pure pain cross his features.

"I think you know that, or you wouldn't be here." His voice had changed, too. If she wanted serious, she'd gotten it.

"You're not the first person to shoot and miss," she said. *God! Now I'm trying to cheer him up.*

"I didn't miss." He turned away from her. "I hit. Trouble is, what I hit was the hostage instead of the suspect."

"It wasn't your fault. It's the kind of shit the bumper stickers say happens. How were you supposed to know someone was going to move at the same time you squeezed the trigger?"

"It was my job to know, just like it's your job to be here and work at making yourself a pain in the ass. Which, as far as I'm concerned, you are not." He wasn't looking at her. Staring out the window. "I didn't do my job. A woman died. Case closed."

Without realizing she'd crossed the room she was at his side, touching his shoulder. "Then let it be closed. Stop torturing yourself about it."

He turned slightly so he could look at her, his smile faint and sad. "It isn't that easy. Guns can kill or maim in a lot of ways. Isn't that the hypothesis—rogue cop tortured by guilt goes crazy and starts shooting people?"

"Not my hypothesis."

"What's yours?"

"I don't have one yet. I'm doing my job, like you were doing yours when you got unlucky."

"We talk an awful lot about the Job."

"People are what they do," Meg said.

"Did. Now I create things out of wood."

"With sharp tools."

He glanced at her. "Somebody been murdered with a band saw?"

"I don't even know what a band saw is," Meg said. "But I can't imagine you murdering someone set to music."

He moved away from her and sat down in a chair, crossing his legs. "Then you've never really listened to the blues."

"Oh, but I have."

He regarded her without changing expression. "What I sensed about you from the start is you might lie to me, but you're honest."

"Of course. I'm a cop."

The sad smile again. "We keep things light so we don't sink in quicksand."

"Lots of us play it that way," Meg said. "The cop's world is a kind of swamp."

He didn't answer and wasn't looking at her now. She knew where he was. Back in his personal swamp he could never quite escape, where he would eventually fall prey to the thing he kept alive there.

She walked to the door. The motion stirred enough air to raise again the acrid but pleasant scent of turpentine and freshly hewn or sanded wood. She imagined his muscle-corded arms and powerful hands working the wood, shaping it, creating . . .

"Interview over?" he asked, sounding disappointed.

"For now."

"Learn anything?"

"Yeah."

"Got any wise words for me?"

"Yeah." She opened the door and looked back at him before stepping into the hall, giving him a mock serious expression. "Don't leave town." A touch of humor to show he could get out of the quicksand if only he'd try hard enough.

It hadn't quite worked. She felt as if she were slowly sinking with him.

He nodded as if giving her instruction careful consideration. "Okay. Don't be a stranger."

Back in the unmarked she sat squeezing the steering wheel with both hands, staring straight ahead at nothing beyond the windshield.

I'm falling for him. A suspect in a serial murder investigation.

Be careful here. Be careful.

23

Kelli Wilson and her ten-year-old son, Jason, left Grand Central Station after riding the train in from Stamford. They took a cab to the Frick Museum, Kelli's favorite. The museum was open extended hours to accommodate public demand for its Impressionist Masters exhibition.

Kelli and Jason spent almost three hours roaming the spacious rooms. Kelli was an amateur painter and knew she didn't have as much talent as Jason, whose art teachers at the Bennett School were mightily impressed.

So Kelli was the mother of a superior child. Thinking about it made her smile. She liked to remind herself and smile. Heredity could be a wonderful thing.

Jason liked art, and loved painting almost as much as playing ice hockey. He was receptive when the recorded voice in the earphones of the tape players worn at the Frick explained the histories of the paintings and their creators. Kelli enjoyed watching the expression in his guileless blue eyes as he listened while he stared at the paintings with something like religious awe.

When they left the Frick the evening had turned cooler,

and she was glad she'd brought her retro mink jacket into the city. Kelli was an attractive blond woman in her forties and had never owned anything mink before the jacket. Always she'd been antifur, but when she had a chance to buy the jacket at an estate sale, she reasoned that it was secondhand, the minks used to make it were long dead, and there would be no real difference in the world if she wore the jacket or if someone else did. The jacket was made of light-colored female mink fur and was incredibly soft. It looked just right with her pale complexion, and it did the magical thing expensive mink could do for a woman. When she wore it, she looked and felt ten years younger, and far more beautiful than she knew she actually was; the mirror didn't exactly lie, but it became her friend.

Kelli put her hand on Jason's shoulder to get his attention, and they stopped at the corner and moved out of the flow of pedestrian traffic. She dug her cell phone from her purse and speed-dialed the work number of her husband, Warren, who was an architect with Lohan and Berner. Warren had been with the firm almost five years, and lately was doing very well. Which was how they'd managed to buy their eighteen-foot cabin cruiser *Dream Waver*.

They kept the boat docked in a slip at the Seventy-ninth Street Boat Basin. When Warren had to work late, which was often, he would stay in the city and spend the night on the *Dream Waver*. The boat slept six, so there was plenty of room on the nights when Kelli and Jason took a train into the city and met Warren for a late supper. The family would sleep on the boat. Kelli had resisted the idea at first, but Warren explained that the hotel bills they saved on the times he'd have to spend nights in the city would help to defray the cost of the boat.

The three years they'd owned the boat had proved him right. Not only that, Kelli came to love sleeping on the boat, feeling the gentle bobbing as water lapped at the hull, hearing the soft and subtle sounds of strain on wood, metal, and fiberglass. She also discovered that sex on a small boat was great, though not exactly private. Of course, it only happened on those rare nights when Jason wasn't aboard. Kelli wondered if they might call Jennifer, the babysitter who sometimes stayed all night with Jason. Jennifer understood—

Warren picked up on the third ring.

"I'm in the middle of a meeting right now, hon," he said, when he heard Kelli's voice.

"Sorry. I'll keep it short. We still on tonight for dinner at Four Seasons?" Kelli had never dined at the famous and expensive restaurant. This was to be a special dinner, celebrating the third anniversary of their purchase of *Dream Waver.*

"We're still on. But I'm gonna be tied up here for a while longer discussing soil samples and city ordinances. I called and changed the reservation for eight-thirty. That okay with you?"

It has to be. But Kelli was only mildly annoyed. "Kind of late for Jason."

"He never minded staying up past his bedtime."

"That's for sure. Jason and I can find someplace to kill time."

"There's a big new toy store over on Fifth Avenue."

"I know the one you mean. We can cab over there and explore. But I can't promise not to buy something."

"With Jason along, it's a given. Listen, I really gotta get back."

"Of course. We'll meet at Four Seasons a little before eight-thirty. Love you."

"Love you back."

The connection was broken.

"So what're we gonna do?" Jason asked, as Kelli flipped the cell phone closed and slipped it back in her purse.

"Oh, I'm not sure. Maybe we could go explore a new toy store."

"Kids' toys?"

She had to grin. "I sure hope so."

"We gonna buy something?"

She tried to ruffle his hair but he pulled away. Grinning, though.

"It's a given," she said.

The Night Sniper overheard most of what Kelli had said on the cell phone, her side of the conversation, on the corner near the Frick Museum. And he'd overheard both sides of the brief conversation between mother and child.

Time, place, opportunity. How carelessly people revealed themselves.

Crouching on the rooftop in the cool wind, he fitted the barrel and scope onto the collapsible aluminum stock of his custom-made Italian game rifle and smiled. The rifle was one of the more valuable in his collection, and it had a wonderful provenance. It had been a gift from Mussolini to Hermann Goering, himself an avid hunter, in 1939, only months before the beginning of World War Two. It was perfectly balanced, its hand-tooled components precise, its trigger pressure slight. So smooth was the mechanism that it was a pleasure for the Night Sniper to squeeze the trigger when the rifle was unloaded, simply to hear the buttery working of steel on steel. Steel that was machined to infinitesimal fractions of an inch.

Perfection.

The Night Sniper worshipped perfection.

And he'd found the perfect sniper's nest, high enough to be unnoticeable from the street during the few seconds he'd be sighting in and vulnerable. Low enough so the angle of his shot was a good one. He had an unobstructed view of the corner of East Fifty-second and Park Avenue, and the entrance to the Four Seasons. The night was clear, and even on the rooftop the breeze was no more than a velvety caress of his bare wrists. Perfect.

His wrists had always been sensitive to even the slightest movement of air, which is why he always shot with his sleeves turned up.

They weren't turned up now, because he had plenty of time. He glanced at the luminous dial of his watch. He was wearing his Tag Heuer chronograph tonight. It kept perfect time, and it indicated precisely fourteen minutes before 8:30.

Approximately fourteen more minutes for his target to live.

And counting.

Jason had fallen in love with a scaled-down radio-controlled model of the red Ferrari Formula One race car driven by his hero, Michael Schumaker. Kelli knew it probably cost more than Warren would have approved of on the spot, but since it was for Jason and it was a fait accompli, he wouldn't be upset. The agreement between Jason and his mother was that Jason would carry the car, and it would remain in the box until they boarded the *Dream Waver*.

He didn't have to carry the car far, because three cabs were lined up outside the toy store. No doubt the drivers knew that almost every adult who entered the store with a child would emerge with at least one bag or package. Pay or schlep.

When she bent over and climbed into the back of the cab after Jason, Kelli noticed the dashboard clock. Ten minutes past eight. They might get to Four Seasons before Warren, but that was okay. They could have something cold to drink while they waited for him, water or Sprite for Jason, a Bloody Mary for Kelli.

As the cab pulled slowly away from the curb, then lurched

slightly as the driver nosed into the flow of traffic and accelerated, Kelli smiled.

Usually Warren chided her about arriving late for restaurant dates.

Not this time.

Repetto, Lora, and Zoe were halfway through their drinks, which were in oversize martini glasses. They were in the Campbell Apartment in Grand Central Station, a plush, secluded bar specializing in creative drinks. Repetto had ordered a regular gin martini. Lora and Zoe had drinks with chunks of fruit on toothpicks in them. Repetto had been here before and liked the ambience, lots of rich wood paneling, soft light, and a patina of wealth and excellence from a time when railroads ruled. Chairs comfortable enough to sleep in were arranged around low, generous tables where conversation came easily for lovers or various other kinds of people on the make. However, the conversation around this table had been strained, probably mostly because of Repetto. He'd been quieter than usual, wondering where the evening was going. He knew there was a reason Lora had pushed for this meeting with Zoe.

It was Zoe who'd chosen the place they were to meet. Through Lora, she was having too much influence on the Night Sniper case. And surely the case was the reason they were here. He thought he might as well be the first to mention the subject.

"Are you still sure our killer won't shoot a child?" he asked, sipping his martini. He studied Zoe as he sipped. She seemed relieved that she hadn't had to broach the subject. Lora was looking warningly at Repetto.

"Still am," Zoe said. "He's simply not a child killer. Or if he is, he breaks the pattern."

"New patterns are made all the time," Repetto said.

"No, not often." Zoe reached for her stemmed glass and almost drained what was left in one long series of swallows. She'd gotten here before them; Repetto suspected it was her second drink. Did she need nerve for this conversation? "Serial killers are trapped in patterns along with their victims."

"Profilers can be trapped in patterns along with serial killers."

Zoe smiled to show him she wasn't perturbed. "Along with cops."

Repetto could have cut rope with the look Lora gave him.

Zoe hadn't taken her eyes off Repetto. "I wanted to talk to you about another aspect of the case."

"Another insight into the killer?"

"Into his motive."

"Well," Repetto said, "that's the heart of it." *More speculation.* "But remember, if we're a few degrees off when we sail, we could wind up on another continent."

"What does that mean?" Lora asked.

Zoe looked at her and smiled. "Your husband's telling me to be careful with my assumptions. And it's good advice." She again focused her attention on Repetto. "It occurred to me there was something interesting about the crime scenes and the victims. The murders all occurred in different parts of town, and to a variety of people. The victims seem to have had absolutely nothing in common, and that in itself is unusual."

She did have Repetto's interest. "You think the shootings aren't random?" he asked.

"They might not be at all random. The shooter never happened to kill . . . say, two unemployed men, or two recently engaged women, or two garage mechanics or insurance salesmen or whatever. Isn't that worth noting?"

Repetto thought about it. "I'm not sure."

"There is *some* coincidence in the world," Lora said.

Repetto looked from one woman to the other. "I assume you two have talked this over."

They both nodded.

"The victims are representative," Zoe said.

"Of what?"

"Different worlds," Lora said, "but all clustered together here in New York. So, in a sense, one world."

Repetto stared at her, trying to figure out exactly what she'd said.

"The victims are various ages, races, and stations in life," Zoe said, "composing a diverse cross section of people living, working, or visiting New York City. And they were shot in different neighborhoods. It's as if the sniper wants to stop tourism and local commerce, as if he has a grudge against the city." She played with the stem of her martini glass. "Viewed in that light, the murders fit the pattern of revenge killings."

Repetto sat back in soft, padded leather. "It's a possibility, if the killer hates everyone enough to kill them."

Lora smiled.

Zoe didn't change expression. "Just *almost* everyone— the people who represent the city's makeup. He's attacking, in his own way, the city itself."

"You really believe that?"

"I believe it enough to press."

At least she was being honest. "What exactly do you want?" Repetto asked, getting to what he knew was the real reason for this friendly meeting over drinks.

"For you to take the theory to Assistant Chief Melbourne. Get him to use his authority to open confidential city records so we can search for anyone who might have a grudge against New York City."

"That'd be half the goddamn country," Repetto said.

"You know what she means," Lora said, throwing in with the enemy. "Personnel files."

Zoe leaned forward. "We need to find out about seriously disgruntled employees, but just as importantly, *former* employees. People who left under the worst circumstances, and carrying a load of acrimony."

"You're asking for a lot of time," Repetto said. "A lot of work hours."

"It might be worth it," Lora said.

"What about Zoe's previous theory that the killer's insisting on game playing, so we should concentrate on that aspect of his personality?" He was asking Lora, not Zoe. Lora the turncoat.

"It could still be true," Lora said. "So could this theory."

"It could also be true that the Sniper might start killing children."

"The two theories could coexist," Zoe admitted. "We're talking about probabilities."

"You are. I deal in hard facts, then put them together to make an arrest that'll stick in court."

"I'm suggesting a way to get at the facts," Zoe said.

Repetto finished his drink and signaled the waiter for another.

"Better go easy," Lora said, touching the back of his hand. "I love you and don't want to have to wrestle the car keys from you."

Repetto had to smile. What chance did he have?

"Okay," he said, "I'll talk to Melbourne and see what he thinks about raiding the department's confidential personnel files."

"Not just the NYPD files," Zoe said.

Repetto waved a hand like a surrender flag. "I know, I know. . . ."

Zoe grinned. Lora sighed with satisfaction. She was a woman who reveled in manipulating and outmaneuvering her mate. Or was that *all* women?

Zoe said, "Thanks," looking at Repetto. Then she glanced

at her watch. "Almost eight-thirty. I've gotta meet somebody at nine for drinks on the other side of town." She dug some bills from her purse and laid them on the table to pay her part of the check. "You two stay and finish your coffee." She stood up.

"A date?" Lora asked.

"A date," Zoe confirmed.

That didn't sound right to Repetto. He never imagined Zoe with any kind of social life, though she was single and certainly attractive. There was probably a lot about Zoe he didn't know.

Zoe nodded good night to Repetto, then leaned toward Lora. Repetto thought she was going to peck her on the cheek. Instead he heard her whisper, "Your husband's a hardhead, but he's actually quite nice."

She didn't look back at them as she walked away. However many drinks she'd had, she was moving in a straight line and with a hip switch and grace that could only be called sexy.

"A seductive redhead," Lora said, probably reading Repetto's mind. "I've sometimes thought of dying my hair red."

"What did she just whisper to you?" Repetto asked his wife, refusing to be distracted by her diversion.

"You know what. You overheard. I was watching and could tell by your expression." Lora rested her hand on Repetto's arm. "I'm proud of you. You handled that well."

"Well, I handled it," Repetto said.

24

It was almost 8:30, and the cab was caught in stop-and-go traffic on East Fifty-second Street. Kelli was sure that getting out and walking would get them to Four Seasons earlier than if they stayed in the cab and gained ground ten feet at a time. Besides, Jason was beginning to fidget, his fingers absently working on the box containing his new radio-controlled car. No doubt he was thinking that Michael Schumacker in his red Ferrari race car would figure out a way to roar through or around this traffic.

"We'll get out here," Kelli told the driver, as the cab rolled forward a few feet, then lurched to a stop inches from the rear bumper of the car ahead.

"We're almost there, lady. Another block."

"Here'll do fine," Kelli said, digging in her purse. She handed the driver a ten-dollar bill and told him to keep the change.

She climbed out of the cab first, standing holding the door open while Jason slid across the backseat and scampered out, still tightly gripping the box from the toy store. Heat was rolling out from under the cab, warming her ankles, reinforcing her decision to leave the cab now; the vehicle could overheat if traffic didn't start to move soon.

Kelli made sure Jason was clear, then shut the cab door and stepped up on the curb. They began walking the block and a half to the restaurant. After sitting cramped in the cab for so long, it felt good to Kelli to be stretching her muscles. She really should exercise more. She'd been slacking off lately, skipping some of her scheduled workouts. Her chiropractor had given her a large inflatable ball to use for low-impact exercises. It made working out seem like play and might help her resolve.

They were standing on the corner with a man and three women, waiting for the signal to change so they could cross Park, when Kelli released Jason's hand and touched her chest high between her breasts. She'd felt a sudden, sharp pain and was having difficulty breathing.

Heart attack?

Not in my family.

The light changed to WALK and the people around her began crossing the street. Someone behind bumped her hip as they danced around her, a large woman in a hurry and not slowing down or saying excuse me.

"Mom?"

Jason. Why did he sound so far away?

She started to look down at him and noticed the bright red on her soft brown mink jacket.

What on earth . . . ?

"Mom?"

Kelly touched the red brilliance and stared at her stained fingers when she withdrew her hand from the wet fur.

Blood?

"Mom?"

Blood?

Before she could figure it out, she was dead on the sidewalk.

* * *

"A vendetta against the city?" Meg said, when Repetto called and told her about Zoe's revenge theory. It was almost nine o'clock. The windows were black mirrors. She'd been dozing when the phone rang. Now she was sitting on the edge of the sofa, clutching the receiver and watching on TV a man in a dark suit, a vaguely familiar political pundit, frowning fiercely and waving his arms behind the yellow letters MUTE.

"That's the angle we're going to start working tomorrow," Repetto said. "Disgruntled former city employees."

Meg tried to shake off her sleepiness. "If Melbourne goes for it."

"Melbourne will go." Repetto was at his desk in his study, thinking about smoking a cigar, thinking maybe he shouldn't. Things were going more smoothly with Lora now that he'd agreed to lay out Zoe's theory to Melbourne and request additional help.

"There must be a lot of disgruntled former city employees," Meg said. "Just cops alone . . ."

"Not a lot of them with the makeup of a serial killer."

"How we gonna know we're looking at that makeup if we come across it?"

"There's the question."

"You think there's actually anything to it?" Meg asked. "The revenge motive?"

"Might be. There's enough to it that Melbourne will have to cover his ass and send us searching."

"Seems like a fuckin' waste of time," Meg said, thinking about a disgruntled former city employee with the skills and makeup of a long-distance killer. *Comes back to Alex.*

"It's what profilers do."

There was a god-awful taste in Meg's mouth. She ran her tongue over her lips and teeth and made a face. She'd fallen asleep too early and would have a restless night. Nothing to read. Nothing on TV but the same news over and over, the same conversations about the same subjects, sandwiched between the same commercials. That was the news: everything's going to hell in the same way.

"Wait a minute," Repetto said. "My cell phone's ringing."

Meg could hear it faintly in the receiver. Repetto's phone wasn't ringing, it was chiming, the first seven or eight notes of a tune she couldn't quite place. Some kind of march. *Figures.* Repetto must have pressed a button and the musical alert stopped.

Now Meg could hear him talking on the other phone but couldn't make out what he was saying.

A few minutes later he was back on the line with her. "That was Melbourne. Another Night Sniper victim. A woman. Shot on East Fifty-second near Park."

"Melbourne say it was our guy?"

"No," Repetto said, "but it was. Can't you feel it?"

Strangely enough, she could.

Kelli Wilson's body was lying beneath a black rubberized tarp large enough to cover most of the bloodstain. Something on the order of a hundred people were crowding the yellow crime scene tape, staring at the lumpy black material. Repetto thought there would have been more if the streets in this area were as traveled as usual.

He elbowed his way through the crowd, past a uniform who recognized him and nodded deadpan, big man in his forties, with a receding chin and droopy eyelids. Meg and Birdy followed in Repetto's wake. An assistant ME Repetto knew, a tall, husky woman named Charlize, was standing with her fists on her hips, talking with a couple of white-uniformed EMS attendants. About ten feet from them, a female uniform was down on one knee, obviously consoling a dark-eyed boy about ten who was in apparent shock.

Repetto prayed the dead woman wasn't the boy's mother.

Charlize left the EMS guys and walked over. She cocked her head briefly toward the boy. "His mother's the one on the sidewalk."

"I was afraid of that," Repetto said.

The uniform who'd recognized Repetto joined them. "I'm Calvin. Me and my partner Len were first on the scene."

"What do you know?" Repetto asked, making sure Meg and Birdy were within earshot.

Calvin gave them the woman's name, along with the name of her son. "The kid says he and Mom were on the way to meet hubby at Four Seasons."

"They almost made it," Meg said.

"They were gonna have dinner, then spend the night on their boat."

Repetto glanced at him. "Boat?"

Calvin shrugged. "So the kid said. It's supposed to be docked at the Seventy-ninth Street Basin."

"Hubby hasn't arrived?"

"Not yet. Len's at the restaurant waiting to intercept him, then bring him here so he can get the bad news."

Birdy looked at his watch. "Hubby's late, or the vic and her son were half an hour early."

"I'd guess he's late," Calvin said. "While the ME was examining the body, the dead woman's cell phone in her purse started to ring. By the time we got to it, the ringing had stopped."

Meg must have known what Repetto was thinking. "The killer wouldn't call," she said.

"Maybe this one would," Birdy said. He was absently making those odd pecking motions with his head, thinking about it, how the killer they were chasing wasn't standard issue.

"What did the kid see?" Repetto asked.

Calvin glanced in the boy's direction. "Saw his mother

fall over, is all he says. He's in shock, wants his dad. Maise over there"—he pointed toward the boy and the kneeling policewoman—"is telling him Dad's on the way."

Meg looked over at the woman and boy. There were tears now in the boy's eyes, and wet tracks on Maise's broad cheeks. Meg looked away. "God *damn* this bastard!"

"We'll get him," Calvin said. He had a kind of drawl, like a cowboy, that made you tend to believe what he said.

Repetto got down on one knee and lifted a corner of the tarp. A blood-soaked fur jacket or some such thing made everything messier and harder to analyze. Kelli Wilson was on her back, one leg bent awkwardly beneath her, one arm thrown sideways, the other resting across her breasts. Her eyes were open, puzzled for eternity. Repetto wanted to close them but didn't. Instead he went about lifting the other three corners of the tarp, getting a full view of the body.

"Medium-caliber bullet high on the chest," Charlize said. "My guess is it clipped the heart and she was dead within seconds. But I'm talking on just the prelim, understand."

"Understood," Repetto said. He dropped the tarp.

Someone was calling his name.

He looked to his right and saw a cluster of journalists, two TV cameras, all set up a few feet off the curb in the street.

"Captain Repetto? Can you confirm this was the Night Sniper?" The questioner was a well-dressed man with incredibly fluffed hair, standing with one foot up on the curb.

Repetto ignored him and motioned Calvin back over. "Round up a couple more uniforms and keep the media wolves at bay. I especially don't want them talking to the kid."

Calvin turned and hurried away to get it done.

"One wound?" Repetto asked Charlize.

"That's the way it looks. We were waiting for you before we moved the body."

"Captain Repetto . . . ?"

Fluff Hair again. Repetto didn't acknowledge that he'd heard. "You done here?" he asked Charlize.

"Yeah. So are the techs."

So's Kelli Wilson.

Repetto knew the area around the dead woman had yielded all it was going to, which wasn't much. "Get her out of here then, away from all these people. Leave the purse." Repetto turned to Meg. "Go talk to the boy. Stand so he can't see them moving his mom."

"I'll be gentle," Meg said, and went to join Maise with Jason. Jason without a mother.

While the EMS attendants worked what remained of Kelli Wilson onto a stretcher and loaded her into the ambulance, Repetto and Birdy stood looking around the area for potential sniper nests.

"Like all the others," Birdy said. "He coulda been anywhere."

"Which means we'll have to look everywhere," Repetto said.

Meg walked back over. "Jason's in shock, trembling."

"We need to get him to a hospital," Repetto said.

"I dunno. He keeps repeating he wants his dad. Maise wants to wait with the kid in her car in front of the restaurant, stop the dad before he goes in. I don't think it's a bad idea. Those two are gonna need each other."

"Go with them," Repetto said. "Tell Maise to drive around the block. Maybe that'll shake the media types. Make it as easy on the kid as you can, and watch how his father takes the news. Ask if that ringing cell phone in the victim's purse was him calling to say he'd be late."

"Will do."

Repetto and Birdy stood watching the ambulance drive away, then the ME's car. Behind them, making a show of it for the media types, was Maise's cruiser with Jason and Meg inside.

The remaining cops who weren't holding the gawkers back began removing the yellow crime scene tape, taking it down with one hand, holding it bunched and tangled in the other. Somebody from somewhere appeared with a bucket and broom and was told it was okay to start cleaning up the sidewalk. A big bald guy dragged a hose from a shop on the corner and called back for somebody inside to turn on the water.

Repetto watched them hose down and sweep the sidewalk. Red-tinted water trickled down the curb and ran in the gutter. A life's blood, a life, being cleansed from the earth. The two TV crews were getting it all on tape.

"Ashes to ashes, blood to sewer," Birdy said glumly. The flesh beneath his right eye did a crazy dance.

"Harsh," Repetto said.

"Harsh."

Lazy-eyed Calvin and another uniform were talking to the three witnesses, two men and a woman, who'd stayed around.

"Let's go over there and see what we can get," Repetto said.

What they got was pretty much what the boy Jason had said. An echoing shot like thunder that could have come from anywhere. Then "Mom fell down."

"Know what I'm wondering?" Birdy asked, as he and Repetto were walking toward where the unmarked was angled in at the curb. The car was partially blocking traffic that was beginning to flow again on the block.

"I think so," Repetto said. "Is it possible Jason was the target?"

"Right. The child angle."

"I rule it out," Repetto said. "It was a heart shot, and we're dealing with a killer who hits what he aims at."

"Has so far," Birdy said. "But everybody misses sometimes."

"Besides, Zoe assured me again, this guy's not a child killer."

"Everybody misses sometimes," Birdy repeated.

"It's something to keep in mind," Repetto said. "I'll go talk with the media and tell them we don't have any hard information yet and we're finished here. On the sniper shootings in general, we're making progress."

"Lie to them."

"Allay their doubts with partial truths," Repetto said.

Birdy chuckled.

"Let's call Melbourne and get some more uniforms down here so we can canvass those buildings."

"We do a lot of that."

"It's what the Sniper wants," Repetto said. "We do a lot of that."

In his luxury East Side apartment, the Sniper sat at a glass-topped table and cleaned his Italian rifle. He reamed the barrel carefully with a soft cloth, then lightly oiled the mechanism and marveled again at its deadly precision.

When the rifle was reassembled, he put on the sterile white gloves he usually wore when handling his collection and wiped down the barrel and stock where his hands had touched. Oil from fingers could be a destructive element over time. Then he went to the gun room and replaced the rifle in its glass case.

The Night Sniper poured himself two fingers of premium scotch, added a splash of water to bring out the taste, then went into the living room and swung open the hinged frame of a numbered Marc Chagall print. Behind the print was a flat plasma TV. The Night Sniper sat on the sofa, used the re-

mote to find the local channel he favored, then sipped scotch
and watched reports on developing breaking news: the Night
Sniper had claimed another victim. Cable news already had
a photo of the victim, Kelli Wilson. Wonderful! Reporters
had tried to interview the victim's son, Jason, who was still
at the scene of his mother's death, but police kept them away.
Police also kept journalists away from investigating officers
headed by Captain Vincent Repetto. Repetto had glanced at
reporters but refused comment and kept his distance until
the body was removed.

Then there was a brief interview with Repetto, heavy
midtown traffic moving slowly in the background.

The Night Sniper sat forward and stared at Repetto.

*He looks tired. Frustrated. Craggier than ever. Gaunt like
a fleet predator. Losing weight? On a worry diet?*

Don't be deceived, overconfident.

The Sniper used the remote to increase the volume.

Repetto said every way he could into a phalanx of microphones that he and his team of detectives knew nothing yet
for sure. Was this shooting the work of the Night Sniper? It
was too soon to know for sure. Did police know where the
shot was fired from? Not for sure. Were they making progress
on the Night Sniper investigation? Satisfactory progress, yes,
but an arrest wasn't imminent. Were there any suspects? Not
for sure.

So it went—not for sure, not imminent, not for sure. The
only thing Repetto *was* sure of was that an arrest was simply
a matter of time. Sorry, it was too soon to comment on this
latest shooting. Too soon to know anything for sure. He
turned away from the microphones.

"Thanks, Captain Repetto!" called the blond woman
from Channel One. That surprised the Night Sniper. He'd
glimpsed her in the background and assumed she was Zoe
Brady, the profiler. Both of them were lookers, and in the re-

flected roof-bar light of a police car, the blond woman's hair had appeared red like Zoe's.

A quick grin from Repetto. "Sure."

Turn on the charm for that one.

The Night Sniper smiled, sipped, smiled.

Lies, lies, lies . . .

This time the theater seat note was found in the orchestra section of the off-off-Broadway theater MindWell: *Solving the puzzle should be child's play.*

The play at the MindWell was *Ripples*, and was about how an abused child grew up to abuse his child.

"Children again," Meg said, in the gloomy basement confines of the precinct office. "He had to go out of his way again to find a play about children." She found herself looking at the patch of green mold in a corner near the ceiling. It had grown three or four inches down one of the walls. *Some headquarters for a major investigation.*

"I still don't think he was aiming at Jason," Repetto said.

"Jason was there, though. A child."

"No denying that."

Birdy was standing at the narrow sidewalk-level window, staring outside at the gray rain, tapping his foot on the floor, wondering if he should start smoking again. "Lucky Jason," he said glumly.

Seated at his desk with the lamp on, Repetto was looking at the unpromising results of inquiries into disgruntled present and former city employees. The list of possibilities wasn't yet half explored.

"Here's a familiar name," Repetto said, scanning down the list. "Alex Reyals."

Now and then, Birdy decided. A cigarette now and then never hurt anyone.

"I'm thinking of taking up smoking again," he said.

Repetto didn't react, still staring at the list in front of him.

But Meg looked positively distressed. "I don't think there's much future in that," she said.

Birdy thought it was nice that she cared.

25

Dante Vanya lost his youth in a matter of months. The city saw to that.

Now people looked away from him or through him as he plodded wearily toward the Thirty-third Street subway stop, wearing the ragged clothes he'd stolen or scrounged from curbside trash. He was like all the others now, he thought. What the people he passed saw, if they saw him at all, was simply another lost and damaged human being who could never be fixed. One of a defeated and hopeless army.

They wouldn't notice Dante was younger than most. His face was dirty, his hair lank and unshorn, his eyes old and hopeless. He was simply another of the city's sick and despondent, lost and waiting for their time somehow to expire. In Dante's dismal world everyone was the same age, calculated not from the beginning of life, but from the much more imminent end.

Over the past nine months, since he'd fled terrified from the apartment of his dead mother and his doomed father,

Dante learned how to panhandle, then to steal. Then he'd resorted to making money selling sexual services, mostly to male clients. Now his health and appearance had declined so even that was impossible. He knew that if people looked directly at him, he in some way frightened them even through their superiority and disdain. Most of those he implored to help him usually decided not to part with their change as they hurried past.

Dante had been abused and humiliated in every way possible. What was left of him was rock-bottom tough and cynical, and he knew with fierce certainty that his father had been right about this city and the people in it.

In the winter, he'd learned to live underground, in subway tunnels that were abandoned or under construction. There was a dark, rat-and-roach infested city beneath Manhattan, where people kept to themselves as much as possible, preferring their own pain to the dangers of association. Strength was respected there, and privacy was defended. There was little sharing, because no one had anything to share. If crowding was inevitable, which happened if the weather above was severe, it was wise not to sleep. This was especially true on cold winter nights. In the dark shelters belowground, death was always near and not at all selective. Everyone was there for one reason: it was preferable to freezing to death aboveground.

But tonight was warm. And still cloudless. Dante was probably one of the few homeless who happened to have heard the weather report was changed and thunder showers were now in the forecast. The abandoned subway stop might be crowded later tonight, but for a while there should be plenty of space.

When he lifted the two loose boards that allowed entry into the abandoned subway stop, there were only a few other dim figures in the darkness.

He edged around frozen turnstiles and made his way

down a still escalator to the platform and tracks. The closest other homeless person to Dante was at least a hundred feet away.

Dante went to the base of the concrete steps leading down to the platform. He'd been here before and knew there was space beneath the steps, where it would be shadowed and darker, more private than simply lying down near one of the steel supporting posts.

He squatted low and stared into the darkness beneath the stairs, making sure the space wasn't already occupied. Nothing visible. No movement. No sounds of stirring or breathing.

With a quick glance around, he scooted into the narrow space beneath the steps. There was a strong smell of urine there, but it at least overwhelmed the faint odor of rot that might have been something dead.

Dante struggled out of the threadbare jacket he'd been wearing despite the heat—it was always safer to wear what you intended to keep than to carry it—and laid it out on the hard concrete.

His hand brushed something and he jerked it back. Then he reached out cautiously and felt the object.

This was good. Among the trash that littered the floor was an approximately two-foot-square sheet of plastic bubble pack. The bubbles had all been crushed in one corner, but the rest still trapped air and, if the sheet were folded, it would provide a makeshift pillow.

Dante curled on his side on the jacket. He folded the bubble pack in half, then in quarters, and worked it beneath his head.

Soft. Almost like a real pillow.

He settled in and exhaled loudly. This was the first time he'd had a chance to rest since morning, when the cops patrolling the park at dawn failed to notice him. Someone coughed, but the sound came from far away down the tunnel. Dante pressed his legs together and folded his arms, then closed his eyes and lay listening. It was a long time before he fell asleep.

Two hours later Dante awoke from the horrors of his dreams, choking, struggling to breathe, in terrible pain. Around him was light. Dancing shadow.

Fire!

The litter and debris on the tunnel floor was on fire!

So was the plastic bubble pack he was using as a pillow!

Fire!

Pain was his world. Pain and panic.

There was no thought, no plan, only terror and instinct. Dante sprang to his feet, banging his head on the underside of the concrete steps, spun screaming until he had his direction, and ran. There were screams other than his own, other cries for help, but he didn't hear them or even his own shrill screams as he fled to street level, the smoldering, melted plastic clinging to his face like a ferocious, chewing beast that would never let go.

In a way, it never did let go.

Dante learned weeks later that faulty wiring had caused the fire, and that electrical service to the abandoned subway stop should have been shut down months before.

The city's mistake, and Dante's bad luck for trespassing.

The city's mistake.

26

Late morning sunlight seemed to cleanse and purify Park Avenue, glinting off cars and striking silver rays from the buildings towering against a high blue sky. The green ribbon that was the broad avenue's median looked mowed, trimmed, and freshly planted. New York might have been built yesterday.

Repetto was alone with Meg, driving along Park, Meg at the wheel, when he decided to bring up the subject.

"Do you know who Dwayne Easterbrook is?"

Meg skillfully passed a slow-moving van and slipped back into the stream of traffic. She smiled faintly, pleased by her driving ability. "Sounds familiar."

"He's a detective out of Homicide. Melbourne assigned him to help out with the disgruntled former city employee list."

"And?" Traffic was slowing for the light at the Fifty-third Street intersection.

"He interviewed Alex Reyals yesterday. The former NYPD sharpshooter."

They were approaching the intersection too fast. Meg braked hard and barely avoided missing the bumper of a cab in front of them that had already stopped for the red light.

"I already talked to Reyals," she said.

"More than once, according to Easterbrook."

"Reyals is a suspect."

"Easterbrook said you talked to him several times."

Meg stared straight ahead. "Fuck Easterbrook. Where's he getting his information?"

"From Reyals."

Meg knew what must have happened. Easterbrook was a good cop and had picked up vibes from Alex. Vibes that suggested there was something more than a cop-suspect relationship between Alex and Meg.

What really annoyed Meg was that part of her was pleased there was something in Alex for Easterbrook to home in on.

She turned her head so she was looking directly at Repetto. "I'll say it once. There was nothing improper about my interviews with Alex Reyals."

"You visited him three times in his apartment."

"He lives in his apartment."

"Meg—"

"There's nothing improper going on."

Horns began to blare. Engines raced.

"Light," Repetto said.

"Huh?"

"The light changed."

Meg goosed the car and it jerked away from a dead stop and almost ran up the back of the cab again. The cabby noticed this time. She saw him glaring at her in his rearview mirror as he increased the distance between the two vehicles.

After a couple of silent blocks: "You believe me?"

"Of course," Repetto said.

And he did believe her, she was sure.

But this didn't bode well. Damn it, this didn't bode well!

"Captain—"

"Enough said, Meg."

Repetto hadn't asked her to stay away from Alex.

Here was Meg again, pressing the paint-clogged intercom button for Alex's apartment, taking the elevator to Alex's floor. Meg where she shouldn't be. Meg sticking her neck out again. It was the kind of thing that often got Meg in trouble, and that she couldn't stop doing.

Nothing improper. That was true. That was goddamn true, and still her ass was in a sling. Or sure felt like it was.

Alex was waiting for her with the door open, smiling when she walked toward him. He was in jeans and a blue Yankees T-shirt, and had a sharp-looking chisel in his right hand. There were tiny wood chips trapped in the hair on his muscular forearms. His smile faded when he noticed the expression on her face.

He stepped back and let her enter. "You okay?"

"Question is, are *you*?"

He was smiling again, amused by her anger even though he didn't know what caused it. That was really annoying.

"You here to arrest me?" he asked.

"Just maybe. Why did you tell Easterbrook I'd been here to visit you three times?"

"Because he asked me how many times you'd been here. I couldn't lie to him, Meg. I'm a suspect in a series of homicides." A serious look crossed his face. "Easterbrook giving you trouble?"

"He mentioned his talk with you to Repetto."

Alex thought about that for a few seconds. "He had no

choice, Meg. Like I had no choice but to be honest with him. You know how lies are, like cockroaches. When there's one, it always seems there are more."

He was right and she knew it. And it was *she* who'd decided to keep coming here to his apartment. At least he hadn't pointed that out to her. Lucky for him.

"I don't blame you for being angry," he said. "In fact . . ."

Don't say it.

He tucked the chisel in his belt and gently placed both his hands on her shoulders, probably getting wood chips on her blazer. She didn't move when he bent down and kissed her lightly on the lips.

This visit wasn't turning out anything like she'd planned.

She kissed him back.

Hadn't planned that, either.

She stepped away from him, and he lowered his arms in a way that suggested hopelessness.

"I've been working," he said, smiling a certain way. "Want to come see what I'm doing?"

She stared at him for a long time, into his eyes.

"I'm getting the hell out of here," she said.

He nodded. "I have to admit it's the smart thing to do."

She turned away from him and moved toward the door and opened it. Turned back. "Thanks."

"For understanding your position?"

"For not telling me I'm beautiful when I'm angry."

"I was thinking it."

She slammed the door on the way out, thinking her visit had accomplished absolutely nothing.

Still, she was glad she'd come.

That was the problem.

A neatly folded fifty-dollar bill got the Night Sniper into the exclusive Club Cleo on the Upper West Side. He sat alone now at a small round table by a wooden rail separating seating from the spacious dance floor. The walls were oak paneled. The music was soft rock, sometimes even romantic ballads. Sinatra would have dug it. Long red drapes hung from the high ceiling, lending the illusion there were windows behind them. The lighting was soft and there were more tables in a gallery upstairs, from which customers could look down at the dance floor. Drug transactions and usage were discreet and not done in the restrooms, where there were attendants.

Club Cleo wasn't exactly for people on the way up. It was more for those who were clinging near the summit, a very private way station on the way up, or down, the steep mountain of success.

Connections could be made here. More than once, the Night Sniper had made them.

An exotically beautiful woman, dressed as a jockey in silks that were the brown and red colors of Club Cleo, took his drink order, and he watched the rhythmic switch of her hips beneath taut silk as she walked away. A riding crop was tucked in her belt.

The band was playing something by Duke Ellington. A raven-haired woman in an emerald-green dress was dancing with a short balding man in an expensive-looking suit. When the dance partners separated for a few seconds, the Night Sniper saw that the man's dark maroon tie matched the handkerchief barely peeking from his suit coat's breast pocket. Subdued elegance. The Night Sniper approved.

He was wearing his blue Armani suit, Gambino Italian loafers, and sipping sixteen-year-old Lagavulin scotch. On his wrist was an antique Patek Philippe watch that kept precise time. His neatly knotted blue tie was pure silk and cost 120 dollars. His dark hair was medium-length and impeccably styled. Only the most discerning eye would notice it was a wig.

The Ellington number was over. The Night Sniper saw the woman with the lustrous black hair talk briefly to the balding man, then turn smiling and walk away. The man seemed disappointed as he returned to a table on the far side of the dance floor and sat down with three other men. They all glanced over at the woman, who sat alone at a small table not far from the Night Sniper's.

The black-haired woman, Mary Maureen Kopler, recently of Atlanta, had just finished her third martini. Maybe that was why she didn't notice anything special about the man seated at the nearby table, watching her, other than that he was flawlessly groomed and almost too handsome, with kind dark eyes and smooth, tanned skin. When he turned away from her, he displayed a profile that belonged in a museum of Roman artifacts.

She thought he was interesting, even if he did seem the type that spent hours getting together an outfit every morning in order to achieve male perfection. He was almost, but not quite, beautiful enough to appear feminine. Mr. Metrosexual. Maybe he was some kind of model. She'd met such men before. Often they were rich. She looked in his direction without moving her head, then waited until he glanced at her. Even before there was eye contact, she lowered her gaze and looked away.

It was enough. She knew it would be. The men who frequented Club Cleo were aware of life's subtleties. That was why she came here.

Drawing a deep breath, staying outwardly oblivious, she waited.

She saw the slight shift of light and shadow and knew he was there even before he spoke:

"Mind if I sit with you for a moment?"

Good start. Simple and direct. Nicely modulated voice.

Educated. Mary Maureen preferred not to waste her time with simpletons.

She looked up as if noticing him for the first time. Gave him a smile, ever so slight. "Are you selling something?"

"Other than the obvious?"

Widen the smile. "I will say you're honest. Go ahead and sit." *For more than a moment.*

She liked this man. He looked clean, smelled clean, and was incredibly handsome. Of course, he'd eventually reveal himself to be too good to be true. Like the rest of them.

But right now, what wasn't there to like?

She was even more beautiful close up, he thought, as he sat gracefully in the chair across from her. "Your accent is charming. Louisiana?"

"Georgia. Atlanta. Well, just outside Atlanta, really. Rome."

"I've been there."

"Not hardly."

Not hardly? She was playing it folksy, he knew. Trying to snag him with her southern manner.

"You're probably thinking of the other Rome," she said. "The big one."

"No. That one's full of Italians now."

She giggled but kept it controlled, not wanting to come across as an airhead.

"I know my Romes," he said. "I've been in Rome, Georgia. What are we drinking?"

"I'm having martinis."

"Then so am I." He turned and motioned to one of the servers.

This was working well, he thought. She'd already had too much to drink. He could smell it on her breath, see it in her labored eye movement and body language, now that he was close to her.

The woman dressed as a jockey brought the martinis. He tipped her lavishly, knowing his southern belle was watching, probably contemplating his gross income and sexual potential.

Within five minutes the Night Sniper knew he could have this woman. And he knew their relationship would be brief. He didn't completely understand what attracted women to him in the first place. Maybe it was a beauty-and-the-beast allure. She had to see beneath his skin, what he was; nothing like that could ever be made completely invisible or was ever completely gone. But women *were* attracted to him; it was undeniable.

He sipped his martini and watched her sip hers. The woman would leave Club Cleo with him and they'd spend the night together where she lived or in his luxury condo. A one-nighter, whether she wanted it that way or not.

They chatted easily for another fifteen minutes, exchanging smiles and tentative touches across the table. He noticed the slight slur that had worked its way into her musical drawl. She squeezed his hand hard and gazed soulfully at him as if she owned him. No, as if she wanted *him* to own *her*.

I'm not buying, only renting.

Halfway through their drinks, they left together.

In the back of his mind he knew that someday she'd discover the true identify of the man she'd lain with, and the knowledge thrilled him even more than what he knew was to follow when they reached their destination.

27

Meg changed into sweatshirt and pants and ate leftovers from the Chinese takeout she'd had for dinner night before last. She didn't mind the hurry-up meal. Some of that Chinese stuff tasted even better after two days in the refrigerator and two minutes in the microwave.

When she was finished, she washed and dried the stainless steel fork and the empty milk glass she'd used, then put various white cardboard cartons into each other, then into the trash. After a gentle, ladylike burp, she went into the living room and switched on the TV to watch local twenty-four-hour cable news.

There was more on the Sniper killing of Kelli Wilson, with tape of onlookers at the crime scene. A brief shot of Repetto ignoring the media types; they might as well have been parking meters standing there. Meg had to smile.

She watched the news until a piece about a dog trapped by a rushing creek in New Jersey came on the second time. She waited until the dog was once again rescued with the aid of some sort of crane and sling; then she punched the remote. The dog, a mottled black spaniel of some kind, had its head turned and was gazing forlornly at her as the picture faded. It seemed almost as if it hadn't wanted to be saved.

In the silence wrought by the remote, Meg yawned, got up from where she was slouched on the sofa, and ambled over to her desktop computer by the window. When she switched on the lamp, she saw her reflection in the dark glass, a weary, rather grim-faced young woman lowering herself into a chair. Meg almost expected the woman in the window to give her a nod of recognition and greeting.

When she'd booted up the computer and was online, there was an e-mail from Alex Reyals:

It was my great pleasure seeing you again, despite the circumstances.
Alex

Polite. Even formal. Not at all threatening. Yet Meg sat shaken. How had he gotten her e-mail address? Did he have NYPD connections that good? Her hand went to the keyboard but her fingertips hovered half an inch above it.

She shouldn't reply to him. She couldn't!

Should she phone and demand to know how he'd discovered where to e-mail her? Not only might she learn more about him, it would give her an opportunity to talk with him again.

But that, too, seemed unwise, especially after her conversation with Repetto.

Finally Meg decided her only course of action was inaction. Her job, her professionalism, demanded that she let the Alex Reyals matter lie. At least until the Night Sniper investigation was resolved.

But what if he was guilty of murder?

She didn't believe it, but the cop in her didn't completely disbelieve it.

Nothing. All she could do was nothing, and hope she was

right and Alex didn't turn out to be the Night Sniper or a copycat killer. A killer whose advances she should have used to her advantage, to find him out and stop him from committing more murders.

Meg told herself again that Alex wasn't involved in any way with the Night Sniper killings, or with any other murders. That was what she damned well *believed*.

She clung to that certainty.

Near-certainty.

She shut down the computer, watched a TV reality show so inane she muted the last five minutes, then went to bed.

It was a long time before she dozed off, and then her sleep was shallow and laced with dreams and worries. Whenever she rose to the surface of wakefulness, she tried to concentrate on practical matters and control her errant thoughts.

Thoughts about Alex.

It was my great pleasure seeing you . . .

The Night Sniper lay in bed in almost total darkness and made no sound, watching the woman from Club Cleo collect her clothes from the floor and chair and tiptoe nude into the bathroom.

As she silently closed the door behind her, he glimpsed her shapely form that was subtly highlighted by the night-light, giving it a lushness he remembered from only hours ago. He glanced again at the red numerals on the clock by the bed. It was 3:30 in the morning. A quiet time.

He lay listening to his heartbeat, the occasional noises from the street far below, and the faint sounds of Mary Maureen dressing behind the bathroom door.

Then the door opened on darkness except for the illumination of the dim night-light. She'd switched off the light above the mirror beforehand, not wanting to wake him. He lay with his eyes open, knowing he was in shadow, and observed her move silently across the room, then go out without looking back.

A minute later he heard the soft sounds of the door to the hall opening and closing.

He switched on the lamp by the bed and sat up.

Other than thrown-back sheets, and impressions in the mattress and pillow, there was no sign that the woman had been in bed with him. He climbed out of bed nude and went into the bathroom. No note, no message in lipstick on the mirror. Nothing. He padded quickly, barefoot, into the living room.

Nothing seemed to have been disturbed. The woman had simply left quietly, sneakily.

He wondered if he'd satisfied her. She'd seemed to enjoy everything they'd done. She'd stroked his face as he was fucking her, moaned unintelligible vows. Her passion had been real and transforming.

But she had left him in the night.

He knew what must have happened. She'd seen him for what he'd been, for what he was, the ugliness so near the surface, the *differentness*.

Some things are indelible, he thought.

Some things are forever.

He cupped his face in both hands, squeezing until it hurt, and he began to sob.

Over an hour passed before he stood up and trudged back to bed. But exhausted as he was, he couldn't sleep. He climbed out of bed and began to pace, drank a glass of milk, paced some more. Tried to read. Tried to watch television. Paced.

Cleaned his rifles.

28

A problem. The shot was impossible from the roof, so the Night Sniper decided on another course of action.

The entire top two floors of the Edmont Arms Apartments were being renovated, and a series of terraces were created as the building stair-stepped down. The terrace of one of the top-floor apartments under construction allowed the Sniper to move out another ten feet toward the sidewalk. He wouldn't be seen there, and the building's roof could be reached without risking having to break into the apartment.

He simply took the fire stairs to the roof, then lowered himself with a rope down to the terrace. When it was time for him to go, he would simply force open one of the French doors leading inside from the terrace, and leave through the apartment's door.

He hadn't been noticed several nights ago when he visited the prospective sniper's nest to make sure it would be adequate. It was no problem entering the building; one simply had to wait until the lackadaisical doorman was otherwise occupied, smoking or gossiping, then slip in through the tinted glass doors. Doormen paid a great deal of attention to people arriving, but they paid less attention to anyone leaving a building. And they had to see them leave, in order to recall them. The problem was that in leaving, there was no way to know where the doorman would be, or what he would be doing—or what he'd see and remember.

The Night Sniper had experienced no problem entering the building either time, or making his way to the roof, then the terrace. Leaving meant running a slight risk, but it would take days to determine the source of the shot, if it ever were determined. The Night Sniper knew that was all he needed, days, before the police talked to the doorman. If the doorman had happened to notice him leaving, by then memory and description would be questionable. Eyewitnesses were unreliable even under the best of circumstances.

A large bird flapped silently past off to his left, startling him. High for a pigeon, he thought. Maybe it had been a falcon. The Night Sniper knew there were falcons living among the ledges of New York's tall buildings. The city was a man-made, ideal environment for predators.

He sat down, getting comfortable, then assumed shooting position, using his knee to support his right elbow and steady the rifle. Feeling the high, cool breeze on his back and bare arms, he sighted through his rifle's night scope. Even from the terrace parapet, this would be a difficult shot from a cross street, vectoring across a triangle at a corner of Central Park, and partially blocked by tree limbs. It might be an impossible shot if the target weren't seated and still.

It would require patience, waiting for the precise moment, when the shot was not only possible, but couldn't miss: the confluence of breeze and action and time, when he *knew* where the bullet would end its flight. The Night Sniper was an observer of people. He knew that in groups of four or fewer there was always a time when conversation flagged, when sound and motion ceased, if only momentarily. A tableau. In that brief moment, the only thing alive with vibrant motion would be the bullet that raced to its target even before the sound of the shot.

The tableau would end in death.

The Night Sniper leaned back, glanced at his watch, then slipped a single round into the rifle's breech.

And waited.

The evening was ideal for dining outdoors. The maitrè d' showed Lee and Marta to a table near the decorative wrought-iron rail that separated the restaurant's dining area from the rest of the wide sidewalk.

Fortunately they had reservations. Every one of the round, cloth-covered tables was occupied. As Lee and Marta sat down at the table and a waiter took their drink orders, Lee glanced inside through a window and saw that the restaurant's interior was less crowded. Only about half the inside tables were in use, and there were fewer than a dozen people at the bar.

But Lee decided it was too pleasant out here to go inside. There was only the slightest breeze. The mild temperature, the soft light from candles burning in the center of each table, the scent of spices, the contented buzz of conversation, was all very seducing. Lee thought that with this kind of ambience, how could anyone not like the food?

Lee Nasad and Marta Kim had made the date two days ago to meet here at Peru North. They were uncommonly busy people, and the location was convenient for both of them. Besides, Marta wanted to try the new Peruvian restaurant everyone at Kolb Research Hospital, where she worked as a forensic medical technician, was raving about.

Though they were casually dressed—Lee in tan pleated pants and a black blazer over a dark pullover shirt, Marta in jeans and a white blouse—and gave no outward appearance of great success, this was a couple about to enjoy the pinnacle of accomplishment.

Their respective climbs had been difficult.

Lee Nasad's mother was born in Jamaica, making him a first-generation American. A delicate child, and still on the small side, he'd fought his way out of a tough neighborhood in Newark and attended school on grants and scholarships. He earned his MBA from Harvard and made good use of it. Recently he was promoted to financial stocks analyst at Cornog and Stoneman Investments. Lee had always enjoyed writing, and after two failed attempts to break into print, he seemed to have reached out from the carousel of chance and grabbed the golden ring. *Where the Money Is,* his book on the coming boom in financial stocks, was published six months ago, at approximately the same time his lone and much-derided call for a 20 percent increase in stock prices, led by financials, came to pass.

Lee guested on one financial talk show after another, and his book was on several best-seller lists. The entire experience hadn't yet sunk in. All of a sudden he was a financial genius, or so people thought. Genius or not, his bloated royalty check arrived from his literary agent last month. He was twenty-eight, rich, and fully invested.

Tonight he was going to propose to his longtime and faithful lover, Marta Kim, the beautiful daughter of a long-dead British war correspondent and his South Vietnamese bride.

Marta had been born in South Vietnam, educated in England, and had been in America five years on a temporary visa. Her professional accomplishments were drawing attention. Marta was as much an expert in DNA analysis as was Lee in equities. Not that she'd need the money success in her field would bring.

Of course, she didn't know that yet for sure.

Tonight, when the time was right, Lee would suggest to Marta exactly that—the time was right. There was no doubt she'd say yes. Not only did the couple dearly love each other, but their marriage would automatically make her eligible to become a U.S. citizen. And a wealthy one.

After their pleasant meal, the time seemed perfect. The waiter had just delivered their coffee, and mood and opportunity coincided. Lee wanted to prolong the moment before reaching into his blazer pocket for the obscenely expensive diamond ring he'd bought just yesterday.

"You're happy?" he asked.

She smiled. "Generally and specifically, I couldn't be happier."

"Spoken like a research scientist."

"God, yes, I'm happy!" She stretched her arms over her head, causing her breasts to be accented by the strained material of her blouse, and glanced around. "Who wouldn't be happy? A magical night, a wonderful meal, a beautiful life."

"You never know, it might get better."

"Oh, I doubt it. I don't see how it could."

The light from the table's candle enhanced Marta's smooth complexion and vibrant beauty. Lee couldn't look away. Marta was seated motionless, gazing back at him.

He drank his coffee black and knew it would be hot.

So as not to spill any, he sat very still and slowly lifted the cup to his lips, staring at his wife to be, his life to be.

The candle flame was perfect. It helped the Night Sniper to gauge wind drift precisely as he eased the crosshairs in his scope slightly to the left.

He'd know when the profound moment came, as he always did. His gift.

Steady . . . steady . . . patience . . . patience . . .

He held his breath, maintaining stillness and oneness with his target.

Like freezing time.

Until his finger tightened on the trigger.

The bullet struck Lee in the side of his neck an instant before the distant *crack!* of the rifle, severing his carotid artery before ricocheting off bone down into the chest cavity. He slumped dead facedown on the table before Marta. She sat stunned, her eyes horrified and her mouth slack with shock, as around her people ran or crawled screaming for cover.

In less than a minute, the entire tablecloth was red with blood.

29

Repetto stood and watched the city begin to reassimilate the place where Lee Nasad had died. Soon people passing the restaurant in cars or on foot would cease to glance in its direction. Conversation would shift to other, more immediate subjects. Diners at the outdoor tables where violent death had visited would enjoy their meals unaware of any infamous past or association with the site. The name of the victim, the sense and presence of him, would fade except in the minds of those who'd loved him. New York would remain New York, where, if you dug long enough and deeply enough, you might find that any block harbored a history of violence.

The block where Lee Nasad died had been closed at both ends, but was in the process of being reopened for traffic. The first vehicle, a cab, went swishing past on the pavement and was soon followed by a pack of cars, then a work van with a ladder rack on top but no ladders.

The ambulance, flashing emergency lights but with siren muted, had left ten minutes ago with Lee Nasad's dead body. Marta Kim was with police, a man whom Repetto thought was identified as her uncle, and with friends from the hospital where she worked. Repetto was told that one of those friends, a doctor, had sedated her.

Lee Nasad had been a celebrity. Already the media was frenzy-feeding on this one and salivating for more. There was still a TV camera crew across the street, taping Repetto, Meg, and Birdy simply standing there inside the yellow crime scene tape and surveying the spilled food and overturned tables and chairs outside the closed restaurant.

"He was about to take a sip of coffee," Repetto said. "Sitting ramrod straight, according to his fiancée."

"Almost fiancée," Meg corrected. "And isn't that some diamond ring she was about to get?"

"The guy was a financial wizard and a hotshot writer," Birdy said. "Money up the wazoo."

"And more on the way," Repetto said. "Some great future that'll never be lived." He propped his fists on his hips and looked around, as if assessing the scene for the first time. "So we know precisely where Nasad was sitting, and the position of his body when he was shot. The bullet angled in from above, so the shooter had to be high, which means he didn't fire from the park. We catch a break. The area of the park reduces by half the potential sites we have to consider. We can recreate the shooting and limit possible sources to five or six buildings in the next block."

"Or taller buildings behind them," Meg pointed out.

Repetto had thought of that. He was hoping the Night Sniper went for the nearer, easier shot. It was the sensible thing to do, and even in the irrational act of murder, people often did what was sensible.

Meg was staring at the bloodstained concrete and thinking of Alex. Could the man she knew have callously, eagerly, snuffed out two bright futures? She reassured herself that he had alibis for most of the previous Night Sniper murders, whatever their credibility. But there was always the possibility of a copycat murder. Or murders. More than one sniper.

To be a murderer, Alex needn't have killed *all* the victims. The Night Sniper shootings were just the sort of crimes to provide the tickle or jolt that would compel a copycat killer, with the know-how and problems possessed by Alex, to start a secondary, parallel series of murders.

And an ex-cop with connections could learn, and emulate, the Night Sniper's moves.

Meg wished she could purge her mind of these thoughts, but she couldn't. Nor could she accept them.

Beside her, Repetto sighed and dropped his arms, then buttoned his suit coat. "Work to do."

"Always," Meg said.

"The world," Birdy said.

Bobby Mays stood in an Upper West Side doorway and watched a windblown sheet of newspaper flutter against the base of a traffic light, then surrender to the breeze and skitter across the street. The backwash of a passing car altered the paper's direction slightly, and the breeze seemed to shift. The newspaper page attached itself to a man's leg like a lover, pinned there by the wind, but he kicked it loose and it sailed directly to Bobby and wrapped itself around his ankles.

What'm I, a subscriber?

Bobby leaned down and got a firm grip on the errant sheet of newsprint before it could sail away. He held it up and saw that it was from the *Times* and was two days old. It featured a story about a Night Sniper victim shot at an outdoor restaurant.

Bobby wished he hadn't broken his reading glasses last month. He had to hold the paper well away from him and squint in order to read it.

It seemed to him that he'd already known about this shooting, but how could he have? Another thing was that reading about it reminded him of the homeless man he saw hurrying on the other side of the street. Some street. Somewhere.

Bobby lowered the paper. How long ago was that? Had he seen the man after a different shooting, or had it been this one? There was something, some connection here, that Bobby couldn't grasp. And the paper had come to him as if fate were blowing it along the streets. It all had to do with the homeless man Bobby was sure wasn't really a homeless man.

The newspaper page was fluttering and flapping in his hands now, trying to escape his grasp and sail free. He folded it in half, then in quarters, then in eighths, and stuffed it in a pocket of his worn-out jacket. Maybe he should see a cop. Tell a cop about the man.

He had an obligation, a duty, sort of, considering he was a former cop himself.

He hunched his shoulders and walked toward Broadway, keeping an eye out for blue uniforms.

There, finally, was a uniformed cop standing on a corner, giving some tourist types directions.

Bobby waited. The cop talked, pointed, talked some more. Then the tourist types, the cop, everybody smiled at each other, and the tourists—if that's what they were—hurried away.

Bobby approached the cop, a tall man with a long nose and a dark mustache. He reminded Bobby of that old-time actor who used to play Sherlock Holmes, Basil Rathbone.

The cop glanced at him and made a kind of face Bobby didn't like.

"I got some information," Bobby said.

The cop kept looking at him, dark eyes hard.

"This shooting thing . . ." Bobby yanked the newspaper from his jacket pocket. "I seen a guy—"

"Guy with a gun?" the cop interrupted.

"No, listen, I seen this guy . . . he wasn't right."

The cop nodded. "Lots of those kinds around, buddy."

"He was hurrying."

"Look around. Ain't everybody hurrying? Don't ask me why."

"I'm not. No. This guy wasn't right. I been reading about this Night Sniper, you know the one."

"Don't we all?"

"Yeah, but—"

"I need to get to Riverside Park, Officer."

A pretty girl about sixteen had approached for directions. Two other girls were with her, standing off to the side as if too shy to talk to the cop. They were all about the same size and build, and Bobby thought except for their hair they might have been triplets.

"You keep walking just the way you're going," the cop was saying.

"Hey, listen, this guy—"

The three girls looked at Bobby, registered distaste, then looked away. He no longer existed.

"Straight down this street." The cop pointed.

Bobby no longer existed to the cop, either.

Give it up. Nobody cares. Fuck 'em!

Bobby shambled off. No one tried to stop him.

It made him angry, what had happened. But it didn't surprise him. He wandered around for the next hour and had just about forgotten what he was angry about, when he saw a precinct house down the street.

Bobby took a deep breath, continued down the block, then entered the building.

It had been a long time since he'd been in a police station or precinct house. This one was like a lot of them. Waiting benches off to the side, a low wood rail with a gate in it, so not too many people could approach the desk at one time and make things confusing or even dangerous. There were rows of desks beyond where the desk sergeant sat, and doors

leading to offices and interrogation rooms. On the wall between two doors was a framed photograph of Yankees shortstop Derek Jeter holding a bat and wearing an NYPD cap.
From somewhere and everywhere came the muted chatter of
radio traffic as cars were directed by a dispatcher. It was a
sound that made Bobby miss being a cop.

A woman sat at the end of one of the benches. She had a
bruised face and her legs were drawn up so she was hugging
her knees. She looked ashamed and embarrassed. A couple
of uniformed cops walked past, swerving to avoid Bobby,
who knew he didn't smell so good indoors, then went outside.

The cop behind the tall desk noticed Bobby and frowned
at him. He was a big guy with gray hair and a smooth,
flushed complexion. Irish-looking guy. A nameplate toward
the front of the desk identified him as Sergeant Dan O'Day.

"Lookin' for a shelter?" he asked Bobby.

"No. Looking to pass on some information. I used to be a
cop."

No change of expression on the Irish face. "Don't say.
Where at?"

"Philly."

"So what happened?"

Bobby shrugged. "I'm not a cop anymore."

"Yeah, well . . . Then maybe you oughta go on outside
and move along."

Maybe I oughta. Maybe coming here was a big mistake.
One last try: "I said I had information."

Sergeant O'Day had begun to write something, thinking
Bobby was on his way out. "That's right, you did."

"These shootings . . ." Bobby paused, searching for words.
Damn it, his mind, his throat, always locked up at times like
this.

"Night Sniper shootings?" the desk sergeant asked.

"Yeah. Those. Anyway, I been seeing this so-called homeless man. And once I saw him in the neighborhood right after I heard a shot."

"Why so-called?"

"Huh? Oh. He was walking with too much haste and purpose."

O'Day looked at Bobby. *Too much haste and purpose.* The words might have been out of a police report, the kind of language cops used when converting experience to official text. Could be this guy actually had been a cop.

"You mean he was running like hell?" the sergeant asked. "Jogging along, walking fast, what?"

"Too much haste and purpose."

"Yeah, you said."

"Walking like he had some place to go."

"Maybe he did."

"Not if he's really . . . like me. That's the thing, I know he's not like me. Not homeless. Not really. Clothes not right, too clean. Shoes not right. I couldn't tell you why. Too much not right. I know this guy doesn't fit. I can tell. I still got the eye. I know."

O'Day looked at him, not smiling, not frowning, nothing. Cop's blue eyes made more blue by the blue shirt. Blue, blue, in the blood. Bobby's blood, still. Always. While his heart still beat.

"I don't hear nothing yet we can use," the sergeant said. "But I'll pass it on."

Bobby knew he was lying. The man behind the desk hadn't believed his story, or hadn't thought it important if he had believed it.

"What's your name?" Sergeant O'Day asked.

Bobby backed away. "Never mind." There was nothing in it now for him or for anybody else. He'd made a mistake coming here, imagining he'd be believed. "Too much haste and purpose. I still got the eye. I know. That's all. I just wanted to help." Bobby was moving toward the door. Nobody—not

O'Day, not another uniformed cop who'd just walked in from one of the offices, nobody—tried to stop him. Nobody gave a fuck. "I still got the eye," Bobby repeated.

"Maybe you do," said the sergeant in a patient, kind voice. But not the kind of voice he'd have used if he believed. "Maybe you do, son."

"Not son," Bobby said. "Don't give me that shit."

"Okay, I won't."

Bobby was out the door, down the steps, back in the night air and smells and sounds of the city. Back on the street.

Where he knew he belonged.

"That one's not ripe," the man said.

Zoe was in the produce department of the neighborhood grocery store, actually shopping for food this time. She put down the casaba melon she was considering and looked at the man who'd spoken to her.

My, my! He was about average height and extremely handsome; one of those men so perfect that there was a suggestion he might be effeminate. But there was also something about this guy that said otherwise—that shouted otherwise. He was wearing an obviously expensive tan raincoat, unbuttoned to reveal a dark suit, white on white shirt, and silky red tie. A gold ring, then a gold watch, glittered as he pointed at the melon.

"Sorry to interrupt your melon squeezing," he said with a great smile, "but I already tested that one."

"I don't resent a kind gesture," Zoe said, scrambling to maintain her mental balance. "Kindness is what makes the world go round."

"Don't we all wish?"

"*Should* make the world go round," she amended. This was a fish she didn't want to swim away. "What I was really looking for was arugula. I'm going to a dinner party and I promised the hostess I'd buy some for the salad. I was too ashamed to tell her I didn't know what it was. Do you have any idea what it looks like?"

He studied her with steady, calm eyes, so appraisingly, the way he might size up the produce.

His smile again, wider. "You know perfectly well what arugula is."

Huh? She shifted her weight from leg to leg like an embarrassed schoolgirl. "Yeah, I guess I do."

"That's not to say there's nothing I could teach you," he said, still smiling.

Zoe was grinning now. She knew this drill. "Aren't you the bold one?"

"The realistic one. Maybe the simple one."

"Simple?"

"When I see a woman as desirable as you, I try to get to know her better. Simple as that."

"Suppose I'm attached, maybe married?"

"You're not. I've seen you shopping in this grocery store before."

"Alone, you mean?"

"I don't want you to walk out of here and out of my life," he said, ignoring her question.

"That isn't likely," she said.

"I didn't think so," he said.

Now Zoe sat at her dresser, brushing her long red hair. She wanted to finish with her hair, get it just right, before slipping into the black dress she was going to wear tonight. She was sure she could work the dress over her head without having to rearrange her hair, and this way there wouldn't be any brushed-out hair on the dress's shoulders.

The last date she'd had, with an intellectual type who was an out-of-work museum curator, hadn't developed into anything near the kind of relationship she sought. Zoe didn't give up. Single women living alone and working in New York didn't lose spirit easily, or they wouldn't live in New York.

This man she'd picked up (or maybe he'd picked her up) at her favorite hunting grounds, the neighborhood grocery store, was an exception. Maybe *the* exception. Of course, she'd thought that before about men she'd met in the produce aisle. There had been more than a few such men. She wasn't sure why the produce aisle was such a good place to meet men, but she sensed it had something primal to do with the juxtaposition of women and raw food. At least in the minds of men.

Zoe knew little about this one other than that he was smooth, extremely handsome, and if his clothes were any indication, very rich. His pickup patter was intelligent and charming, and disturbingly knowing. Definitely a guy worth taking a chance on, since he seemed harmless.

She smiled at the thought of her dinner date also dressing to impress her before coming to the apartment. If he wasn't married, gay, or terminally ill, he had to be one of the most eligible bachelors she'd ever met. Handsome, rich, and intelligent. The trifecta. Now if only he was honest and had a kind heart. Something about him made her think he might have both those attributes.

She did suspect that he might wear a toupee, but nobody was perfect.

30

Nothing came easy. Working from diagrams and the autopsy report, Meg, Birdy, and half a dozen uniforms took almost a week to locate the sniper's nest.

It was Officer Nancy Weaver who found it. At least, she was the one who called Meg on her two-way.

When Meg and Birdy got to the address, Weaver led them upstairs to the top two floors of the building, which were being renovated. At the end of the hall on the top floor was an apartment with the door standing open.

Weaver stepped aside so they could enter.

No furniture. A newly drywalled, unpainted living room. There was old padding, but no carpet on the floors. The place smelled like plaster dust. More than smelled. Meg sneezed. Birdy hoped God would bless her.

"They're renovating all these places," Weaver said. Another uniform, who'd been securing the apartment, nodded in somber verification. The light streaming through bare windows didn't shine on anything that would reflect it other than steel staples in the carpet pad.

"Looks like work stopped some time ago," Birdy said.

"Four months," Weaver confirmed. "The manager told me the owners ran out of money. They're trying to get refinancing now."

Meg walked back to the hall door. "Lock looks okay."

"Not this one," Weaver said, and led them into a bedroom.

Meg saw what she meant. The locking latch on one of the French windows leading out to a terrace had been forced. There was some furniture in the bedroom, an abandoned dresser without drawers, a wooden headboard with the veneer peeling off. The furniture was dusty and hadn't been touched in a long time. Carpet padding in here, too, prevented any footprints.

"Looks like he fired from the terrace," Weaver said. "Out there at the corner."

Meg went out onto the terrace and imagined herself lining up a shot at someone in Peru Norte's outdoor dining area. She leaned forward slightly and could barely see the restaurant. The sidewalk table area had been cleaned up but was still closed. The table where Lee Nasad and his fiancée had sat was visible.

Backing away from the terrace's low parapet, Meg shielded her eyes from the late afternoon sun and looked straight up. Had to be.

Weaver had been watching her figure it out. "I've been up there," she said. "The Night Sniper lowered himself from the roof to the terrace, then let himself into the apartment so he could make his getaway. Probably just took the elevator down and left without anybody seeing him."

Meg thought about it. Uh-huh, it would work. The Sniper was probably out of the building before anybody at the restaurant fully realized what happened. Shock played hell with logic. Eyewitnesses, too.

"Reminds me of that Night Spider case," Weaver said,

"where the killer dropped from the roof on a line, like a spider, and entered the victims' bedrooms through their windows."

"Sort of," Birdy said. "But looks to me like the Sniper was just following the easiest course of getting into firing position without attracting attention."

"He was probably here before the night he fired the shot, too," Meg said. "Figuring out where he wanted to shoot from. And he didn't want to walk away leaving a sign that one of the apartments had been broken into."

"Say what?"

Repetto had arrived. He nodded to Weaver, then listened while Meg and Birdy filled him in.

"Nice work again, Weaver," Repetto said.

"Thanks. But there's more." She walked carefully across the carpet padding toward a spot near the French doors. Meg and Birdy exchanged looks. Weaver had obviously waited until Repetto had arrived to spring her big find. The woman wanted a promotion. Meg had to smile. She begrudgingly admired Weaver at the same time she resented her ambition and manipulation. Reminded her of someone a few years ago, before that someone had wised up.

Or maybe after.

They followed Weaver until she stopped and pointed. "See? Look careful and there's a muddy footprint."

They did look.

"About size ten," Repetto said.

"Narrows it down to a few million guys and me," Birdy said.

"There's more of what looks like that kind of mud on the roof, where someone would be if he were attaching a rope to lower himself to the terrace. I checked the elevator, but it's been used too many times to give up anything."

"Gotta be the killer's print," Birdy said, "if it's the same kinda mud that's on the roof."

"It wasn't raining the evening Lee Nasad was shot," Repetto said.

"That's what makes it odd that there's mud," Weaver said. "But it's on the roof and here in the apartment. Out on the terrace, too."

It occurred to Meg that Weaver shouldn't have taken them out there without telling them about the mud. But maybe she would have warned them if they were about to step on any evidence. That's what Repetto and Birdy would say, anyway, if Meg said anything critical of Weaver. The little schemer worked these guys as if they were sock puppets without eyes.

The mud was on the edge of the parapet, and more or less all over the terrace.

"Techs are on the way," Repetto said, "but I don't think they'd mind this." He used his forefinger to scoop a tiny amount of mud from the parapet. "Let's go to the roof, see if this matches whatever's up there."

The mud did match, at least to the eye and feel. Light brown and gritty. More like clay. Meg wasn't surprised by the match. Probably Weaver had already been up here with her own mud sample, or she wouldn't have mentioned the mud.

When they went back down to the apartment to wait for the techs, the light had changed somewhat. Something tiny but with almost luminescent glitter caught Meg's eye. Something near the forced lock of the French doors. She moved to the side and could no longer see it.

But when she walked over to the door, there it was again. She leaned close and peered at a three- or four-inch strand of black hair stuck in the space where the brass handle rotated. There was something about the hair . . .

Everyone had stopped talking and joined her.

She didn't touch the hair, but pointed it out to Repetto.

"Let's find out if the previous tenant or any of the workmen who were in here wore a hairpiece," she said. "Unless the lab proves me wrong, I'm going with this not being a human hair."

31

1990

Dante spent a month in the burn unit of Roosevelt Hospital, then was transferred to the Holmes Burn Clinic in New Jersey. Another three months of skin grafts and pain followed. Hell was a lasting thing.

At first Dante was in a ward, then a semiprivate room he shared with an old man who'd been in a gas fire. But soon he was in his own room, and able to get up and walk to his meals and for some of his medical procedures. For a long time he thought being burned had become his life, and he was ready for it to end anytime.

The nurse who'd been assigned to his case kept his spirits up at least high enough to get him through his ordeal. Her name was Jane Jones. She was in her early thirties and liked to read to her patients, who were all burn victims. But Dante she enjoyed reading to more than anyone. He had an amazingly quick and bright mind and was often ahead of her in whatever story she was reading. He was particularly good at discerning the endings of mysteries.

It didn't hurt their relationship that she was an attractive, willowy blonde, and Dante developed a crush on her. She was something to think about other than the pain.

One morning when Jane came into his room and sat in the chair by his bed, it was obvious she'd been crying.

Dante wanted to help her but felt inadequate to the task. "You okay?" The question seemed awkward and inane.

Jane smiled and touched a knuckle to the corner of one eye. "The thing is that *you're* okay now, or getting to be."

Dante didn't think he was okay. Not when he looked in the mirror. One side of his face was a drooping red and purple scar, and his hair grew not at all on the left side of his head, and only in patches on the right. He didn't know how Jane could stand to look at him.

She leaned forward in the chair and locked gazes with him. "You're getting better fast now, Dante. It's time for you to become an outpatient."

"What's that?"

"It means you won't live here at the clinic anymore."

A sob lodged in his throat. It hadn't occurred to him—not consciously, anyway—that he'd ever have to leave here. It was possible that, despite the pain, he'd been safer and happier here than anywhere else. "But I'll come in every day for treatment? Is that what you mean?"

"Yes and no. You'll be an outpatient, but you'll live and your treatment will be in Arizona."

Dante let his head rest back on the pillow and tried to comprehend that. Arizona. He knew it was another state, but it might as well be another country. Desert and cactus, cowboys. A place you visited if you were rich, but no one really wanted to live there.

"Why Arizona?" he asked.

"That's where the Strong Foundation is. Their headquarters is a ranch where the boys and girls live while they receive their remaining treatment." She paused. Dante was looking blankly at her. "The foundation's been paying your medical bills, Dante. Your treatment in New York and your stay here at Holmes."

It hadn't actually occurred to Dante that someone must be paying his medical expenses. He thought it would be the state, or some other government entity. Or maybe the hospital and clinic themselves. Wasn't that what hospitals and clinics did, made people well? "I don't understand this foundation."

"It was started years ago by a very wealthy man named Charles Strong. Mr. Strong died long ago, and now the foundation's managed by his son, Adam. Its mission is to save homeless children and provide whatever opportunity is left for them."

"A ranch. I'm supposed to be a cowboy?"

Jane laughed. "Not exactly, though it is a working ranch that raises cattle. And you and the other children you'll live with will work. That's part of the reason for the ranch, to teach work and responsibility."

"Is everyone there sick or injured?"

"In some way, inside or out. The foundation tries to make them whole again."

Dante turned away from her and gazed out the window at the branches of a willow tree. "It sounds like an orphans' home."

"I suppose it is, in a way. But it's also something more than that."

"The other kids there? Are they orphans like me?"

Jane seemed to search for words. "They need someone to care for them, Dante. They have no one else."

"I have you."

"I'm your friend. We'll remain friends. But I can't care for you forever. I can't afford it, and I have a life outside the clinic. . . ." Jane's voice broke. "Are you crying?"

"No!"

"You'll like it at the ranch, Dante. In fact, you'll learn to love it there. Other kids have. Are you crying? You can't go back to living on the street. It's dangerous. You're too young. Nobody, whatever their age, should have to live on the street. Damn it, Dante, are you crying?"

She leaned forward so she could see his face and kiss his undamaged cheek.

He was crying.

32

The present

Meg stopped the unmarked for a traffic light and watched through the metronomic sweep of the windshield wipers as pedestrians stepped over a puddle near the curb and crossed the street. She'd taken the car home last night and was on her way this rainy morning to pick up Repetto. They were to meet Birdy at their precinct office.

When she pulled the car over to the curb in front of Repetto's house in the Village, she saw him standing with Lora in the shelter of the small awning over the entrance. As soon as the car stopped, he leaned down and kissed Lora, then took the concrete steps to the sidewalk with the casual adroitness of a much younger man.

Lora followed, teetering on high heels and balancing her purse as she opened a black umbrella while on the way down the steps. A multitasker. She was on her way somewhere work-related, Meg thought, wearing a blue raincoat and dress-up shoes of the sort Meg could never wear to work unless going undercover as a hooker. When she saw Meg, Lora smiled and waved. Meg lifted her fingers that were curved around the top of the steering wheel and wagged them.

Repetto opened the passenger-side door and slid into the car, bringing heft and moisture and the scent of wet clothing with him. He shut the door in a hurry, trapping the dank morning scents inside the car.

"Lousy morning," Meg remarked.

"You were right," he said, smoothing back his damp hair with both hands, then glancing at his wet fingers. "About the hair."

At first Meg thought he was referring to *his* hair; then she realized what he meant.

Repetto brushed his hands together to dry them. "The dark hair you spotted caught in the door latch in the apartment the Sniper used—it turned out to be synthetic, just as you predicted."

Meg felt a flush of satisfaction. "So our guy wears a hairpiece or wig."

"Looks that way, though he wouldn't necessarily wear one all the time."

Meg thought about Alex and his military buzz cut. Ideal hair to wear beneath a wig.

Repetto wasn't finished with his good news. "You were right about the mud in the apartment, too. He must have tracked it in from some place in the neighborhood, or more mud would have come off his shoes before he entered the building. Mud on the lobby floor, incidentally, suggests that's how he got into the building. He must have simply walked in when the doorman was occupied and wouldn't notice him. Easy then for him to take the elevator to the top floor and make his way onto the roof. From there he dropped by rope to the terrace outside the apartment. There were traces of mud there, too, where he would have knelt or sat in order to shoot."

"That mud could have been tracked out onto the terrace

by me or Birdy, or one of the uniforms who got there before us."

"Possibly," Repetto said, "but Weaver said she was the only one who went out there after spotting the forced lock on the French window, and she was careful."

"She would be." In the corner of her vision, Meg saw Repetto glance over at her.

"What's that supposed to mean?"

Huh? "Weaver's ambitious, is all."

"What is this, catfight time?"

Meg grinned. "You know me better than that. I think Weaver's a solid cop. It's just that she has . . . ambition."

"Like you don't?"

Does this guy want *to argue?* "You're the one—"

"Okay," Repetto said. "Enough. The mud matches, and Weaver's sure she didn't track any out on the terrace. And you're right—I shouldn't compare. You and Weaver are two different people entirely."

Meg said nothing. She was irritated mostly at herself. Sure, Weaver was ambitious. So what? It wasn't lack of ambition that had kept Meg down in the ranks. It was resistance to playing the political game.

And something else.

Maybe in comparing her to Weaver—Weaver of the flirtatious grin and the reputation for merriment and sleeping around—Repetto was trying to tell Meg that she, Meg, was too cynical. The male chauvinist might be saying the Job, on top of a rough marriage and divorce, could make a woman too hard, if she let it. Her mind, her thought processes, could become too rigid.

He might be right. Or she might be making too much of a chance remark.

Not that Repetto made many chance remarks.

Meg looked over at him and modulated her voice. *Make-nice time.* "Maybe this is a good morning to see if we can find similar mud in the neighborhood, someplace where water might stand for a few days and leave mud even during a short dry spell."

"It'd be better to wait till tomorrow, when it's not supposed to rain and most of this mess has dried up. Then we can go on a mud hunt."

"True," Meg said. *At least I found the synthetic hair.*

She braked for a school bus, breathing the yellow monster's exhaust fumes that made their way into the car.

"Smells like Lora describes my cigars," Repetto said.

Meg was watching half a dozen kids about the same age— eight or nine—emerge from an apartment doorway and trudge toward the waiting bus single file and perfectly spaced, like ducks in the rain.

They all looked glum; they were on their way to school. What did they know from real worries?

To be a kid that age again . . .

A memory dropped like a coin in the back of Meg's mind. It took her a few seconds to realize what it meant.

"Meg?"

Repetto was nudging her shoulder. The school bus had pulled away.

A horn blared behind Meg, and she spun the unmarked's tires on wet pavement as she tried to get up to speed.

It was still raining when they reached the precinct house. They trudged through the area in front of the desk, then the detective squad room where a cluster of plainclothes cops sitting or leaning around a computer glanced over at them. A couple of uniforms guided a dejected-looking guy handcuffed and with arms covered with tattoos outside to drive him to Central Booking.

Repetto led the way downstairs to their basement office. It smelled mustier and more oppressively than usual this rainy morning. Former Police Commissioner Kerik, in his framed photo on the wall, appeared moody and depressed by the weather. The green mold in the corner up near the ceiling had thrived and was now about six inches down one of the walls. Meg wondered sometimes if they were in a race to solve the Night Sniper case before the mold took over the office.

Birdy must have just arrived and was finishing hanging up his wet raincoat as they entered. He used his hand to brush drops of water from it onto the floor. While Repetto briefed him on the hair and mud news, Meg examined the Night Sniper murder files. She wanted to make sure she was right about what she suspected after seeing the school bus and kids had jogged her memory.

Birdy slapped a hand to his forehead, as if he'd just remembered something himself, then went to a desk and opened a white paper bag. The scent of coffee wafted over to Meg, chasing away some of the mustiness. Birdy got three Styrofoam cups from the bag, handed one to Repetto, then walked over with another for Meg.

"The next Night Sniper victim will be low on the economic ladder," she said casually, accepting the coffee and nodding her thanks.

She removed the cup's plastic lid, waiting for Repetto to come over to her desk, knowing he'd overheard what she said to Birdy. *If you think the synthetic hair was impressive . . .*

He was standing there giving her one of his level looks, as if he were a master craftsman trying to line up something delicate.

"Explain," he said, taking a careful sip of his coffee.

She took a sip from her own cup. No need for caution. It was lukewarm. "Our Sniper is very much into playing games."

"What he lives for," Birdy said. "And Repetto is his opponent, at least in his mind."

"And his mind is what we're trying to get into. He gets his jollies planting clues, leaving us riddles to solve."

"And you solved one?" Repetto asked.

"I just checked the murder files to make sure," Meg said to both men. "If, in the Sniper's mind, the game actually began when Repetto came to the case, the first victim was Vito Mestieri."

"Sniper pretty much made that game thing clear," Birdy said. "It started with Mestieri."

"So to this point the victims are, in order, Mestieri, who owned and operated an appliance and TV repair shop. Ralph Evans, buyer for a chain of men's clothing stores. Candy Trupiano, editor and National Guard corporal. Kelli Wilson, who sometimes spent the night on her boat docked in the city. And Lee Nasad, millionaire author. Tinker, tailor, soldier, sailor, rich man—"

"—poor man, beggar man, thief," Repetto finished for her.

Meg nodded. "Child's play."

33

Strong Ranch was 590 acres of flat, arid land roughly between Phoenix and Tucson in the Arizona desert. It was bisected by an arroyo that ran with water about twice a year during unusually heavy rainstorms. On one side of the arroyo was the main ranch house, the boys' barracks, and various outbuildings including a tractor shed and hip-roofed barn. On the other side was the smaller, girls' quarters, a scaled-down version of the boys' stucco-and-lapboard one-story structure with rooftop air-conditioning units and solar panels.

The barracks were divided into separate cubicles that afforded some privacy, and it was in one of those cubicles that Dante Vanya spent most of his time alone after being transferred to Strong Ranch. Being by himself was what he wanted, or told himself so, and the ranch wasn't the kind of place where friendships were easily formed.

In the dining area, Dante ate alone at a table away from

the other ten boys currently at the ranch, his fellow . . . he wasn't sure if they were prisoners or patients.

With each passing day, Dante became more determined to go it alone at Strong Ranch. The others might have their problems, but none of them had Dante's disfigurements.

On the third day, a hulking fifteen-year-old named Orvey tried to pick a fight with Dante by perpetrating a shoving match. Instead of shoving back, Dante kicked him hard in the shin, then advanced on him. Dante wasn't angry, and not at all frightened. He was obviously resigned to taking a beating from the much larger boy, but determined to give back what he could.

The fight didn't last long, and Dante was saved from a serious trouncing when two of the older boys separated the combatants out of fear the confrontation would draw attention and result in punishment.

From then on the other boys, including Orvey, granted Dante his privacy. They also respected him. They recognized toughness born of hopelessness and knew that whatever they started, the quiet boy with the sparse hair and hideous left profile would match them in meanness.

The week after Dante's arrival, a commotion outside his cubicle made him curious. The other boys were obviously pleased by something, judging by their loud voices and laughter.

Dante ventured out to see what was going on.

A tall, broad-shouldered man with curly blond hair stood in the center of the main room. He was wearing a western-style tan shirt, cowboy boots, and jeans with a big silver belt buckle.

When he saw Dante he smiled. "Ah! Our newest arrival!" He walked over to stand near Dante, seeming even taller. "I'm sorry I wasn't here to meet you, but I had to be in Europe on business. I'm Adam Strong." He extended his hand.

Dante took it, and they shook. Strong's grip was firm but he didn't squeeze Dante's hand like some people who tried to establish that they were in charge.

"This is Dante Vanya," Strong said, releasing Dante's hand and straightening up. He formally introduced the other boys, one of whom, Kerry, was bald. Dante learned later he'd lost his hair because of some kind of cancer treatment.

"What we do here," Strong said, "is let you continue to recuperate, if you arrive with physical problems, and we help you find yourselves, no matter how you arrive." He grinned. It scrunched up his cheeks and made his pale eyes tilt so he looked like a cat. "No doubt you've heard that 'finding yourself' malarkey before. What it means here at the ranch is that you learn what you like to do, then learn how to do it well." He looked directly at Dante. "This is a working ranch, so we expect something in return for your stay here. There'll be chores. You'll act and talk like gentlemen. And we expect you to take part in activities." The grin widened. "But don't let me scare you, Dante. The main idea is for you to learn how to live, and to enjoy living."

Strong looked at his wristwatch. It was big and seemed to have been made from a gold coin. "I've got work to do now. Vic will assign chores for the day."

Vic was an older boy, about eighteen, who slept in the main house and also dressed like a cowboy. Dante thought he looked something like the gunfighters he'd seen on TV, only without the guns.

Vic read from a wrinkled sheet of paper. Nobody complained when they heard what work they were assigned, whether it was cleaning stables, milking cows, or helping to dig a new well. Dante drew kitchen duty in what everyone called the mess hall. In the biggest kitchen Dante had ever seen, a fat woman named Allen, even though she was a woman, gave him a paring knife and sat him down to peel potatoes for lunch. It would be a month before Dante learned that Allen was her last name and that her first was Lil.

Dante still kept to himself, but after a while he didn't much mind being at Strong Ranch. The routine was morning chores, then various activities, and in the evenings reading or sometimes movies for both the boys and girls.

One of the girls, a redhead named Verna, was pretty in a storybook princess way, and Dante wished he knew her better, but after one look at his burned face she didn't seem interested. He heard that her father was dead and her mother had sold her for crack money when she was six years old, to a man who'd kept her prisoner in a trailer court until she was nine. "Poor Verna can't ever love anyone," Dante overheard Lil Allen say one day, "'cause she can't trust anyone. Not all the way."

Dante could understand that. What he didn't understand was that Verna must also betray everyone.

After the first month at the ranch, the school year began, and boys and girls together rode a bus every day into Nailsville, a small town about twenty miles away. There, with a lot of other kids, they attended school in a long, flat-roofed brick building with narrow, horizontal windows.

Despite having missed a grade, Dante found school easy enough, especially math. One day his math teacher handed him an envelope with instructions to give it to Adam Strong. Dante thought he might be in some kind of trouble, and since the envelope was unsealed, he opened it and read the note inside. His gaze fixed on the word *amazing*. The teacher thought he might be some kind of genius at mathematics.

Genius. Dante didn't know what to make of that. All he knew was that he comprehended what he was taught, especially in his math class. It made sense, so why didn't everyone comprehend it?

Early one evening, instead of the usual softball or soccer

exercises, or track and field competition, Adam Strong had something different in mind. He drove up in his dusty white Ford pickup to where the boys were assembled, then lowered the tailgate and stood there with his fists on his hips. In the truck's bed was a folded blue blanket. When the boys had all walked over to him, Strong unfolded the blanket to reveal a dozen rifles.

"We're going to target shoot," Strong announced. "Shooting's a sport I used to be good at, and I know it's a fine sport, no matter what you might think of guns, or what other people have told you."

"I'm gonna join the army!" a tall, skinny kid named Charley announced loudly. Not meaning it. Smarting off in a way that had gotten him in trouble with Strong before.

"Not a bad choice," Strong said. "They'll know just what to do with you."

When the other boys were finished snickering, Strong continued. "These are not new weapons. In fact, they are quite old. They are army surplus M1 rifles, and you need to understand them before you use them. Before we actually shoot, I want to show you how these rifles work, how to take them apart and put them together, and most of all, how not to accidentally shoot yourself or anyone else."

"The girls gonna shoot?" one of the boys asked.

"They were told they had the opportunity," Strong said. "They all chose other activities. That's okay. They don't like guns."

More snickering.

Strong ignored it. He picked up the nearest rifle and handed it to Charley, then gave out the other rifles. When he handed one to Dante, Dante hesitated, remembering the gun his father had used.

But this wasn't like that. This was another kind of gun. A rifle. And Adam Strong wasn't his father. He accepted the rifle but knew Strong had noted his reluctance.

When everyone was armed with unloaded rifles, Strong sat down on the truck's open tailgate, a rifle across his lap, and said, "Gather round."

They spent the next three days learning about the rifles, how they were different from shotguns or handguns, and how to aim them, allowing for wind and distance. They learned how to lead a moving target. It struck Dante that shooting a gun wasn't so complicated. It was mathematical, a matter of angle, speed, time, and distance. And variables like wind and the rhythms of motion and momentum.

He also learned from Kelly that Adam Strong had been an alternate small-bore rifle shooter on the 1976 U.S. Olympic team that went to Montreal. He hadn't actually shot in competition there, but he'd been ready.

On the fourth day, Strong gathered the boys around the back of the pickup and said, "Today we shoot bullets. I have targets set up beyond the barracks, against a safe backdrop. Vic will lead the way, and I'll follow in the truck, where we'll leave the rifles for now."

When they reached the new target range ten minutes later, Dante saw that the tractor sat nearby and now had a scoop on it like a bulldozer's. It had been used to create a bank of earth about eight feet high. In front of the banked earth were bales of straw, and on each bale was a sheet of paper with a target on it, a series of circles around a red bull's-eye. At intervals Dante later learned were twenty, fifty, and a hundred yards were low stakes in the ground with twine strung tautly between them, marking lines for the boys to shoot from.

They shot first from a distance of twenty yards, using the standing position Strong had taught them. Dante sighted carefully, squeezed the trigger gently as instructed, and felt the rifle's stock buck against his shoulder. He winced, and his ears buzzed from the explosive bark of all the rifles firing almost at once.

"Not bad," Strong said. "We'll examine the targets later."

Beginning with his second shot, Dante tried to factor in all the conditions he was shooting under. It wasn't difficult, since it was a calm day and wind had little effect. That left the simple geometry of sending a predictable moving object toward a stationary one. He held his breath and felt an unexpected connection with the target, as if a wire were strung between it and the gun barrel, and squeezed the trigger, ready this time for the bark and buck of the old M1.

He felt a rush of excitement. He *knew* that this time he'd hit the target. And could do it again.

Every boy fired from standing, sitting, and prone positions at varying distances, a total of twenty rounds of ammunition.

Strong walked out and collected the targets while Vic and the boys stood and watched.

When Strong returned, he held all the targets but one in his right hand. In his left hand was Dante's target.

He looked at Dante and said, "Holy Christ!"

All the boys froze. They had never before heard Strong utter a profanity.

"Eighteen out of twenty in the target, four in the bull's-eye," Strong said. "Holy . . . Toledo. Have you shot before, Dante?"

Dante shook his head no.

Strong stared at him for a long time, silently, with something like doubt and with something like wonder.

Then he said, "Okay, let's go back to the barracks. Remember to be neat. Pick up your shell casings."

It was an instruction Dante never forgot.

34

The present

There was a small savings and loan on the ground floor of the Maigret Building on West Twenty-third Street. Repetto entered through a door alongside it, which led to an unadorned foyer lined with mailboxes. A narrow stairway led to offices above, which were identified by a directory that had yellowed over the years beneath the clear plastic plate protecting it from theft and graffiti. The directory informed him that B. Grams, Inc., was on the second floor.

That was fine with Repetto. There were six floors and no elevator in the building, and he didn't feel like climbing stairs. Also, he didn't feel like being reminded of how he was getting older.

Last week Repetto had happened across one of his long-time snitches, a burglar and sometime fence named Artie Silver. Artie was smart enough to fence stolen goods of all sorts without leaving a trace, so, if there was going to be an actual prosecution, it was necessary to nail him while he still had the loot in his possession. It had never happened. Another way Artie had of insuring himself against a conviction if he did get caught was to sparingly provide police with information about some of his clients, both buyers and sellers. He was a discreet snitch, and through the years Repetto had been discreet with his information.

Repetto actually liked Artie, and had been talking with him about things in general, while both men stood in the sunlight and ate knishes from a sidewalk vendor on the corner of Third and Fifty-fourth Street. This was New York at its best: vendor food, warm sun, and an endless variety of people streaming past, as if it could all last forever for everyone.

So why not do a little business, Repetto thought, for old times' sake? He asked Artie if he knew any gun dealers or collectors specializing in rifles.

"Almost always it's handguns or automatic assault weapons," Artie said, with an exaggerated shrug that was pure Artie. "Rifles are something else altogether, more for hunting than the kinda thing that'd interest you." He wouldn't cheapen what he had by giving it away too quickly.

Repetto chewed a bite of knish and waited in the warm sunlight.

Then, as in the past, Artie smiled thinly and gave Repetto a name: "Boniface Grams."

"Dealer," Repetto asked, "or collector?"

"Facilitator. If he can't help you, he might be able to tell you more than I know. Guns wouldn't be my specialty, if I had a specialty. I don't like the things around. I'm all for the Brady Bunch Bill."

Repetto wasn't sure if Artie was joking, so decided to let that one pass.

Artie put on a pious expression. "Like everybody else in this town, I'd like to see you collar the Night Sniper."

"Are guns this Bonepart guy's—"

"Boniface."

"—guy's specialty?"

"Are they ever!" Artie took a big bite of knish and chewed enthusiastically with his mouth open. "And I tell you," he said around the knish, "he's mostly legal. His expertise is in obtaining valuable pieces for serious gun collectors."

"Sounds all the way legal."

"Well, sometimes the guns aren't legal, or maybe they're from a museum or who knows where. Maybe the collector doesn't have a permit. I don't know, mind you. I'm speculating."

"So speculate as to where I might find Boniface Grams."

Artie gave Repetto the Twenty-third Street address.

"I have to level, Artie, I'm not sure if I can do you any good if you're angling for payback. I'm not with the NYPD anymore on a permanent basis."

"I know. I read the papers. Which is why I wanna help, so you can stop this Sniper prick and the city can get back to normal. It was after dark, I wouldn't be standing here eating this knish."

"Boniface," Repetto said, folding his paper napkin so he could write on it. He unclipped a pen from his pocket. "How do you spell that?"

Artie told him.

"He French?"

"If France is in Africa."

The steps hadn't been too bad. Not breathing noticeably harder, Repetto found himself at the end of the hall on the second floor. The door to B. Grams, Inc., had cheap brass numbers on it and fancy black lettering spelling out the name of the company. Repetto opened the door and stepped inside, expecting some kind of anteroom, maybe even a receptionist.

Instead, a tall, spiffily dressed black man not yet thirty was seated on the corner of a desk, reading a newspaper. He was wearing pleated gray slacks, a white shirt, and colorful blue and yellow suspenders. His black, cap-toed shoes were shined to a blinding gloss. A suit coat that matched the pants was draped over a hanger dangling from a brass coatrack.

He looked up in mild surprise and removed dark-rimmed reading glasses as Repetto entered. "You got an appointment?"

"Does anyone?" Repetto asked.

The man grinned handsomely with perfect white teeth. He had a trimmed little brush mustache that made him look something like Errol Flynn. A guy his age, Repetto bet he'd never heard of Errol Flynn. "Cop?" he asked Repetto. As if he didn't know.

Repetto nodded. "Boniface?"

The man placed the newspaper on the desk and stood up all the way. Repetto took that for a yes.

"I got a soft spot for cops," Boniface said. "My brother was one in L.A. and got shot to death by some drug-freaked asshole. Mom never got over it."

"Too bad," Repetto said, doubting if any of it was true.

"Had a helluva funeral. VIPs and LAPD brass and bagpipes and everything. What can I help you with, Detective Repetto?"

Repetto hadn't given Boniface his name. "Want to see some ID first?"

"Don't need that. I seen your photo in the papers and on TV. Knew you was the dude soon as you walked in. Anyways, you got cop stamped on your forehead."

Repetto believed him there. "You strike me as a smart guy."

"Course."

"You know why I'm here?"

"'Cause you think for some reason I might be able to help you."

"Why would I think that?"

Boniface smiled and shook his head. "Never did like to dance. So let's say somebody told you my company sometimes deals in firearms, and you think I might know something about where the Night Sniper dude's getting his arsenal."

"We think he might be a collector."

"Well, I ain't no collector."

"But you supply them. You're a buyer for them."

"Well . . . sometimes. They're looking for something rare, I locate it for them. That's not illegal, though."

"Not if the guns are legal. And the sale is legal. And the transportation of the guns is legal. And there's no hard-ass homicide cop who might get on your case in a major way if you don't tell him what he asks."

Boniface leaned back so his haunches were against the desk, then crossed his arms over his colorful suspenders and floral-pattern tie. "Point taken."

"You supply any illegal collectors? I'm not asking names. Not yet. It's the Night Sniper I'm interested in, not some redneck who likes to collect guns."

"I don't supply any collectors like you're talking about," Boniface said. "Some secret collectors, yeah. But there's nothing about them I know's illegal. They just wanna keep their collection a secret 'cause of the bias against guns in this country. Don't want their pansy-ass friends to know, you follow?"

Repetto didn't answer. The river was flowing.

"And I deal mostly in handguns. Some long guns, though. Sometimes. But I ain't dealt long guns in over a year. Year at least. That's God's truth, dude."

Repetto thought you seldom heard *God* and *dude* in the same sentence. He fixed Boniface with a stare that obviously made him uncomfortable. "Talk some more. On your own. Tell me something that'll brighten my day. Your day, too."

"Kinda collector you're looking for, I don't know," Boniface said. "Truth is, most of my customers are legal, got permits, licenses, the whole shebang. Also, the kinda collector you're talking about don't figure to be a serial killer. Ones I met, they're so interested in guns they wouldn't have time to go on a killing spree. Some of the really expensive collector pieces come from Europe, too. Dueling sets, blunderbusses, that kinda thing."

"I'm not looking for blunderbusses, Boniface. You aren't helping me."

"Well, the kinda help you want, I can't give, 'cause I don't know the answers to your questions." He uncrossed one arm and stood like Jack Benny, thumb and forefinger cupping his chin. He was thinking deeply, and just for Repetto. "Lemme put it this way. You ever do any hunting?"

Repetto stared at him. "You mean birds and animals?"

"Whatever. Things you'd use a rifle on."

"Not in a long time."

"If you were an avis hunter—"

"You mean avid? Avid hunter?"

"Yeah. You'd know from the bullets, the Sniper dude ain't using hunting rifles. They're target rifles."

"Target . . . hunting . . . what's the difference?"

"Mostly the caliber or millimeter. The bore. Target rifles use those offbeat, smaller-size rounds, nothing like most hunting rifles. Plinker size but powered by large loads so they got muzzle velocity. Foreign make bullets, too."

"You saying the Sniper collects target rifles? The shooting-for-sport kind?"

"Maybe not *only* target rifles. There are rifles made specifically for sniping, too, with some of the same characteristics, and he might have a few of them. But mostly from the bullet sizes the papers are saying, my guess is the rifles are manufactured for target shooting and are expensive."

"What do you mean by expensive?"

"Four, five figures almost certainly. Up from there. What I'm saying, Detective Repetto, is the Sniper dude, if he's a collector—and he probably is—he's one rich mother to own the kinda guns he's been killing with so far."

"Where would he obtain them?"

"Oh, there's all kinds of bad, bad people in the arms business, and all over the world. And I can tell you there's some rich collectors avis enough to buy stolen collectibles and keep 'em just so they can get 'em out once in a while and play with 'em."

"Avid."

"What you say."

"So we're looking for a rich gun collector who specializes in target rifles."

"Way I see it. I'm talkin' about rifles that are rare, and they're legal—not assault rifles or anything. But like I said, the way some gun buffs are, they don't wanna advertise. 'Nother thing they're afraid of is attracting thieves."

"Thieves who might steal their guns and sell them to other collectors."

"Why, yes, that could happen. Then those other collectors 'specially wouldn't want anyone to know they owned those particular guns."

Repetto reached into his coat pocket. Boniface drew back as if he thought a gun might emerge. Instead, out came a business card.

"I'm gonna give you my number," Repetto said. "Two of them. Cell phone's in pencil. You come across anything else I should know, you call me."

"Course."

When Repetto was at the door, Boniface said, "One thing *I'd* like to know, who told you about me?"

"One of those secret collectors," Repetto said. He glanced at the open door. "You really incorporated?"

Boniface laughed. "Hell no! Don't even know what it means."

Repetto doubted that.

* * *

NYPD Patrolman Michael Skeppy woke up sweating.

Damned air-conditioning was falling behind again. The bedroom was way too warm, and beams of light angling in along the edges of the black shades hurt Skeppy's eyes.

He squinted and looked at the clock on the nightstand.

Damn!

He'd overslept again. *Gonna catch hell from the sergeant, never get off traffic detail.*

Where the hell is Maggie?

He sat up on the edge of the mattress, a fleshy but powerful man in his thirties, with pleasant but homely features reminiscent of an amiable bulldog's. Sitting there in only his jockey shorts, he knew he'd never get to the precinct on time. He needed a shower, a shave, something to eat.

Maggie.

He called her name, then stood up and plodded to the door and opened it.

She was asleep on the sofa, in the middle of the afternoon.

Irritated, he called her name again, louder, and her dark eyes opened wide and she sat up. She looked at her watch. "Oh, damn! I didn't mean to fall asleep. I'm sorry."

"Doesn't help," he mumbled, and plodded toward the bathroom to shower.

"I'll fix you something to eat," his wife said behind him. "You're gonna need your energy."

"Damned straight," Skeppy muttered to himself, wondering which of Manhattan's busy intersections were going to demand his services this afternoon and evening.

Twenty minutes later, showered, shaved, and in uniform, he made it a point to kiss Maggie good-bye before leaving for work on the afternoon shift. They had their problems right now, plenty of them. And he knew how she hated it when he worked this shift. It meant she had to sit alone most of the evening and wait up late if she wanted to see him at all that day.

A cop's wife, Skeppy thought. A hard life.

But not as hard as standing on your feet all day waving your arms at people who'd just as soon run you over.

Alex made sure the door to his workshop was locked. He wouldn't want Detective Meg to enter unexpectedly, as she might very well do. It seemed to be her nature. The cop in her.

The hiss of fine sandpaper on the custom gun stock he was toiling over soothed him as his hands lovingly worked the fine walnut. He'd created the stock out of a single block of prime wood over a yard long. Hours with the saws, the lathe, the sander, and now his hands separated from the wood only by the flimsy, clothlike sandpaper that allowed him almost to feel the grain. The graceful gun stock, of Alex's own design, was for a .280 Remington rifle with an extended barrel. After the fine sanding, he'd get his wood chisels and spend long hours engraving the stock with exotic, sometimes erotic designs. It would become a work of art that Detective Meg might not comprehend.

There were plenty of ready customers for his custom stocks. Lots of people understood, like Alex, the fascination and repulsion of long guns that delivered death from a distance. While in a sense he loathed such weapons, he was also drawn to them, and he didn't want to consider too carefully the depth of satisfaction he got out of creating beautiful wooden stocks for such firearms. Hate and love, fear and love, were sometimes so similar as to be indistinguishable. Like opposite sides of a rapidly spinning coin.

Detective Meg wouldn't understand that.

Or maybe she'd understand it too well.

He sanded until the muscles in his arms began to cramp, thinking about Meg.

After a dinner of potatoes, broccoli, and cheese, all mixed in some kind of casserole she'd learned about on one of those half-hour-recipe TV cooking shows, Meg surveyed the mess in the kitchen and vowed never to make the dish again. It hadn't been bad, but then it hadn't been good. It had tasted like potatoes, broccoli, and cheese, and so what?

Well, there was enough of the stuff left over for tomorrow night, that was what. And these days Meg had a lot on her mind and was mostly eating for fuel rather than pleasure.

After cleaning up the kitchen and putting the leftover casserole in the refrigerator, she went into the living room.

She didn't feel like watching television; she'd had enough of the world outside the apartment and didn't want to watch news or some idiot's idea of reality. Instead of sitting down on the sofa, she went to her desk chair, booted up her computer, and was told she had mail.

E-mail. One message from AR3276@Kno.com.

Alex.

She fought against opening the e-mail, then admitted to herself that eventually she was going to read it anyway, so why not soon? She moved the mouse on its *Dilbert* rubber pad and clicked.

Alex's message was brief, like most of his others: *Thinking of you.*

Meg deleted it from her e-mail but not from her mind.

She leaned back in her desk chair, thinking of Alex. Damn him! Why couldn't he leave her alone? At least until the Night Sniper case was solved? He'd been a cop. He should understand.

She shut down the computer, went to the sofa, and used

the remote to turn on the TV in order to pass the time and not strain her brain. A commercial was playing, a woman sitting on top of a speeding car with her legs down through the open sunroof. A handsome young guy was driving while fondling her bare feet. They were both grinning. Music blared and another, identical car was speeding toward the first, driven by a woman. A handsome man was sitting on that car with his legs down through the open sunroof, and the woman driving was fondling his bare feet. They were smiling, too. Everyone was smiling and speeding. Both men needed to shave. Both women looked as if every hair other than the ones on their heads had been depilatoried out of existence.

Meg wondered what any of this had to do with cars, then stopped watching and listening, and saw and heard nothing more of it. With so much else to occupy her thoughts, there was no way she could concentrate on television fare.

Thinking of you . . .

35

To Adam Strong's amazement, Dante's performance on the target range wasn't a fluke. He continued to shoot well, though he was such a natural shot that learning the fine points only marginally improved his aim. He was phenomenal at both skeet and still target shooting, accurate with a handgun, but particularly efficient with rifle or shotgun. And Dante continued to grow scholastically, especially in mathematics. Calculating distance, speed, and angles in shooting, and taking aim at solutions requiring similar calculations in mathematics, were talents that nourished each other.

Dante became increasingly important to Adam Strong, and Strong made it obvious. It was as if he'd found a son, and Dante had a father again. Dante grew in confidence and ability. The other boys respected him, especially when he began to defeat them regularly in the games they played. In everything from matchstick poker to chess, Dante became an obsessive and fiercely competitive opponent. He seldom lost. Then, after a while, when he had the measure of each of his opponents on the ranch, he never lost.

Strong gave Dante much more individual attention than he did any of the other children, and none of them complained. They all seemed to see something special in the relationship of Strong and the boy with the scarred face. Or maybe they figured that Dante had an extra measure of grief in the world, the way his face was, so he deserved special attention.

After one of their shooting expeditions plinking varmints—mostly jackrabbits and voles—on the ranch's outskirts, Dante and Strong were walking side by side toward Strong's pickup truck. The Arizona sun was brilliant and the temperature high. Neither Dante nor Strong was perspiring, but the heat still had to be taken into account. It worked internally and created a slight nausea. It discouraged fast or sudden movement.

They walked leisurely without talking, as they often did, content and comfortable with silence and each other's company. The only sound was the regular slapping of their leather boot soles on the dry ground. Rooster tails of dust sprang up at their heels and settled back to earth slowly in the dry, still air.

Strong was wearing jeans, a western shirt, and a broad-brimmed straw hat. Dante had on jeans and a sleeveless T-shirt and was wearing a long-billed baseball cap.

Beside Dante, Strong slowed his pace slightly. He had his European single-shot breechloader broken down and balanced over his shoulder, freeing both his hands. This enabled him to remove his hat with his right hand and simultaneously swipe his left forearm across his forehead, where the hat's leather brim had left a red indentation.

"Sun bother your scars?" he asked Dante.

Dante momentarily broke stride, surprised by the question. His burn-scarred face was something Strong never mentioned. Everyone on the ranch had learned not to mention it.

"Some," he said, hoping Strong wasn't going to pursue the subject.

"I been talking to some doctors in Phoenix," Strong said. "Will you hear me out on what I learned?"

"Don't I always hear you out?"

Strong smiled. "Yeah, I guess these days you do."

"What kinda doctors?"

"The kind that can repair the damage to your face. It's their specialty, helping people like you."

Dante stopped walking. He swallowed. "I don't wanna hear no more. Nothing about plastic surgeons."

They began walking again. Strong said nothing for another dozen steps.

Then: "You scared?"

"It isn't that."

"Okay, we'll let it drop."

Neither of them spoke until they reached the truck.

"Not plastic surgeons, though," Strong said, as they made sure their rifles were unloaded and placed them in padded cases, then in blankets in the pickup bed. "Cosmetic surgeons, they call themselves. They showed me pictures. They can show them to you. It's amazing what they can do."

"I thought we were gonna let it drop."

Strong slapped the side of the pickup, startling Dante. "Listen, I know how you feel, and I'm only gonna push this so far. But I'm duty-bound because I'm fond of you, Dante. I want you to hear the facts, to think about them. Affection works both ways, you know. You really oughta give me a chance."

Dante looked off to the horizon. The distant mountains were purple. The sun would be setting soon.

"I'll listen," he said.

For the next twenty minutes, then on the drive back to the ranch house, Strong told him what the doctors in Phoenix had said. They couldn't make Dante perfect, but there'd been important advancements in dealing with scar tissue, and burn scar tissue in particular. They could make him normal.

It was dark when Strong parked the pickup alongside the tractor shed, in what he knew would be morning shade. He and Dante got out and walked around to the back of the vehicle to remove their rifles.

Strong smiled. "You gonna think on this, Dante?"

"Not much use. I've done some reading about it myself."

"Then what do you mean, not much use?"

"I know how expensive it is. And I know I'm here because I don't have any money."

Strong removed his rifle from the back of the truck and shook his head. "I've got money, Dante."

"Foundation money. You fix my face, you might have to do stuff for everyone here."

"My money," Strong said. "It'll be my personal money."

Dante stared at him in the dying orange light. "Why would you do that?"

Strong bit his lip. "Because I . . . think of you as a son." He reached out with his free hand and drew Dante close, hugging him.

Dante hugged him back. They stood that way for a long time, each awkwardly clinging to the other with the arm that didn't hold a rifle.

Dante began to cry. Strong held him even closer until he gained control of his emotions.

It was several minutes before the sobbing stopped. By then Dante knew he'd do whatever Strong wanted.

He knew that this time the father-son bond would never break.

36

The present

Officer Michael Skeppy was dropped off by a radio car at his intersection at eight that evening. Con Ed was doing street repairs in midtown, and select strings of traffic signals were scheduled to go black a few minutes past eight and remain so until ten o'clock. For two hours, that section of Manhattan would have to do without electric signals and rely on old-fashioned traffic cops.

Skeppy had drawn the busy intersection of Fifty-fifth and Lexington. He stood on the corner observing the still-functioning traffic signals, noting that there were still a lot of vehicles on the street despite the end of the after-work rush. Pedestrians veered around Skeppy's stolid blue form with a glance; he was as much a part of the New York scene as the Empire State Building or Radio City Music Hall—the fabled New York cop. You could buy into whichever fables you chose, from Serpico and corruption, to the Twin Towers and incredible heroism. Skeppy could study the faces passing him by and pretty much know what their owners thought.

There were variations, unless they needed directions or had just had their pockets picked. When people needed help, the faces were the same.

A subtle change in the rhythm of the passing traffic, then the distant blaring of horns, told Skeppy that the signals up Lexington were going dark one by one. Time to do his thing. He waited for a break in traffic, then strode like an emperor out into the middle of the intersection, whistle clamped in his teeth.

He surveyed the traffic, reading what must be happening blocks away on Lexington, then gave a shrill blast with the whistle and took charge. He raised a hand and fixed the driver of a minivan with a neutral but stoic stare, stopping traffic from turning off Fifty-fifth onto Lexington. Then he waved on the twenty or so cars that had raced the last block to arrive at the intersection and were waiting at the blank signal.

Skeppy knew how to direct traffic. A part of him even enjoyed it, when the weather was good like this evening. He used his hand signals expertly, getting into the rhythm, extending a hand palm-out, using his other arm to wave through vehicles waiting to make a left turn. In heavy traffic, like tonight, it could be almost a dance. Skeppy didn't hotdog it like some of the cops working traffic, but he definitely was into it. So much so that a few people stopped and watched his skillful ballet done to the tempo of traffic and the shrill music of his police whistle.

They watched him spin like a dancer and wave an arm gracefully but decisively for a stopped truck to make its left turn, then come square with Lexington traffic, and with a blast of his whistle summon waiting vehicles on with both hands raised to shoulder level. Husky as he was, he possessed the elegance, balance, and daring of a matador. Onlookers watched as he demonstrated an amused disdain for speeding cars that almost brushed his clothing as they passed. They watched him not so much ignore danger as embrace it.

They watched him drop to his knees, as a sudden, reverberating crack like near thunder rolled and echoed along the avenues.

Skeppy kneeled there with his arms limp at his sides as traffic streamed around him. A few drivers glanced over at him as they passed and their expressions changed slightly. Inside their cars they'd heard the report of a rifle and knowledge was beginning to sink in.

Onlookers up on the curb saw the blood on Skeppy's chest and the growing puddle of scarlet at his knees. They saw the police whistle drop from his lips and dangle on its cord slung around his neck. Then they saw him pitch forward and his chest and face strike the concrete hard. He hadn't moved his limp arms or turned his head to avoid contact with the pavement. There was a collective gasp when he fell, because the way he fell, everyone somehow knew he was already dead.

Traffic began moving disjointedly on Lexington, and a scattering of blasting horns became a chorus, then became a crescendo and filled the warm evening.

Within minutes traffic had stopped. Three men on the sidewalk took advantage of the stalled traffic to run out in the street to see if they could help Skeppy, but when they reached him they saw that was impossible and simply stood staring. Sirens screamed and yodeled, making their way toward the dead man lying facedown in the middle of the intersection. Since traffic was stalled up and down Lexington, as if it might never move again, a few drivers got out of their cars and stood a respectful ten feet or so from Skeppy and his would-be saviors.

There were noticeably fewer people on the sidewalks, and a growing number of drivers and passengers were abandoning their stalled vehicles now and entering buildings. Some of them were walking swiftly, glancing uneasily around as they made their way to shelter. Word was spreading fast about how the dead cop had gotten that way.

By the time the first radio car arrived, after a twenty-minute journey through nightmare traffic, cops from the surrounding blocks had made their way on foot to Fifty-fifth and Lexington, and were standing in a circle around Skeppy, guarding his body and preserving the crime scene. They appeared angry, many of them looking around at surrounding tall buildings as if daring whoever had killed Skeppy to show himself, to take a shot at them.

It took another twenty minutes for the crime scene unit to arrive, and for the ME to reach the scene and pronounce Skeppy dead. While they worked, traffic was rerouted and began to flow again.

Shortly thereafter, Skeppy had been removed, and vehicular traffic streamed down Lexington and across the Fifty-fifth Street intersection. The river of traffic parted to avoid a small area in the center of the intersection, marked with yellow crime scene tape, and with NYPD sawhorses ten feet on either side of the cordoned-off square of pavement where Skeppy's blood was still soaking into the concrete.

Repetto stood with Meg on East Fifty-fifth Street and looked out at the intersection where Skeppy had lain. There wasn't much to say, because most of it was beyond words. The investigation had become intermittent, tragic routine. Melbourne had no trouble procuring uniformed officers, who were already canvassing neighboring buildings. Eventually they'd find where the Night Sniper had concealed himself while aiming at Skeppy and squeezing the trigger. It would tell them nothing. Perhaps there would be a smeared print from a latex glove, or faint evidence of someone kneeling or standing. They might even figure out where the Sniper had rested the barrel of his rifle to steady it. None of this would lead anywhere they hadn't been.

"We learn only what he wants us to learn," Repetto said.

Meg looked at him, not liking the expression on his face. "He's controlling the game."

"We have to figure out how to get control away from him."

"We'll find a way," she said.

"It's reached the point where he tells us what he's going to do, and we still can't stop him."

"The rich man, poor man nursery rhyme . . . maybe we shouldn't have given that to the media."

"They'd have it anyway," Repetto said. "What the NYPD does world-class is leak."

Meg had to agree. It had even leaked her phone number and e-mail address to Alex.

Repetto's cell phone chirped, and he pulled it out of his pocket and answered. The flip-up phone seemed toylike in his big hand as he pressed it to his ear.

As he spoke, he absently drifted away from Meg, not as if he didn't want her to overhear, more because of an impetus to walk and talk at the same time, as if one made the other easier.

Within a few minutes, he broke the connection and she saw him slip the phone back in his pocket. He looked around as if he'd just awakened and found himself ten feet away from her.

"That was Birdy," he said, when he'd returned to stand in front of her. "Mrs. Michael Skeppy's been told."

"Jesus!" was all Meg could think of to say. How must it feel to answer the phone or open your door and *know*, and then be told? Like drowning, Meg thought. It must feel like drowning.

"She's in a lot of pain," Repetto said, "not making much sense."

"What happened to her doesn't make much sense. Did Birdy break the news to her?"

"No. Melbourne did. But Birdy accompanied him. She'd already heard on the radio about a cop being shot, and she had a feeling it was her husband."

Meg wondered if every cop's spouse or lover who'd heard the news had experienced that feeling.

"Birdy did find out one thing," Repetto said. "He checked the public record to make sure it was true. The Skeppy family filed for bankruptcy two weeks ago."

Meg stared out at the yellow crime scene tape flapping in the wind and cordoning off where Michael Skeppy had died. Hallowed ground for another half hour or so, until the sawhorses were picked up and the tape removed. The thought sent a twist of pain through her. "Rich man, poor man . . ."

"I'm getting tired of that one," Repetto said with a quiet anger. "Have you heard the one about how an honest cop is a poor cop?"

"I've heard it," Meg said. "The rest of it is, *But he sleeps well.*"

"We can hope Michael Skeppy's sleeping well," Repetto said, "because it's going to be forever."

Bobby Mays had dozed off seated on his coat spread out on the sidewalk, his back against a brick wall. It was early evening. He hadn't begged enough money to pay for his prescription medicine, but he knew where he could buy a single Ambien to help keep the demons at bay.

The pills had worked well enough before, but they made him sleepy. He'd taken his last one this morning, but its effects were wearing off. Now he was wide awake, with a fierce headache, and with a terrible taste along the edges of his tongue. His legs, his pelvis, were numb. He wished he had a watch so he could know how long he'd slept sitting up against the building.

Bobby observed the people walking past. They didn't return his gaze. He looked at the streetlights, the sparse traffic. The evening was warm, but hadn't it been warmer when he sat down? He remembered taking up position on the sidewalk about seven o'clock. Now it *felt* much later than that.

He shifted his weight slightly to confirm that he was too numb and stiff to stand up right away. The way he was sitting now, though, circulation would return in his lower body and he'd soon have some mobility. The back of his thumb made contact with something, and he looked down to see his coffee mug. There were some crinkled dollar bills in it, and bright loose change visible at the bottom.

That was as good a measure of time as he had, so he picked up the cup and counted the money.

Four dollars and sixty cents, in bills and change. And something else. He felt and traced the familiar contours with his fingers.

An empty shell casing. As sure as he was sitting here.

He glanced down and saw the brass color in his hand.

A shell casing.

Then he looked more closely. The object wasn't brass at all. It was copper. A copper penny. His fingers, his mind, had played a trick on him again. It was happening more often.

The object even felt different now. It felt exactly like a coin. Why hadn't it felt like a coin before?

Bobby threw the penny away in despair, hearing it nick off the sidewalk. A woman striding past glanced down at him in alarm and picked up her pace, unconsciously clutching her purse closer to her side.

Bobby looked past her, across the street, and there was the raggedy man who walked with too much purpose. The homeless man who didn't belong even in that anguished and desperate society. The man was moving too fast, with his gaze fixed straight ahead—not glancing around, not wary. *Not right. He doesn't fit. Bobby knows. Bobby's got the eye.*

Had the eye.

This time Bobby wouldn't let himself be taken in. He couldn't deny the evidence that he hadn't been thinking straight lately. He'd been losing yesterdays, imagining todays. This wouldn't be like the shell casing that turned out to be a bullet. No, a penny. A coin that felt like something shaped completely unlike a coin.

How could my mind do that to me?

As he watched, the raggedy man went down the steps of a subway stop and disappeared.

He was there; then he was gone.

That was when Bobby was sure the man wasn't real, because the subway stop was closed.

37

"C'mon, Dante! The girls are waiting!"

Orvey was eager to leave. The ranch was holding what had become its annual mixer, an outdoor dance in the cool December Arizona evening. The girls from across the arroyo would be there, along with a five-piece band trucked in from Tucson. Strong had determined that all his charges on the ranch would learn to dance at least well enough to negotiate a crowded floor. This dance floor wouldn't be crowded, but there'd be few standing and watching instead of struggling to keep time with the amateur band's persistent tempo.

Dante didn't bother answering Orvey. He finished brushing his teeth, then rinsed out his mouth with Listerene to ensure good breath. Wiping his lips with a towel, he smiled at himself in the mirror. A tanned, handsome youth smiled back at him. In fact, dressed as he was in a blazer and tie, his black wig perfectly adjusted to blend with his sideburns, Dante was incredibly handsome. Possibly knowing the pain caused in his young life by circumstances, then by hideous scarring, the surgeons had gone too far, made him somehow too attractive. His were the kind of features that graced movie posters and romantic fantasies of foolish girls.

Verna wasn't foolish and didn't think Dante was too attractive. She'd made it clear she'd be waiting for him tonight and expected the first—and the last—dance. This was the closest thing to a date the protective and puritanical Strong would allow.

The other boys were jealous but didn't act on it. Dante, with his accomplishments and new handsomeness, had reached a place in their estimation where he was untouchable. And if anyone did cause pain or even inconvenience for Dante, they would have to deal with Adam Strong.

Strong made no secret of his favoritism when it came to Dante. He even from time to time slipped and referred to him as his son. He figured Dante, unlike Strong himself, had earned the hard way everything he had.

Dante's long and often agonizing series of cosmetic surgeries to restore his burned features had been at the Strong Foundation's expense. The result was the handsome reflection in the mirror. The effect could be ruined only if he removed his wig. Because of his burns, hair grew only over half his skull. Unless he kept his head cleanly shaved, the odd pattern of hair growth was obvious and, along with the unusual smooth texture of his flesh, gave the definite impression that he hadn't been born with his good looks. Rather than shave his head almost daily, Dante often wore a wig.

Despite the nearly perfect image in the mirror, he sometimes looked more closely and could see beneath the surface of his new flesh and form. If he failed to look away, the old Dante emerged through the thin surface flesh and grinned hideously at him, and sometimes wept.

That was happening less often lately, but still it was happening.

Not tonight, though.

Not tonight.

"C'mon, Dante!"

Orvey again.

Dante switched off the bathroom light and hurried through the barracks and outside to join the other boys.

There were half a dozen of them, lounging around in sloppily knotted ties, and blazers that didn't quite fit, all waiting for Dante. They seemed oblivious of the moths circling and darting around them in the pool of light cast by the barracks' outside fixture. Hanley, a skinny six-footer from South Carolina, was smoking a cigarette, keeping it cupped in his hand so the ember wouldn't be visible, fooling no one.

"You busy jerkin' off or somethin'?" Orvey asked jokingly. The others laughed. "We're already late."

"What's it matter?" Hanley asked. "Who else they gonna dance with?"

"You guys don't wanna go, I'll dance with all of 'em," someone said.

Dante didn't bother joining the banter.

With his friends, his admirers, he strolled through the cooling evening toward the distant music, voices, and softly hued light from colored paper lanterns, toward Verna and a dream almost real.

In the years that followed, nothing could stop Dante. Perhaps it was the successful surgery—that certainly had to help. But he grew in confidence and ability every year. He graduated from Nailsville High School with honors, then left the ranch to attend Arizona State University. Weekends he drove home from college in the old Ford pickup Strong had given him and stayed at the ranch.

Maintaining a 4.0 grade point average was no problem, and Dante dated as often as he chose. But it was still Verna he thought of and saw most often. She planned on remaining at the ranch until she began college next year, when she thought she'd be psychologically strong enough to go out on her own, attending the same school as Dante. He'd already made up his mind that if she weren't accepted, he'd go to school elsewhere, so they could be together.

It was a rainy weeknight, and Dante was stretched out on his bunk in his dorm room, reading *Ecce Romani*, when he took Adam Strong's phone call.

As soon as he heard the tone of Strong's voice, Dante sat up and the book hit the floor. He suspected something was wrong, but he would never have guessed what. He was afraid to guess.

"Verna has left the ranch, Dante."

Dante lay back, stunned. "Left? Why?"

"She went to live with relatives."

"She doesn't have any living relatives."

"Apparently she does."

"Where?" Dante's questions were automatic; he was still trying to digest this.

"She'd rather keep it a secret."

Relatives. Verna had never talked about relatives. None she cared about, anyway, or who cared about her. "So where were these relatives when she needed them?"

"Not helping her as they should have. But that's beside the point. They want to help her now."

"When she doesn't need their help."

"She needs it, Dante. She's going to have a baby."

Dante's mind whirled. Each time he'd made love with Verna he'd used a condom. She'd also taken birth control pills. They both knew how an early, unwanted pregnancy could alter their lives. Neither wanted to take the chance.

But nothing was perfect. *God! A baby! Maybe one of the condoms—*"

"Orvey's left the ranch, too, Dante."

It took Dante a few seconds to grasp what Strong had told him. "You mean with Verna?"

"No. Maybe that's what he should have done. He said he didn't have it in him, that he was afraid and couldn't make it. And Verna didn't want him. I think probably they were both right."

"Damn it!" Dante said. He kept repeating it, slamming his fist into his pillow.

Strong must have heard the softened blows over the phone. "You want to come back to the ranch for a few days, Dante? Your grades can take it."

"You sure Orvey isn't with Verna?"

"He went the opposite direction." There was disdain in Strong's voice.

"Then Verna's all alone with this."

"It's how she wants it. And she's got family, Dante."

"I oughta . . . God, I don't know!"

"She doesn't want to see you again. She's thought it out. You've gotta respect her wishes, Dante. She . . . left a letter for you. I mailed it yesterday, figuring once I did that, I'd get up the courage to call you rather than have you read it cold. It should be in today's mail."

"Damn it, Adam!" Dante couldn't hold back the sobs any longer.

"C'mon home, son. Come home to the ranch."

Dante didn't answer until he got his gasping sobs under control. He felt cold, but he noticed with surprise that his hands were sweating, slippery on the phone. "This weekend," he said. "I can't get there till this weekend. I've got a big calculus test."

"Whatever you want," Strong said. He sounded as if he might start sobbing himself.

"Goddamn that Orvey! Why the fuck—"

"You've gotta get used to it, Dante. It's something that

happened. A part of life you've got no choice but to learn to live with."

"Don't I know it?"

"You gonna be okay there by yourself?"

"I've always been okay by myself."

"Dante, that's not right. You don't have to think like that anymore."

"I know, Adam." Dante wiped his nose with the back of his wrist. "Thanks for calling and letting me know."

"I wish it hadn't been necessary. I sure as hell do."

Though his eyes brimmed with tears, Dante had to smile. Adam Strong using profanity. It didn't happen very often. That touched Dante more than anything.

Verna, Orvey, they didn't just mess themselves up; even if they didn't mean to, they hurt a lot of people, caused so much pain. It might go on for years.

A part of life . . .

"Thanks again," Dante said softly, and hung up.

He felt so much older lying there. Like an old man who'd somehow found himself in a young man's room. He realized he'd been old the first day he arrived at the ranch. Too much of him had died after his father killed his mother.

He'd begun to die when the gun his father aimed at him clicked on a bullet that hadn't fired.

Verna's letter wasn't in that afternoon's mail, but it arrived the next day. Dante didn't open it. He knew why Verna didn't want him, the only reason it could be: she'd seen beneath the thin new skin to the old Dante, the real Dante. He'd stared into the mirror last night and seen the real Dante himself, like sharp bones pushing through the flesh of a corpse.

He used both hands to crumple the unopened envelope

with Verna's handwriting on it into as small a damaged object as possible, then dropped it in one of the trash receptacles that were placed around the campus.

Verna was simply something that had happened.

Something in the past.

38

The present

This time when the Night Sniper's simple typed note bearing a theater seat number arrived in Repetto's mail, they didn't have to waste time figuring out which theater.

"This is it," Repetto said, standing up from his desk chair and showing Meg and Birdy the note. "Let's go."

"Where?" Meg asked, replacing the plastic lid she'd just removed from her Styrofoam coffee cup. She'd been prepared to sit at her desk, get her caffeine fix, and work the phones.

"We don't have to play by his rules this time." Repetto pointed to the *Times* on his desk, open to the page with theater listings.

Meg and Birdy looked. A play at the off-off Broadway theater Candle in the Night was circled: *Beg, Borrow, or Steal.*

"If he stays true to form, the Night Sniper's next victim's going to be the beggar man," Repetto said.

"Big *if*, with this sicko," Birdy said.

"Everything is," Repetto said. "That's one way he yanks our strings. But this is the only play listed with 'beg' in the title. It might not be the only place we have to search, but it should be the first."

Fast and sure, when he decided it was time to move, Meg thought. It was one reason she respected Repetto.

He was already on his way out.

Meg and Birdy followed, Meg taking a hurried sip from where the tab was bent back on her cup's plastic lid and scalding her tongue.

Candle in the Night was located in SoHo, in what used to be a restaurant. Repetto remembered having dinner there years ago with Lora and one of her clients, who was writing a book about cops and pumped him for information. There were show posters outside it now, advertising *Beg, Borrow, or Steal.* One of them featured the play's stars, a handsome young guy wearing spiked hair and a tuxedo, who was handing a necklace to a beautiful young woman with platinum-blond hair and oversize blue eyes. Repetto noticed her name was Tiffany something. Near the bottom of the poster was a *Village Voice* review blurb that said, *Delightful . . . clever . . . scintillating.*

The theater was larger than it appeared from outside. Stepped wooden platforms had been installed to provide unobstructed seating. The stage was narrow and seemed to be at a slight angle to the audience. There was lots of lighting equipment in shadows overhead, and the set, what appeared to be an English drawing room or club, was surprisingly professional and richly detailed.

The seats on each side of a center aisle were a bit worn looking and had probably been acquired when an older, larger theater uptown had been renovated or demolished. They were bolted to the plywood risers and still clearly numbered.

Repetto led the way to 12-F, the number in the Night Sniper's note, and raised the seat to check beneath it.

He looked, felt.

"Nothing."

"I think you better talk to Irv," a voice said.

Repetto turned and saw Jack Straithorn, the young production manager who'd met them at the theater entrance to admit them. Lurking behind Straithorn was a short, potbellied man in a gray work outfit that was too tight on him everywhere. He had a slightly crooked, smarmy smile that Repetto figured stayed stuck to him even when he slept. Irv, Repetto assumed.

Correctly. "I found this 'bout twenty minutes ago when I was sweepin' up," Irv said, holding out a tightly folded scrap of paper. "Had some tape on it, but I tore it off."

Meg moved out of the way so Repetto could accept the note from Irv. He thought about lecturing the man on tampering with evidence but figured it would serve no purpose.

"I was gonna call you guys," Irv said, reading Repetto's mind.

Repetto simply nodded as he unfolded the note and read: *The show will go on.*

He handed the note to Meg, who read it with Birdy peering over her shoulder.

"So what's it mean?" Birdy asked.

"Irv looked at the note earlier," Straithorn said in a voice spiked with irony. He made a theatrical motion toward Irv, who was smirking.

"Means he's gonna kill again," Irv said. "There's gonna be another act, and ain't nothin' nobody can do to stop it."

* * *

The Night Sniper stood at a bus stop down the block, watching the entrance to Candle in the Night, with its make-shift marquee and movielike glassed show-poster frames. He was wearing a black beret and the Madre Verdi sun-glasses he'd bought last year on the *Costa del Sol*. The glass's lenses were dark green mirrors on the outside, but he could see out quite clearly.

Meg Doyle emerged from the theater first. Then Repetto and Birdy Bellman. The opposition. The Night Sniper smiled. They thought they were taking control, having figured out early this time which theater to go to and find his message. They didn't know he'd been waiting for them here.

A bus rumbled up and he moved back, making it clear to the driver that there was no need to stop.

But there had been a need. The bus's air brakes hissed, and it pulled up to the curb. Its rear door opened and a large woman laden with plastic shopping bags stepped down onto the sidewalk. The woman stood with her feet far apart and looked around, as if trying to orient herself, then walked swiftly away in the opposite direction from where the Night Sniper stood. She'd only glanced over toward where he stood and paid him little attention. The bus roared and belched foul exhaust fumes, then lumbered away.

Repetto and his team were still standing in front of the theater. It looked as if they were studying the message that had been taped beneath the theater seat. Repetto was holding what appeared to be a slip of paper while Meg was pointing to it and talking. When she was finished, Birdy Bellman began to speak. Repetto was the listener. It amused the Night Sniper to see them standing there discussing his message. If they only knew, they could simply walk half a block down and discuss it with the man in the dark beret and sunglasses. If they only knew.

Repetto refolded the message, then slipped it into what looked like a plastic folder—an evidence bag—and slid it

into an inside pocket of his sport coat. When the coat
flapped open, the Night Sniper got a brief view of a handgun
in a tan leather shoulder holster.

The three detectives crossed the street toward a white
Ford sedan, their unmarked car for the day. Detective Meg
got in behind the steering wheel. Repetto sat up front on the
passenger side, Bellman in the rear.

The Night Sniper watched as the car's tailpipe emitted
faint dancing fumes. A few seconds later it pulled away from
the curb.

He had his own car parked nearby, but he made no attempt to follow. He'd come here to make sure they'd figured
out the correct theater, that they were moving along the tracks
he'd laid. Mission accomplished. Anyway, he knew where all
three of the detectives lived, knew more about them than
they dreamed. If he wanted them, he could find them.

Right now, he didn't want to find them. He had other
things to do.

He glanced at his watch and began walking down the
block at a brisk pace. He had a luncheon engagement, and he
didn't want to be late.

Zoe's apartment this time. Her new lover wasn't only
handsome, he somehow knew precisely what she wanted,
and how much and when and where. She lay on her back, her
bare legs clamped around his sweating body as he thrust into
her again and again. Her arms were twisted over her head
and somehow he managed to clasp both her wrists together
with one powerful hand as he skillfully altered his rhythm
and force so she remained on the edge of her third orgasm.
Each time she almost climaxed he tightened his grip on her
arms so the brief pain brought her back; then he slowly
began to take her up again. The bedsprings sang as if in
accompaniment to the internal crescendos of her body. Even

as she lay there suffering so wonderfully, a part of her thought that he must have a lot of experience to be so good at this.

He drove into her harder and more determinedly, relentlessly, and she knew that this time he would let her reach the peak.

Afterward she was too exhausted to move. He released her limp arms, kissed her perspiring forehead, then unwound her legs from around him and rolled off to lie beside her. The ceiling fan played cool air over the length of her sweat-damp body. She felt empty. Spent. When she tried to speak, she was unable to find words. She turned to him, and as if expecting it, he kissed her lips, then the tip of her nose, and lay back. It was like a routine he'd practiced.

"You're all right?" he asked.

"Better than," she said, her breath still ragged.

He propped himself up on an elbow and gazed down at her. "You're a wonderful creation, Zoe." She felt his hand slide over her left breast, gently squeezing her nipple, then moving lower.

"I'm a creation that's going to be late for work," she told him with a weak smile, grasping his wrist.

He immediately withdrew his hand, knowing when not to pressure her. "Want to shower together?"

"I should say no, but I won't."

"That's my Zoe."

She was, of course, much later getting back to her office than she'd planned.

She also hadn't planned on drinking a martini and two glasses of wine at lunch, then going to her apartment and getting her brains fucked out. The drinks they'd taken into the shower hadn't helped, either. She was sure she no longer smelled of sex, and wasn't tipsy enough for anyone to notice, but it wouldn't hurt if she had about an hour alone in her private office to let the effects of the afternoon wear off.

After telling her assistant she wasn't to be disturbed, es-

pecially not for phone calls, she closed her office door and
went to her desk. She had to be especially wary of the phone,
since she might unintentionally slur a word. Settling back in
her leather desk chair, she sighed. Now she was getting
sleepy. Great.

*Resolution: No more love in the afternoon. It's all too . . .
inebriating.*

She caught herself smiling and felt a twinge of anger.
What was she thinking? It made more sense to chastise herself. She covered her face with her hands, which were unexpectedly cool.

*Damn, I didn't want this to happen today. Where was my
vaunted willpower? Am I sorry it happened? Of course not.
Okay, then. You've been a big girl for a long while. Stop your
bitching, Zoe. Self-recrimination is nothing if not self-
defeating.*

How does he do this to me?

Peeking through her fingertips, she saw a file folder on
her desk that hadn't been there when she left . . . over two
hours ago.

She leaned forward and opened the folder. Repetto had
sent her a copy of the latest Night Sniper theater note, as
they'd agreed. It had been located in a theater called Candle
in the Night. She picked up the note and read. *The show will
go on.*

She smiled. Substitute "game" for "show." He was taunting them now. The note was the kind of thing that must make
Repetto furious. He was like so many of the old-time, hard-
ass cops. Dinosaurs. Too proud for their own good.

But one thing about them was, they never gave up. Never.
And when it came to focused and applied obsession, Repetto
was their leader.

Zoe sat back in her comfortable leather desk chair and
wondered if the Night Sniper truly understood that about
Repetto. Repetto might seem primal, but he was locked onto

his target like a heat-seeking missile, and the Night Sniper was burning hotter and hotter with his own detectable obsession.

She fell asleep wondering.

Some of the actors who played at Candle in the Night ate regularly at the diner on the corner. Like most actors, they'd had their hard times, and they knew homeless Joe DeLong and helped him out whenever they could. Joe had told them he'd been an actor himself long ago. He knew they didn't believe him. But then they couldn't completely *dis*-believe him.

Joe would do his panhandling across the street from the diner, a bit diagonally so the people in the window booths wouldn't have to look at him whenever they glanced outside. At the same time, he wanted people to know he was there. Often, after the ten o'clock curtain for whatever was playing now at the theater, half a dozen of the actors, including Tiffany Taft, the star, would make their way to the diner for a late-night snack.

Tiffany was in her twenties, with bright blond hair and wide blue eyes to go with a gorgeous figure. Not scrawny like a model, but with lots of curves, the way Joe liked his women. Whenever he thought about women these days. He'd studied her on the blown-up photo on the show poster in front of the theater. He liked the sassy way she stood, with her knees locked and her rear end stuck out. He liked the way she pouted up her little mouth. There wasn't much he didn't like about Tiffany.

And she must like him, at least a little. She'd smiled at him once. And when she ate at the diner, he could count on her leaving a white takeout container on top of the trash receptacle on the corner.

After they'd all departed, Joe would pick up the takeout boxes left by the actors, but he was always careful to know which one was Tiffany's. She sometimes left him almost complete portions. Once he'd even found a chocolate after-dinner mint in with some untouched pizza slices.

At times Joe thought that if he weren't so fucked-up, he'd approach Tiffany, introduce himself properly, and try to get to know her. As it was, he'd probably frighten her to death, and that would be the end of the takeout containers. It didn't matter. He wasn't ever going to talk to her unless the voices informed him it was okay to do so.

Every night, or so it seemed to him, Joe would sit on the curb near the Aal Commerce Building, an ornate, iron-fronted structure on Broadway. High on the building was a tall metal antenna with a light on top that blinked red in the darkness. No voices emitted from the antenna during the day, but at night, when Joe sat on the curb leaning his back against the light post, the transmission would be just for him. Some of the voices even referred to him by name. They warned him who to watch out for, who was on the side of his enemies. Tiffany, the voices assured him, was not one of the rude people that made his life, and the lives of countless others, so difficult.

Joe DeLong's schizophrenia hadn't presented itself until he was in his early twenties—about the usual age for males, he'd learned later. The disease ran in his family, on his mother's side, so he shouldn't have been surprised. His uncle Roger had spent most of his life in a sanitarium in Virginia, and Great-Aunt Vi, whom he'd never met, was rumored to have committed suicide when she ran her car into a bridge abutment on her way to see her psychiatrist. But schizophrenia was a subject seldom discussed in Joe's family. His wife, Eva, had never heard the word in his presence until three years into their marriage, when Joe became difficult and she had to turn to someone for help. After her phone conversation with his mother came the first visit to the psychiatrist.

When the disease struck, it struck hard. It shook Joe's life and turned it upside down. Medication helped, the increasing dosages of lithium, but he couldn't remember to take his medicine every time. You had to do that, take it every time you were supposed to. It said so in the instructions right on the vials or bottles, even though you were too sick to pay much attention, which was why you needed the medicine. Sometimes the voices helped him to remember. They gave him guidance.

The job went first. Who needed a phone solicitor who might say anything at any time, and to anyone? Eva left him; then Joe drove wedge after wedge between himself and the rest of his family. He began deliberately refusing his medication. Alcohol was almost as good. Alcohol was more socially acceptable than mental illness. Alcohol temporarily relieved the fear. But alcohol was sneaky, invented by the enemy. Alcohol exacted its price.

After one of the increasingly frequent arguments with his mother, and a fistfight with his father, Joe left home for good with nothing but a suitcase full of clothes and a wallet containing almost a thousand dollars—all the money left in his savings account.

The money lasted less than a month, as Joe sank deeper into alcoholism. Some of it went for booze and rent, and some even went for food. Hamburgers and French fries at first, then canned stew, then watery soup.

When there was no more money, he left the fleabag hotel where he'd been sleeping and began his life on the streets. It wasn't as if he had a choice. He was broke, and the voices said his family, even if he *had* wanted to talk to them, were away somewhere on a ship. Eva was married now to a surgeon in Warsaw. The voices spoke of him as "the sawbones in Warsaw." Joe always smiled when he heard that.

Joe's luck didn't last much longer than his money. He was mugged one night in Washington Square and walked thereafter with a slight limp. The pain never left his right hip.

Wine helped that, when he had enough money to buy some. The wine dulled the pain and helped to keep his mind from shattering. The food left by the Candle in the Night actors helped to keep his body from destroying itself. The voices said that's what the body did when it couldn't get enough to eat: it digested itself. Joe often had bad dreams about that.

When the weather was nice, like this time of year, he didn't think it was such a terrible life there on the streets. He'd perfected techniques for panhandling, for begging directly to carefully chosen fellow citizens. He could tell by their shoes, sometimes by their aura, if they'd part with some pocket change. Often enough, he was right. He took an odd kind of pride in being an effective beggar. Pride in what he did for money. That was a part of his soul that begging couldn't smear.

Joe had in his possession about a third of a bottle of Pheaser's Phine Burgundy. Now and then he'd duck into a doorway and take a carefully controlled sip. He suspected that when the wine ran out, his luck for the day would run out at the same time. He didn't want that to happen before the actors came out of the diner and left their takeout containers. He was hungry.

So far, he wasn't worried. The voices had predicted he'd be hungry. Joe laughed and spat on the sidewalk. That was an easy call. Sometimes he wished he could talk back to the voices and actually record their conversation and play it back over and over. But, if he wasn't mistaken, something about that was against the law.

It was almost midnight when the actors emerged from the diner. Joe had been seated on the second step of the dark doorway he would occasionally back into to take sips of wine. He didn't move when they came out the diner door, talking and laughing. His heart fell when he saw no white containers. Most of the actors had on dark clothes, like people wore in New York, as if they were mourning, and if they'd had containers, he would have seen them.

This wasn't right! This was goddamned—

There was a flash of white against Tiffany's dark jacket.

Yes! She was carrying a takeout container between her coat and her black purse. That was why Joe hadn't seen it.

When the cluster of actors reached the corner, then crossed without waiting for the traffic signal to change, Tiffany unobtrusively and daintily placed the container on top of the day's trash in the wire receptacle.

Joe stood trembling, waiting until the shadowy figures had disappeared in vaster darkness down the street; then he hurried toward the trash receptacle.

It was going to be a good night after all.

39

After Verna's departure, Dante applied himself all the harder. He focused on himself, on what he could and would do, and thought of the past as what it was—something that no longer existed. It was a delicate and protective attitude, but one he could maintain. If only he didn't have bad dreams.

He graduated magna cum laude from ASU in three years, then promptly earned his MBA from the Wharton School. Corporate recruiters saw him as prime cut. A month before his graduation from Wharton, he had a position secured as a bond analyst in the Chicago financial firm of Koch and Banks.

Dante liked Chicago and was soon making a six-figure salary. Koch and Banks profited from his talents, and was generous in its bonuses and stock options. Investing was a game he found incredibly simple, and his own holdings grew exponentially. He wasn't yet as rich as he wanted to be, but only because he hadn't had time. For Dante, money wasn't going to be a problem.

At least once a month he returned to the Strong Ranch

and saw Adam. His mentor and surrogate father couldn't have been more proud of Dante, and was still providing a kind of permanent home both physically and spiritually. Though he lived in a luxurious Lakeside Drive penthouse apartment, the ranch remained Dante's still point in the universe, where he could always retreat to and regenerate himself when life became difficult.

On one of these visits, when Dante was temporarily escaping a bitter Chicago winter for the warmth of the Arizona sun, Strong seemed markedly older and unlike his usual self. During their stint at the target range, he'd missed almost a quarter of his shots.

Their rifles propped in the crooks of their arms, the two men were walking side by side toward Strong's dusty, three-year-old Ford pickup. It was a walk they'd taken together many times, and usually it soothed Dante's soul. This was how he always saw Adam in his mind, striding tall and powerful alongside him, rifle or shotgun broken down and slung over his shoulder or, as today, cradled in the crook of an elbow. The Arizona heat, the sun, the dust he could feel when he licked his teeth, the vast expanse of sky stretching to distant mountain ranges, it was all part of why he came here. It was reassuring to Dante. It fed the soul.

"You're quiet, Adam," Dante said, "even for you."

One, two, three paces before Strong spoke: "I suppose I should tell you things aren't going well, Dante."

Feeling a cold dread, Dante glanced over at him but didn't break stride. "Your health?"

"No."

"Good. Then whatever it is, it's not serious."

"Oh, it's serious, all right. Most of my money—the ranch's money—was invested in Global Venue."

Dante stopped and stood still. Global Venue was a publicly traded capital management firm that controlled the resources of major clients, including some of the country's largest pension funds. Global had hedged its clients' billions of dollars in investments with complex money rate plays, and in an ironic, and illegal, round-robin sequence, with some of Global's own stock. The company was under federal investigation. Most of its major clients had left, and Global stock had plunged almost 90 percent and would soon be delisted from the New York Stock Exchange.

"You mean Global Venue was investing some of your money for you?" Dante asked.

"Not exactly. I figured I wasn't smart enough to place my eggs in different baskets myself, so I thought it'd be simplest to buy GV stock. When the trouble started with the government, the accusations and indictments, I kept thinking the stock would stop falling, that I could recoup at least some of my losses. This was one of the biggest companies in the world, Dante. It was about to become one of the Dow Thirty."

Dante rested a hand on his rifle's warm walnut stock and shook his head sadly. "I don't need to tell you, you can't sell *was about to*."

Adam looked off to the left where a turkey vulture circled in the blue void beyond the ranch house. "They're right when they say the hardest thing about investing's knowing when to sell."

"I . . . we never talked about it, Adam. I knew about your wealth and assumed you were a sophisticated investor, or that what you had was in a trust."

"I took it out of the trust some years ago, when I saw so many people I knew getting rich overnight on tech stocks. Thought I could build up some wealth and put it in the ranch. Even managed to do that some. You notice the new dam and culvert to divert water when the arroyo floods?"

Dante had noticed. He figured the object was to eventually create a lake. "You had tech stocks when the bubble burst?"

"Quite a few of the biggest losers. Peanuts compared to

Global Venue stock, though. I'm ashamed to tell you what percentage of my holdings were in that single stock, in a company I thought was internally diversified enough to protect me."

"You're not the only one who made that miscalculation about Global. Lots of smart people rode it up and rode it all the way down. Do you still own the stock?"

"Yeah. Most of it. For what it's worth."

Dante knew it was worth about five dollars per share and falling. A little over a year ago, Global Venue's stock price had been over eighty dollars per share.

"I've been selling my shares off a little at a time to keep the ranch going. We've got eleven kids here now, and three more on the way." Strong quit staring at the distant vulture and looked at Dante. "You think there's any chance the stock'll come back?"

Dante shifted his weight in the hot sun, not wanting to answer. "It won't come back. Global's going down for corporate malfeasance. When the regulators and lawyers are finished with it, some board members will be sent to prison and the government's gonna dismantle the company. If you hang on to the stock, you might receive par value."

"Next to nothing."

"About a dime a share. That's if there's anything left after bondholders and preferred stockholders take their meager cuts. My guess is none of you is going to get even the dime."

"So I should get out?"

Dante smiled sadly. "You should." He felt a dark remorse move through him, and an ugly guilt. He'd been paying so much attention to his own affairs, he'd never discussed Adam's with him. It had seemed like two different worlds, Chicago and the ranch. Dante had always assumed Adam was well invested, that he'd brought the same common sense and prudence to managing his wealth as he exhibited in every other facet of his life. Dante should have known better. He'd learned that when it came to money, people weren't always in character. He could have prevented this.

"Even after I sell," Strong said, "I'll be down to my last hundred thousand."

"That's something."

"Not much. The ranch is an investment that eats hay, as they say in this part of the country. And the bank's pressuring me on some loan payments. I'm afraid I'm not good for more than a few more months."

"*Months?*"

Strong could only swallow. He looked back toward where the buzzard had been circling. There was only empty sky.

"We can't let that happen, Adam!"

"I wish to God I knew how to prevent it."

"You've taken the first step, Adam. You confided in me."

Strong smiled. "I always loved your grit, but not everything's possible. And the last thing I'd do on earth is borrow money from you, Dante. Not that anything other than a financial transfusion from a small country would help."

"Sometimes it's hard to know what will help. You're right, I'm doing well, but much of it's in options that are locked up for the next few years. I don't have the kind of money that would bail out the ranch. But I want to see your books, Adam. A financial statement. Everything.*"*

"Dante—"

"This is what I do, Adam. And nobody's better at it. I want to help. I owe it to you, and we both know that's a fact."

Strong stared hard at the ground, chewing the inside of his cheek. Then he reached out and clutched Dante's shoulder and squeezed. "All right, Dante. Thank you. I won't be proud."

"Bullshit!" Dante snapped. "You can be proud."

* * *

Dante had been prophetic. After months of negative publicity, then indictments and a long series of trials, Global Venue was dismantled. Shareholders of the common stock received nothing.

Dante had reallocated the foundation's investments, and was beginning to pump financial lifeblood back into the ranch, but no one could have planned for the events of September 11. The terrorist attacks, and the resultant reaction in the markets, devastated the rest of Adam Strong's holdings.

There was enough remaining to keep the ranch solvent awhile longer, but while most of the market gradually rebounded, Wall Street seemed to have turned against Adam. Even the skills of Dante Vanya couldn't prevent foreclosure.

Adam Strong was ruined. Dante could only watch, and bear some of the responsibility.

40

The present

Joe DeLong waited until Tiffany and the rest of the Candle in the Night cast members had clambered into two cabs that had arrived outside the diner.

The cab's taillights flared red, then drew close together and disappeared as the vehicles turned the corner. Joe stepped out of the shadows. The street seemed so silent and empty after the cabs' departure. It was no surprise. Even Joe, who never watched TV news and seldom read a newspaper or magazine, knew why the streets were less crowded than usual after dark. He'd heard snatches of conversation, and sometimes Tiffany left a folded newspaper with the takeout box, knowing Joe could use it to insulate his thin clothing if the night grew cool. Even if you only used newspaper to wrap fish or help stay warm, it was difficult not to have read at least something about the Night Sniper.

Joe waited for his hip to stop aching from standing so long in the dark doorway; then he shuffled along the sidewalk in the direction the cabs had gone. He'd seen Tiffany leave the group outside the diner and walk down to the corner where the trash receptacle sat near the traffic signal. He knew where she was going; she'd often done this before for him. He'd watched as she placed a takeout container on top of the day's refuse before hurrying back to the others.

And there was the takeout box, one of the square flat kind, resting right on top of the trash that filled half the wire container. He reached down and lifted the white foam box, surprised by its weight.

When he opened it, he smiled. Inside were two large slices of pizza, the thick-crusted kind with sausage and mushrooms. They were still warm. Joe had been hungry; now the aroma of the pizza made him ravenous.

He moved away from the brightly lit corner, wolfing down the pizza as he walked, then sat on the concrete steps of a boarded-up shop halfway down the block and licked his fingers before starting on the cloverleaf roll that was in the box with the pizza. If only he had something to drink, a cold beer, life would be perfect for a while. That was all other people had, Joe knew, a perfect moment now and then in an imperfect world.

It wasn't so late that he couldn't walk to where there were more people, then set up on the sidewalk and wait for contributions. Or maybe he could use the ethnic approach, walk up to someone who was obviously Jewish or Asian or Hispanic and plead for enough money to buy chicken soup or chop suey or a burrito. Of course, what Joe would buy was a bottle. Beer if it was all he could afford, wine if he got lucky.

He was about to stand up and set out for brighter, busier streets when the voices began. They were trying to tell him something, but it was as if they were speaking another language. It was a language Joe knew, if only he could focus his thoughts.

He decided to make his way to the Aal Commerce Building and sit beneath its tower.

Maybe there he could understand the voices.

The Night Sniper decided not to interrupt the beggar's last meal. Besides, where the Sniper was set up to fire the fatal shot, it would be better if the target came closer. For several nights the Sniper had observed the beggar and knew his habits. When the destitute man had eaten his fill and did get up to go elsewhere, the odds were he'd move in this direction, toward the waiting rifle. And if he did happen to set out in the other direction, the shot would be only slightly more difficult. A second bullet might be necessary.

The beggar set aside the white takeout box and sat with his head bowed, as if listening to something. Then he stood up slowly, as he always did, and waited for the stiffness in his body to abate, as he always did, and began walking.

With the odds. With fate.

Toward death.

The Night Sniper steadied the rifle and sighted through the night scope at the slowly approaching figure on the dark street below. The night was still, and the target was walking so slowly and at such a slight angle, it was almost unnecessary to lead him.

The Sniper was patient. He'd sense when the moment arrived, when his finger should tighten ever so slightly on the trigger, almost of its own volition.

Patience . . . patience . . .

Once he sighted in, the moment always arrived.

The voices were louder, urgent, a cacophony so frantic it was almost a buzzing. Joe still couldn't make out what they were saying, but somehow he knew it was important. The pizza and bread had made him dry, and he tried not to think about how thirsty he was as he listened to the voices. The message, the answer, was so nearly understandable beneath the buzzing.

There! Something . . .

He paused and bowed his head, listening, listening . . .

Tiffany was in the back of the cab that stopped five blocks from Candle in the Night to drop off Yancy, where he lived with his uncle who wasn't really his uncle. John Straithorn, the producer and theater manager, actually lived closer to the theater than Yancy, but he'd arranged for the cab's route so he'd be alone with Tiffany. Tiffany had listened to his circuitous instructions to the driver and pretended not to notice.

As soon as Yancy was inside his building, and the cab made a sharp U-turn to drive back the way it had come, Straithorn kissed Tiffany on the ear. As she turned her head away, she smiled. She knew what was in his mind. He had only a short time to convince her she shouldn't go home, but should spend the night with him in his apartment. While the cab was bouncing over potholes and accelerating to make traffic lights, he'd be working desperately to make the deadline.

She knew he'd make it.

The cab was only a block away from Straithorn's loft, and Tiffany was locked in a frantic kiss with Straithorn, when the lovers heard a sharp, echoing report over the roar and rattle of the cab.

Neither paid it the slightest attention.

* * *

On the cruel streets of New York, Joe DeLong had somehow survived frostbite, beatings, near starvation, the voices of madness, and episodes of violence with real or imagined enemies.

The beggar man didn't survive the bullet fired by the Night Sniper.

41

Meg watched the ambulance make its way to the end of the block and turn the corner. Driving slowly through the gray dawn, with emergency lights and siren muted, the vehicle was a somber sight. Across the street from the crime scene, a group of onlookers stood quietly like mourners. The police hadn't yet identified the homeless man found shot to death on the sidewalk, but he was almost certainly a victim of the Night Sniper.

"The beggar man," Birdy said next to Meg.

"Down on his luck as far as he could go," Meg said.

A ten-year-old but immaculate black Buick rounded the corner and parked in a loading zone. Repetto's personal car that Lora usually drove. As Meg and Birdy watched, Repetto climbed out of the hulking car and straightened up as if his back hurt, then walked toward them. He had a long raincoat on today to guard against the forecast of showers, and with the gray light behind him he reminded Meg of one of those western movie gunfighters wearing a duster.

"Looks like he just rode in on a horse," Meg said.

Birdy glanced at her. "Huh?"

When Repetto got closer and his shirt and tie were visible, the effect was lost. Meg decided not to explain it to Birdy.

Repetto nodded to them and looked over at the techs and ME departing the scene, then at the bloody concrete where the body had lain. A radio car was parked at the curb and a uniform was still standing guard near the crime scene tape that would soon be removed so the sidewalk could be hosed down.

"Our beggar man?" Repetto asked. He'd been rousted out of bed and his hair was recklessly combed.

"'Fraid so," Birdy said. "He didn't have a dime on him, and the Salvation Army woulda turned away his clothes. We don't have an ID yet. Died sometime between ten and midnight last night. He was shot once in the chest, dead center through the heart."

"The ME said he was dead when he fell," Meg said.

Repetto squinted and peered up and down the block. It was early, and people were still asleep. The scene reminded him of a stage set before the actors appeared, other than the mournful supporting cast of onlookers on the opposite sidewalk. "Nobody called this in until this morning?"

"That's how it went," Meg said. "A woman in an apartment at the end of the block's the one who broke the ice. She said she heard what sounded like a shot a little before midnight. Didn't think much of it and went back to sleep, then got to worrying this morning when she was taking a shower. About the time she called it in, a cleaning woman going to work early found the body and used her cell phone to call the police."

"The midnight shot dovetails with the approximate time of death," Repetto said.

"When we talk to people in the buildings around here that have apartments, we'll find more who heard the shot," Birdy said confidently. "They don't like getting involved, but when they learn they weren't the first to talk to the police, and won't have to make a statement or testify, they'll open up some. Like always."

Repetto simply grunted his agreement. The neighborhood was still waking up. The knot of people that had gathered on the other side of the street had finally dispersed, now that the body had been removed. The last of them, a woman walking a small, poodlelike dog on a short leash, disappeared into a building diagonal from where the body had lain. An occasional car passed, headlights still glowing even though it was light out. Half a dozen pedestrians were visible down the block, near the intersection. A tall woman wearing incredibly high-heeled boots and low-cut jeans strode past across the street, staring straight ahead and moving fast, as if she had to be some place soon.

"How do women get into jeans that fit like that?" Birdy asked, watching the woman. He was shaking his head in disapproval at the same time he was making his habitual pecking motion. It made him look like one of those wobbling dashboard dolls that didn't stop motion until after the car had been parked awhile.

"Last time I heard that question," Meg said, "I was sixteen."

A patrol car slid into a parking space behind Repetto's Buick, and four uniformed cops climbed out. They walked toward the three detectives. Meg noted that the sun was high enough to have ruined the silhouetted gunfighter effect.

One of the uniforms was Nancy Weaver. Meg thought she looked pretty good for such an early hour. Or maybe she hadn't slept at all last night. A woman like Weaver, who knew where she'd been, what she'd touched?

Meg looked over and saw that Birdy was smiling at her, watching her watching Weaver.

The smile widened. "Thinking catty thoughts?"

"Like maybe I'll claw your throat out," Meg said.

Weaver nodded good morning to Repetto and gave him a big grin.

"I'm glad you're on this," Repetto told her.

The bastard!

"Fill Weaver in so she can instruct the others," Repetto told Birdy.

Birdy winked at Meg and moved about twenty feet away so he could talk privately with Weaver.

"Familiar neighborhood," Repetto said to Meg, who'd been watching Birdy and Weaver.

Meg realized what Repetto had said and refocused her attention. "We're only a few blocks from the Candle in the Night Theater."

"In this city," Repetto said, "the Sniper had plenty of beggar man targets to choose from."

"You think there's a connection between our dead beggar and where the Sniper left his last theater seat message?" Meg asked. Repetto was going somewhere with this, and she was intrigued.

"Could be."

Waiting. Letting me run with it. "Possibly the Sniper lives in the neighborhood," she suggested. "This particular beggar was convenient."

"I doubt it," Repetto said. "Bad guys of all sorts tend not to foul their own nests. It's human nature, even with the inhumane."

"Then maybe it was like you said. There are plenty of beggars to shoot. The Sniper was in the neighborhood to see the play and plant his message, and he didn't have to go far to settle on his next victim."

"He didn't kill on the same night he planted the theater seat note," Repetto said. "He had to have spent time in the neighborhood, seen the beggar man more than once, or he wouldn't have known his haunts and habits, where he'd likely be so he could be shot."

"The victim might have had some connection with somebody in the play," Meg said.

Repetto didn't answer. She looked at him. He was still regarding her with a faint, anticipatory smile. Wherever he wanted to go with this conversation, they weren't yet all the way there.

Meg felt something cold walk up her spine. "The Sniper was hanging around the theater to see us! He's watching us. The bastard is watching us. Maybe he has been for some time."

Repetto nodded, and the smile stayed but his eyes changed. "Maybe he's watching us right now."

Canvassing the neighborhood where the beggar man had died garnered nothing, other than substantiation of the time when the Sniper squeezed the trigger. Half a dozen apartment dwellers reported hearing the shot, and at the same time—a few minutes before midnight. Because of the acoustics of New York, the echoes and reverberations of the shot made it impossible to home in on its source. By the end of the day, they still hadn't found it.

That evening Repetto drove to Candle in the Night, arriving an hour before curtain, when most of the cast would be present. He was armed with morgue photos of the dead homeless man. They'd done their usual good work at the morgue of making such photos as bearable to view as possible, and these were more pathetic than gruesome. The dead man appeared shrunken and forlorn, as if he were holding back a lifetime of tears that would never be shed.

Straithorn seemed annoyed by Repetto's presence, but he made the best of it and took him around to show the morgue photos to cast and crew.

There was no reaction until Repetto was introduced to Tiffany Taft, who was fitting herself into a sequined black dress. Tiffany smiled at Repetto as she took a deep breath, exhaled, and with perfect timing a woman from wardrobe zipped up the dress's back. Repetto returned the smile, thinking Tiffany was one beautiful young woman.

When Straithorn and the woman from wardrobe left, and they were alone in Tiffany's small dressing room, Tiffany sat on a bench in front of a vanity with a many-lightbulbed make-up mirror that looked like something out of *A Star is Born*. She worked her dainty feet into black high-heeled shoes. She had perfectly turned ankles.

"I happen to be a theater buff," Repetto said, "and I think on looks alone, you'll go far."

Again the incandescent smile. "That's so nice of you, Detective . . . ?"

"Repetto."

"But it takes acting talent, too."

"I'm sure you have it."

"You're very kind."

"You might not think so after I show you these." He handed her the morgue photos.

"These are of the homeless man who was shot last night?" she said, accepting them.

"I'm afraid so."

When she looked at the top photo, she gasped.

Repetto studied her eyes and knew she'd recognized the dead man. He waited.

"I don't know his name," Tiffany said. She seemed genuinely moved by the man's death. Repetto reminded himself that she was an actress.

"It's Joseph DeLong," he said. "He was identified by his fingerprints."

"He was a criminal?"

"No, he was in the military. His prints were on file." Repetto didn't mention the two pandering convictions.

"Joseph . . ." Tiffany looked at herself in the mirror, then in the mirror at Repetto. "I never asked his name. I should have."

"You knew him?"

"Only as a homeless person who hung out in the neighborhood. After curtain, some of us usually go to a restaurant over on Twelfth Street and have a late snack. I usually left something for . . . Joseph . . . in a carryout box."

"You talked to him?"

"No, I left it on top of the trash basket on the corner. He often rooted through its contents. I put the box right where he could reach it. He was almost always outside the restaurant when we came out. He stayed away until we were gone, like he was afraid to talk to us. Or like he was . . ."

"Too proud?"

"Maybe."

"And you never attempted to speak to him?"

"No. Never." She sounded defensive.

Repetto smiled at her. "You showed him kindness. There's no reason to think you should have done more. I'm sure he was grateful."

She bent down and put on her other shoe.

Repetto wanted to make sure of what she was saying. "So Joseph was a fixture in the neighborhood, especially around the restaurant. And he regarded you as a benefactor."

"I guess he could count on me for food, if that's what you mean."

"I do mean that, and it's something." Repetto had the information he wanted confirmed. The beggar man was a neighborhood fixture, and was usually outside the restaurant where Tiffany dined. Repetto wondered if the late and unmourned Joseph DeLong had been in love with Tiffany. Probably, he thought.

He stood up. "I'll leave you to concentrate on your performance. It's been a real pleasure, and I'm sure I'll see you uptown onstage sometime in the near future."

She handed him back the morgue photos, having looked at only the top one, and with her smile melted him in a way he'd have thought unlikely. "I hope you're right," she said. "And I hope whoever killed Joseph . . . you find him."

"We will," Repetto told her. "You can be sure of it."

He didn't tell her she and her beauty and generosity had been the magnetism that had kept Joseph near, and made him predictable prey.

"Good-bye, Detective Repetto."

He told her good-bye, then almost gave her the traditional Broadway *Good luck.* "I won't say it," he said, pausing at the dressing room door.

She looked puzzled, then grinned. "Oh, that!"

"Your legs are too beautiful."

Another breathtaking smile. This time with a touch of shyness.

Joseph DeLong hadn't had a chance.

42

The view from the brick passageway between the leather goods shop and the closed Zippy Dog fast food restaurant remained the same. People passed without glancing into the shadowed passage, and if they did chance a look, all they saw were a few rubber trash containers and a pile of black plastic trash bags that had evaded months of pickup. The bags were old enough to be beyond odor, though a few rats that had scurried away must have scented something of value in them.

What the Night Sniper saw from where he sat, with his back resting against the mound of plastic bags, was the view across the street, into a similar but wider and well-lit passageway. Opening into that passageway was the unmarked steel door that he knew was the stage door of the Bellam Theater. Right now the door was closed flush with the building's brick side wall. Its flat gray surface was unbroken. It had no knob and could be opened only with a key or from the inside.

Truly, no one sees the homeless, the Sniper reflected, slumped against the pile of trash bags. No one had so much as glanced at him as he'd shuffled down the street and entered the dark and dangerous access.

Before he'd discovered the passageway, he had taken a position on the sidewalk, seated on his folded thin coat, his chipped ceramic cup set out for donations. He had his feebly scrawled AIDS sign out, which not only elicited sympathy but also seemed to repel the police, but hours on the sidewalk had garnered him only a few dollars in his cup.

Not that he cared, sitting there watching New York stream past. His clothes were ragged and artfully stained, but clean against his flesh. They were the only part of his wardrobe he didn't send out to be cleaned, but washed and dried in his condo's laundry room off the main bedroom's bath. He carefully maintained the garments' threadbare, quasi-soiled condition and was sure they'd pass muster as throwaways even if someone with a trained eye looked closely at him.

Of course, in the evenings he'd spent on the sidewalk across the street from the Bellam Theater, no one had looked closely at him. That was the genius of his disguise. That and the fact that no one who knew him would ever dream he'd be sitting on the sidewalk in such a subservient position, begging.

Seeming to beg.

During the day he worked out of his condo or his Wall Street office, where he'd become one of the most highly regarded money managers in Manhattan. In only a few years he'd made dozens of clients rich, and himself even richer. Now he led the life of an Epicurean in the city made for dissolution, enjoying women, clothes, fine liquors, art collecting, and his secretly acquired gun collection, the basis of which had come to him by way of Adam Strong. He was now a model man, leading a model life of urban sophistication.

But occasionally he glimpsed his younger self on the street, and when he looked in the mirror he sometimes saw the scars and felt the unhealed wounds of the past. And felt the rage.

For a moment he considered using his vantage point as his sniper's nest. A victim taken from street level. Something new and puzzling for Repetto and his detectives. So difficult for them, in the game that kept changing.

Then he decided the rooftop he'd scouted out and accessed twice, easily, would be the safest course of action, and would almost guarantee his escape. There were unacceptable risks here at street level. People were unpredictable. Coincidence might gain the upper hand. Besides, he couldn't be sure of the echoing effect of the rifle's report down low, how difficult it would be to guess its origin.

Play it safe. Take more of what luck has granted you. In everything, it's imperative that luck and genius be friends and accomplices, so each can alleviate the others' shortcomings.

He settled deeper into the concealing mound of formless plastic bags. They gave for him, welcoming him, their contents cooperating in his merging with them so he'd be invisible in the shadows. A feeling of power, of control, surged through him. What he attempted, he accomplished.

In the game whose rules he set and employed, and in which his pawns and opponents had no choice but to play, he was fate itself.

He smiled as he continued his watch on the Bellam Theater's stage door, waiting, accumulating information on his target's haunts and habits, becoming one with his prey.

She had no idea that her future had been decided, and that it was brief.

Meg sat in the unmarked across the street from Alex's apartment building. She wasn't sure why she'd driven here instead of home, but that shouldn't surprise her, because she had no idea how she really felt about Alex.

She'd received another e-mail from him this morning, imploring her to see him again, this time in an unofficial capacity. She'd caught herself smiling after reading it, and deleted it immediately and left to meet Repetto and Birdy.

Who did Alex think he was? He'd been a cop, and he knew she was a cop. There was no way she should even consider beginning the kind of relationship he obviously had in mind. She also didn't care for the way he assumed he could push her buttons and she'd respond. Meg figured she'd had her share of that kind of love.

Yet here she was with her motor idling—the car's motor—and the air conditioner keeping the heat and humidity at a minimum. Meg had figured out which of the windows facing the street were Alex's, and saw that a light was on inside the apartment's living room. She was about to look away when a figure passed the windows, moving in a way that, even from this distance, left no doubt it was Alex.

Now she couldn't drive away. Couldn't look away. She knew why. She had to find out if he was alone.

An idiot. I'm acting like a jealous idiot. As if he doesn't have a perfect right to see whoever he chooses.

Five minutes passed, and Meg's neck was getting stiff from the way she had to sit to stare up at Alex's windows.

There he was again! Alone.

But the glimpse wasn't enough. Meg stayed.

A minute or so later, Alex crossed the windows going the opposite direction. Alone again. Three times. That should be enough even for the most masochistic, jealous fool. And though she'd seen him only briefly each time and hadn't absorbed detail from this distance, she was sure he was fully dressed.

She looked away, raising an arm and using her right hand to massage the back of her neck, then put the car into drive.

A final glance up as she was about to pull away from the curb stopped her.

Alex had crossed the window again—she was sure it was Alex. And he'd been carrying a long object. *A rifle or shotgun?*

A crutch? A closed umbrella? A saw?

This is stupid! This is goddamned stupid!

Enough!

She concentrated on the view out the windshield and accelerated away from the curb.

A horn blasted and made her jump when the car had traveled only about ten feet. A cab roared past her with another, abbreviated note of its horn, its driver chastising her with an automotive expletive.

She hadn't checked the mirror or glanced over her shoulder before pulling out into traffic.

More careful now, remembering to look before stepping down on the accelerator pedal, she joined a string of vehicles that had just been set free by the signal at the corner.

Part of the flow of traffic now, Meg relaxed somewhat.

She was sure she hadn't seen Alex carrying a rifle.

In retrospect, she couldn't even be sure she'd been looking at the right window. The man—if it had been a man—carrying the long object might not even have been Alex.

The rest of the drive home she tried to put her mind at ease.

It didn't work.

"You want the rest of this cinnamon bun?"

Repetto was seated across the table from Meg the next morning, in a maroon-upholstered window booth at the Harrison Diner on First Avenue. The place had a double door to form a kind of air lock, but each time someone entered or exited, a breeze played over his ankles. Since the air conditioner hadn't yet chased away the heat left over from yesterday, it felt pretty good. The sweet scent of the oversize,

overiced bun on his plate dominated even the grilled bacon
smell permeating the diner.

"They heated it up," he added.

Meg silently shook her head no.

Repetto had been studying her since she'd slid into the
booth. Her hair wasn't as neatly combed as usual, and her
eyes had a weary, dreamy quality. He had to admit it made
her more attractive.

Then it struck him. He knew the look. She was in love. Or
something like love.

Not like Meg the terse. Meg the cynical.

A new Meg?

"You seeing someone?" Repetto asked, and took a sip of
his coffee. Repetto driving to the point.

She looked sleepily at him. "Seeing—oh, you mean *seeing* someone."

"Uh-huh."

Her face reddened and he knew he'd struck a soft spot.
"Does my personal life have something to do with my work?"
He could see her confusion. She didn't know what to say or
do, so she feigned anger.

"You know it does."

"Do I ask *you* if you're *seeing* someone?"

"You can."

"Are you?"

"No. My wife would kill me."

Meg noticed the expression on his face didn't change.
What did his words mean? Men were such accomplished de-
ceivers. It was fucking genetic. "Look," she said, keeping
her tone level, "if my personal life starts getting in the way
of my job, I'll let you know."

"But will *you* know?"

"Whether I will or won't, I just told you the way it is."

Feisty but controlled, letting me know I crossed the line.

He stared at her, trusting her. She might be in love or in heat—he knew the signs—but she wasn't going to let it interfere with the investigation. That was all he should be concerned about and all he needed to know.

Repetto took a sip of coffee and sat back. *Who might be her secret love interest?* Since they'd teamed up, Meg had spent most of her waking hours with him or with Birdy.

Repetto felt a sudden alarm. Might Meg feel that way about him, Repetto himself?

No. He didn't think so. Not judging by her reaction to personal questions that maybe he hadn't had a right to ask.

Birdy?

It was difficult to imagine the fidgety, wary Birdy being involved in a secret extramarital affair with Meg. Nobody Repetto knew was more *married* than Birdy. Besides, he and Meg both knew the rules. They both knew what this investigation meant.

No, not Birdy.

But Repetto had seen unlikely relationships develop between seemingly incompatible partners on the Job. He knew how sex and love could turn people into . . . other people.

He used the back of his forefinger to nudge his plate toward Meg. "You sure you don't want the rest of this cinnamon bun? They're really good. I'm just not hungry."

"No means no," she said, not smiling.

There was no part of that Repetto didn't understand.

On the roof of the Myler Building, high enough above the turmoil of the Times Square area that it seemed isolated, the Night Sniper shifted his weight, achieving comfort and balance. The rare Azner Line Premium rifle was assembled, its scope adjusted, and it now rested against his thigh.

A cloud passed over the moon, then moved on quickly in

a light-hazed night sky. A warning to the wise. This one would be an easy shot, so he mustn't let himself become complacent.

He felt confident, though. Even smug. He remained a step ahead of Repetto and his team.

Where they might assume he'd leave his next note, was where they would, in fact, find his next victim.

Too late.

The entire audience in the Bellam Theater rose to its feet, applauding, shouting approval, exhorting the cast to come back onstage for yet another curtain call.

The cast obliged. The star of the hit Broadway musical *American Cat Burglar in London*, Libby Newland, was center stage, hands joined with the cast members on either side of her. She was smiling big and meaning it.

This was the way every performance of *Burglar* ended, with what in these uneasy times was a good house, more than half the seats sold, everyone on their feet and applauding. But Libby knew that financially the play was struggling to stay in the black. What a hit it would have been if the Night Sniper creep wasn't out there somewhere, scaring the hell out of everyone as soon as the sun went down, holding people prisoner where they lived, or making them simply decide not to drive into the city after dark. Even Libby had to admit it wasn't worth the risk, though she never shared that thought. She didn't think you should let other people tell you how to live, especially people with guns. She hated guns.

The cast gave a final bow from the waist, then jogged offstage in a way that made it clear they were spent from the performance, but still spirited. Some of them waved their appreciation of the audience's response, or maybe of the audience's courage in attending the theater.

As the houselights came up, the audience, smiling and making favorable comments, began filing toward the aisles and exits.

"Another one down," Libby's leading man, Victor Tobin, said, as she made her way to her dressing room. He was a tall man with generous actor's instincts and ever-present Listerine breath. Vic was a little short in the voice department but could dance like Najinsky. He was, more than anything, a pro. Libby thought sharing the stage with him was a pleasure.

"It'd be nice to play to full houses," she said, stopping for a moment to let two black-clad stagehands pass with a plywood prop.

"It seems odd," Tobin said beside her, "to be playing to full-house matinees and half-house evening audiences."

"Night Sniper asshole," Libby said, by way of explanation. She opened her dressing room door.

Tobin grinned. "Dead on, Lib." He bent down and gave her a peck on the cheek before moving on.

As soon as she was alone in her dressing room, Libby got a chilled bottle of carbonated water from the tiny refrigerator and downed half of it. It was too warm in the room, so she switched on the floor fan in the corner, wishing these old theaters would work on their air-conditioning.

There were three knocks on the door; then it opened and Beth from wardrobe entered.

The play had run long enough that there was no need for words between the two women. Their actions after each performance had become routine. The elderly, saturnine Beth helped Libby out of the tight black Lycra costume she'd worn in the closing dance number, then draped it over a padded hanger on the metal rack against the wall. After taking a few garments from the rack that needed cleaning or sewing, she waited to see if Libby required anything more.

Libby glanced around, smiled, and shook her head no,

and Beth withdrew to help someone else with awkwardly placed Velcro or zippers.

Leaving the door open a crack to facilitate the flow of air from the fan, Libby sat down before her lighted mirror and looked at herself, the ultimate London cat burglar. Elfin, mischievous, even feline.

Anyone would pick me out of a lineup as a cat burglar. Maybe I missed my calling.

Nobody in the theater world would agree with that last part.

Time to disassemble the cat burglar. Libby carefully removed her wig and placed it on its form for Beth to comb tomorrow morning. Since the shedding of the Lycra dance costume, Libby was wearing only panties, no bra, and decided to stay that way to remain cool while she removed her makeup.

The door opened all the way and a male dancer named Edmund stuck his head in. "Oops! Wrong room," he said. "Sorry."

"You don't seem sorry," Libby said, smiling as the young man closed the door.

When she was in her street clothes, her dark, short-cropped hair a charming mess, she put on an ankle-length light raincoat, tinted glasses, and a jaunty denim cap. She had an appointment to meet her agent and a TV producer in Marteen's Lounge, where they would have a few drinks and talk over a possible television series based on the success of *Burglar.*

Libby was sure nothing would come of the idea, but she knew this was the way it went in her business. Meet someone over drinks or food, then listen, talk, listen, forget it, take a phone call six months later, and you had work. The acting life. She loved it, and finally it was starting to love her back.

She adjusted the angle of the denim cap that made her

look sixteen and as if she should be hawking newspapers, then lowered the dark glasses on her nose so she could peer over the tops of the frames at her image in the mirror.

Nothing left of the cat burglar.

"Good to go," she said to herself, then left the dressing room and made her way to the glowing red exit sign, saying good night to people as she went. She was sure no one would recognize her on the street when she left by the stage door on the side of the theater.

She was wrong.

After closing the heavy steel door behind her, she turned around and felt a terrible pain in her chest. Her thoughts went flying. Her heart began a wild hammering.

Beyond the mouth of the passageway, almost everyone dropped flat or sought cover at the crack of the shot Libby had barely heard in her sudden shock. She felt dizzy, completely . . . disoriented. She heard someone whimper—*probably me*—and with a dancer's grace she sat down cross-legged on the hard concrete.

Libby lost her grip on time and didn't know how much of it had passed. Her heartbeat was deafening and becoming more irregular, and that terrified her. She was only about ten feet back from the sidewalk and tried to call for help, but she could make no sound other than the soft whimpering.

Several minutes had passed since the echoing report of the rifle, and out on the street and sidewalk people were beginning to raise their heads and look around, or stand up uneasily and move on. None of them seemed aware that Libby had been shot. None of them happened to glance into the lighted passage where she sat bleeding.

Warm . . . warm . . . Am I bleeding?

She extended her forefinger and tried to touch the wavering red brilliance spreading all around her. She couldn't reach it. Much too far away.

When she looked up she saw on the other side of the street a ragged derelict staring directly at her while hurrying along under the burden of a dark backpack.

He knows I'm here!

The way he's staring at me . . . we both . . .

Nothing more.

43

"We got trouble," Melbourne said.

He was standing behind his desk in his spacious office. The desk was a slate-topped, massive mahogany affair he'd paid for himself. There was a bank of file cabinets along one wall, and a smaller desk nearby on which sat a closed notebook computer and a neat stack of green file folders. The other walls were festooned with photographs, framed news items, commendations, trophies, and personal letters from celebrities. The rewards of ambition and political acumen.

Repetto sat in one of the burgundy leather chairs facing the desk, his legs extended and his ankles crossed. His heels were dug into the plush carpet. "I guess by that you mean *more* trouble."

"We should never have clued in the media on the nursery rhyme thing."

"We had no choice," Repetto told him. "They would have caught on to it anyway. Besides, would you want to take the heat if people were killed and we might have warned them?"

Melbourne ignored the question. He glared at Repetto from beneath eyebrows his barber had obviously forgotten to trim; then he leaned forward and supported himself with the knuckles of both hands on the desk, the way an alpha gorilla might stand. "The Night Sniper chose one hell of a victim last time out."

"The thief," Repetto said.

"So all the morning papers tell me. But Libby Newland wasn't your ordinary thief. She was a scene stealer. The public loves—loved—her. The public is pissed off. That piss gets on the pols, who pressure the department higher-ups—"

"You," Repetto interrupted.

"Me. Who, in turn, diverts all that piss and pressure to?"

"Me?"

"Uh-huh. The downhill theory."

"More than a theory," Repetto said.

"Right you are, there at the base of the hill. The stakes have been raised. We have to nail this guy, Vin."

"Or I re-retire?"

That seemed to sober Melbourne. "No, no . . . But I need something for the wolves that are snapping at me, so they can play show-and-tell with the others. Some meat to throw them."

"Like the Night Sniper himself."

"That'd be prime steak. Are you any closer?"

"With every victim," Repetto said, "but it's a hell of a way to gain ground."

"Why couldn't you figure out he might kill somebody in a Broadway show with *Burglar* in the title?"

"Because in the past he only used theater and play references to give us clues so we could find his messages." Repetto uncrossed his legs. He stared at the photographs of Melbourne receiving awards, Melbourne posing with NYPD elites and the city's top political figures. Not a stupid man, Melbourne. "You ask a good question, though," Repetto said. "He took a chance killing such a famous thief, gambling that we wouldn't anticipate it and be ready for him."

"You haven't figured out how he thinks," Melbourne said, "but he's figured out how you don't think. He's inside your mind, and at this point you're supposed to be inside his."

"I am to an extent," Repetto said. "He's not the sort to take that kind of chance."

"But Libby Newland's dead. She had no police protection, and the Sniper's escaped as usual."

"I don't buy that *knows how we don't think* premise of yours," Repetto said, "but at the same time, I agree with you. It's as if he knew we weren't thinking along those lines. As if he could be confident there wouldn't be any sort of trap if he tried for Libby Newland."

Melbourne straightened up, then sat down hard in his padded desk chair and stared hard at Repetto. "You saying what I think I hear?"

"I don't know. But maybe the Sniper has police contacts, knows somebody in the department, has at least some inkling of how we're playing the game."

"That word again."

"That's how he sees it—a game. And it's one that, right now, he's winning."

Melbourne let out a long breath. "I won't tell you the NYPD doesn't leak. Do you have any facts to base your theory—"

"Not even a theory."

"—your notion on?"

"No."

"Then don't let it get outside this office. I—we have enough pressure. Libby Newland was one of the most popular celebrities in New York, a city that worships celebrities. Media and political pressure have intensified like water trying to reach a boil. There's growing economic pressure here, too, Vin."

"I'll bet."

"They think business is bad now, it's gonna grind to almost a dead stop after dark. The city at night belongs to the Sniper."

To sudden, random death, Repetto thought.

Melbourne stood up again behind his desk, so Repetto stood also.

"We'll take back the city," Repetto said flatly.

Melbourne gave him a crooked smile, like the one in all the wall photos. "I'll tell the mayor that when I see him."

"Quote me," Repetto said, and left the office.

Zoe Brady was asleep when she should have been showering and getting ready to go to her office. Her latest produce department conquest lay beside her and listened to her breathing. He was an expert on the breathing of sleepers; he'd crept out of dozens of apartments while women lay sleeping. And he had lain beside them weeping as they slept.

He wasn't leaving this apartment. Not yet.

He looked over at Zoe's relaxed features, her slightly open mouth near the top of the thin sheet, as if she were about to nibble at the linen. Her rhythmic breathing made the edge of the sheet near her lower lip flutter in time to her exhalations. Besides the three glasses of wine she'd had for dinner, Zoe had consumed, in the plastic bottle of diet cola he'd brought her after sex, two powdered Ambiens that he'd crushed between two spoons. He thought it would be at least ten o'clock before she woke up on her own.

Confidently but quietly, he eased onto his side, then swiveled his nude body so he was sitting on the edge of the mattress. The slight stirring of air brought scents and memories of last night. The woman was perspiring slightly and still smelled of sex. She moaned softly in her sleep as if sharing his recollection.   .

He stood up slowly and moved away from the bed, then padded barefoot into the living room. Zoe kept her laptop computer on her desk that was concealed behind a four-panel Chinese screen. During his last visit he'd discovered her ISP password, along with various Web site passwords, written on a piece of paper hidden beneath the base of the brass desk lamp. So many of them hid passwords beneath nearby lamps.

He booted up the small but powerful Toshiba computer and within a few minutes was online and had access to all of Zoe's files.

Her document files were informative. They included working notes as well as personal letters, and summaries of conversations concerning the Night Sniper. He simply scanned the documents, then plugged the zip drive he'd brought into the computer's USB port and copied them. He would peruse them later in his apartment, along with several other files that were encrypted. He was confident he'd soon be able to break the encryption and read all of Zoe's secrets. If he couldn't solve the puzzle of encryption, he'd have to steal the computer and delve deeper into its system. There was always a way, though often it was time-consuming.

But that was a problem for the future, if it came up at all. Right now, a cursory look and a later, more careful examination of what he'd copied, would do for a start.

He was pleased to find Zoe's links to NYPD databases. Pleased also that she had extensive clearance. It took only a few mouse clicks to see there was plenty of information on the Night Sniper case. Intrigued, he spent almost an hour linking to various NYPD sites.

When he was finished, he removed the zip drive and shut down the computer. The drive was small enough to fit into its slim leather case and be concealed in the inside pocket of his suit coat that was draped over a living room chair.

He rearranged the carefully folded coat, then went back behind the screen and closed the computer's lid.

Back in the bedroom, he stood by the bed and studied the

sleeping Zoe. Her left arm was still slung carelessly above her mussed red hair. One pale leg protruded from beneath the even paler white sheet. She was still breathing evenly. She hadn't moved. She still smelled of recent and vigorous sex.

He lowered his weight gently onto the mattress, listening to the muted ping of bedsprings, then gradually moved his nude body so it was pressing lightly against hers. The slight contact with her seemed to ignite dreams.

Zoe shifted her hips in her sleep, sighed, and turned to face away from him. As he wedged up against her he could feel himself getting erect, but he decided to ignore the temptation. He slid a hand around her, over her smooth, rounded belly, and up to gently cup one of her breasts. His mouth was near her ear.

"Hey, sleepyhead," he whispered. "Time for us to get up and you to go to work." He kissed her ear gently, then flicked it with the tip of his tongue.

She opened her eyes, smiled, and turned her head so she could kiss him back.

Her warm body jerked and he knew she'd noticed the clock on her side of the bed.

"Damn! If I don't get moving I'm gonna be late."

"Told you so."

"So you did."

He kissed the nape of her neck. "Maybe we should share a shower, save water, save time."

"I'm not so sure we'd save time," she said. She wriggled out of his clutches, then sat up and winced. "God!"

"Headache?"

"Whole ache. And I feel like I could sleep another eight hours."

"I warned you about drinking too much wine at dinner."

"Did you? I don't remember."

He grinned. "Bad sign."

Zoe stood up and held a hand to her forehead. "Ouch! You must have been right about that wine." She began massaging her temples with her fingertips.

He got out of bed nimbly and moved to stand next to her, supporting her.

"I'm not gonna fall down," she assured him, giving up on her temples and dropping her arms.

"You never know," he said. "Could be dangerous. You shouldn't be in the shower alone. C'mon." He began leading her gently toward the bathroom.

"No funny stuff in the shower," she said.

He laughed. "Do I have to promise?"

"Of course. I can't be late. I really can't."

"I know. You're working on an important case."

"Nutcase who's shooting people," she said. A hint of irritation had crept into her sleep-thickened voice, either at the killer or at being unable to speak or think coherently so soon after waking.

Now that she was up, he didn't want her to suspect anything. Best if she came all the way alert as soon as possible. "We'll take a shower," he said. "Then I'll call for my car and driver so you won't be late for work."

She stopped moving and stared up at him, impressed as she often was by this man she barely knew. "You can do that?"

He gave her his perfect smile.

"For you," he said, "I can do that."

44

He was pleased by the results of his latest kill.

The Night Sniper settled back in the soft support of the leather sofa in his East Side luxury apartment, sipping expensive scotch and watching the plasma TV screen that took up much of the living room's south wall. Local cable news was on, covering almost nothing other than the Libby Newland shooting.

The popular actress's death had caused such outrage in the city that the police and political machines were running wild with frustration. The serious blond woman on the screen proclaimed this with exaggerated lip and chin motion, beneath eyes that were obviously reading. Many businesses were deserted after dark. They were reconciled to great financial loss and closed early every day. Serious Blonde segued to an interview with a mayoral aide, an angry-looking man with a shock of gray hair who said the city was considering shutting down the theater district. Those in the theater world could hardly object. Tickets were being scalped at a third of their box office price, and with Libby Newland's death, fewer than half the seats were occupied. Tourism and business travel were dropping off precipitously. Aircraft were landing at JFK and LaGuardia with more empty seats than anyone had seen in a major airliner in years.

Wonderful!

The Night Sniper took a sip of aged single-malt scotch and congratulated himself. Things were going better than planned.

He stood up and carried his glass to the window that provided the broadest view of the night-bejeweled city and wondered who his next victim should be. The nursery rhyme required a doctor. He knew a doctor. In fact, he was currently having an affair with one.

Too close to the bone. Too risky.

Now wasn't the time to increase risk; it was the time to reduce it.

Why not change the game at this point? Or at least the rules? The Night Sniper enjoyed the advantage and always would, if only he'd use that advantage. He who controls the rules controls the game.

He looked out over his vast view of the city and again pondered the identity of his next victim. Possibly his hand-picked nemesis, Vincent Repetto?

No, not yet. Killing Repetto would almost be like destroying himself. Besides, it would precipitate a new game, and the Sniper was enjoying this one too much to end it and start over with new, untested opposition. Perhaps opposition that wasn't up to the task.

Lora Repetto! There would be an interesting choice, the beloved wife who was now and then mentioned in the press as Repetto's aide and confidante, and who herself had been fond of Repetto's dead protégé, Dal Bricker. Like a son to them. First a son, then a wife. Terrible loss. Poor Repetto.

But an even more terrible loss was possible. If Repetto couldn't actually lose a son, he could lose a daughter. Amelia Repetto. Lora would blame her husband for their daughter's death, and Repetto's marriage would disintegrate before his eyes. First his daughter, then his wife would be lost to him.

Loss. The Night Sniper knew loss as Repetto never could. He caught a glimpse of his reflected self in the dark window-pane and felt his heart grow cold. Staring back at him was his other self, his true self.

He made himself smile, a death's-head grin in the glass, and raised his tumbler of whiskey in a silent salute.

But the transparent figure in the glass didn't raise his drink in response, and now appeared to be weeping. Loneliness. The glittering night world of the city was spread out behind him, and he was alone, fragile as the glass itself.

He turned away, swiping a tear from the corner of his eye with a finger of his free hand.

There on the TV was another City Hall spokesperson, this one a severe-looking middle-aged woman with dark bangs. She was speaking earnestly into a microphone held by one of the male journalists who appeared regularly on local TV, but too softly to be understood. The Night Sniper went to the sofa, picked up the remote, and increased the volume:

". . . for the Take Back The City rally," the woman was saying. "It will be at Rockefeller Center on a date to be determined. Its purpose will be to demonstrate that life can go on as usual in New York despite the Sniper murders."

"Has the mayor okayed this idea?" asked Media Man with the microphone, a male version of Serious Blonde.

"Not only has he okayed it," said the woman with the bangs, "he'll personally speak at the rally."

The Night Sniper suddenly became as still as if he were sighting in on a difficult target.

A juicier target than either Lora or Amelia Repetto.

He switched off the TV and went into his combination office and collection room. With the practiced ease of a surgeon, he slipped thin, flesh-colored rubber gloves on his hands. From a cabinet beneath a bookshelf he got out the ancient Royal typewriter he'd bought at a roadside antique shop in New Jersey for twenty-five dollars. He'd made minor repairs on the manual typewriter himself, then bought a ribbon at an office supply store and fed it onto one of the old reels. The typewriter worked fine and was perfect for his purpose. Let the police trace the typeface of a fifty-year-old machine in the century of technology.

No point in wasting time. He placed the typewriter on his desk and got an envelope and sheet of paper from a bottom drawer. He addressed the envelope, then rolled the paper onto the machine's platen.

The note he typed was brief:

Game changed. Stakes Higher.

When the paper was folded and sealed in the envelope, he placed the envelope in an inside pocket of one of his blue blazers. He removed the gloves from his hands and stuffed them into a side pocket.

After shrugging into the blazer, he lightly tapped its pockets to make sure nothing had fallen out.

Then he left to buy a theater ticket.

45

"Game changed," Meg said. She dropped the copy of the latest Night Sniper theater note back on Repetto's desk in their precinct basement headquarters. It caught a draft and almost slid off the back of the desk. "Do we all agree on what he means by that?"

"Next target's gotta be the mayor," Birdy said. He was perched on the desk corner, absently working one foot as if trying to shake something from his sole. "Why the idiot had to announce when and where he was gonna be is beyond sound reason."

Repetto was standing over by the window, blowing on his coffee and waiting for it to cool. He shrugged. "It's what mayors do."

"Man's got the brain of a piss ant," Birdy said.

Meg grinned. She kind of liked the mayor, who wasn't pure politician. "Are you politically motivated, Birdy?"

Birdy snorted, stopped with the foot, and began pumping his leg nervously. "I got enough trouble motivating myself to make it through the day."

The air conditioner clicked on and a cool breeze wafted

from the vents near the ceiling, bringing with it the scent of the booking area above: stale perspiration mixed with desperation. Repetto thought there really might be a smell of fear, and that it lingered.

"We all know the next line of the nursery rhyme," Meg said. "*Doctor, lawyer, Indian chief.* That schedule of victims seems to have been abandoned. What the mayor did accomplish is to take a lot of pressure off doctors."

"There are scads of doctors," Birdy said, "only one mayor. No brain."

"I stayed up late last night," Meg said.

Birdy winked at her. "That mean you're gonna be short with us?"

"It means I was busy." She'd been waiting to tell what she'd figured out, knowing it would top whatever the amorous and ambitious Weaver had done lately.

Birdy started pumping his leg faster and grinned. "You gonna tell us about your love life, Meg?"

Odd thing for him to say if they were having a secret affair, Repetto thought. *Maybe not. Probably not.* He looked at Meg, waiting.

"I checked all the Sniper crime scenes," she said. "Wanted to make sure of something. For each murder, the most likely area of the shot's origin has been worked out. In each of those areas is a permanently or temporarily closed subway stop."

Birdy stopped his leg and stared at her. She knew he hadn't reasoned out where she was going.

It took Repetto a few seconds; then he smiled at her like a proud father.

"The muddy footprint on a dry night," he said. "In the apartment after the restaurant shooting near the park. Lee Nasad."

"Right. I didn't want to say anything until I had all the facts. I obtained a sample of mud from the closed, partly renovated subway stop in that neighborhood yesterday and dropped it by the lab. Then I got confirmation this morning. It matches the mud left by the Sniper's shoe." *Take that, Weaver.*

Birdy stood up from the desk corner. He was chewing on his lower lip, turning over in his mind what Meg had done. He stopped chewing and looked at her admiringly. "I like it, Meg."

She gave him a slight nod to acknowledge the compliment. "I bet our Sniper's using deserted subway tunnels for shelter and to get around the city unseen."

"Which would explain why we button up a crime scene area minutes after the shot, and he's gone," Birdy said.

"Uh-huh. Poof, like that."

Repetto was facing away from them now, staring at the slender bar of sunlight fighting its way in through the narrow, ground-level window. "Maybe something's turned," he said thoughtfully. "Maybe for once we can get out ahead of this bastard."

"It'd make a nice change," Birdy said.

"I'll pass on this information to Murchison," Repetto said, still staring at the light as if fascinated by it.

"Who's he?" Birdy asked.

"Captain Lou Murchison. He's going to be in charge of TBTC security."

"Take Back The City rally?"

"Yeah. It's already got an acronym."

"No stopping it now," Birdy said.

"Murchison'll notify the mayor's personal security so they and the NYPD can coordinate efforts."

"Maybe the mayor will change his mind," Meg said.

"No mind," Birdy said.

"Something else," Meg said. "Two blocks from Rockefeller Center there's a subway stop closed for future renovations."

Repetto turned back around. Birdy returned to perch on

the desk and started pumping his leg again, faster and faster. He noticed what he was doing. Kicked the desk once, hard.

"Closed subway stop could be good or bad," Repetto said.

"That's what I thought," Meg told him.

"Bad," Birdy said.

A doughnut bag! That was good. Bobby wondered why so many people often threw away doughnut bags with one or two doughnuts still in them. Bought more than they could eat, maybe. Or calorie guilt caught up with them and they left a doughnut or two to reassure themselves they were still on their diets.

Bobby didn't care. He reached farther down into the trash receptacle and pulled the crumpled white bag out from beneath a warped and water-stained old paperback somebody had thrown away. He glanced at the title: *Six Rules for Sensational Sex.* Self-help. Fuckin' joke.

He ignored the book but did remove one of several discarded newspapers in the wire basket. This one, a *Post,* was barely used, as if whoever had thrown it away merely glanced at the headlines, then discarded it.

With the folded paper tucked beneath his arm, he opened the doughnut bag. Half a powdered jelly. Okay, that'd do.

Bobby shuffled down the block until he came to the doorway of an import shop that had its steel shutters down over the windows. He sat back so his lower legs wouldn't be out on the sidewalk where he might trip somebody, then bit into the doughnut. Great. Still fresh.

It took him only a few seconds to down what was left of the doughnut. After swiping his hands together to brush away the sugar, he licked a stubborn glob of jelly from a knuckle, then leaned back against the shop door and unfolded the *Post.*

"Shit!" he said, loud enough that a guy in a dark business suit walking past turned his head and gave him a look.

Right there on the front page was more news about the Take Back The City rally, under the headline NEW YORKERS FIGHT BACK. Thousands were expected to attend.

Thousands of targets, Bobby thought. No, *one* target, really. TBTC, as it had come to be known, had seemed to Bobby a bad idea from the beginning. Somebody should have talked to the mayor and made him see reason. He was taunting the Night Sniper, the deadliest killer the city had seen in years, and a real sicko. Bobby was no profiler, but there was no doubt in his mind a guy like the Sniper couldn't pass up a challenge like this one.

Across the street, a young woman hurrying toward a bus stop casually left behind a plastic water bottle on a display window ledge. Even from this distance Bobby could see that it was almost half-full.

He was thirsty, after the doughnut.

He stood up and stuffed the crumpled, empty doughnut bag into his hip pocket to be thrown away later. (Bobby was neat; didn't foul up his city.) The newspaper he refolded and tucked beneath his arm. He'd read it later in the park.

When there was a break in traffic, he crossed the street to get the water bottle, still thinking about the TBTC mass of humanity that was going to be in Rockefeller Center. A wonderful place to die.

The mayor had balls. Bobby had to give him that. Maybe Bobby would even register so he could vote for him in the next election, if they were both still alive.

"This is a nightmare," Captain Louis Murchison said to Repetto. He was a tall man with the slimness of youth and steel-gray hair. Repetto had seen him around over the years, usually in uniform. Today he had on a well-tailored gray suit and looked more like a Wall Street baron than a cop. "We don't have enough people to cover every rooftop and window the Sniper can use for cover."

The two men stood on Forty-ninth Street, adjacent to Rockefeller Plaza, and surveyed the surrounding neighborhood. Repetto saw that Murchison was right; this was one of the busiest areas of Manhattan and was vertically developed. There were possible shooting points from overlooking buildings even blocks away, taller than the buildings between them and the Plaza.

"I've got something that might help," Repetto said, and told Murchison what Meg had figured out about the Sniper using closed tunnels and stops in the subway system to move around town.

"Interesting," Murchison said. "He can get in and out of the crime scene fast and unseen, and it minimizes the risk of him carrying a rifle both directions."

"Whatever weapon he's using," Repetto said, "it probably breaks down. Target rifles often do, for travel."

"So he can kill somebody, then carry away the damned weapon in his pocket."

"They don't break down quite that far," Repetto said. "But maybe some of them fit in a shopping bag or attaché case."

Murchison stared down thoughtfully at the pavement between his feet. "I wonder how many closed subway stops there are."

"At present, permanently and temporarily, fifteen," Repetto said. "I checked with the Transit Bureau."

"You ask them how many miles of track there are?"

"No," Repetto admitted.

"Damn near 240. My brother-in-law used to work for Port Authority told me that a while back. There's another city underneath this one, Repetto. Our sniper has plenty of room to roam."

"Still," Repetto said, "knowing where he roams makes it easier."

"Yeah," Murchison said despondently, "we might be standing only a few hundred miles from him right now."

Repetto decided not to point out to Murchison about miles as the crow flies, and that the crow didn't fly underground. The subway system was laced with a crisscross pattern of tracks. They might be standing on top of the Sniper right now.

Murchison slipped his hands in his pockets and glanced up again at the surrounding buildings. "Our sniper roams high, too. Planning and preparation go into everything he does. He might be watching us right now."

"Makes me glad I'm not the mayor."

"If they'd take my advice," Murchison said, "this rally would be canceled. But the mayor won't hear of it."

"Maybe he figures he's in too far to back out."

"No, not him. He *wants* to do this. And not only for political reasons. He takes it as a personal affront, what the Sniper's been doing to his city."

"So do I," Repetto said.

Murchison looked at him to be sure he was serious.

Repetto was.

"You and the mayor," Murchison said with mock disgust.

"You too," Repetto said.

"Yeah, maybe. But I go only so far. Gotta give Hizoner credit for guts."

"Gets my vote."

Murchison turned and motioned toward Rockefeller Plaza, where a restaurant was serving outdoor diners in the sunken area where the ice rink was during the winter months. It was also where the city's official Christmas tree would be displayed later in the year.

"We're gonna set up a podium down there in the Plaza,"

Murchison said. "Make the speakers, including the mayor, tougher targets below ground level."

"Good idea. But probably not enough."

"Probably not, but thanks to your man—"

"Woman. Detective Meg Doyle."

Murchison nodded. "I'll remember the name. What we'll do is pull some people off the immediate area to cover the subway stops in the neighborhood. Have them look for anything suspicious, especially if it involves somebody possibly carrying a rifle—even one that's disassembled."

Repetto said he thought that was a good idea. He also knew the long odds against results, in a city where everyone schlepped everything.

"You'll be in charge of subway stop security," Murchison told him. "I'll clear it with Melbourne."

Repetto was surprised but didn't argue. Daunting as the assignment might be, it was one he wanted. *His* city. His and the mayor's.

Murchison waved an arm in an encompassing gesture. "We'll have the area around the Plaza flooded with uniformed and undercover cops. Spotters and SWAT snipers will be stationed strategically in, and on, surrounding buildings."

"The Sniper will be expecting that," Repetto said.

Murchison nodded agreement. "That's why the subway information and your assignment are so important."

Repetto knew what Murchison meant, but Murchison went ahead and said it: "It'd be nice if we nailed the Sniper *before* he kills the mayor."

The object of the game, Repetto thought.

The game.

46

The Night Sniper sat back from his typewriter and checked his letter to the *New York Times*. In it he complimented the mayor for his wisdom and fortitude in speaking at the upcoming TBTC rally. It was a time for strong leadership and the mayor was providing it. The city couldn't let itself be held hostage by fear, and only someone with courage could break the chains of that fear through bold and definitive action. The mayor made the letter writer proud to be a New Yorker.

The letter was unsigned.

The Night Sniper doubted the *Times* would print such a letter from an anonymous source, but they'd count it in their pro and con survey. It would add weight, however slight, to the mayor's political responsibility.

It would contribute to maneuvering the mayor closer to the point of his death.

* * *

The morning before the TBTC rally, the Night Sniper made his way on foot across town toward Rockefeller Center. He'd noticed a uniformed policeman stationed near the closed subway stop that provided access to a tunnel leading downtown. The subway tunnel was the route the Night Sniper had intended taking.

He stood looking at the policeman, a young man with a seriousness and tenseness about him. As if he expected trouble and perhaps wanted it.

Not willing to take a chance, the Night Sniper walked to his secondary entry point.

No uniformed cop there, but a decidedly suspicious businessman seated on a nearby bench and pretending to read a magazine while sipping water from a plastic bottle. He looked, he *felt,* like an undercover cop. And if he wasn't, what about the homeless man with the good haircut slouching near the corner?

No problem, the Night Sniper told himself.

But as he walked toward Midtown, he saw that other subway stops were staked out by the police. No mistaking it now; they must at least suspect he was using the subways for shelter and to move about, especially the deserted tunnels and stations.

This shouldn't be a complete surprise. Repetto wasn't a fool. That was why he'd been chosen.

The Night Sniper walked on.

He finally found a long-deserted stop his pursuers had overlooked, on East Fifty-ninth Street. The surface structure leading to the stairwell was razed, its rubble piled nearby. The entry to underground was shielded from sight by a raised plywood walkway, the access to the stairwell covered by a square steel plate. The construction walkway was flanked by four-by-eight plywood sheets propped on their sides and nailed tight to upright supports, so that only the upper bodies of passersby were visible.

When no one was on the angled walkway, the homeless man with the backpack dropped down out of sight. The steel plate was screwed down, but was easy to pry up from the weathered wood walkway. He quickly slid the plate to the side, then lowered himself into the darkness beneath. Just as quickly, but with considerably more effort, he slid the plate back into place from below so it could be walked upon. In darkness, he began descending rusty steel rungs protruding from an old concrete wall that curved to remind him of a well.

The last ten feet of the ladder was smooth steel, as the entry widened to twice its diameter. The ground below was muddy but with a firmness just below the surface.

Standing at the base of the ladder, the Night Sniper could hear the muffled roar of subway trains. He got his small mag light from his backpack and shone the thin beam about.

He knew where he was. In a tunnel with unused tracks leading to a stop near West Fifty-first Street—not far from Rockefeller Center.

This was his world. He felt safer here. Heartened, he strode confidently into darkness, playing the flashlight beam ahead of him so he wouldn't trip over something or twist an ankle on a piece of debris. The tunnel smelled musty and faintly of something rotting. A familiar and comforting smell.

After a while, the unused tunnel veered left into the operational tunnel leading to the subway stop. Trains ran regularly along this route, so he had to stay alert.

Minutes later the Night Sniper stopped and stood with his back pressed against the tile walls of the Fifty-first Street subway stop. He was on the shadowed edge of light from above, waiting for the opportunity to emerge from the tunnel and climb onto the concrete platform. He knew he'd be seen by at least a few people, but they'd quickly looked away from his shabby clothes and threatening demeanor and put him out of their minds. It was no secret that many of the homeless spent their days in the subway stops, and perhaps he'd dropped something near the tracks, or spotted a coin, and had pocketed it and was climbing back up onto the platform. It was no concern of theirs, not in the real world where they lived their lives of relationships, appointments, and responsibilities, the world that mattered.

The time came and the Night Sniper moved smoothly to the steel maintenance ladder near the end of the platform and began climbing it. He was noticed by another of the homeless, a large African-American man preparing to panhandle on the next train, and an older white couple who looked like tourists. The woman had a camera slung around her neck. The Night Sniper hoped she wouldn't attempt to use it. He'd been photographed before, as part of the flora and fauna of the city, and he'd gone to some trouble to steal the camera, a digital one, so he could destroy the image. Cameras could see deeply, beyond flesh and posture and into the real self.

Everyone who noticed the ragged figure climbing onto the platform quickly turned away with the same curiously wooden features that routinely rejected him as a fellow human. Only a blond girl about ten, standing behind the tourist couple, continued staring curiously at the Sniper.

She stared until a train rolled in and she boarded with a man who was probably her father.

The Night Sniper joined the throng of passengers who left the train and made their way toward the Fifty-first Street exit.

A few minutes later he was in sunlight on the surface, sure he'd drawn no undue attention. He'd scouted the neighborhood and knew where he was going, to a private spot behind a Dumpster where he could quickly change clothes and his homeless persona.

For now, though, he was one of the untouchable and unseen. He felt safest this way. The police knew the various rifles he used were expensive, so they were searching for a man of wealth. That deliberate misdirection was part of the game. The Sniper hardly appeared wealthy now, shuffling along the sidewalk with his thirty-thousand-dollar J.G. Anschutz target rifle—once owned by a member of Saddam Hussein's cabinet—broken down and fitted into his worn backpack.

He was only blocks from Rockefeller Center.

Deputy Mayor Marcus Pelegrimas stood watching the mayor stand erectly to his full height before the mirror in the room adjacent to his office, where he often rehearsed his speeches.

"Night must not be synonymous with fright!" the mayor proclaimed, raising a finger.

He turned to Pelegrimas, a much taller man with a shaved head and a studied expression of impartiality. "Should I do that, Marcus? With the finger?"

"Never wise to give the voters the finger," Pelegrimas said, deadpan.

Hector Chavez, the mayor's on-duty bodyguard, glanced at him and smiled. He was a medium-height, blocky man with impeccably combed black hair that matched his impeccably tailored suit. He had about him the air of a man who didn't move around much, but when he did move, it was fast and with purpose.

There was a slight noise from the office on the other side of the door. Chavez immediately locked the door between the office and the room they were in, then slipped out an opposite door.

Pelegrimas and the mayor stood silently. Then there was a soft knock on the office door and it opened just far enough so that Chavez could squeeze back in.

"It's the people from the Committee to Revive the Southern Tip," the bodyguard said.

Pelegrimas nodded to the mayor. "I'll deal with them, sir."

"Fine, Marcus. Tell them I can give them ten minutes, starting in a few."

"Yes, sir." Chavez stayed with the mayor as Pelegrimas opened the door to the office.

"Do I smell smoke?" the mayor asked. "Is someone smoking out there, Marcus?"

"No, sir," Pelegrimas said, and closed the door behind him.

When he returned, the mayor was back before the mirror, trying the "Night must not be synonymous with fright" line again, only without the raised forefinger.

"You're really going to do this, sir?" he asked.

"I didn't point the finger that time, Marcus," the mayor said.

"I mean the speech itself. You're going to take the risk?"

"I didn't get elected to sit in my office in a flak jacket," the mayor said.

"Ready for tomorrow?" Melbourne asked Repetto.

They were in Melbourne's office, along with Lou Murchison. Melbourne was seated behind his big desk, making a tent of his fingers and barely turning this way, then that in his swivel chair. Repetto and Murchison were in the leather chairs angled toward the desk. The swivel chair squeaked. The office smelled faintly of cigar smoke, making Repetto wish he had a cigar. Not one of the ropes Melbourne smoked, though.

"There's no being all the way ready for something like this," Murchison said.

Melbourne stopped swiveling and gave him a cautioning look over his tented fingers.

"Our SWAT snipers know their stations and have their instructions," Murchison said. "The Rockefeller Center area's flooded with NYPD, in uniform and undercover. We've synchronized with the mayor's security and know the schedule, but you know how these rallies can get out of hand."

"I don't care how out of hand this one gets, as long as the mayor survives," Melbourne said.

"Two of his security men have that special responsibility," Murchison said.

At first Repetto didn't know what he meant. By the time he'd caught on, Murchison was explaining.

"One on each side of the mayor is assigned to take the bullet."

"Jesus!" Melbourne said.

"They're gung ho," Murchison said.

"Mostly gung," Repetto said. "By the time they can react, the bullet'll be in the mayor."

"Guts, though," Melbourne said.

Probably all over the podium, Repetto thought, but knew better than to say.

"Ten minutes before the mayor speaks, we go on high alert," Murchison said. "We stay that way until he gets his political tail away from the podium."

"Will he be wearing a protective vest?" Repetto asked.

"No. Says it'd be noticeable under his suit coat and ruin the effect of what he's trying to do, which is to show the Sniper the city can't be scared into shutting down."

"More guts," Melbourne said.

"Votes," Murchison said.

"You're a cynic."

"I'm a cynic. Maybe it's the job."

Melbourne turned to Repetto. "How about the subway system?"

"It's been staked out the last couple of days, especially the closed stops. If our sniper does travel by abandoned train tunnels, he probably enters and leaves them at closed stops."

"Are there that many abandoned or temporarily closed subway tunnels?" Melbourne asked.

"Miles of them."

"And all we've got suggesting the Sniper's using them is that match with the mud."

"All we've got so far. Are any of the names on the disgruntled employee list transit workers?"

"Some. But they've been ruled out. And the list goes back ten years." Melbourne rooted through a file on his desk and leaned forward to hand a copy of the list of names to Repetto.

Repetto's gaze played down the column of thirty-seven names, complete with last-known addresses. Thirty of them had been lined out. The name Joel Vanya did not appear.

"Why only ten years back?" Repetto asked.

Melbourne made a dismissive motion with both hands, as if flicking away something that was closing in on him from all directions. "Long time to hold a grudge. You gotta figure, more than ten years, the Sniper would've struck back at the city a long time ago."

Repetto didn't answer. He saw that Alex Reyals's name hadn't been lined out. The former cop. Meg had been assigned to that one; Repetto would have to ask her about him.

"Here's something else both of you should see," Melbourne said. "An anonymous letter written to the *Times*. A journalist there with sharp eyes and a curious mind saw that the note was typed rather than done on a computer printer. The newspaper doesn't get many of those these days. He also noticed the similarity in the typeface with the previous Sniper notes. The lab confirmed the same typewriter was used. *Times* doesn't know that yet."

"Our killer's actually urging the mayor to speak at the rally," Murchison said disbelievingly, handing the note back to Melbourne. "The bastard has some gall."

344   John Lutz

"Either that or he's a great admirer of the mayor," Repetto said.

Melbourne looked at him, doing the tent thing again with his stubby, powerful fingers. "What do you think?"

"I think he's gonna be there tomorrow," Repetto said. "He might even have wanted us to figure out this letter's from him. And if he didn't want it, he sure as hell doesn't care about it, or he wouldn't have sent it."

"He could be daring us," Murchison said.

"Oh, with every breath."

"We gonna be ready for him?" Melbourne asked, looking from one man to the other, and sounding too much like a desperate football coach exhorting his team to overcome a lopsided score.

Murchison nodded and held up crossed fingers on each hand.

Repetto said, "If he shows, we act. He won't get away via the subway system."

"And how we gonna know if he shows?" Melbourne asked.

Repetto and Murchison exchanged glances. It was Murchison who said it:

"The only plan with a reasonable chance of getting our man is one that concentrates on what happens *after* the mayor is shot."

Not what the coach wanted to hear.

47

At the plush Marimont Hotel on West Forty-eighth Street, a block south of Rockefeller Plaza, a handsome man wearing sunglasses and with a slight foreign accent paid cash for a requested suite on a high floor. He was carrying a large gray Louis Vuitton duffel bag and politely refused a bellhop's offer to take it to his room.

The hotel was too far from the Plaza to provide opportunity for an accurate rifle shot, made even more difficult because the shooter would have to aim over shorter buildings between rifle and target. This apparent impossibility was exactly why the Night Sniper had chosen the Marimont. That and the fact that a serial killer would be highly unlikely to check into such an exclusive hotel. The mayor's security wouldn't consider the site a threat.

Upon entering the spacious and tastefully furnished suite, the Night Sniper placed his bag on the bed and unzipped it. He seemed to know exactly where everything was in the bag and didn't unpack completely, only removed a pair of jeans, a dark T-shirt, and worn jogging shoes. From his pocket he withdrew a pair of flesh-colored latex gloves and slipped them on. From now on he would be extremely careful about what he touched in the suite, or he would be wearing gloves.

After changing clothes and hanging his tailored suit in the closet, he went to a window, opened it, and looked out at the tar and gravel roof of the setback in the building's construction. There was a drop of about three feet from the window ledge to the roof. The Night Sniper sat on the ledge, swiveled his body, and stepped down onto the firm, rough surface.

He'd scouted the location carefully. It would do, but barely—which was exactly why it was ideal. After tomorrow night, his reputation as a marksman would become legendary, and fear would know no bounds. The roofs of surrounding buildings were all much lower than the outcropping on which he stood, and behind him the Marimont rose another five stories of blank brick wall. No one could peer up at him, or down. The Sniper was invisible to anyone earthbound, but there was always the possibility of a police helicopter spotting him, some observer being alert for anything suspicious even this far from Rockefeller Plaza.

He glanced at the sky uneasily, then went back to the window and hoisted himself back up into his suite.

He returned to the bag he was carrying when he checked in. He felt around in it carefully, then removed a light aluminum frame and a small tool kit. Carrying frame and tool kit, he went back out onto the outcropping roof.

It took him only a few minutes to screw four steel brackets into the roof, then fit the legs of the metal frame into them. On the frame's top cross braces, he attached with thumbscrews two small but sturdy vises, then returned to his suite and assembled the custom target rifle.

On the roof again, he checked the sky to make sure there were no helicopters about, then went to the edge of the roof, where he'd bolted down the frame and vises. Making sure the telescoping aluminum frames were tight in their brackets, he adjusted the frame so it was slightly higher than the parapet, then fitted the rifle firmly in the vises.

With another glance at the sky, he crouched low and peered through the rifle's telescopic sight to the corner of a distant building, adjusted the sight, and could see the plaza where the podium was being constructed for tomorrow night's TBTC rally. He knew his bullet would have to barely miss the distant building's corner that was almost in line with where the lectern would be, and where the mayor would stand to speak. The Night Sniper thought again that any skilled marksman would assess this as an impossible shot, and would be correct, which was why the Marimont wasn't being factored into rally security plans.

He waited patiently, sighting through the scope, an ear attuned to any sound in the sky.

The sounds below were from Con Ed continuing lengthy repairs that entailed tearing up the sidewalk near the hotel with jackhammers. Con Ed, the city, his unknowing accomplice. He was amused by the notion.

The Sniper waited for the pounding of the jackhammers to cover the report of the rifle, then squeezed the trigger.

Carefully maintaining the position of the rifle in the vises, he unlocked the legs of the framework from its brackets affixed to the roof. Carrying rifle and framework as one inflexible piece back to the window, he returned to his suite.

Now for perhaps his biggest risk. He placed frame and rifle on the closet floor, then left the suite. The DO NOT DISTURB sign was still on the door, but there was always the off chance that a maid or maintenance crew member would for some reason enter the suite and look in the closet. A slim possibility, but the Sniper knew it was such possibilities that posed the most danger. Enough of them, and the odds tilted.

Wearing his sunglasses, he elevatored to the lobby and left the hotel. He walked the three blocks to the blank brick wall he'd just shot. Standing nearby with his arms crossed, his sunglasses hooked over the neck of his T-shirt, he glanced around and above like a tourist taking in the city. It was easier than he'd anticipated to see where the soft bullet he'd fired from so far away had chipped the brick surface, six inches from the building corner it must barely clear. The rifle was shooting true, as he knew it would.

He returned to the hotel, then patiently, patiently, repeated this process three more times. Each time he removed the inflexible frame with vise-attached rifle from the roof brackets and concealed it in the closet, walked the three blocks to the corner, and observed the results of his shots. Each time he calculated trajectory, angle, and windage. The wind, of course, would be the only variable, but the weather report for tomorrow night was a virtual repeat of this evening's. Fate was cooperating.

His last shot had struck the wall less than an inch from the building's corner. When he returned to the hotel, the slightest adjustment of the precision scope, the precision rifle, its frame secure in its roof brackets, was all that was needed, and he could be sure.

Precision.

He felt a warmth spread in him, and a confidence. He'd figured out how to make this seemingly impossible shot. He'd make it by not making it.

Well, not exactly.

In a sense, he'd already made the shot, or at least set it up, though it had taken him four tries. Next time he wouldn't have to sight in and aim, because that had already been done.

When he squeezed the trigger tomorrow night, he wouldn't have to rely on the bullet going to the mayor, because the mayor would have gone to where the bullet would be.

The Night Sniper would stay with the firmly mounted and aimed rifle now; it needed only have its supporting frame affixed to the metal roof brackets to duplicate today's shot. Until the time of the mayor's death arrived, the Sniper would remain behind the DO NOT DISTURB sign, wearing surgical gloves even while eating crustless sandwiches and drinking Evian.

While he was confident about the shot he'd make tomorrow night, it bothered him that the subway stops were being watched. It was something he hadn't planned on. He'd been counting on his frequent manner of traveling underground and avoiding attention and capture after a shooting; his *homeless* clothes and backpack were in the Louis Vuitton bag. The cloth bag itself would fold and fit neatly into his backpack, along with his rifle, when he left the hotel via a side door.

He shrugged inwardly, knowing nothing other than vengeance was writ in stone. Perhaps the tight subway security necessitated a change of tactics. He had some ideas in that regard.

Placing his water bottle on the carpet, he walked to the window and looked out at the descending night and the array of lights that lay before him like a kingdom he'd sworn to destroy. His was a life unwasted. A life that meant something grand. Pride stirred deeper emotion. For a moment a yearning for his dead mother and his wronged and lost fathers rose like fire in him and he thought he might cry.

Instead he smiled, liking the way his plans were shaping up, admiring his own nimble adaptation to his opponent's every move.

Murder was so much like chess.

He went down to the lobby for only a few minutes to use a public phone.

48

By 7:30 PM, the area around Rockefeller Plaza was teeming with over twenty thousand people. Various speakers found their way to the podium: various rights advocates, councilmen, and other city officials spoke briefly to demonstrate their confidence and courage, some of them unconsciously slouching as if to make themselves smaller targets. One of them, a councilman from Brooklyn, actually dived to the plank floor when a nearby balloon popped; then he managed to rise and toe the floor as if he'd slipped on a protruding nail or a wrinkle in the green outdoor carpet. Not a few in the crowd had reacted the same way, so he was greeted with only sporadic boos or laughter.

The speakers appeared not only live but on four large digital TV screens raised and angled so everyone could see who was at the massed microphones. News channel trucks, local and national, were parked as near as possible to the podium, some of them with their large tower antennae raised high above the masses. Now and then someone emerged from the crowd to invade the small area roped off for the trucks, cameras, and crews, then mug or go into a wave-and-smile routine.

"They're acting like it's a St. Patrick's Day rally," Meg said to Repetto. They were standing on Forty-ninth Street with a view of the Plaza.

"They know there's only one true target," Repetto said. "I wonder how many of them are here hoping the mayor is shot."

"Plenty," Meg said. "It's the way people's minds work."

"Some people, anyway."

"You sound less cynical than I am," Meg said.

"I am, Meg. Haven't you noticed?" He smiled at her. "On the other hand, you seem more . . . contented lately."

She stared at him. What the hell did Repetto mean by that, with a kind of smirk she'd seen on men before?

By the time she'd decided to ask him, he was speaking into his cell phone and had moved away into the crowd.

At 8:30 one of the mayor's aides began to introduce him. The crowd's mood changed. Those farthest back pressed forward. Those nearest the podium massed closer to it.

The aide, a pol Repetto knew as one of those who gave the NYPD the most heat from City Hall, made a grand gesture and raised his hands high to lead the applause. The crowd roared, some riding the shoulders of others and obscuring Meg's view. She focused on one of the wall-sized screens and saw a small, gray-haired figure in an immaculately tailored dark blue suit stride toward the podium. The crowd noise became deafening.

The mayor grinned wide and raised a hand high with his fingers in the victory sign, then made a damping, downward motion with both hands so the noise might subside enough for him to begin his speech.

It took several minutes for the crowd to become orderly enough that he might be heard.

* * *

Almost three blocks away, on the setback roof of the Marimont Hotel, the Night Sniper crouched behind the rifle set by vises in its rigid aluminum frame. The frame was mounted firmly and immovably to the blacktop and gravel roofing material and the planking beneath it. The frame, the rifle with its night scope and flash suppresser, composed a virtual one-piece unit that was as steady as the building itself.

The Sniper, peering intently through the telescopic sight, saw and heard nothing other than the figure of the mayor at the lectern and the distant roar of the crowd. He hadn't counted on the oversize TV screens, but fortunately they didn't block his incredibly narrow field of fire.

Motionless as the lethal creation he'd attached to the roof, he waited for the moment he knew would be his. He wanted to read the mayor's body language, to feel, to know, that the mayor wouldn't move suddenly and avoid his fate.

Even from this distance he *could* feel it; he was inside the mayor's mind. Hunter and prey were one, and the bullet would travel the arc of connection between them as surely as if it were on tracks.

The metal frame and vises held the rifle firmly. His eye was less than an inch from the scope. The only part of the rifle he touched, ever so lightly, was the trigger.

Elated by the turnout and crowd enthusiasm, the mayor raised both hands high and then lowered them palms-out. There was something like silence from the boisterous crowd.

He placed both palms on the lectern and glanced at his notes, leaning slightly forward to be closer to the microphones:

"Citizens of New York. This night we lay claim . . . "

He lapsed into silence and looked around as if astounded, then slumped over the lectern and slid to the floor. His notes fluttered down around him like white birds in the night as the echoing report of the rifle reverberated along the avenues. Women began to scream.

Meg saw the mayor's security rush forward. Several of them stood over the fallen mayor and desperately scanned the surrounding buildings. It was impossible to know which way to look for the source of the shot.

The aide who'd introduced the mayor was suddenly at the microphones. "Ladies and gentlemen, please stay calm. All of you, damn it! We've got an emergency here!"

Buffeted by the crowd, Meg saw the TV screens above the podium go blank. She tried to call Repetto on her cell phone but it was knocked from her hand. A big man in a yellow shirt elbowed her aside and she punched him in the ribs.

Be professional!

She gave up trying to retrieve the cell phone; it was probably trampled flat anyway. Instead, she began fighting her way through the crowd toward the podium, not sure what she'd do when she got there. She could hear sirens wailing in the distance now, converging on the Plaza from every direction.

Why didn't they plan for this? It was sure to happen. They should have had an ambulance waiting nearby.

But somebody at City Hall was ahead of Meg. Men and women were frantically clearing away the lectern and chairs on the podium, creating a large, flat platform. Blue uniforms and suited security surrounded the platform, moving back the crowd, sometimes not so gently.

Lights, a loud fluttering sound, and a helicopter dropped almost straight down from the night sky. Its skids settled perfectly on the stage that had become a landing pad, and within less than a minute the mayor, already on a stretcher, was transferred to the chopper through a wide side door.

* * *

Three blocks away, the Night Sniper saw the helicopter approach from beyond the Plaza and drop between tall buildings to land on the platform. *Very efficient.*

He removed the frame from its brackets and scooped gravel over them so they weren't visible from inside the hotel.

The Sniper was back in his suite before he saw the helicopter, with what surely must be the mayor's body, rise back into the dark sky above the bright haze of the city.

He was more excited than he'd anticipated as he broke down the frame and rifle, then fitted them in his Louis Vuitton bag.

There had been a change of plans. He was sure he hadn't been spotted outside, and with the flash suppresser, even if someone had been looking in his direction from the distant podium, they wouldn't have seen the muzzle flash. He felt safe at the hotel, at least for a while.

He began undressing, trying to stay calm. *Jesus! This is something!* His fingers were trembling as he fumbled at his belt buckle.

The mayor! This is something!

He heard a high-pitched giggle and was startled until he realized it was his own.

Not good! This wasn't like him. He had to gain control of himself, of his actions, during the rest of the evening.

He worked his legs out of his jeans, then sat on the edge of the bed to change socks. He glanced at his watch. More time had elapsed than he'd thought, but he refused to make himself hurry. Every move was deliberate and economical.

Get hold of yourself, of your emotions. Not like you. Not like you. Get hold.

Jesus, this is something!

* * *

Twenty minutes later, the Night Sniper looked nothing like the homeless wretch he usually became immediately after claiming a victim. He was wearing a navy blue Armani suit with a subtle black weave, black Italian leather shoes, a white shirt with gold cuff links, and a maroon and black silk tie. His wig was neatly affixed and almost impossible to distinguish from his real hair. He was tanned, smoothly shaved, and carried the faint scent of cologne.

He took the elevator to the lobby, to make sure nothing he should know about was occurring.

Everything seemed normal, considering the news was out that the mayor had been shot. People were clustered in small knots and talking to each other, some of them standing and staring at a TV screen in the lounge. Outside, beyond the hotel's bank of tinted glass doors, two valets stood beneath the awning talking to half a dozen teenage girls, while a third valet was trying unsuccessfully to hail a cab.

He'd managed to hail two cabs, and the girls were piling in, when the Night Sniper pressed the Up button.

As he waited for the elevator that had just descended to empty out, an attractive, midtwenties woman, escorted by an older man, glanced at him appraisingly and smiled as she walked past. He smiled back, used to being noticed by women. She glanced back at him as two businessman types stepped into the elevator, and one of them held the door so it wouldn't close until a woman who might have been an airline attendant made it inside. Moving into the elevator, the Night Sniper saw that she not only had the sort of folded hanging bag used by flight attendants, but there was an American Airlines employee's tag on it. She thanked the man who'd held the door, then noticed the Night Sniper paying attention to her and smiled at him. "I was checking out and remembered I left something in my room," she said, as if he'd asked her a question. "I'm a flight attendant. Gotta get to LaGuardia. Not that there'll be anything flying out for a while, after what just happened."

He merely nodded, not wanting to be remembered by the woman if she was asked about him later.

"What just happened?" one of the business types asked.

"The mayor was shot while he was giving a speech."

"That rally thing?" the man asked.

The woman nodded.

"Damn! The mayor of New York . . . He dead?"

"Dunno." She glanced at her watch.

"Your room near the elevator?" the man asked. "We can hold it here for you while you get whatever it is you forgot."

"Thanks, but don't do that. It'll take me a while, and I might make a phone call."

She got off on the tenth floor. The businessmen—if that's what they were—got off on the twelfth. As they strode together down the hall, they were talking about the mayor being shot, wondering out loud if he'd been killed.

Natural enough, the Night Sniper thought. He was wondering the same thing.

But there would be time to learn the mayor's condition. The connection had been made, the bullet sent true to its target. Despite the difficulty of the shot, he was reasonably sure the mayor was dead.

He rode the elevator all the way up to the hotel's Pot-O-Gold Room, for dining and dancing with the woman he'd arranged to meet there.

He was confident of how the rest of the evening would go. The mood in the Pot-O-Gold Room would be subdued at first, but the pianist and cabaret singer who'd been performing there for years would manage to lift spirits. The food would be delicious, the wine at least acceptable, and when the singer finished his set, his four-piece backup band would play soft music.

The Sniper and his companion would sip champagne and dance and stay late and have a grand time.

Zoe would get a little drunk.

The Night Sniper wouldn't.

49

Captain Lou Murchison was standing back beyond the podium where the press couldn't get to him. Even from this distance he looked as if he'd just been sentenced to be hanged. The cops around him were keeping their distance; they knew what Murchison had and didn't want to catch it.

Melbourne sat in one of the radio cars behind the wheel. Repetto was beside him, Meg and Birdy in the back. Meg didn't much like it, sitting back where the suspects rode.

The least of her troubles.

"Looks like the mayor's got a slim chance," Melbourne said. "Bullet entered his side and missed the heart. It's still in a lung. Nicked an artery, and they're trying to stop internal bleeding. Touch and go." He was staring out the windshield at the stragglers who were left after the Plaza was cleared, at the techs and plainclothes detectives milling around up on the podium. "Fuckin' mess!"

"Murchison did what he could," Repetto said. The car's police radio was on low, like background conversation in a restaurant, only more abrupt and with the occasional crackle of static.

"Fuck Murchison."

Repetto knew that pretty much summed up what was left of Murchison's career.

"What about the subways?" Melbourne asked.

"Locked down tight as soon as the shot sounded. The Sniper would have had a hard time using the subways to get out of the area."

"He didn't have to go underground," Melbourne said. "The way all hell broke loose and there were people running every which way, he could have simply joined the crowd."

"Could have," Repetto said, "but I doubt he'd have counted on it ahead of time."

Melbourne was staring at Murchison again. "Murchison was supposed to prevent this, or at least nail the bastard that did it right after."

Repetto said nothing, simply sat watching two of the plainclothes detectives on the podium stare up and around, trying to figure out where the shot might have originated. They might as well have been figuring the odds on rain.

"Ball's in your court now, Vin," Melbourne said. The threat was implicit. Repetto could become the next Murchison.

"I've already got the uniforms you gave me canvassing the surrounding buildings."

"And doesn't that sound familiar?"

"I need more people," Repetto said. "Maybe more than you can give me."

"For this I can supply warm bodies."

"We'll keep on the surrounding buildings, even the ones we had covered before the mayor's speech. Also question the NYPD sharpshooters stationed around, see if they spotted anything unusual. If we don't find anything tonight, tomorrow when it's light out, we'll use the extra uniforms to widen the circle of our investigation to take in even the unlikely places the Sniper might have been when he squeezed the trigger."

"I thought we had everything covered that was on a line from the lectern and within range. That's what Murchison assured me."

Repetto wished Melbourne would get off Murchison. "Maybe the Sniper's even more of a marksman than we thought."

"If he can shoot through solid walls, he is."

"We've been looking into former SWAT snipers and ex-military types. Professionals. Possibly we should be looking at amateurs."

"Amateurs?" Melbourne looked first disbelieving, then nauseated. Or maybe it was the reflected alternating red and blue light from outside the car.

"Competition shooters," Repetto explained. "Olympic athletes. They might be better shots even than the SWAT or military snipers. We got any present or former Olympic-caliber target shooters in the area?"

"We'll sure as hell find out," Melbourne said. "If we have anybody left tomorrow who's not out examining buildings for blocks around."

Repetto thought about suggesting Melbourne set Murchison to the task. *No, no . . .* He rested his arm on the seat back and twisted around so he could see Meg and Birdy.

Meg came hyperalert, knowing Repetto was looking for suggestions. Or volunteers.

"How 'bout that uniform's been so capable," Birdy said, "Weaver? She's a smart one."

Meg glared at him. *Prick!*

"Officer Nancy Weaver," Repetto explained to Melbourne. "She's hot to get out of uniform and back into plainclothes, and she's got good skills and instincts."

"Give *that* one a list of top amateur shooters in the area and she'll have 'em lined up like ducks in a gallery," Birdy said.

Such enthusiasm. Meg wondered if Birdy was sleeping with Weaver. Or was he just in line?

"You like Weaver for it, put her on it," Melbourne said to Repetto. "I'll get the computer whizzes on the hunt, soon as I make a phone call. We'll sic this bloodhound Weaver on the names tomorrow morning."

Bloodhound. Meg liked that.

"I don't exactly see her as any kinda hound," Birdy said. "'Specially since she's pretty much a looker."

Repetto locked eyes with him in the car's outside mirror until Birdy looked away. *Might Birdy be sleeping with Weaver?*

"Then she's a pretty little poodle," Melbourne said. "Long as she can do the job, I don't care what breed she is." He worked the handle and opened the door. "I'll call you when we have the list for Weaver," he said to Repetto. "Right now I'm gonna meet with the commissioner and activate the entire available force. You'll have plenty of uniforms, plain-clothes, and undercover cops here at your disposal before you know it."

He climbed out of the car, then leaned down and stuck his head back inside before shutting the door. "Anybody asks, tell 'em nobody in the NYPD better even think about sleep until I sleep, and I'm not gonna sleep for a long time. The mayor's been shot. Sleep's not an option."

They watched Melbourne hurry away to avoid a pursuing woman who looked like a journalist.

"Sleep is not an option," Repetto reiterated.

"Guess we're gonna have to catnap," Birdy said.

"Not unless you have nine lives," Meg told him.

By the time she'd heard the mayor was shot, Zoe had already consumed one gin martini and half of another, while waiting for her dinner date to arrive in the Pot-O-Gold Room on top of the Marimont Hotel. *The mayor shot.* She should go in early tomorrow, or possibly cancel the dinner and leave the posh restaurant right now. Such a momentous occurrence, it didn't seem right to be sitting here sipping drinks and looking forward to a romantic evening. She could leave a message with the maitre d'. On the other hand, she was a profiler, not assigned or needed to respond to emergencies.

All thoughts of cancelation left her when her date walked into the restaurant. Not a few women's heads turned so they could stare at him. He looked more handsome than Zoe had ever seen him. He was fit, tanned, and downright gorgeous in an obviously expensive dark suit, white shirt, and a tie that matched the handkerchief peeking out of the suit coat pocket. When he walked, the swing of his arms made gold cuff links glitter.

Rich, Zoe thought. That was the word that came to mind when she looked at him. *Rich*. That and another word.

"Been waiting long?" he asked, sliding onto the chair opposite hers. The petite tables were round, with yellow and white china, silver flatware, and cut crystal glittering on white cloth. They were small enough so that two people seated opposite each other could lean forward and kiss, made for romantic assignations.

"Awhile," Zoe said, "but it was worth it."

In so many ways!

The evening progressed with a smile and a peck on the cheek, another drink, smooth conversation, a white and a red wine with a delicious meal, then an after-dinner port.

Zoe consumed another drink gradually, then champagne between dances. She tried to stretch the time between sips, but slowing down didn't help. The alcohol had her now, and she knew it.

The mayor shot . . . mayor of New York . . . The concept knocked on the door of her consciousness from time to time, but she didn't invite it in.

She danced, she drank, she gazed hypnotized into eyes like blue ice. God, he was handsome! He could even dance well. He was perfect!

By the time they rode the elevator up to his floor, she thought tomorrow would be soon enough to worry about the mayor.

At 3:00 AM Repetto crawled into bed alongside Lora, trying not to make the springs squeak. A calmer Melbourne had relented on his rash and impractical no-sleep policy. When mind and body were dead tired, both were trudging along in place, not tending to business but trying to ride the treadmill to some future respite that never quite arrived.

The area around Rockefeller Plaza was frozen, cordoned off by yellow crime scene ribbon, isolated from pedestrian and vehicular traffic by NYPD sawhorses and sleepy cops in parked patrol cars. What a nightmare the rerouted traffic would cause tomorrow morning, when people tried to make their way to work.

In the morning the investigation would begin again full force. The search area around the Plaza would be widened. The Night Sniper might seem like a phantom, but the bullet that struck the mayor was real and had to have come from *somewhere*. And *somewhere* could be found.

Repetto hadn't been this exhausted in years. He sighed as he settled down on the mattress and pulled the light sheet up around him. Cool air from the vent near the ceiling flowed lightly over him, soothing him through the thin linen.

Lora stirred beside him. "You just get in?"

"A few minutes ago," Repetto said. "I made straight for the bed."

He heard her roll onto her side and felt the sheet pull taut. "So how's the mayor?"

"They think he might make it."

"Good. He's not a bad guy. Not that I'm gonna vote for him." She raised her upper body, dug an elbow into the mattress, and cupped her chin in her hand, staring down at Repetto. "Any progress finding out who shot him?"

"Not so far."

"Others still working?"

"No. Skeleton crew's got the area secure. It all starts again tomorrow morning."

"It's already tomorrow morning."

"Um."

She was silent for a while, unmoving. "I take it you don't want to talk."

"Too tired."

Her lips were cool on his forehead, and he heard and felt her lie back down beside him.

Weary as he was, Repetto knew he wouldn't fall asleep easily. Still too much adrenaline in his system.

"I'm worried about Meg," he said.

Linen rustled, Lora sitting up now.

"She's acting peculiar," Repetto said. "Like she's . . ."

"In love?"

Repetto didn't lift his head from the pillow, but craned his neck so he could look at Lora in the dimness. "Why do you say that?"

"I've had lunch with her a few times recently. I know the signs."

Women and lunch, Repetto thought. If Lora wasn't lunching with Zoe Brady, she was lunching with Meg. He really didn't mind now, perhaps because he knew he was helpless to control the female tradition that kept so many Manhattan restaurants in business. Besides, food and gossip could be a revealing combination, and he was curious about both women.

"Also," Lora said, "I shouldn't tell you, but she mentioned to me she might have found someone."

Repetto was wide awake now. "Ah! She say who?"

"No, she was very secretive."

"That's it?" Repetto asked. "Meg told you that much, then stopped talking?"

"About that subject, yes."

"So why did she mention it to you in the first place?"

"She's a woman. We all like to share the good news."

Repetto lay for a few minutes listening to the faint and distant traffic sounds drifting on the night. New York. Never completely silent or completely still. Never completely predictable. Like people.

"What about Birdy as Meg's secret suitor?" he asked.

"Be serious. Anyway, he's married."

"They spend a lot of time together."

"Okay, they do. And love can be random. Do *you* think Meg might be involved with Birdy?"

"No."

"I can tell you one thing for sure," Lora said. "She's hooked."

We're all hooked, Repetto thought. He listened to a siren wailing off in the distance. Trouble never let up, never eased up on people.

Resting a hand on Lora's thigh, precious contact with the person he loved more than his life, he dropped into dreamless sleep.

Sooner or later, one way or another, we're all hooked. . . .

Safely back in his suite, lying beside the sleeping Zoe, the Night Sniper watched the silent TV screen beyond the foot of the bed. Zoe's bare foot extended from beneath the sheet so that her toes blocked his view of the screen's lower right quarter.

A muted blond anchorwoman with seriously collagened lips was smiling widely as she soundlessly mouthed the news. The TV was set for closed caption. He read in white capital letters on a black background that the mayor was expected to survive.

The Sniper had to contain himself to keep from cursing out loud and waking Zoe.

No, she wouldn't wake up. Not after all the alcohol she'd taken in tonight. Zoe was a smart, competent woman, but early in their relationship he'd noticed she liked to drink, maybe even had a developing problem. It was a weakness he'd homed in on, knowing its usefulness.

It hadn't been difficult to accelerate her drinking. After a while it was no longer even necessary for him to be subtle. Zoe might have an understanding of the criminal mind—the *average* criminal mind—but like so many people, she was blind to her own vulnerabilities.

Her drinking made her easy to convince, and to manipulate. Usually they ended their dates in her bed, and while she lay in an alcohol- and sex-induced slumber, he would log on to her Toshiba laptop and learn what he could about the NYPD's progress in the Night Sniper case. Those files he thought might be of further use to him, he copied.

Zoe snored softly, and her breathing became even deeper and more regular. She was hours away from so much as fluttering her eyelids.

The Night Sniper gazed again at the TV and he did curse out loud. He'd missed his shot. Not completely, but he had missed. It was unacceptable. He directed another expletive at the TV screen. Zoe didn't stir.

He laced his fingers behind his head and stared at the ceiling, thinking. So his shot hadn't been perfect and the mayor would survive. Perhaps, considering the innate difficulties and the variables, the shot actually *was* impossible. Maybe he'd asked too much of himself.

He smiled in the soft, flickering light from the TV, then scooted back on the mattress so he could watch the screen through eyes that weren't narrowed by angle. He saw that mayoral aides and assorted sycophants were huddled grimly in what looked like a hospital waiting room. They knew that whatever the mayor's chances for survival, the game wasn't over.

The Sniper would settle on another target to strike soon and make up for the mayor's narrow escape (so far) from death. Perhaps the target should be Repetto, who'd already lost his surrogate son and protégé.

No, not Repetto. Not yet. Repetto deserved not death, but another loss, as the Night Sniper had lost two fathers.

The police would expect him to try for Repetto. Zoe might even tell them it was in the Sniper's character and methodology. In fact, he might be able to steer her in that direction, advise the NYPD on how best to apprehend him. *Intriguing idea.* He absently reached over and gently twirled a long strand of Zoe's red hair.

The Night Sniper's genius was in doing the unexpected.

He knew what Zoe didn't know. What the police didn't know.

Repetto deserved more grief, more pain, another loss. And just when he was getting so close—or thought he was.

Loss, not pain.

The game had changed and the Sniper had even left Repetto clues to tantalize and torment. That was another good reason to save Repetto for later. He should suffer. He should *know* he'd been outsmarted. Let the law and the media think the Sniper was displaying the serial killer's well-known subconscious desire to be stopped, to be caught. Zoe might even tell them that, encourage them. *Wonderful!*

But it was the game. The vengeance game.

Another loss for Repetto. Another grave. Another emotional bullet to the heart. No blood, no pulped flesh, but another rend that would never heal as long as Repetto lived.

Lying silently in the dim room, listening to Zoe breathe, the Night Sniper quietly composed in his mind his next theater seat note:

Rapunzel will take a tumble.

50

Bobby spent the night in the Dismas Shelter in Lower Manhattan. Ordinarily he preferred the street, especially during those times of year when the weather was bearable. But with the rally uptown, he thought the entire borough would be too active, not only with the people who roamed the streets before and after the affair at Rockefeller Plaza, but with those who saw them as prey. With all the muggers, rapists, pickpockets, con men, car thieves, and various other criminal types on the prowl, the shelter was a safer place.

The food was miserable but free—if you didn't count the sermon—and the beds were little softer than park benches or subway seats. But once you warned away the crazies and resolved to sleep lightly, the shelters would do for a night or two.

The coffee was free that morning in small Styrofoam cups. Bobby took his outside the shelter, sniffing cool morning air that smelled fresh after the dormitory scent of stale booze, vomit, and pine-scented disinfectant he'd just left. Sipping the strong black brew, he trudged two blocks across town, then uptown, putting distance between himself and others who'd ventured from the shelter at about the same time.

No one had mentioned the news while Bobby was in the shelter. It was a place where life-changing events were smaller and more personal, and horizons nearer. When Bobby noticed a harried-looking business type dropping a folded *Times* in a trash basket, he stopped walking. He went to dig out the paper before it might become damp from discarded garbage, and saw for the first time the headlines proclaiming the mayor had been shot.

There was no place nearby to sit down, so he leaned his back against a building and read, ignoring the glances of people hurrying past on the sidewalk.

The mayor would live. That was good. The asshole Sniper had missed for the first time.

Why?

Too much security, Bobby figured. He knew a few things about being a sniper. It must have been necessary for the Night Sniper to set up and shoot from farther away than usual. And of course, if he'd set up too close to the Plaza, he'd have a harder time getting away after the shot.

Bobby read that the police thought the Sniper might be using subway tunnels to get around. Even hiding out in subway stops that were permanently or temporarily closed. Bobby had spent his time down there. It was a rough place to live. The Sniper was one tough guy if he was using subway stops and tunnels for shelter and to travel on foot.

It could be done, though, Bobby thought. It could be done. He recalled seeing the ragged man who didn't fit his surroundings going down into a subway stop. Bobby had assumed the man wasn't real, but now, considering what was in the paper, *maybe he had been real.*

Bobby's legs and feet were beginning to ache. He folded

the paper and tucked it beneath his arm to read more carefully later, then pushed away from the building and stretched
in the warm sun heating up the concrete.

It took him about twenty minutes to get to Washington
Square, where he found a bench, shooed away half a dozen
lethargic pigeons, and sat down. Tired as he was, he didn't
lie down; he didn't want to be chased. He sat leaning back
with his eyes half closed, his face to the heat of the sun.

After a while he felt stronger, but he was hungry. He'd
have to scare up some food, or the money to buy some,
pretty soon. He remained on the bench, but he kept his eyes
open for someone throwing away anything edible—a doughnut or breakfast muffin or pizza slice. It was amazing how
many students from NYU liked cold pizza for breakfast.

So the ragged man is real.

Bobby couldn't get the man with the hurried gait and the
worn-out backpack out of his mind.

A girl about twenty, college girl probably, wearing a tight
T-shirt and jeans that were slung low on her hips, walked
past. Bobby's gaze went with her. She had some kind of tattoo
just above the crack of her ass. And she was talking on a cell
phone.

"Way, way wrong!" a female voice said nearby. This
woman was wearing a business suit and carrying a leather
case in one hand. Her other hand held a cell phone pressed
to her ear. She ignored Bobby as she swished past on high
heels. She was built better than the college girl and he
wished she were the one wearing those jeans.

He noticed that beyond the woman a man stood talking
on a cell phone. Bobby settled back on his bench and studied
the people around him in the square. It was amazing how
many of them were talking on cell phones.

He watched the woman in the business suit lower the
phone from her ear and place it in her purse. She left the
purse open as she strode from the square and began moving

faster, flailing an arm in an attempt to hail a cab. A woman was seated about two benches down, reading a magazine, her purse beside her, a small leather case that probably contained a cell phone alongside the purse.

Bobby was no thief. It wasn't that he was so honest, more that he was stubborn. Despite his lowly position in life, he held on to his essential self. Or so he told his essential self. He drew lines. He didn't cross them. He might be down on his luck, but he wouldn't let circumstances make him a thief.

But this was different, what he had in mind. This was one of those rare times when the end actually did justify the means.

He knew he was going to steal a cell phone.

Repetto immediately understood the meaning of the note. Another nursery tale: *Rapunzel*. The beautiful girl held captive by a witch in a tower. The girl who let her braided golden hair grow so long that her lover could climb it and join her.

Only the witch had foreseen what would happen. The witch was in control.

Repetto knew who Rapunzel was in the Sniper's note, in his mind, in his sights: Amelia Rapetto.

"You've got to move out of this apartment," Repetto told his daughter, after showing her the note. "We can get you someplace safe."

Amelia didn't stir from where she sat on the sofa. "It wouldn't do any good. The Sniper might simply follow me. Or find out where I went. From what you say, and what I've read about him in the news, he might even have sources inside the police department."

Repetto couldn't deny it. He was amazed that she didn't seem frightened. Her features were so composed, so calm. He found himself proud of her, even if he wanted to grab her long braid and drag her out of this apartment. Maybe he'd do just that, to save her life.

"I have a life to live, and I'm not going to let some sick killer decide how I'm going to live it. People aren't like chess pieces he can move around anytime however he wants."

"Amelia—"

"I'm *twenty-one,* Dad."

"Meaning I can't make you move out, even for a while?"

"Awhile?"

"Until this killer is caught."

"That could be forever."

"We're talking about your *life*, Amelia."

"Yes, my life. And I'm not going to let *anyone* dictate how I'm going to live it."

"I'm not trying to do that. I'm trying to preserve your life. And the Night Sniper's not trying to dictate how you live. He's planning to end your life."

"If I'm the Rapunzel in the note."

"You don't believe he means you?"

She couldn't lie. Absently her right hand touched her luxurious long braid, slung over her shoulder and falling almost to the waist of the faded Levis she wore without a belt. "I suppose he means me."

"Then you'll get out?"

"No."

Repetto felt like kicking a piece of furniture. Kids! Teenagers! No, Amelia was no longer a teenager, no longer a child. She was an adult making an adult decision, albeit a bad one. "You're just like your mother."

"I'm like my father. Maybe I'll even be a cop someday."

Here was something new. Repetto was thrown. The women in his life seemed to keep doing that to him.

"Will you at least accept police protection?" he pleaded.

"Of course," Amelia said in an unemotional voice. "I'm not suicidal."

"Could have fooled me."

"Then you are fooled. I want to live, just like anyone else. Any of the other victims."

He watched her throat work as she swallowed. A pale shadow seemed to move across her face, and for the first time he saw fear.

But beneath the fear, the courage.

He pulled her to him and hugged her tight.

"I admit I'm afraid," she said. "Okay?" As if she were admitting getting home past curfew.

He kissed the top of her forehead. "Anyone would be. Will you at least not attend classes for a few days, stay here out of sight? For me and your mother?"

"Of course. I don't want to cause either of you any pain. And I really don't want to die! I don't! More than that, I don't want you to think that's what I want. It's just that I'm an adult. I have to make my stand here or I might regret it for the rest of my life." She stared up at him so much the way Lora did sometimes. "Please try to understand, Dad."

"I understand," Repetto assured her. He knew she was wrong, that she wouldn't always regret leaving, that this wasn't her young life's Waterloo. There would be plenty of other crises, other battles. He also knew he could never explain this to her so she'd believe it.

He held her tighter and waited until her sobs had quieted and her body had stopped shaking. The longer he held her the more he hated the idea of her staying here, in this street-level apartment. He wished Dal were still alive. He wished—

Fuck it! Dal was dead, and Repetto wanted Amelia to remain alive.

"I'll have Birdy and Meg guard you in shifts, along with some uniforms outside."

She nodded. The admission of fear had at least made her that compliant.

"Follow their instructions," Repetto told her. "In the

meantime, if you insist on staying here, don't go near the windows, and of course make sure everything stays locked. Promise?"

"Promise."

"I'll call Birdy, then talk to Melbourne and get things set up. While we're waiting for your angels to arrive, I'll make sure the apartment's sealed tight."

"Angels?"

"The ones with guns who'll be protecting you."

"I'll try hard to believe in angels," Amelia told him. She almost managed to smile. "Better guns than wings."

Repetto already had his cell phone out and was contacting Birdy. He explained the situation and told Birdy he couldn't rule out another change of tactics by the Night Sniper. Maybe he'd start killing at close range, indoors, during daylight hours, with a handgun. Nothing seemed beyond him. Repetto told Birdy to stay inside the apartment with Amelia, not even to go out for food.

"This is my daughter," he reminded Birdy.

"Then—if you don't mind my asking—why don't you get her out of there?"

"I would if I could and be sure she wouldn't return. She considers this her date with destiny. Leaving isn't what she wants. And she reminds me she's twenty-one."

"Ah, they do keep reminding you when that happens, whenever the shit gets deep. The good ones, anyway. Her father's daughter."

"Goddamned right."

Repetto told Birdy he could have food delivered, or help himself to whatever was in the refrigerator.

He was to eat with his 9mm beside his plate.

51

"Look at this," Meg said.

She was standing at the window of a high suite in the Marimont Hotel, pointing outside to the roof of a setback in the tall building.

Repetto looked. He saw shorter buildings beyond the parapet, and blue sky beyond buildings off in the distance.

"I mean look at the roof," Meg said, noticing where he was staring.

At first Repetto didn't see it. Then he noticed an irregularity in the tar and gravel roof, something small protruding. Another, identical object. Four in all, arranged as if marking the corners of a rectangle.

"So what are they?" he asked.

"We're not sure. One of the uniforms noticed them and told me about them. He came up here to check the windows, to make sure they didn't provide a view of the plaza and podium even though they're three blocks away."

"Be a hell of a shot," Repetto said, "even if the mayor was visible from here."

"C'mon out on the roof," Meg said. She grinned when he didn't reply immediately. "It's only a three-foot drop."

She opened the window, gracefully sat on the sill, then swiveled to step outside. Repetto followed, bumping his head on the window frame.

Meg led him to the four objects on the roof. Repetto stooped low and saw that they were metal painted a dull black so they weren't very visible. Stubby, hollowed, and rectangular. Brackets of some kind.

He looked up and squinted in the direction of Rockefeller Plaza. The podium and lectern hadn't been disassembled. From where he squatted, it appeared that part of the podium and about half the lectern were visible, but he couldn't be sure from this distance. But they *were* what he was looking at; he could see them far beyond the corner of a building two blocks away.

"An impossible shot," he said. "Even if the Sniper got it just right and barely cleared that building corner, he'd have to be unbelievably accurate."

"And lucky," Meg said. "But he wasn't lucky all the way. The mayor *is* still alive."

Repetto straightened up and stared at her. Then he glanced back at the building on which they stood. The window they'd exited was the only one that looked out on the setback's roof, and only blank brick wall towered above. Where he and Meg stood, they were invisible from anyone else in the Marimont or from the surrounding shorter buildings. A perfect sniper's nest. One that had to have been carefully scouted by an expert.

And they were dealing with an expert.

Still, so far away . . .

Repetto breathed in the high, clean air above the traffic-clogged street. They were high enough that not even much sound reached them from below. "You're thinking the brackets were used to support a tripod or something to steady the rifle."

"Something steadier than a tripod. There are four brackets. Some kind of brace might have fit into them, and after the shooting, the Sniper disassembled it and took it with him."

Repetto squinted again toward the Plaza and held his hand in saluting position over his eyes to shield them from the sun. "It still doesn't seem possible, Meg. Did you ask anyone from the hotel what those brackets were?"

"I described them downstairs to some of the maintenance crew. Nobody seems to know what they are. No one could come up with any possible use for them."

Repetto folded his arms and stared toward the Plaza. "You're theorizing that the Sniper broke into this suite—"

"Or got a key somehow. I examined the lock, and there's no sign it's been forced. He didn't lower himself from the roof above. The hotel restaurant's up there, the Pot-O-Gold."

"So he must have sneaked into the suite somehow and gained access to this roof. If it were two blocks closer to the podium, it would have been a perfect place to shoot from, but then it would have been checked out and covered by us."

"That might be exactly what appealed to him. It would have been written off as a threat. And this far away, it would've been easy for him to slip out of the hotel and disappear after firing the shot."

"But how could he be sure we wrote it off? Simply the seeming impossibility of the shot?"

"That, or maybe he has a contact in the NYPD."

Always possible, Repetto knew. "Suppose he did have a key, Meg? How could he know he wouldn't open the door and be face-to-face with a guest?"

"He might work for the hotel."

"It would have to be in a capacity where he could control who stayed in which room or suite. That's the only way he could plan on this suite being unoccupied during the time he needed it. Did you check at the desk and see if anyone was staying in it at the time the mayor was shot?"

"Yes. It was registered to someone, but there's no guarantee the guest was in the suite at that time. In a busy hotel like this, people come and go unnoticed."

"Has anybody stayed in the suite since the mayor was shot?"

"No. It's expensive and isn't occupied as often as ordinary rooms."

Repetto shook his head. "Even if the Sniper did manage to get in here, then out on the roof and use something to help brace his rifle, it still looks like an impossible shot."

"The Sniper's the sort who might enjoy the challenge."

"Now you sound like Zoe."

He was beginning to make Meg doubt. "Zoe's not always wrong." She was becoming argumentative, she knew, sounding petulant. But damn it . . .

Repetto went back inside, careful not to bump his head this time, and Meg followed.

"Expensive suite, all right," he said, looking around at the tasteful furniture and wall hangings. He could imagine celebrities and political dignitaries staying here.

Repetto glanced at his image in a gold-framed mirror across the room and saw that his hair was mussed from the breeze out on the roof. He smoothed it back so he didn't look so much like a wild old cop. It stuck back out. *Stubborn as Meg.*

"Maybe the Night Sniper himself registered and stayed here," he said, watching her in the mirror.

She looked surprised, then grinned. "That I kinda doubt."

"Zoe would say he'd see it as a challenge, taunting us."

"We'd have his fingerprints."

"He'd be careful ahead of time, use only one or two rooms, then wipe them down carefully before going out on the roof to take his shot."

"He does wear rubber gloves," Meg said.

"Did the maid say the guest slept here?"

Oops! "I didn't ask. Didn't imagine—"

"We're here," Repetto said. "Let's go find out."

It didn't take them long to locate the maid who'd cleaned the suite that morning. She was a heavyset Hispanic woman with strong, beautiful features and graying hair. Fifteen pounds and years beyond being a beauty queen. In an accent that was pure Brooklyn she told them the bed had been slept in, probably by two people.

"It was registered as a single," Meg told her.

The maid stared at her as if she were unbelievably naive. "Uh-huh. Single male, what I was told. Sometimes they find company, y'know?"

"You clean the entire suite?" Repetto asked.

"Sure. Even though most of it didn't need it. Did my usual thorough job. Only room that was really a mess was the large bedroom. Bedsheets all tangled like there'd been some heavy action there."

"You sure he wasn't alone?"

"Not 'less he tossed an' turned all night an' used two pillows. Sheets had a certain kinda stain and smell about 'em, too, if you know what I mean."

"You change the sheets?" Meg asked.

"Now whaddya you think?"

"They been laundered yet?" Repetto asked.

"Long time ago. Just like them towels."

"Towels?"

"There was a lotta damp towels piled in the bathtub. Like somebody took a bath or shower every couple hours."

Repetto and Meg looked at each other. Both understood the towels might have been used to wipe the suite clean of prints.

"You happen to see the suite's occupant at any time?" Repetto asked the maid.

"Never. He had the do-not-disturb sign out mosta the time. The kinda guests we get, we gotta pay attention to those signs."

They thanked the maid and let her return to work. She pushed her linen cart along the hall, appearing to be leaning hard on it and deliberately making one of the wheels squeak.

"Woman's got a burr up her ass," Meg said.

"Some do," Repetto said, giving her a look. "Let's check at the desk and see if anyone remembers the suite's occupant."

Meg felt her heartbeat quicken. Repetto suddenly seemed to be taking seriously the possibility that the Sniper was a registered guest. He was making Meg a believer. She had to walk fast to keep up with him on the way to the elevator.

They got lucky. The same desk clerk was on duty who'd checked in the suite's occupant.

"Here's where he signed in," the clerk said. He was a small man with dark hair combed straight back and shiny as patent leather, a narrow nose too long for his face. He swiveled a large black registration book for Repetto and Meg to read.

"Not many hotels still use those," Meg said.

"We don't usually, because most of our guests pay with plastic and that creates its own record. But some still use old-fashioned cash."

Meg and Repetto glanced at each other. "He paid cash?"

"Certainly did."

Repetto and Meg looked at the registration book as the clerk touched a manicured finger to the correct line. The man's name was neatly printed: *Ott Eperrepinsi*.

"Sounds foreign," Meg said. "Maybe Ott's a nickname for Otto. Maybe he's from one of those Balkan countries that're so hard to pronounce."

"Or his German mother married an Italian," Repetto said. To the desk clerk: "Do you recall what he looked like?"

"Vaguely. About average size. Dark hair. Well groomed and very fashionably dressed in suit and tie. He was rich, I'd say. Not to be crass, but we develop a feel for that here, being able to guess at net worth. We can come pretty close."

"I'll bet. Anything unusual about his appearance other than his wealth?"

"Wealth isn't unusual here at the Marimont. He was a handsome man, women would say. Had a bold bearing about him. Something else about him that isn't that unusual here. He was wearing a topper."

"Topper?"

"A toupee. I can spot them easily because I used to wear one myself, before I got my hair transplant." He absently touched his luxurious dark hair.

"That's really something," Meg said, genuinely impressed.

"Science," said the desk clerk.

"Did you happen to see him with a woman?" Repetto asked.

The desk clerk stroked the bridge of his narrow nose, giving that one some thought. "No. I only noticed him once or twice more after he checked in, going or coming. He didn't check out. Not that it was necessary, since we use electronic card keys and he paid in advance and with cash. But usually our guests stop by the desk."

"You're sure he didn't?"

"Oh yes. I was on duty that morning from early morning until past checkout time."

A man and woman arrived at the desk with a flurry of luggage wielded by an eagerly helpful bellhop. Repetto nodded to the clerk so he could move to the opposite end of the desk and check them in.

"Doesn't feel right," Meg said.

Repetto got out his wallet and removed one of his cards. "I wanna write down this guy's name before I forget it."

He leaned over the open registration book and used one of the hotel's ballpoint pens to copy the guest's name on the back of the card, then suddenly stopped writing, staring at what he'd done.

"Get some uniforms and freeze that suite," he said. His features had become hard.

Meg was too surprised to move right away.

"Asshole and his games," Repetto muttered. He finished writing on the card and looked up at her. "Zoe was right about this guy." He handed her the card.

Meg stared at it and felt a chill ripple up her back. Beneath his first writing of Ott Eperrepinsi's name, Repetto had written it again, only backward, adding comas:

I, Sniper, Repetto.

52

"My professional opinion," Meg said to Amelia, "is that you should get out of the city until we catch this guy."

They were in the Amelia's West Side apartment. Meg had caught a few hours of sleep earlier and come in to spell a haggard-looking Birdy. Though it was still light out, the blinds were closed and lamps and fixtures supplied most of the illumination. The cheaply furnished living room, with its mismatched furniture, museum posters, and shelves and stacks of books, mostly paperback, seemed smaller to Meg than when she'd first entered, more a trap than a refuge. Along one wall was a narrow table with an Apple computer on it. There was a stereo on one of the sagging bookshelves, with speakers so large they were unsettling. At least Amelia didn't have the damned things on.

"I've been informed of the dangers," Amelia said, "and my dad and I agreed to the precautions." She was sitting in a gray wing chair, her face sidelighted by a reading lamp so she was even more beautiful than usual. Her hair looked like the spun gold of fairy tales. What a shame, Meg thought, for somebody so young, vital, and attractive to die when it wasn't necessary.

It kind of irritated Meg, the way people who decided to place themselves in this kind of danger always seemed to agree only grudgingly to protection, as if they were being put out, as if a few cops or more weren't laying their lives on the line to keep the intended target alive. Still, this was a kid, too young to have developed good survival skills.

"I know what you're thinking," Amelia said, "that I'm a lot of unnecessary trouble. But I've got a right to live where I choose." Something in her voice was like her father's.

"So you're sticking," Meg said. "You know what that makes you?"

Amelia smiled sadly. "Stubborn?"

"Well, that too. It also makes you an easy target."

"So I've been told," Amelia said. She knew the neighborhood was flooded with cops, in uniform and plainclothes, and of course there was protection right here, inside the apartment. "I feel safe, Meg, with what's outside, and with you inside."

"I know how your dad feels about this," Meg said. "What about your mom?"

"She hates it, but she knows it's my decision."

"She try talking you out of it?"

"Only until she went hoarse."

Meg gave her a level look. "You really understand what's at stake here?"

"Yes, but I'm also skeptical of the notion that with all this obvious protection, the Night Sniper would dare come anywhere near here."

"You don't understand him," Meg said. "It's the difficulty that would attract him. The challenge. He's a risk taker."

"You sound as if you admire him. I've picked up the same thing sometimes in my dad's voice. And in Birdy's."

"If we admire him," Meg said, "it's only as an adversary, not as a human being."

"Whatever he is, I feel safe enough from him." Amelia curled her legs beneath her in the chair and yawned. Her long braided hair was arranged now on the back of the chair and on one shoulder. What Meg wouldn't do for hair like that.

"Not been sleeping well?" Meg asked.

"All right. I think your friend Birdy is nervous enough for both of us."

Both women jumped when the doorbell rang.

"Almost nervous enough," Amelia added.

"Bedroom," Meg said.

Amelia immediately rose from the wing chair and disappeared down the hall.

Meg went to the door, stood to the side, and knocked three times on the inside.

There was an answering knock. "It's Knickerbocker," came the voice from the other side of the door. "Mr. Chicken."

Meg squinted through the peephole and recognized the uniform outside. Ben Knickerbocker, with the fried chicken dinners from the corner deli.

Knickerbocker knew she was looking through the peephole. He made a loud clucking sound.

She unlocked the dead bolt and chain and opened the door. Cooler air wafted into the apartment, emphasizing how stuffy it had become. Knickerbocker clucked hello.

Meg accepted the two white takeout boxes from him. He was a young guy, handsome, with too much mouth on him. "Do I get a tip?" he asked through a wide grin. *Guy must have fifty, sixty teeth.*

"You would have," Meg said, "but you put me in a fowl humor. They have everything the targ—Amelia requested?"

"Roger that. I made sure you'd both be happy."

"How is it out there?"

"Normal enough," Knickerbocker said. "Not dark yet, so the streets are still fairly crowded. Sniper'll stand out more if he stays with his after-eight-thirty MO."

"I wouldn't count on anything with this guy."

"We aren't," Knickerbocker said. "You on the inside can count on us on the outside. The kid holding up okay?"

"Amelia? Sure. I don't think she fully recognizes the danger. Thinks she does, but she doesn't."

"Just so she follows the rules," Knickerbocker said. He touched the bill of his cap in an oddly old-fashioned mannerism. "Enjoy dinner."

Meg called Amelia back in from the rear of the apartment.

"Who was it?" Amelia asked.

"Mr. Chicken."

They went into the kitchen to eat at the table. Amelia unscewed the cap on a bottle of cheap red wine while Meg spread out the chicken, slaw, potatoes, and rolls, placing them on china plates from one of the cabinets.

Amelia poured the wine and they sat down to eat.

"Not so bad," Amelia said, raising her glass. "To safety and freedom from fear."

And to an admirable show of bravado, Meg thought, deciding to go easy on the wine.

She clinked her glass against Amelia's in a toast, thinking the mayor might have raised a glass after similar words at dinner the evening he was shot.

53

The next day, Bobby sat on a bench in a pocket park on East Fifty-third Street, where office workers from nearby buildings went to eat lunch or simply rest in the shade provided by small trees or the buildings bordering the park. There was a flat-surface waterfall at the far end of the park that supplied relaxing burbling and lapping sounds. A very restful atmosphere in the beating concrete heart of the city, and one where people tended to lower their guard.

Lunchtime seemed to be when these people in suits, blazers, and ties wanted to make personal calls on their cell or satellite phones. Bobby slumped on a bench as if half asleep, watching two women in particular through half-closed eyes.

The nearest was a lean, high-powered executive type with a pale complexion, startlingly blue eyes, and black hair short and parted on one side. She wore matching blue slacks and blazer and navy high-heeled pumps. All business, at least during working hours.

She was the first to end her conversation. Flipping the phone's lid-earphone closed, she replaced the unit in her purse.

The second woman, young and with her light blond hair combed straight across her forehead and over one eye in a way that made her look like Martha Stewart, wore slacks, a gray blazer, and white jogging shoes. She completed her conversation and absently laid her phone alongside her purse on the bench where she sat. The bench was near the edge of the park, and Bobby thought it would be easy to create some kind of diversion, or simply walk past and scoop up the phone while her attention was elsewhere. If he did happen to be noticed, he'd simply hand the phone over to the woman with a smile and pretend she'd knocked it on the ground and he was retrieving it for her. Even if she didn't believe him, she probably wouldn't raise much of a fuss. Something about her made him think she wasn't the type. And it was almost as if she wanted to have the phone stolen. She even made it easier for him by pulling an envelope from her purse, opening it, and becoming engrossed in a letter.

Bobby nonchalantly rose to his feet and shuffled at an oblique angle toward the bench. None of the park's other occupants seemed to be paying much attention to him. He wasn't the sort whose gaze anyone wanted to meet.

Within a few seconds he was only about ten feet from the bench. The woman continued to sit hunched over her letter, gnawing on a sandwich now, the black and purple cell phone resting near her right hip like a bright piece of fruit ready to be plucked.

The trouble was, Bobby wasn't a thief.

He walked slowly past the bench, unable to act.

He *couldn't* reach for the phone. He thought he'd reasoned it out and decided the end justified the means. But there was still a part of him that he held sacred and protected, that the city in its cruelty and hardships hadn't claimed, and wasn't up for compromise.

He hadn't backslid that far. He hadn't gone over to the other side. Not Bobby Mays.

Try as he might, *he* goddamn well wasn't a thief!

Bobby kept walking, past the unsuspecting woman on the bench, out of the small, narrow park, and into the throngs of people passing on the sunny sidewalk.

Half a block down, he stood off to the side and with his fingertips counted the change in his pocket. A couple of dollars. If he set up with his sign and cup on a busy corner, like the one across the street, he could raise more.

Maybe enough for what he had in mind.

Within a few hours he had a total of fourteen dollars and thirty-five cents. It would have to be enough. After a subway pay-for-ride MetroCard bought from a machine, he was down to slightly over ten dollars. But he was soon uptown, in the 140s near Broadway.

There was a guy Bobby had come to see, a black man going by the name of Meander. Sometimes, when Bobby couldn't afford his prescription medicine, Meander sold him pain pills. Only last week Bobby had bought some Darvocet from him, a few weeks before that some cherry cough medicine heavy with codeine that had not only relieved pain but given Bobby a bit of a buzz. Once he'd simply purchased Tylenol that Meander had probably stolen that morning from some retailer's shelf.

Meander didn't only specialize in medicinal aid to the hapless and homeless; he also dealt in stolen cell phones. These phones had a shelf life before they were noticed missing and the provider was alerted. They depreciated accordingly. Some of the phones had been bought cheap by Meander from desperate thieves laying them off for a few dollars for food, booze, or drug money. Others Meander, an accomplished pickpocket, stole himself. Pure profit, those.

Meander had an assortment of chargers and kept the phones' batteries up. Usually the buyer could count on a few days of use, sometimes longer. Longer was always riskier. It didn't take much time to run up astoundingly high phone bills, never to be paid by the illicit user.

Bobby wandered the neighborhood for about half an hour, then spotted Meander at one of his usual places of business, the doorway of a blackened brick building that had been damaged by fire a few years ago and remained unrepaired. The building had housed a small auto supply shop that had been a front for drug dealers. The oil and other petroleum products had made for quite a fire.

Meander was a short, thin man with heavy-lidded, lazy eyes and a goatee that lent his narrow face a bored yet satanic expression. He was about forty, wearing jeans so baggy they were almost like the gangsta pants worn by the younger thieves and thugs of the neighborhood. He also had on a black T-shirt three sizes too large, and a gray baseball cap worn sideways on his head so that the bill was cocked low over his right ear. The cap wasn't precisely a baseball cap; it bore the words *Shit Kicker* instead of a team logo. Bobby couldn't imagine the mentally active but physically lazy Meander kicking anyone who might kick back, or playing any game that required exertion, unless it was Run From the Cops. A few feet behind him, in the shadow of the deep doorway, was a tattered cardboard box Meander would disavow any connection to if he happened to be rousted by the law. In this box were his wares—phones on one side of a cardboard divider, medicinals on the other.

Standing slouched against the building near the doorway as if he were glued to it, Meander watched Bobby approach. His heavy-lidded eyes didn't blink.

"You hurtin' agin, my man?" he asked, when Bobby was about twenty feet away and obviously had come to see him.

"Came for something else," Bobby said.

"I axed was you hurtin'?"

"So you did. I'm always hurting."

"Not if you take the medicine I sell you."

"That's some bullshit," Bobby said.

Meander grinned. "Tha's to say, if the expiration dates on the bottles ain't more'n ten years old."

"Which they are sometimes."

"Which they are," Meander agreed. "What you need, Bobby, you po homeless fucker?"

"I need what you sell. A phone."

Meander looked surprised—for him. His eyelids raised to the three-quarter-open position, then dropped back to half. "Who the fuck you be callin' on the phone, walkin' bundle of rags like you?"

"My broker?"

"You broke, all right. You can't afford no phone."

"I got ten dollars."

"That be different, but it still ain't enough."

"It's all I've got."

Meander remained slouched, but he crossed his arms over his bony chest. "It still ain't enough."

"Look in your box and I bet you'll find something in my price range. Do it as a favor."

"Mean you gonna owe *me* a favor?"

"That's the idea," Bobby said. "How the world is greased."

"You ain't a cop or nothin', so what the fuck good's a favor you owe? You jus' a po fool like I used to be 'fore I became a businessman."

"I used to be a cop."

"Like I used to be police commissioner. 'Sides, you a cop once, you always a cop."

"Whatever. Let's trade favors. I'll owe you one in return for a ten-dollar phone."

"Ain't no such thing as a ten-dollar phone, Bobby. Ain't you kept pace with technology?"

"I'm trying to gain ground. That's why I wanna trade favors. Your favor'd be a discount on the phone, and mine'd be something you need in the future."

"Trade favors, my ass. Cops don't do that kinda deal."

"Sure they do. Anyway, like you said, once a cop . . ." Bobby glanced meaningfully at the incriminating box full of stolen wares.

Meander straightened up from the wall, somehow still slouching. "You fuckin' threatenin' me?"

"Just pointing out about how favors work between friends." Bobby *was* threatening him and both men knew it. Bobby twisting an arm, working the street again. Bobby back on the Job. It felt good, throwing a scare into a booster like Meander. It felt right.

"Now, that the kinda deal a cop makes," Meander said. "Do the favor or fuckin' else. That what you're sayin', Bobby, my man? That what I'm hearin'?"

Bobby merely stared at him. Fixed him with the dead-eyed look that might mean anything, including explosive danger.

"Maybe I got a spare phone at that," Meander said, squinting slightly as if for the first time bringing Bobby into focus. "Be an Amickson clamshell, *ob*-tained yesterday."

"Never heard of an Amickson."

"It be a good brand, made in North or South some country or other."

"Does it work?"

Meander appeared internally injured. "Do it *work*? Fuckin'-A right it work! Ain't no *Mo*-torola or *No*-kia. Tha's why it's cheap, why we can *do* the deal. That an' I got no way to charge up the motha."

"Huh? You wanna sell me a dead phone with no way to charge the battery?"

"Dead? Ain't dead, man. I say dead? Got some power left. Got a rabbit."

"What's that mean?"

"Battery indicator uses little rabbit icons. Five rabbits be fully charged. You got a whole rabbit left. Might last a few minutes, maybe an hour. Hell, you might be buyin' half a dozen phone calls. Cheap at the price. Couldn't sell it at such a discount, 'cept it was dropped. I acquired it myself, an' no sooner it hit the pavement, I put it right back together."

"You mean you dropped it when you were running away from whoever you stole it from."

Meander scratched his head. "That what I mean?"

"Anything else I should know about this phone?"

"Nothin'. Oh yeah, the six don't work. Button don't press no more."

Bobby summoned up the phone number he might have to call. "That'll be okay. Just the six not working?"

"Got my fuckin' word. You a good customer, Bobby, so why'm I gonna piss you off?"

"Amusement?"

Meander chuckled. "Fuckin' 'musement!" He turned and rummaged around in the box, then held up the phone for Bobby to see. Small, black, with blue buttons. It looked okay, though it wasn't the clamshell flip type as Meander had said. Lying could become an addiction.

Bobby leaned closer and peered. The 6 looked like all the other buttons. The phone appeared not to have been dropped hard enough to damage the case or cause much interior damage. There were small red letters across the top. "Amickson," Bobby read aloud. The script looked Gothic. The screen glowed and a small rabbit appeared in the upper left-hand corner. One of its ears appeared to be missing.

Meander did a tight little dance. "You want it or not? Gotta get off the stool, man. No more negotiation. I'm doin' business here an' the shit I sell's of the highest quality. Tell the truth, you ain't shoppin' Cadillac, 'cause you one po motha. You want a phone be an off-brand, got no spare battery that'll fit it, got no charger an' jus' a little charge, no number six button—price be ten dollars. An' it's guaranteed. It don't work, you can bring it back." Meander grinned. "Ain't about to git your money back, though."

Bobby fished the ten dollars—three crumpled bills and the rest in change—from his pocket and handed it over. "You're all heart, Meander."

"All head's what I be. All business. Anyways, what difference it make? What party a loser like you gonna call? What you up to, Bobby? You talkin' to Mars? Or maybe *Ur*-anus?"

"Maybe Mars," Bobby said.

"Well, here's your space phone." He stuffed the money from Bobby in his pocket before handing over the phone. "Be the special of the day, price you paid. Now git on. I don't want no homeless motha hangin' round, be bad for business. I'm done with charity for today."

"Charity? I thought you didn't have a heart."

"Huh? I say that?"

Bobby slipped the phone into the pocket that had carried the money to buy it, then nodded to Meander and moved away down the street.

Considering what the ten dollars might have bought, the phone could be a bargain.

If it worked when it was needed. If the rabbit didn't die.

Lora was perched on the window seat, her back to Bank Street. Her shoulders were hunched, helping to add ten years to her age in the failing light, and her gaze was solemn.

She said, "This is driving me goddamned crazy, Vin."

"Both of us," Repetto said, pacing.

"Why don't we go grab her by both arms and force her out of that apartment? That death trap?"

"That'd be against the law."

"Then we break the fucking law!"

Repetto stopped pacing to face his wife squarely. "She'd go back. She can do that. She would do that."

Lora lowered her gaze to the floor. "This is your decision, not mine."

"It's Amelia's decision," Repetto said. "If it was mine, it'd be the same as yours."

After a long pause, Lora said, "You're right." She began shaking her head from side to side. "It's just so damned hard to swallow."

Repetto began pacing again, wondering if she really had swallowed it. Beyond her hunched form framed by the window, he watched night begin to fall.

Just from reading the papers it hadn't been hard for Bobby to figure out the identity of the Sniper's next intended victim. And to know from reading between the lines that Amelia Repetto might still be in town, refusing to be run off by fear.

If true, she was one gutsy young lady. Not stupid, from everything Bobby had read about her, so it must be courage.

Bobby had figured out her address easily from what they said about her neighborhood in the paper, and from the *A. Repetto* listed in the phone directory. Easy for him, easy for the Sniper. Bobby knew how the police would think, how they'd lay out their protection. He was walking the neighborhood of Amelia's apartment, not getting too close, prowling the perimeter and gradually working his way inward. The lowering evening was cool enough to be comfortable, moonlit and without much of a breeze. A shooter's night.

He touched the hard plastic of the cell phone in the pocket where he usually kept the handouts he'd garnered. He thought about the Sniper. And Amelia Repetto. *So maybe this'll be the night. Or maybe he'll let her sweat awhile longer. Let everybody sweat.*

Or maybe she wasn't sweating. At twenty-one, he'd thought nothing could kill him. Amelia Repetto might still feel she was immortal.

All the more dangerous.

Bobby had a feeling about tonight. His rusty instincts from when he was a cop in Philly were working well and governing his actions, his plan.

He felt good tonight. Meander had been right with his "once a cop always one" remark. Even a dickhead like Meander had that one figured out.

Bobby was back even though he'd never really been away.

Tonight, every night, he was a cop.

"I know I shouldn't call and tie up her line," Lora said. "I'll call her cell phone."

She was on the cell phone now. With Repetto. He was in an unmarked vehicle half a block down from his house, where Lora was inside and on the phone, but she didn't know that. A radio car would arrive soon to take his place. Lora had to have police protection, too. In case the Sniper's stated intention to try for Amelia was a feint. Repetto and Lora hadn't discussed that possibility, but he knew she must be aware of it.

But Repetto didn't think the threat to Amelia was a feint. That wasn't the way the Sniper would play the game. Not this stage of the game, anyway.

"I want to go to her, Vin." Lora said. "Every fiber of me wants to."

"That's the last thing you should do. Maybe the thing the Sniper wants most."

"I tried again to talk her into leaving the city, but she wouldn't listen."

"I tried too. She's—"

"Bullheaded, like you."

Repetto didn't argue with her.

"All right," Lora said with a sigh, after ten or fifteen seconds of his silence. "I'll get off the phone. But I want to know what's going on."

"You will know," Repetto said. "I promise."

"Our daughter—"

"Only daughter," Repetto said. "She has guts."

"Don't give me that bullshit, Vin. I want her to stay alive. Dal had guts and look what happened."

Repetto really, really didn't want to get into this. He felt his grip tighten on the phone.

"I'm sorry," Lora said, as if she were right there in the car with him and had seen the effect of her words.

"That's okay," Repetto said. "It'll all be okay if we let the police do their job."

He sounded as if he really believed it.

The Night Sniper sat at the antique oak table in his gun room and worked the ramrod that was reaming the barrel of the Webb-Blakesmith competition rifle that was from his collection. This rifle didn't disassemble down to caseable components for travel like a lot of the custom-made weapons in the collection, and wouldn't fit in his backpack; but he wanted to use this particular weapon for its accuracy, and because it was one of his favorites. For such an important shot, there could be no other choice.

As he usually did with rifles that wouldn't break down and fit into his backpack, he would wear his long, light-weight raincoat to conceal the weapon. It could be carried in a sling beneath the tattered coat. That was easy to do, with the stock tucked in his armpit, and the sling's hook run through the trigger guard behind the trigger. He could hold the rifle tight against his side beneath the coat and walk with the defeated shuffle of the homeless. He didn't mind using the concealed sling, because he had no illusions about tonight. It would be best to keep the rifle handy in case he had to shoot his way out of an unfortunate situation. The odds were with him because he planned carefully, but still there was always the unexpected challenge.

In the bright lamplight, he admired the cleanly designed and constructed steel mechanism of the rifle, the precision firing pin and gas ejection breech, the lightly sprung trigger and long, blued barrel with its matte black sights that reflected no light that might disrupt aim. Wonderful! Man had devised few mechanisms as precise and reliable as the firearm.

Drawing the ramrod from the barrel, he sat back for better light. He examined the square of white cotton on the end of the ramrod and saw no dark markings. The rifle was clean. Ready and reliable. Still, he fitted a new square of cloth over the end of the ramrod and reinserted it in the barrel.

For a long time he sat at the table in the lamplight, working the ramrod back and forth in the long, grooved barrel, thinking about tonight.

About Amelia Repetto.

Rapunzel.

54

Amelia was having a migraine this evening, which Meg understood. The young woman's head should be splitting open with fear. Right now she was lying down in the dim bedroom with a cold compress over both eyes. The drapes were closed, the bedroom lights turned low, and the windows locked. Amelia was protected not only by the NYPD personnel in the neighborhood, but by locked doors and steel-barred windows, and by Meg.

Meg was confident and relaxed. That was partly because her charge, Amelia, was cooperative and at least temporarily safe from harm, and partly because Meg had, at Amelia's insistence, sipped half a glass of what was left of last night's cheap red wine with Amelia, while Amelia had three glasses in a futile attempt to fend off her developing headache. Probably, Meg thought, it had made the headache worse.

No one had called or knocked on the door since Knicker-bocker—Mr. Chicken—had delivered the nightly takeout meal, most of which was now in the refrigerator. Meg was tired but had no desire to go to bed like Amelia. Instead she sat on the sofa and found herself staring at the phone.

Found herself thinking about Alex.

It couldn't have been the few ounces of wine she'd sipped to pacify Amelia, not even enough, to Meg's way of thinking, to constitute drinking while on duty. So maybe it was the situation, the tension. Whatever the reason, she couldn't stop thinking about Alex and had to fight an almost overwhelming desire to go to the phone and call him.

If she could simply hear his voice, it might help. She might be able to chase him from her thoughts.

It would be so easy to pick up the phone and call.

Insane to think this way.

But it would be so easy.

Then she realized the apartment's phone line might be tapped, in case the Sniper called. Not his MO thus far, but as he'd warned in his note, the game had changed. And he seemed to be the maker of the rules.

Of course, Meg could always contact Alex with her cell phone. That call wouldn't be picked up with a wiretap. Amelia was probably asleep, but even if she weren't, she was unlikely to come out of the bedroom for quite a while. No one would know if Meg made a brief phone call. What was there to lose?

She got up from the sofa and moved to a wing chair farther from the door, where her call was less likely to be overheard.

Meg hesitated, knowing the possible consequences, but she had no real choice. Her heart was in control.

She watched her hand, like someone else's hand, peck out Alex's number on her cell phone.

He picked up on the second ring.

Meg didn't say anything after he'd identified herself. Then she said quickly, before he might hang up, "It's Meg—Officer Doyle."

"More questions, Meg?" Alex sounded unsurprised to hear from her, even faintly amused. At the same time, she was sure she picked up pleasure in his voice, knowing she'd called him.

"Yes. I had a few spare minutes and thought—"

"You'd spend them with me."

This is hopeless. I'm hopeless. "All right, yes. That's exactly what I thought. Spend them with you on the phone, I mean." *Why am I always so flustered around this man?*

"Good. So how's the Night Sniper investigation going?"

Now he wanted to talk business. "We're progressing."

"That's the sort of thing you tell the media."

"Or a—"

"Suspect," he finished for her. "Only you don't really take me seriously as a suspect, do you?"

"I phoned you," Meg said. She heard his low laughter.

"There's an oblique answer. Looks to me like Repetto's daughter might be the Sniper's next target. I hope she went somewhere safe."

"She didn't—listen, that's not why I called."

"Wait a minute. You mean the daughter—what's her name?—is hiding out someplace in New York City?"

"I didn't say that and didn't mean it."

"Where are you calling from, Meg?"

"I can't say."

"I can guess. Jesus! Doesn't Repetto have enough sense to—"

"That isn't what I called about, Alex."

He sighed. "Okay, I'm sorry. I hope you called just to hear my voice, and so I could hear yours."

Which was true, but Meg didn't want to admit it. "I think we need to be realistic. I admit I'm attracted to you."

"Then why don't we—"

"Because I'm a cop working an open homicide case. A lot of open homicide cases."

"And I'm a suspect?"

"Back to that again, are we? I'm not worried about you being a suspect."

"Then you're worried about what would happen to your career if someone found out about us."

"No. Well, yes. But that's not all. It simply isn't right. We're goddamn adults, Alex. We can wait until this investigation is closed."

"*You* called *me*, Meg."

"Because sometimes I'm stupid."

"I don't think so. But what if the investigation's *never* closed? I've been a cop, Meg. I know how many unsolved homicides there are out there. How many nutcase killers are never caught. This sicko might stop killing people; then the news about him would taper off, something else newsworthy would happen, and that'd be that."

"He isn't going to stop. He can't."

"Because some profiler says so?"

"No. Because I say so. You don't know all the details or you'd agree."

The sigh again, like a rush of warm air in her ear. "Okay, Meg. But I'm glad you called. You don't know how glad."

"I hope as glad as I am. When this is over . . ."

"Until then, do you want to have phone sex?"

"Alex!"

He was laughing.

"Phone sex wouldn't be bad," she said, "but I'm too busy."

"Right after I met you, Meg, I bought a bottle of the best champagne I could find, and I'm keeping it iced up for as long as it takes until you're back here with me. Until we're together. Really together."

"Alex—"

She heard a noise from the bedroom.

"I have to hang up," she said, almost in a whisper.

"I understand. Call again when you can. Promise me."

Meg didn't answer, but quickly broke the connection and slipped the phone back into her purse.

The bedroom door opened and Amelia stood there. She was barefoot and her clothes were wrinkled from her time in bed. Her hairdo was flat on one side. Her eyes and forehead were reddened and she held the ice-filled compress in her right hand. She was squinting either from the comparatively bright light or because of pain, and had her head tilted back slightly as if from the weight of her long braid.

"Headache better?" Meg asked.

"Monstrous," Amelia said. "I need more ice."

Meg rose to get it for her.

An RMP car patrolled the blocks south of the Repetto apartment, while another drove regularly back and forth along the blocks to the north. All the while the precinct car regularly assigned to that area drove its usual routes, with the addition of several passes in front of the apartment containing Amelia Repetto and Meg. There were undercover cops borrowed from the Vice Enforcement Division at each end of the block, one hanging around the deli, the other in a parked cab that wasn't really a cab. Inside the Repetto apartment with Amelia was Meg. Across the street in another, vacant apartment was Birdy, watching the street. Repetto oversaw it all, roaming the area in a five-year-old Dodge minivan borrowed from the Motor Transport Division. If anything suspicious occurred, more NYPD could be called in to seal off the area as quickly and completely as possible.

The life of the neighborhood had to go on with at least the outward appearance of normality. Though darkness had closed in and there were fewer people and vehicles on the streets than there would be without the Night Sniper threat hanging over the city, the area seemed no different essen-

tially from any other New York neighborhood. Delivery vehicles made their stops with takeout food, taxis haunted the
streets like restless yellow spirits, the homeless wandered,
lovers strolled, late workers straggled home from their jobs.

Bumping along in the dirty white minivan that had been
confiscated after a drug bust, Repetto knew it could all
change in a moment. The trap was set.

He didn't like to think about the bait.

Question was, how far could she trust Nancy Weaver?

Answer was, she didn't know but had to find out.

Zoe sat at a corner table in P.J. Clark's and waited nervously for Weaver. Before her was a glass of Guinness from
which she'd taken exactly three sips. She desperately needed
something to relax her, but she also desperately needed to
have a clear head when Officer Weaver arrived.

It was Zoe who'd requested the meeting. Zoe who'd been
unable to sleep since the night the mayor was shot. Zoe
who'd gotten rotten drunk at home when she realized what
must have happened. Her finger touched the cold beer glass.
Only touched.

It was drink that had helped get her into this horrible
mess. So easy to see now, when it was too late. But still she
hadn't learned.

She shouldn't have ordered the Guinness. But she couldn't
climb on the wagon all at once. She goddamn needed *something*.

Maybe a bullet in the head, if she couldn't convince
Weaver to cooperate with her.

She almost did take a drink when she realized the idea
didn't seem so far-fetched.

Zoe hadn't caught on at first when she learned the Sniper
had fired at the mayor from a setback roof of the Marimont
Hotel. She'd entered the same hotel shortly before the rifle

shot. When the bullet had struck the mayor, she was cozily ensconced in the hotel's plush restaurant, having her first cocktail.

A coincidence. One not necessarily worth mentioning.

Then, in a later report, she'd read the room number: *2233*. She actually almost fell out of her chair.

Zoe had known what it meant even before reasoning it out. Suite 2233 was where she and Otto (Everyone calls me Ott) Smith had gone after dinner and dancing in the hotel restaurant. It was where they'd made violent and passionate love. After their lovemaking he'd admitted to her his real name wasn't Smith, but Eperrepinsi, an old Sicilian family name that became his German mother's married name; he seldom used it because it was difficult to pronounce and confused people. There was also an old story about his grandfather being executed by the Mafia for conducting an affair with the don's wife.

It seemed to amuse him, finally letting her in on his secret. Now she understood why.

She reached for the glass of beer with a trembling hand, then withdrew it. She was staring at the end of her career and the ruination of her life. What she needed wasn't more alcohol—it was Weaver. Rather, Weaver's understanding and cooperation. Zoe knew she'd better keep herself together for the most important conversation of her life.

Weaver had come through the bar and was standing at the restaurant entrance. She wasn't in uniform—working plainclothes for the assignment she'd been given of finding and questioning competition target shooters. She looked businesslike in a blue skirt, white blouse, and sensible black shoes. Her hair was short and dark and purposely mussed in a spiky way that made her look devilish. From everything Zoe'd heard about her, she was devilish. Devilish and ambitious. Not so unlike Zoe. Zoe was counting on that.

Weaver saw her, smiled, and walked across the restaurant

to the table. Male heads turned. She wasn't exactly beautiful, but there was something about her; men sensed a vitality in her that was unmistakably sexual.

By all accounts, Weaver made good use of it.

She sat down opposite Zoe, placed a dark purse on the table, and nodded, still with the smile.

"I'm glad you could come," Zoe said. "Buy you a drink? Something to eat?"

"Diet Coke," Weaver said, playing it safe and not drinking alcohol on duty. A hovering waiter heard her and hurried off to fill her order.

"How are you doing in your effort to track down target shooters in the area?" Zoe asked, after a few minutes of nervous small talk.

"There are a surprising number, but a lot of them are connected with law enforcement or security, and we already vetted them. We've got some gun club members and skeet shooters in the new mix. Even a fast-draw artist."

"Cowboys and Indians."

"That's what we play," Weaver said, locking gazes with Zoe. Her expression said she was a busy woman and didn't want to waste a lot of time here, if that was what was going to happen. "You said on the phone you have something to tell me."

"Share with you, I said."

Weaver took a sip of the Coke the waiter had delivered and nodded, waiting.

Zoe took a deep breath and explained.

Weaver sat unnaturally still and listened. She appeared as shocked as Zoe had been, when she'd fully absorbed what she'd just heard. What it must mean.

"You've been fucking the Night Sniper," she said in a stunned voice.

Zoe was calmer, relieved, now that somebody else knew. "I would've put it a different way, but yes."

Weaver sat back and touched a finger to an earlobe, as if she were listening to some faint sound. Maybe the wheels of her mind turning. "He's been pumping you for information. Literally."

"Jesus!" Zoe said. "Can't you think of a better way to put things?"

"No," Weaver said honestly. "I gotta tell you, you're in deep . . . well, you're in quicksand."

"And breathing through a straw."

"I've got my responsibilities," Weaver said, still trying to digest this, figure it out.

"That's what I wanted to talk to you about."

"I'm sure he never gave you his real name."

"He was just Otto—or Ott—for a while. Then that name he signed in with at the Marimont."

"He's quite the gamester, our killer." Weaver wondered if this information, sensational though it might be, was going to be useful, or simply embarrassing and destructive to Zoe. A police profiler sleeping with the killer she was profiling. An earthquake for Zoe, but maybe nothing much for the investigation. Simply another of the Sniper's infuriating taunts.

"I need your help," Zoe said.

Uh-oh. Weaver looked at her. "I think I know the kinda help you want. You don't want to tell Repetto or Melbourne about this."

"Them or anyone else."

"And you want me to keep quiet."

"Yes."

"This is bound to come out, Zoe."

"Eventually, yes. Unless the Sniper is never caught, or is killed rather than be captured."

Weaver was still trying to get a handle on this, figure out where Zoe was going with it. "Why me? Why did you tell me?"

"We're both smart, ambitious women in more or less the same field."

"Wouldn't deny it."

"We can help each other," Zoe said. "This could be a career maker for you, and a way for me to solve my dilemma."

"The Sniper must know you're on to him now."

"Yeah. I won't see him again. I hope to hell I *never* see him."

"If you simply wanted me to keep mum," Weaver said, "we wouldn't be sitting here talking." Another sip of Coke. "Why should I give you anything? And what do you want other than my silence?"

"I think I can give you a direct way to discover the identity of the Night Sniper. You can make the collar every cop in the city dreams about. Think of the publicity and career advancement."

"I'm not agreeing to do or not do anything at this point, but I'm interested. You told me why, now tell me what."

"First I want information. Were my fingerprints found in that hotel suite at the Marimont?"

"Not unless it's being kept secret. Course, Latent Print Section isn't done, but the room looked like it was wiped clean of prints with damp towels. Do you remember what you touched?"

"Bathroom fixtures for sure. And the . . . headboard."

"Headboard was wiped clean of prints. His must've been on it, too."

"They were," Zoe said, looking at the table, yearning for a long pull of that Guinness.

"Everything you touched that he might have, he wiped clean," Weaver said. "He was thorough." She was wondering if she'd already decided to agree to Zoe's proposition. She leaned forward, her elbows on the table. "Listen, did you ever suspect this guy? I mean, all the time he was putting the wood to you . . . the night he tried to kill the mayor?"

"Never. And I'd had too much to drink that night. He saw to it."

Weaver leaned back and crossed her arms. "I've got another question."

"You don't have to ask. Yes, we did it in my bed several times, but considering who he was—is—I'm sure he was just as careful about not leaving prints in my apartment."

"It'd still be worth a look. LPS can work miracles."

"I think we can keep it a more closely held secret than if we gave my apartment prints to the lab," Zoe said. She reached down to where a plastic Barnes & Noble bag containing a laptop computer was leaning against her chair and lifted it to set it on the table. "I got up one night to use the bathroom and was sure my laptop had been moved. I felt it, and it was still warm from use. Didn't think much of it at the time. Ott—he—was asleep, so I figured maybe he'd used it, but so what? He didn't know my password to get online, but maybe he wanted to go online with his service, check his e-mail or something. I forgot to ask him about it in the morning. But I think now, since he was using me to gain information . . ."

"Yeah, it's a sure bet he figured out a way to hack into your computer."

"He had to touch the thing all over, the case, the keys. But he'd figure I'd handle it and smudge all the prints within a few days. I didn't, though. Not much, anyway. Soon as I realized what must have happened, I made sure I didn't touch it again. It's smooth plastic that'll hold prints like glass. Even if he wiped it down carefully, there's a good chance he missed a few prints. Gotta wipe it with the lid up, with the lid down. All those keys. It's not easy to be sure you got everything. The rest of my apartment, if he didn't wipe it, I did, while cleaning or accidentally, or at least I must have smudged everything over the past week or so."

"And I don't suppose you two ever went to his place, or we wouldn't be having this conversation."

"Never. For obvious reasons, he always had an excuse.

He made sure that when we parted I'd know nothing about him."

"So what's the plan?" Weaver asked, already guessing but wanting to hear it from Zoe.

"Mine and his are the only prints that should be on this laptop. You dust it yourself and take any prints you find other than mine and run them through records. If you get a match, you have the identity of the Night Sniper. Later, if you have to explain where you got a print to match, you can say you went to his house or apartment earlier as part of your search for amateur or pro competition shooters. He wasn't home, and you lifted the prints from the doorknob or his mailbox. Very industrious of you, but you've got that reputation."

"I know my reputation. Is this guy a shooter—I mean, some kind of hunter or shooting sports competitor?"

"I don't know. He must be. And it wouldn't surprise me if he's got a gun collection. He's got the money."

"You sneak a peek at his bankbook?"

"I didn't have to. I could tell. He was money. Not necessarily born to it, but money."

Weaver thought about it. The world might be opening up to her here. With even a partial print, she might be able to get a name and address or both; then she could make the collar, say she came across the suspect in her search for target shooters. He *must* be an expert shooter of some sort. She could spook him, then say his behavior under her questioning prompted her to arrest him. She could say he panicked and bolted and she'd stopped him. If he denied it later in court, who'd believe him? And she bet she *could* panic him. As for Zoe, he'd wiped the hotel suite clean of prints, so there'd be no evidence that she was ever there. And the laptop prints—if there were any—would be Zoe and Weaver's secret.

"Can we work together to the benefit of both of us?" Zoe asked. "My salvation and your career path?"

Weaver carefully lifted the plastic bag containing the computer by its handle and stood. She smiled down at Zoe, looking surprisingly young and pretty in the restaurant's soft light. "I think we should see where it takes us."

Neither woman had to tell the other they were in it together now.

"I'll keep you posted," Weaver said. She turned and walked out the door with the laptop.

The restaurant was starting to get busy now. People wanted to eat and get home before it became really dark. A waiter led two men in business suits to a nearby table. They were laughing and yammering about some kind of deal they'd pulled off. Some guy they referred to as a schmuck had signed a contract not in his best interest. Unwise arrangements were made all the time.

Zoe knocked back the rest of her beer and got out of there.

55

Bobby noticed the police cruiser approaching but ignored it, continuing along the sidewalk with his dejected, shuffling gait. It wasn't much of a stretch for him to act harmless, he realized ruefully. His joints did ache, especially his hip, and there was that recurring pain low in his gut that he suspected might be his appendix acting up. Medical insurance was a dream to Bobby, but at least if the damned thing burst he might be able to get himself to a hospital emergency room soon enough to stop the poison from spreading and killing him.

He sensed rather than saw the cruiser slow as it passed him; then it picked up speed and turned the corner two intersections up. Bobby was sure the officers in the car hadn't paid much attention to him; he wasn't the only person on the block. It was even possible the car had slowed down so the cops could appraise the lean Hispanic man down the street, wearing jeans and a numbered sleeveless jersey, dribbling a basketball and dashing around as if to take shots at an imaginary basket fixed somewhere above the concrete stoop of the nearest building. Serial killers had adopted stranger disguises.

Bobby continued to roam with apparent aimlessness, making circuitous routes around the Repetto apartment but keeping his distance. Everything in the neighborhood seemed normal, but he could feel something in the air. It was almost the way it felt years ago, just before a tornado touched down near him in Illinois. Or that time in Philadelphia, minutes before a big warehouse robbery and shoot-out.

He knew this was different. And the Sniper seemed to want his prospective victims, the city itself, to sweat. He was a sadist, though he might not think so. And not stupid. Anxious, but not eager. Probably nothing would happen tonight.

Yet there was that feeling . . . Bobby's cop's instincts reawakened.

With all the security for Amelia Repetto, the precinct basement office was deserted. Glad of the fact, Weaver sat hunched over the glowing computer on the desk. The air in the office was damp and stale and smelled faintly of insecticide or disinfectant, but she didn't notice.

Weaver hadn't been able to lift any prints from Zoe's laptop. But she wasn't an expert, and now that she was in league with Zoe, she didn't want to give up on their scheme. She decided to take someone else into her confidence, someone who couldn't and wouldn't reveal any involvement.

Weaver had once been embroiled in a torrid love affair with a married tech in Latent Prints, so she managed to get a confidential rush job on the laptop. The tech was a man with three kids, still with his longtime wife, so he knew how to keep a secret. Weaver wasn't worried about him talking.

Zoe had spoken the truth. There had been only two sets of

prints on the laptop. But there had been only three prints total, very faint. Two, on the keys, had been Zoe's. The remaining print, on the bottom of the computer, was missed when the laptop was obviously wiped down.

It didn't take much time for Weaver to run the print through Central Records Division and come up with the name Dante Vanya. He'd been fingerprinted on a prostitution charge, which was later dropped, in 1989 as a juvenile. Still as a boy, his prints went on record again when he was in the jurisdiction of the New York Administration for Children's Services, in 1990, after a lengthy hospital stay.

Fascinated, hopeful, Weaver did a search on Vanya and found city records revealing that he'd been treated for burns and later placed in the care of a guardian ad litem, while a trespassing-on-city-property charge was considered. In this case the guardian was a charitable foundation called the Strong Society that provided a home for the boy while he recuperated from his burns. Custody had become long-term. Dante had remained a resident of the Strong Society until he attained legal adulthood.

More computer work. Weaver thought, not for the first time, that the Internet was a wondrous thing. The Strong Society had operated a rehabilitation ranch for children in Arizona that filed for Chapter Eleven in 2001. The steward and CEO of the foundation, Adam Strong, had subsequently committed suicide.

Weaver could feel her heart beating faster. She was closing in on something. Every instinct in her body told her so.

She did a computer search on Adam Strong, her fingers darting over the keyboard almost of their own volition.

Within twenty minutes she found him. Adam Wellmont Strong had been born poor but became a wealthy man in the steel fabrication industry during World War Two. He'd died in 1987 at the age of seventy-nine.

Not Weaver's Adam Strong.

Discouraged for the first time since she'd logged on to the computer, Weaver desperately clicked on various links—until a name jumped out at her: Adam Wellmont Strong, Jr.

She was back on point, squirming now in her chair with eagerness.

Quite a guy, Adam Strong, Jr. He'd been a star quarterback in high school in Flagstaff, Arizona, then suffered a knee injury that ended football for him. But it didn't stop him from attending college, graduating with honors, then spending two years in the Peace Corps. After the Peace Corps, he'd done some government social work, obtaining mortgage loans for low-income families, then gone to work for his wealthy father's foundation. While doing social work, he won several skeet and target shooting titles, then had become an alternate shooter on the U.S. Olympic team.

Weaver found herself grinning wide enough to make her face hurt.

After his father's death, Adam, Jr., inherited both the position as head of the foundation as well as the family land in Arizona, where he created the Strong Society Ranch.

Where Dante Vanya had spent some of his formative years.

Weaver needed to learn more about Dante Vanya. After a more thorough search, she uncovered a *New York Times* article about a homeless boy who'd been badly burned in a subway station fire. A subsequent article revealed that the boy's father, a former New York Department of Sanitation worker, had murdered his wife, who was Dante's mother, then shot himself.

Weaver leaned back from the computer, staring at the monitor. Though the past few hours had required practically no physical energy, she found herself exhausted. Now the air in the office did seem stifling. She was perspiring and her breathing was ragged.

Almost there.

Calmer now, she used the computer to check the various online borough phone books.

No Dante Vanya.

But he could be using a different name. Or simply have an unlisted number.

Weaver went from online phone directories to actual various cross and residence directories.

Dante Vanya didn't have a listed phone number, but he did have an address on the Upper East Side of Manhattan.

She didn't want to get her hopes too high, *but how many Dante Vanyas could there be?*

Weaver couldn't stop staring at the address as she went over what she'd learned about Dante Vanya. A homeless kid; then, judging by his present address, he'd obtained wealth. After the murder of his mother and suicide of his father, a New York City sanitation employee, Dante had spent time on the streets, then in the custody of a world-class competition shooter.

The boy's relationship with Adam Strong, who possibly taught him to shoot, might have been surrogate son to father. Then Strong, like Dante's real father, had committed suicide.

Dante was an Upper East Side New York resident who could probably afford an extensive firearms collection.

Dante might very well be a crack marksman.

Dante's fingerprint was on Zoe Brady's computer.

Gotcha!

Weaver knew she should act fast, not because Dante Vanya was likely to bolt, but because the longer she kept this hot information to herself, the more explaining she might have to do.

She was going to hold what she knew close, then act on it.

Zoe had been right about something else. It would be a career maker for any cop who made the Night Sniper collar.

And I have his name and address!

It took Weaver's nimble and ambitious mind only a few minutes to decide on a cover story. She would stay with the one that had occurred to her even as she was talking with Zoe. After the arrest, she'd maintain that Vanya's name had cropped up when she was investigating target shooters. She'd tracked down his address, then gone there to question him. During their conversation, she began to suspect him more and more as he'd become increasingly nervous and evasive, and when he panicked and bolted, she'd stopped him—either with a shout or a warning shot—then cuffed him and read him his rights. The fact that he ran would open all the legal doors and ensure his conviction.

The only problem was in getting him to bolt.

The only question was whether she would shoot him if he refused to bolt.

She was sure that if she had to make such a decision, it would be the right one.

56

Meg looked up from the sofa, where she'd been sitting watching but not seeing television with the sound off.

There was Amelia, back in the living room. Pretty college girl, showing some fear in her eyes. Meg thought it might be because the reality of the situation was catching up with her. Meg thought Amelia was that dangerous combination of young and nuts, not brave. In her place, Meg would have gotten as far away from New York and the Night Sniper as possible.

Amelia still looked a bit rumpled and disheveled from sleep, but this time she'd left the ice pack behind. She was wearing fluffy white slippers that made her feet look gigantic.

"Headache better?" Meg asked.

"Not much, and it's constant. But I'm tired of lying around in the dark and waiting for it to go away." Amelia's gaze went to the silent TV. "Anything new?"

"New?"

"About the Night Sniper. You're watching the news."

"Oh! So I am. Not really, though. I was just sitting here thinking. Anyway, when there's news on the Sniper, we should hear it before they do." Meg nodded toward the anchor-woman mouthing silently on-screen.

"What were you thinking?" Amelia asked, wandering to the window and parting the drapes slightly so she could peer out.

"How best to keep you safe. Uh, stay away from the window, please."

Amelia let the drape fall back in place. "I just wanted to peek outside, to reassure myself there still *was* an outside." She smiled. "I know I'm a pain in the ass. It's just that I'm not the type to hole up and wait for something to blow over."

"I understand," Meg assured her. "Neither am I, but sometimes people like us have no choice. You'd rather be going about your business as usual, and I'd rather be clamping the cuffs on the sicko who's causing all our problems."

"Most of our problems, anyway."

Meg wondered what she meant by that. What kind of problems could a beautiful twenty-one-year-old woman have, other than being stalked by a serial killer? "It's gotta be tough for you. We all know that. Your dad sure knows it."

"He worries too much about me. So does my mom."

Meg looked closely at her. She didn't appear to be kidding. *Only because a stone-cold killer's vowed to take your life.* "That's because they both know the danger. So do I. It's real, Amelia, believe me."

Amelia hesitated, then nodded. "Oh, I know it's real, but . . . well, I guess I'm a fatalist."

Or a dramatist. Or twenty-one years old. "You're not afraid?"

"I'm terrified. That's why the headache, I suspect. That's why I close my eyes but can't sleep. But at the same time, it's all on a certain level, almost like a bad dream. There's no way I can get my mind around the idea that somebody really wants me dead so much that he'd risk his own life in an attempt to kill me. And if he does, what are the chances of him actually getting through my assigned bodyguards like you?"

"On the level? There's some possibility. You're a cop's daughter. You understand that there's at least some chance he can bring it off."

Meg almost instantly regretted her candidness. Whether she was a dramatist or not, for an instant terror shone through Amelia's pale features; she was an inch away from losing her composure and becoming a sobbing, terrified victim.

"I'm plenty afraid," Amelia said, "but I refuse to give in to panic." She took a deep breath and her entire body trembled. "The truth is, I just want it to end. To be over."

"That's what *he* wants," Meg said. There had been something disturbing in Amelia's voice. And it struck Meg that maybe that was how it worked—the intended victim's fear finally manifested itself in a perverse cooperation with the killer. "*I guess I'm a fatalist.*"

The Sniper would know that and how to use it.

She decided not to mention this disturbing insight to Amelia. But it could be a problem, this condition of fear and impatience, resulting in an eager kind of resignation that made the victim complicit in victimization. It could lead to a sort of deliberate, inviting carelessness.

"What I mean is, I want the tension to end, no matter how."

Meg stared at her. *No, you don't. Not really.*
Or do you?
She watched as Amelia began to pace.

Now that she was here, Weaver was even more impressed by Dante Vanya's address. His apartment was in the Elliott Arms, a soaring structure of glass and steel rooted in three stories of pale stone, with a tinted glass front and a maroon-awninged entrance flanked by twisted green topiary in huge ceramic planters. It took a lot to intimidate Weaver, but as she crossed the street from her unmarked and gained the attention of a rigid, brightly uniformed doorman, she felt like saluting.

The man was well over six feet, with the body of a weight lifter even though he was graying and probably in his fifties. He smiled at Weaver, but surveyed her suspiciously with steel-blue eyes as he held open one of the tall, tinted doors for her.

The lobby was gray marble veined in red, the elevators discreetly hiding out of sight around a corner. Another uniformed man, this one not so grandly clad, sat in the recess of an angle of marble that was a reception desk. A tiny, decorative shaded lamp sat on one corner of the desk, looking out of place in such a vast, cool area.

This guy was also in his fifties, gray and paunchy, and resembled everybody's kind uncle. Weaver relaxed and gained confidence, telling herself she wasn't so crazy coming here.

The man smiled from behind the slab of marble that looked as if it had been lifted from a mausoleum one dark night and finely polished. "Help you?"

Weaver decided not to identify herself as police. Not yet.

"I'm here for Mr. Vanya."

She was sure the man would ask her name, but he didn't. He merely consulted a logbook on a lower shelf behind the marble.

He looked up at Weaver over half-lens reading glasses. "Not in, I'm afraid."

"Is he expected back soon?"

"That I couldn't say. He left about an hour ago."

"I don't suppose he mentioned where he was going?"

"No, ma'am. And we don't ask."

Weaver had her choice. She could identify herself as police and push the issue, but she still couldn't get into Vanya's apartment without a warrant. Or she could play it low profile, leave, and wait across the street in the car for Vanya to return. He might not choose tonight to try for Amelia Repetto, and when he returned home and Weaver tried again to see him, there was no reason he shouldn't invite her up. Especially if she identified herself as on old friend of Adam Strong.

She chose the latter option. With a smile, she said, "It wasn't important, anyway. I'll drop by later."

Back across the street, behind the wheel of the unmarked, she settled down to wait for men to enter who might be Dante Vanya. A photograph sure would have helped, but there hadn't been any in the records, and she didn't want to take time for a broader search.

She tried to get more comfortable, sitting there with her impatience and ambition and hunter's blood. Probably Vanya had gone out to get a bite to eat, or meet someone for drinks. Maybe he'd even return home with a woman. That would sure make things interesting.

She gazed diagonally across the street at the Elliott Arms. The glass and steel entrance gleamed. The doorman stood at parade rest near one of the corkscrew yews.

Some digs, she thought again. There was no doubt Vanya was wealthy enough to be the rare weapons collector, or was at least able to obtain such rifles for his use. There was less and less doubt in Weaver's mind that he was the Night Sniper.

Her way to a brighter future.

Her prey.

The car seemed to be closing in on her and smelled faintly of oil and musty upholstery. Weaver started the engine and turned on the air conditioner, even though the night was cooling down.

Across the street, a man in a tan raincoat and wearing a black beret nodded to the doorman and entered the Elliott Arms.

Not Vanya. Too old. She could tell not only by the fringe of white hair showing beneath the beret, but by the weary set of his narrow shoulders and unsteadiness of his stride.

A while later a woman and a small child entered. Then a man who was also too old to be Vanya.

Weaver yawned, but it wasn't because she was tired. It was nerves.

Surely he'd be back within the next few hours. She could wait, but it wouldn't be pleasant.

Waiting wasn't her game. She was more the type to make something happen.

57

Almost an hour passed before Bobby saw the homeless man who didn't belong. He emerged from a dark passageway across the street, then headed in the opposite direction, away from Bobby.

Bobby squinted at the man. He was real, all right. He had to be real.

Playing it casual, Bobby walked several more steps before pausing and removing the cell phone from his pocket.

He pressed the power button and the tiny screen glowed dimly. One tiny rabbit icon. Still some battery power, anyway. Bobby had committed the phone number of the nearest precinct house to memory. No 6s. He punched out the number and listened to the phone ring on the other end of the connection.

As he did this, he slowly turned and began following the man across the street, staying on the opposite sidewalk and well back, almost out of sight.

He got through to someone who identified himself as Sergeant Britain.

"My name's Bobby Mays," Bobby said in a hoarse whisper, hoping the Amickson phone transmitted as clearly as it received. "I'm at Amsterdam and West Eighty-ninth Street, in Amelia Repetto's neighborhood, and I'm following a man who might be the Night Sniper."

"And why would you suspect him?" Sergeant Britain sounded remotely interested. Probably this wasn't the only Night Sniper tip he'd received this evening.

"He's wearing a long raincoat," Bobby said. "One that could easily conceal a rifle. And he's pretending to be one of us."

"Us?"

"The homeless."

"You're one of the homeless?"

"That's right. And he isn't. I'm sure of it. I'm a former cop, a while back in Philadelphia. I got the eye. This isn't a real homeless man."

"Ex-cop?"

Was Britain hard of hearing? "Right. In Philly. Name's Bobby Mays. I've seen this guy before and he doesn't set right."

"How so?"

"He isn't one of us. He's walking with too much haste and purpose."

Britain waited a few seconds. "That's it? Other than the long raincoat?"

"I've seen him before in the areas of some of the Night Sniper shootings."

"So where is he and where are you?"

"I told you—"

"I mean, are you in a car or a building, looking out a window?"

"We're both on foot. I'm following him along Eighty-ninth Street while I'm talking to you on my cell phone. He's walking with too much haste and purpose."

"You told me that. You say you're homeless, so where'd you get a cell phone?"

"Bought it," Bobby said. "Listen, this isn't about me. It's about—"

"We get a lotta calls," Britain said. His disinterested gaze went idly to a photo of Yankees shortstop Derek Jeter that was hanging on the wall across from the desk. Jeter was grinning, holding a bat, and wearing an NYPD cap. Young stud millionaire, Britain thought enviously. Not a care. "I gotta check."

Bobby forced calm on himself. "Yeah. Sure. But if you don't do something this guy's gonna get away from me. He's average height, wearing a dark baseball cap, green or gray raincoat down almost to his ankles. Got a little hitch in his walk this time, as if he might be carrying a rifle in a sling."

"My, you *are* observant."

"I'll stay on the phone," Bobby said. "I'm gonna keep following him and talk you guys to him."

"No, Mr . . . ."

"Mays. Bobby Mays."

"Right. Ex-cop, Philly. Don't follow him, Mr. Mays. You understand me? That's our job."

"Damn it, you don't believe me! I can tell."

"I didn't say that."

"This time he's real! I know it. He's real!"

"This time? Real?"

"I told you there was another time. I even went to the police and tried to get them to listen."

"Ah."

Bobby didn't like his tone. "Britain. Sergeant Britain. Please, listen, I—"

"You listen, Mr. Mays. I don't want you hurt. I'll see a car is sent. The police'll take care of this matter. Stop following this man, whether he's real or not. Don't interfere in any way. I'm . . . 'elling you for . . ."

Britain's voice was fading. Breaking up.

"Sergeant? You gotta take this seriously."

"I . . . 'sure you I am . . ."

The tone of Britain's voice changed; then the silence in the phone was no longer alive. Bobby lowered it from his ear and looked at the dimming screen. No rabbit. No power. Nothing but a tiny battery icon indicating that the phone needed charging.

The phone was dead.

At the other end of the connection, Sergeant Roland Britain realized he was now talking to himself.

"Don't interfere in any way," he said again into the phone, just in case the caller might hear.

He's real this time.

There was no way Britain could recommend sending a car on the information he'd just been given. And from such a source.

He hung up and forgot about the call.

Disgusted, Bobby wiped his fingerprints from the dead cell phone and dropped it down a sewer grate.

For another two blocks he followed the homeless man who was walking too fast, who didn't quite belong. Then he lost him.

He was like a shadow moving into another shadow, and he didn't emerge.

Bobby retreated into a dark building nook and watched the street for a while, thinking maybe Britain would actually see to it that a car was sent to investigate his phone call.

But a car never came.

Not that Bobby saw.

58

It was almost three hours before the end of his shift, but Sergeant Roland Britain was leaving early to visit his wife, Junie, in the hospital. She'd just had her gall bladder removed by that new kind of surgery where they deflate the thing and pull it out somehow and leave only three or four little puncture holes in her belly. She'd be coming home tomorrow after only one night in the hospital. The insurance company wasn't out so much money that way. Insurance, Britain thought. Everything these days was for the insurance companies. Or the big oil companies.

The deal was, Britain was going to take off for the hospital and buy some flowers on the way, and the sergeant for the next shift was coming in early to cover for him.

Nice guy, Dan O'Day, to agree to the arrangement. Someday Britain would return the favor.

There was O'Day now, coming in through the precinct house door, looking neatly turned out as usual, one of those smooth-skinned, florid Irishmen who aged well and always seemed to dress smartly. Even in uniform, like tonight, creases in his pants *and* sleeves, shoes shined, even a badge that glittered, O'Day stood out among the other cops in the precinct. When he spoke, especially at muster, people listened. Britain figured most of it was Irish bullshit, but they listened.

"Quiet night, Roland?" O'Day asked, as he came around behind the desk.

"So far. Nothing shaking on the Night Sniper asshole looking to shoot Repetto's daughter."

"Maybe he'll choose another night for his sick games," O'Day said. He stood beside Britain and scanned the shift log. Two mugging suspects, an alleged rapist, two drunks, a guy on a domestic violence charge who'd been in at least twice before, three prostitutes (apparently working as a team), and a smash-and-grab suspect in a jewelry store robbery. Quiet enough, O'Day thought.

"All these sterling citizens in the holdover or Central Booking?" he asked, setting aside the activity log.

"Yep. And I already fed the info into the computer. Our wife beater's waiting for his attorney, who's supposed to be driving in from Long Island."

"Must be a friend, coming all that way instead of waiting for morning. Let's hope he's a real estate lawyer."

Sergeant Britain slid down from the high-legged, padded stool behind the desk, and O'Day took his place.

"I 'preciate this, you filling in for me," Britain said.

O'Day waved a hand in dismissal. "I'll give you the chance to return the favor."

"Maybe I'll stand you for drinks sometime at Chargers," Britain said. Chargers was a small but busy bar where many of the precinct cops hung out off-duty.

"That'd do it."

"Oh yeah," Britain said, as he picked up his cap and started to leave. "There was this phone call on the Amelia Repetto stakeout, didn't mean squat." He walked back to the desk and leaned over to check his notes. "Homeless dude, or so he said. I wrote this down left-handed while I was on the phone and can't read my fuckin' handwriting. Can't make out his name. He said he was an ex-cop from Philly."

"Really?" O'Day continued reading the log.

"Nutcase, though. He claimed he was in Amelia's neighborhood, on Eighty-ninth Street, tailing some guy he thought was suspicious, and he wanted me to send a car so he could talk us to him with a cell phone."

"Homeless dude had a cell phone?"

"I wondered about that too. He had an explanation like alphabet soup. Anyway, he wasn't even sure the guy he was following was real."

"That'd make a difference." O'Day turned the page and was glad to find that the next one was blank. He began reading the contents listed in suspect possession envelopes that were stacked in a nearby wire basket. It was good to see that each of the hookers carried condoms. "If Homeless didn't think the guy was real, why was he following him?"

"Said he was real *this* time, not like last time."

"Uh-hm. There's a certain logic in that. Why'd he think the guy was suspicious?"

"Walking too fast, is what he said. Not like one of the *real* homeless. Walking with too much haste and purpose."

O'Day looked up from what he was reading and stared at Britain. "Those were his words? 'Too much haste and purpose'?"

"Those words exactly. Said it twice. Sounds like an ex-cop, don't he?"

O'Day was down off the stool now. "Used to be a cop in Philly, you said?"

"Uh-huh."

"His name happen to be Billy . . . no, Bobby Mays?"

Britain appeared puzzled. "Yeah, that's it. You know him?"

"He was in here before. Not long after a Night Sniper shooting. Mays is homeless, all right, but I gotta say he didn't strike me as a nutcase. Not used up yet. Something about him."

"Still got cop in him, maybe," Britain said. "That came across despite all the real and unreal bullshit." He shifted his weight and glanced at the wall clock. "Listen, I gotta go or Junie'll be after me for missing visiting hours."

"How's she doing?"

"Good, good, fine." Britain had his cap on and was moving toward the door. "I'll tell her you asked about her."

"Do that," O'Day said. "Give her my best. She's a fine woman just for putting up with you."

"Couldn't argue with that," Britain said, and was out into the night.

O'Day sat for a moment looking at the framed photo of Derek Jeter smiling at him from beneath his NYPD cap.

Not thinking about Jeter, though. Thinking about Bobby Mays, about what there was in the poor young guy that made it impossible for O'Day simply to dismiss him from his mind.

Should he believe Mays was sane enough to make sense?

Maybe.

Buy into what Mays had said to Britain?

Maybe.

O'Day was a man who recognized a fork in the road when he came upon one, especially one that might skewer him. He knew he'd be sticking out his neck if he called about Mays's conversation with Britain and got everyone including God and the NYPD stirred up over nothing. Mays was, after all, a homeless man who apparently hallucinated. But considering his previous contact with Mays, maybe O'Day's neck would be stuck out even further if he *didn't* call and the Sniper took a shot at Amelia Repetto.

Maybe was reason enough.

He picked up the phone.

59

Repetto listened carefully on his cell phone to what Melbourne was telling him. He found himself gripping the phone too hard and made a conscious effort to loosen the pressure of his thumb.

When Melbourne was finished, Repetto waited a few seconds, then said, "To sum it up, we've got a homeless man who admittedly hallucinates telling us the Night Sniper is in the neighborhood, might be carrying a rifle, and might be moving toward Amelia."

Melbourne had known Repetto too long to be surprised by this note of skepticism. "We both know it's something more than that."

"Do we?"

"I know what you're doing," Melbourne said. "You're trying to play devil's advocate. Okay, I'll go along. Our homeless man's an ex-cop—"

"Says he is."

"Okay, says so. This is the second time he's reported seeing this guy who doesn't set right with him as one of the homeless, thinks he might be a phony. Both sightings were when the Night Sniper might have been in the area."

"*Might.*"

"Always," Melbourne said. "Something else. We both know what it takes to prompt somebody like this Bobby Mays to contact the police. We're the people who roust him for loitering or panhandling, make his life even harder. Still, he did his ex-cop citizen's duty."

"All kinds of psychos," Repetto said, "imagining and doing all kinds of things."

"All kinds, yes. But Mays isn't imagining he was a cop. Philadelphia P.D. says he was one of theirs, and a good one till a family tragedy put him on the skids."

Repetto's mind was working furiously, listening to Melbourne while unconsciously shuffling facts, priorities, and nuances, trying to synthesize what he knew with what he felt, which was often simply knowing on a deeper level.

"That all we got?" he asked.

"'Bout it."

"No, it isn't," Repetto said, switching positions with Melbourne. "We've got what Sergeant Dan O'Day's gut tells him."

"That make it enough?" Melbourne asked. "What a veteran cop senses is the ore in the rock?"

"I know O'Day slightly. Times I've seen him, he struck me as the type who lives the Job."

"I know him more than slightly," Melbourne said. "He's what you're talking about. He's a good cop. A good man. Ground smooth but not down." Melbourne was silent for a couple of beats. "He's not so unlike you, Vin. I'm gonna let this be your call."

"I'm calling it," Repetto said. "We're going on the assumption the Sniper's in the trap. Let's spring it. Send what we have. We'll cordon off the neighborhood and tighten the perimeter while we search the surrounded area."

"Done," Melbourne said. "Call Amelia and whoever you have posted there and alert them to what's going on."

"Soon as this conversation's finished," Repetto said, and broke the connection.

His blood was racing but his mind was calm. This was what he used to live for, this moment when the balance might be shifting, when he could *feel* it shifting. Everything was suddenly gaining momentum in the same direction, rushing toward the telling instant, like a narrowing focus that would achieve laser intensity. The grueling teamwork of the past long weeks, the breakthroughs and revelations large and small, were all converging.

O'Day's gut instinct had become Repetto's.

As he pecked out Amelia's number on his cell phone, Repetto knew that if it weren't for the danger to Amelia, he'd be loving this.

The Night Sniper was confident as he walked the dark streets of the West Eighties. His opponents knew now where he'd fired from when the mayor was shot, and had his general, useless description, compliments of the Marimont desk clerk. All the better, that description. The contrast between the Marimont shooting and what was about to happen to Amelia Repetto would be too much of a gap for them to leap. As would the contrast between the perceived shooters. Homeless people didn't take suites at the Marimont Hotel. The police knew how wealthy he really was, and their mental image of him would be that of a cultured, influential man in a tailored suit, not one of the helpless and homeless wandering the avenues.

Tonight, in his worn-out clothes, his tattered long raincoat concealing his rifle, he was treading the stage in costume perfect for the role. Beneath the darkened faux stubble that would wipe off easily, he couldn't contain a thin smile.

He feared his pursuers, feared the psychotically resolute Repetto especially, but he did love the game.

When he reached a dark passageway, he glanced about, then entered the shadows and became one. The narrow passageway would take him to the next block, where he knew he could enter an apartment building through a side door whose lock he'd already neutralized.

Good! He was sure no one had seen him entering the building. There was a laundry room in the basement, and he had to get past its door without being noticed. An obvious vagrant in the building would inspire curiosity if not immediate alarm.

His luck held like an omen. Caution wasn't necessary here. No one was washing or drying tonight.

With a small pair of wire cutters from a coat pocket, he disabled the fire alarm system. He entered the interior fire escape stairwell without an alarm sounding and made his way to the third floor. Already in his hand was the key to the sparsely furnished apartment a handsome young executive about to be transferred to New York had subleased for a year. Of course, the information given to the apartment's primary lessee, who'd placed an ad in the *Times,* was false, but that didn't matter now. The information was backed up by competently forged identification, and a deposit check the Sniper knew had cleared a Los Angeles bank. The useless rental agreement would become known within a matter of weeks, but that was okay.

The Sniper had required use of the apartment for only a short time. For the few visits he'd made in order to prepare.

And for tonight.

The apartment was in a vine-covered four-story brownstone diagonally across the street from Amelia Repetto's apartment, three buildings down the block. Though it was on the third floor, observation had convinced the Sniper he could have a clear shot into Amelia's lower-level living room, and into one of the bedrooms.

He went to the window overlooking the street and raised it about six inches, adjusted the blinds, and sat down in a small but comfortable wing chair he'd pulled close. From where he sat he could peer down the street at Amelia's apartment and calculate his shot if the opportunity arose. The angle was acute, but his field of fire would cover approximately a third of both rooms. The challenge was certainly easier than that which he'd faced when he made the mayor a target.

He settled into the softly upholstered chair and propped the Webb-Blakesmith rifle against one of its arms, where he could easily snatch it up.

Though he was relaxed, he was alert, listening to the faint sounds of the city he'd slowed, and the subtle noises of the old building.

He was confident Amelia Repetto was in her apartment across the street. She would be closely guarded, not only by cops on the street, but probably by someone in the apartment with her.

But nobody was careful all the time. The Sniper had tonight and several more nights before the risk of occupying the subleased apartment would become too great to justify. Plenty of time.

Patience . . .

A shooter's patience was usually rewarded.

It was merely a matter of waiting.

Parked across the street from Dante Vanya's apartment, Officer Nancy Weaver glanced at her unmarked's dashboard clock and decided this had gone far enough. She could afford to wait no longer. She had to cover her ass and make the best of what she had.

She'd actually realized this fifteen minutes ago and had been reasoning it out. She'd go back into the Elliott Arms, as a cop this time, and bullshit the doorman and whoever else needed bullshitting to give her access to Vanya's apartment. Once inside, she could maybe find what she needed in order to contact Repetto, who could then obtain a warrant and prompt a wider search.

Not quite legal, Weaver knew. If she found nothing suspicious in Vanya's apartment, she'd politely thank everyone involved, make her exit, and hope for the best. Which would be that an infuriated honest citizen named Dante Vanya wouldn't complain to the department.

If she did find something definitive and incriminating, it might save Amelia Repetto's young life; then Repetto, with Melbourne's help, could smooth out any problems she might have with improper entry.

Like hell he could.

But being responsible for nailing the Night Sniper could overwhelm a lot of mistakes and make a lot of things right.

What she was about to do was risky and Weaver knew it. She also knew she was at a point in her career where it was time to take a risk.

And she *knew* this bastard was the Night Sniper.

Taking a chance, though. Hell of a chance . . .

Weaver glanced across the street at the grandly uniformed doorman standing like a sentinel at the building entrance, looking intimidating, or trying to. He'd be good at his job, but Weaver figured she could get around him, win him over, bully him if she had to do it that way. Who'd he think he was, anyway? Big jerk-off standing there like the president of some country with weapons of mass destruction. She had the entire force of the NYPD behind her. *Fuck him!*

She summoned up her most official attitude, put her shield on display, and climbed out of the car.

60

Amelia's relentless pacing was beginning to get on Meg's nerves. The regular *prushh, prushh, prushh* of her slipper soles on the carpet was almost constant. Twenty-one-year-olds were restless, Meg reminded herself, even if they weren't sniper targets.

It meant Meg could never relax. There was always the danger that Amelia would wander into a far part of the apartment alone and do something foolish, or peer out a window before Meg could stop her, or instinctively answer a knock on the door that led out onto the exposed stoop and sidewalk.

Local news was on TV with the sound off, but there was plenty to learn from the crawl at the bottom of the screen or by lipreading the anchorwoman. Meg, seated on the sofa and trying to keep one eye on Amelia and the other on the TV, decided that all the silent information insinuating itself into the living room might be too much. She used the remote to flip through the channels, stopping at a 1970s repeat of *The Price is Right*. It was all about profoundly excited people who needed haircuts and wore starched-looking loud clothes. They were ecstatic about prizes received if they came closest at guessing prices. Everything in life had its price, Meg reflected. And coming close was about as well as you could do.

Meg's cell phone chimed and Amelia stopped pacing. She stared as Meg pressed the phone to her ear and listened to Repetto.

"We're on high alert," Repetto said.

He told Meg about Bobby Mays, and the homeless man who didn't quite fit even in Bobby's remote and lonely world.

"Doesn't sound like enough," Meg said, imagining dozens of RMP cars and scores of uniformed and plainclothes cops silently closing in on the blocks surrounding where she was sitting. They'd soon establish a loose cordon around the area; then they would inexorably tighten it. Inside its perimeter, others would position themselves near subway and bus stops, halt vehicles at intersections for traffic checks, or walk the neighborhood searching for the homeless man with a rifle who might be real.

Whoever the Night Sniper was—and Meg had private doubts about this homeless guy another of the homeless had described—if he knew the forces closing in on him, he'd wish he'd chosen another night.

"Amelia holding up all right?" Repetto asked.

"Well as can be expected." Meg decided not to mention Amelia's incessant pacing, or the growing apprehension Amelia would describe as simply nerves. *Better than simply terror.*

"Everything still tight there?"

"Like the city budget. Don't worry about this end."

Repetto hung up without asking to talk with Amelia. Things were moving fast and he was busy, his thoughts concentrated. He had to stay that way to remain on top of events that might be about to give him quite a ride. Meg understood. Amelia wouldn't.

"Who was it?" Amelia asked, watching Meg clip the phone back on her belt.

"Your dad. I think he had more to say, but he got called away."

"So why'd he call?"

Meg told her.

"He puts a lot of faith in what he calls instinct," Amelia said. "Or hunches." She began to pace again. *Prushh, prushh* . . . "It's really just subconscious reasoning, what your mind knows before it lets you in on the secret."

Maybe she would understand.

Meg decided it might be a good idea if they talked about this. She switched off the distracting TV, where a woman in an evening gown was grinning and caressing a refrigerator as if she were in love. Woman and appliance shrank and disappeared in a point of light.

When Meg looked away from the blank screen, Amelia was approaching a window and reaching for the heavy closed drapes so she could part them and peer out.

Meg was instantly up out of the sofa, crossing the room swiftly but smoothly, so she didn't spook Amelia and cause her to yank at the drape.

She saw Amelia's fingers close on the thick velvet material and moved faster so she could rest a hand on her shoulder.

"Amelia, don't—"

There was an almost inaudible *snick!* from the other side of the drape, and the unmistakable crack of a rifle shot echoed along the street.

Meg saw the shock on Amelia's face, the pattern of blood on her left cheek.

Then Meg was sitting on the floor, dragging Amelia down with her.

It all seemed to be happening slowly, but disjointedly in a way that ate up time.

Shouts from outside. Running footfalls. Leather soles shuffling on concrete. The doorbell chiming over and over. A pounding on the door.

Meg looked again at Amelia, who was sitting hugging her knees and staring wide-eyed back at her, still with the stunned expression. And something else. A kind of horror mixed with pity.

A pain in Meg's right shoulder made her gasp, and she curled to lie on her side on the deep, roughly napped carpet. She felt for her shoulder and found fiery pain. Blood was thick and scarlet on her fingers, and now she felt the warmth of fresh blood between her breasts, trickling down her ribs beneath her left arm. Her life trickling away.

"Christ! I've been shot. . . ."

"Stay still," Amelia said, calmer now, suddenly older than twenty-one and in charge. Her face was bloody, cut by flying glass. A small shard protruded from just below her left eye. "I'll get help."

"Careful. . . ."

Amelia nodded as she scooted away, staying low, passing out of sight because Meg was too weak to turn her head to follow her movements.

I've been shot . . . Can't be . . . So many things left to do . . .

Motion. Shiny black shoes near her. Big. Men's shoes. Cop's shoes.

Jesus! That's reassuring. . . .

A cop's face looming over her. Knickerbocker's.

Mr. Chicken.

Exhausted, no longer in pain, Meg closed her eyes.

The Night Sniper knew he'd missed. He'd tried to make a head shot and failed. Carelessness of a sort. Or unlucky.

Something made the blond woman in the window, who

had to be Amelia Repetto, suddenly move—only a few inches, but enough to save her life. Life was always a matter of inches.

Lucky Amelia.

This time.

There'll be another time.

Right now the challenge was to get out of the subleased apartment fast. He'd gone over it all in his mind, so his actions were almost automatic. He moved quickly and deliberately, a part of his mind seconds, minutes ahead of where he was and what he was doing.

This rifle had a bolt action, so the Sniper didn't have to use valuable time retrieving a shell casing; it remained in the breech. There weren't as many tall buildings in this area as downtown, which meant the echo effect wasn't as great. It wouldn't take his opponents long to locate the source of the shot. If he weren't fast enough they'd be on his heels.

It was their time of temporary advantage in the game.

Their move.

His risk.

Even as he was reviewing this in his mind, he was heading toward the door to the hall.

He took the fire stairs fast, this time not caring if he made noise.

Past the musty-smelling basement laundry room. *Still unoccupied.*

Out the side door into the dark passageway. The fresh night air.

He hurried toward the paler rectangle of light that was the block behind Amelia Repetto's apartment, his long coat flapping as he took giant strides while fitting the rifle in its sling. Protruding from one pocket of his threadbare coat was a brown-wrapped bottle that would account for the uneven gait caused by the rifle extending down alongside his left leg. Its awkward, shifting weight only added to the suggestion of inebriation. As he walked across a subway grate, he worked the rifle's bolt and let the spent shell drop from beneath his coat to fall into darkness. If he must, he could throw the coat open and raise and fire the rifle in an instant.

If he must.

Right now, he didn't anticipate the need. Though his shooting could have been more accurate, his escape from the area was going just fine. He would stay in his homeless costume this time, and make his way as one of the invisible into the vastness and anonymity of the city.

He forced himself to move more slowly and deliberately, as if he were unafraid, as uninterested in his pursuers as they should be in him.

Another ten minutes and he'd be safe. The ageless equation of the desperate: *time equals distance equals safety. . . .*

He was unaware that a large percentage of the NYPD was in the area. And that they knew more than he imagined.

As Repetto jogged the final few yards to Amelia's apartment door and started up the concrete steps to the stoop, his cell phone chirped.

"We got a name," Melbourne told him.

"We got a shooting here! My place!"

"Amelia okay?"

"Dunno. Gonna find out."

Repetto was through the door now, shoving aside a uniform as he made his way toward the still form of a woman on the floor.

Then he became aware of Amelia standing off to the side, holding a bloody towel to her face.

She came to him and hugged him fiercely, dropping the towel and pressing her bloodied face to his shoulder. He hugged his only child tight, kissing her forehead, then leaned back to stare more closely at her.

She didn't appear to be injured badly, but she'd need treatment. He could see glass shards glittering in the small cuts that peppered her cheek. Outside, sirens were yowling, drawing near.

"We got EMS on the way," a voice near him said. Repetto turned to see a uniform, tried to recall his name but couldn't.

Amelia had moved away from Repetto. A guy wearing a bowling jacket and beard who Repetto knew was undercover was helping her over to the sofa, gently guiding her with a hand on her elbow so she'd sit down.

Repetto began thinking more clearly through his fear and concern for Amelia. He understood now that the woman on the floor was Meg.

He went to her on numbed legs, barely avoiding the blood. *We're going to get the bastard!*

The trap was closing.

We're going to get him.

After making sure her wounds were only superficial, Repetto saw Amelia off not in an ambulance but in a patrol car. He called Lora, talking to her only briefly, to let her know what had happened, to reassure her that Amelia would be all right. Then he called Melbourne back.

"Amelia . . . ?" Melbourne asked, when he heard Repetto's voice.

"She'll be okay," Repetto said.

"Thank God for that."

"Meg's not so good."

After Repetto had brought him up to speed on what had happened at the apartment, Melbourne said, "Our sniper's name is Dante Vanya." He spelled it for Repetto. "Weaver tracked him down. We did a rush through Central Warrants and tossed his apartment, swank place on the Upper East

Side. He's the son of a guy the Department of Sanitation fired sixteen years ago. Dad became depressed and shot Dante's mom, then himself. Dante lived for a while as a street kid, got himself badly burned in a subway station fire, then rehabilitated at a charity foundation ranch out in Arizona. That's where he learned from an expert how to shoot."

An orphan who'd grown up on the street, trying to kill a girl too stubborn to run. Sons and daughters, Repetto thought. Put the tape on rewind, and almost every crime could be prevented. "We sure about all this?"

"We are. You were right about Weaver. She did a hell of a job gathering facts. Vanya's also got a room in his apartment with a door that doesn't look like a door, and inside it is the biggest collection of rifles and shooting paraphernalia you ever saw. Ballistics is gonna be in heaven."

"I take it Vanya wasn't home when you arrived with the warrant."

"No, and we both know where he was."

We know. Repetto felt rage become determination in his gut. "We got his photo?"

"None anywhere in the apartment, which is also curious. Vanya never had much to do with his neighbors—not so unusual in New York—but the doorman describes him as average height and build, in his thirties, black and blue, good-looking guy, and a sharp dresser."

"Get the name out to the media. Spread it all over the city, along with his description. Somebody'll know him and tell us more." Repetto thought about the NYPD personnel stationed in the neighborhood, and the cordon of cops in the wider area, closing in, tightening the trap so there were more and more cops to the square block, the square yard. "We have him. I can feel it."

"When he knows he's trapped," Melbourne said, "he's gonna be desperate and even more dangerous. And he can shoot the buttons off your shirt, only he won't be aiming at your buttons."

"We put out his description," Repetto said, "and maybe he'll surprise us and surrender in remorse."

"I believe you hope he doesn't."

Repetto didn't see any point in answering that one. "Better make sure the public knows he's armed and dangerous."

"Right now I'm making sure you and the rest of your people know it," Melbourne said. "Right now I'm reminding you, this guy is deadly."

Repetto said, "Tell it to Meg."

"Word just came in on another line, she was hit in the shoulder and should be okay. She look to you like she was gonna make it?"

"There is no okay when you've got a bullet in you," Repetto said. "And we'll find out soon who's gonna make it, and who isn't."

61

A chill ran through the Night Sniper as he saw a man carrying what looked like a small duffel bag, crossing the street half a block down. He slowed his pace, stalling until the man had climbed half a dozen steps to a concrete stoop and disappeared into a building.

Relieved, the Sniper picked up his pace.

He hadn't expected this kind of security. Since leaving the apartment across the street from Repetto's, he'd spotted uniformed cops, then people who might be working undercover. Real or suspected, he'd managed to avoid them all.

Other people walking the dark streets, who fortunately weren't police, paid little attention to the homeless man in his long, rumpled coat, shuffling dazedly along the sidewalk. The fact that there were somewhat fewer homeless in New York these days seemed to make him even less noticeable, less of an actual person. He was a problem that was ended, or at least made manageable, and was no longer of concern. If anyone did look at him closely, the brown paper bag jutting from a pocket would explain his apparent disorientation. There was nothing unusual about people like him in New York. They existed in the thousands and drew no particular interest.

Yet he didn't feel the smug invulnerability that usually sustained him when in his homeless persona. His heart was beating faster and he was slightly out of breath, hyperalert. *Adrenaline. Terrifying, but like a drug.*

There was another police car, gliding across the intersection at the next block. The Sniper barely managed to halt and become part of the shadows. Again, he was sure he hadn't been noticed.

Reasonably sure.

How long before they see me? Approach me?

What was going on here? Security in Amelia Repetto's neighborhood, yes. But this sudden and relentless tightening of a net was beyond what he'd anticipated.

What do they know?

How do they know it?

One thing was for sure. They knew something. They'd been ready for him and had a plan that was now in effect. No surprise there. Everyone in the game knew that Amelia Repetto was being used to lure him. Like a staked lamb. But the number and intensity of the Sniper's pursuers were upsetting.

For the first time since the game had begun, his confidence was shaken.

He was frightened.

He had to admit it. *Afraid.*

But, as always, he knew where he was, and what he had to do. He changed direction and walked several blocks to the west. To a subway stop that had been closed for several months, awaiting renovation.

He managed a smile but didn't like the nervous twitch at the corner of his mouth. Like a fox, he'd go to ground and let the hounds pass over him, near him, unaware of his presence, not realizing how lucky they were not to find him. He was pleased by the analogy. He drew comfort from it.

Like a fox. But dangerous.

When he reached the darkened subway stop, he paused near the narrow concrete stairwell descending to the plywood-boarded entrance. No one seemed to be observing him, but just in case, he removed the bagged whiskey bottle from his pocket, pretended to take a swig, then started down the stairs that descended to blackness.

He was in familiar territory now, where a part of him had never left and still knew where it belonged, a discard and a freak hiding away from the rest of humanity.

His probing fingers found a rough wooden edge in the darkness, and he inserted them beneath it and began prying a plywood panel loose on one side to provide entry.

Through his fear he knew he was going home. Home to the ferocious security of a demon in hell.

Vanya. Dante Vanya.

Bobby had heard two guys standing outside Rocko Bill's Sports Lounge talking about this Vanya, about the Night Sniper. They'd observed something on TV inside the lounge and seemed to think Vanya and the Sniper were one and the same.

One of the guys gave Bobby a shit-kicker look, and Bobby moved on.

They were both big and they might have been a little drunk, so he waited until they'd left before returning to the lounge entrance. He edged the door open to the sound of talking, laughing, and a baseball announcer doing a Braves game on the channel out of Atlanta. Bobby had a clear view of one of the big TVs above the bar. There was a news crawl across the bottom of the screen, but he couldn't make out what it said. He did hear the name again—"Vanya"—in the conversation of people seated near the door.

Dante Vanya.

"Hey, you!"

Bobby looked in the direction of the voice. A bald man behind the bar was waving what appeared to be a white towel at him. "Out! Get the fuck out!"

Bobby backed away, letting the door swing shut. Things had changed. Now he—and the police—knew the name of the Night Sniper:

Dante Vanya.

If he *was* the Night Sniper.

If he was the homeless man who didn't belong.

If he was real.

So many *ifs.* Bobby jammed his fists into his pockets and bowed his head as he limped away on newly raised blisters.

That was the trouble. When you went to the police and they didn't believe you, it made you doubt yourself.

Officer Tom Dillon hoped to hell somebody knew what they were doing. He wasn't due at the precinct till tomorrow for his next shift, and here he was looking for a guy named Vanya who might be the Night Sniper.

It was all part of a Special Operations Division plan that had sprung into place because Repetto had called it in after somebody'd shot at his daughter. Dillon had been on the Job only two years, but he'd heard plenty about Repetto. The guy knew his shit, and that was the only thing that kept Dillon from thinking tonight might not be a total waste of time.

Fifteen minutes ago an RMP car had dropped him off three blocks away from the crime scene, and he'd been walking ever since. He'd been assigned to stay on the move, observe, and get the information out fast on his two-way if anything or anyone merited suspicion.

Dillon wished he were home in bed with his wife, Glorianne, who was pregnant. Even in her fifth month, Glorianne was capable of having and enjoying sex. That had been something of a surprise to Dillon. But the doctor had said—

The young officer stopped and stared. He was sure he'd just seen somebody start down the steps of a subway stop half a block away, near the next corner. Which didn't make sense, because he knew the subway stop was closed and boarded up. Had been for months.

Or maybe it had been a trick of his vision, a play of shadow, and he hadn't seen anything at all. Dillon couldn't be sure.

He'd better make sure.

Telling himself this might fall into the category of something that merited suspicion, he went to investigate.

Dillon peered down the narrow concrete stairwell into darkness. There was no sound from below. The acrid smell of stale urine wafted up at him, almost strong enough to make him turn his head.

"Hey!" he yelled. "You, down there!"

If anybody's down there.

He got out his flashlight and aimed it down the stairwell, tentatively descending three or four concrete steps so he might see better.

The figure he'd glimpsed had been real. A ragged, homeless man holding a brown paper bag was just beginning to settle down with his whiskey in the shadows at the base of the steps. He glared up at Dillon, surprised, frightened, and perhaps indignant. The expression on his face suggested Dillon was invading his home.

Dillon was no stranger to the proprietary nature of some vagrants. He relaxed but kept the beam of his flashlight trained on the man. "You! C'mon up here."

The man stood up unsteadily, as if his legs were sore, facing away from Dillon with his feet widely planted. His lower arms and hands disappeared in front of him, a slight bend to the elbows.

He appeared to be urinating, and not for the first time in the odorous stairwell.

Dillon thought about telling him it was illegal to piss down there; then he decided to be patient, let the poor guy finish his business before making his painful way back up to the city's surface world.

That was when the man turned around with a sudden nimbleness that aroused Dillon's suspicion. He saw that the homeless guy hadn't been pissing but had struck a match and was holding it in the same hand that held the brown paper bag.

No, not a match. Too much flame, and growing. A twisted rag sticking up from the neck of the bottle in the bag. *A wick!*

Dillon tried to spin his body and clamber up the steps at the same time, scraping the toe of his left shoe on concrete and going nowhere. His right foot slipped and he banged his shin. He heard his flashlight clatter down the steps.

The explosion was more of a *whoosh!* than a bang. Dillon picked up a momentary stench of gasoline and realized the man had thrown a Molotov cocktail at him, *and he was standing where it had detonated.*

His legs were on fire!

His screams drew attention, and through his pain he managed to wrest his 9mm from its holster and fire several shots blindly through the flames in the stairwell.

The bullets splintered wood but missed the Night Sniper, who had bent down to pick up Dillon's still-shining flashlight and shove it in a coat pocket. He hadn't brought his own flashlight tonight because he hadn't anticipated going underground.

The fire provided enough light to work by.

He got a fresh grip on the crooked panel and was through the plywood barrier and running down a frozen escalator, fumbling for the flashlight he'd need for the total darkness ahead.

It took a few minutes for the cops on the street to reach the subway stop and drag what was left of Dillon up to the sidewalk. Assuming, with a glance at his charred and smoldering body, that he was dead, they switched their efforts to trying to extinguish the fire at the top of the stairwell.

They had little other than the soles of their shoes and a shirt one of them had removed to try to smother the flames, but it didn't take long for the remaining gasoline to burn itself out.

Convinced that Dillon had expired, but also knowing it could be a mistake to mentally pronounce someone dead at the scene of a crime, the three cops decided they couldn't desert him. The shirtless cop, a big African-American named Wilson, was elected to stay with the fallen Dillon to wait for an ambulance.

It was a good thing. As if responding to their decision not to give up on him, the thing that Dillon had become began to moan.

While the other two uniforms made their way down the blackened steps and through the dark gap made by the pried plywood panel, Wilson used his two-way to call for medical transport and to get out the word:

The Night Sniper was in the subway system, on the run and under hot pursuit.

62

The Sniper ran stumbling along the tracks, staying close to the tunnel's dark concrete wall, occasionally bumping it with his left shoulder. He knew that though the stop was closed, the E and V trains still roared through the tunnel. Now and then he thought he could feel the wind pressure of an approaching train shoving cool air ahead of it in the narrow tunnel. But there was no thunderous, clacking roar that accompanied the trains, and no approaching brilliant eye of light.

He knew he could find shelter in the occasional tile maintenance alcove along the tunnel, where he could press himself back while a train passed a few feet away from him. He'd done it more than once during his time as a street kid, and more recently while using the tunnels to get around the city undetected. It was a convenient and private way to move about, once you learned the train times and layout of the underground maze.

What he feared more than the trains was what he knew would soon be pursuing him. There'd been an army of cops in the area, and they'd see where he entered the tunnel. As soon as they'd tended to their burned comrade, and the fire blocking the stairwell was extinguished, they'd be after the cop's killer.

And they'd be motivated.

He could hear his rasping breath, and every few steps feel the bite of sharp or angled rock beneath his soles.

What if I turn an ankle now, fall, and become immobile? They'll have me. Here in the tunnel they'll do what they choose, their own notion of justice.

He ignored the rifle barrel bumping his leg beneath his coat and ran harder, careful to avoid the live rail. Like everyone who'd spent time in the subway system, he'd seen the dead rats on the tracks that had died by electrocution, and it was obvious they had left this world in agony.

His right side began to ache with each step. The intermittent, piercing pain grew sharper, slowing him down, making his stride erratic.

This is insane! Don't panic! Don't!

Think! Plan!

He made himself slow to a brisk walk and worked to regulate his breathing. From a pocket he withdrew a fresh magazine for the rifle. He stopped completely for a moment, removed from the rifle the magazine that was missing the bullet he'd fired at Amelia Repetto, and replaced it with the fresh magazine. Soon, any second, every shot might count. The magazine a bullet short went into his pocket. He fitted the rifle back on the sling beneath his coat.

Under way again, breathing more rhythmically, he picked up his pace and rounded a bend in the tunnel. After another hundred yards he reached a shallow alcove and pressed himself back into it. He switched off the flashlight and tucked it in his belt, then brought the rifle up from beneath his coat.

Shifting position and bracing himself against hard tile, he

raised the rifle and peered through its infrared scope. Whoever was after him would soon be rounding the bend in the tunnel.

It felt good to be taking the initiative instead of acting, *feeling,* like a hunted animal. He had options other than mindless flight. He could plan. He could act.

He could shoot.

Oh, he could shoot!

The Night Sniper felt confidence swell in him like a warm revelation. He'd stopped playing their game.

Now they were playing his.

Their flashlight beams became visible first. Now that he had a fix on his pursuers, the Sniper raised his eye from the scope and waited.

Yellow fingers of light played over the tracks and tunnel walls. Then the figures holding the flashlights came into sight in dark silhouette, one quite a bit taller than the other. One of the yellow beams darted close and momentarily reflected off the damp tunnel wall to reveal two uniformed cops. They appeared to have their flashlights in their left hands, their handguns in their right. Their body language gave away their fear.

The Night sniper squinted again through the night scope and took careful aim. He felt solid, steady, and the moment arrived as he knew it would.

His first shot took down the tall cop, who seemed to melt into a dark heap.

The Sniper worked the rifle's bolt action smoothly, and before the startled shorter cop could get off a shot, sent a bullet into him.

Through the scope, he studied the two still forms on the ground. The tall one had rolled against the tunnel wall and lay motionless. The short one hadn't moved since he'd fallen and lay on his back near the tracks. The Sniper knew he'd hit both targets, and considered sending a shot into each of them to make sure they were dead.

Then he decided against it. If they weren't dead, they were surely wounded, probably unconscious, and couldn't keep up with him.

More confident now, he lowered the rifle and hooked it into its sling, then resumed his journey through the dark tunnel.

He'd taken only a dozen steps before he felt the cool rush of air that told him a train was bearing down on him, coming toward him.

No mistake this time.

Without hesitation he ran back toward the alcove where he'd shot from to bring down the two cops. The rifle bumping against him slowed him down, and he slipped on something and almost fell. He could hear the train now, and feel its subtle vibration. Glancing over his shoulder, he saw a pinpoint of light staring at him like an unblinking hunter's eye.

He reached the alcove, ducked into it, and stood with his back pressed tightly against the tile wall as the train roared toward him. The tunnel shook. The wall at his back trembled.

Then the train was passing him.

Only a few feet away. How near the passengers were as they blurred past in the lighted cars. He knew he wasn't visible to them in the black tunnel as they ticked by unaware, kept company by their reflections in the dark glass.

He'd watched carefully and was sure the conductor in the lead car hadn't seen him.

He could still feel the vibration as he listened to the roar of the train become fainter.

Danger past.

He let out the breath he'd been holding, though even as he did so he knew something wasn't right.

It was the way the train sounded, fainter yet no farther away. And he'd heard an underlying metallic squealing.

When he stepped from the alcove, he was surprised to see that the train had slowed almost to a stop only a few hundred feet away.

Okay, he could start running in the opposite direction and there was little chance anyone inside the last car would notice him even if they could see out into the close and ominous darkness.

Another metallic squeal, and the train began gradually building speed.

The Night Sniper realized what must have happened; the train had made contact with one or both of the dead cops. He remembered the short one who'd fallen near the tracks. Now the train had worked its way beyond the obstruction and was picking up speed.

The Night Sniper was amazed how opportunity, fate, always turned out to be his unexpected ally. Amazed but not really surprised. Fortune favored the brave.

He sprinted toward the last car that was now traveling about five miles per hour. He was aware of something soft beneath his foot as he passed the place where the cops had fallen, and caught a glimpse of the tall cop's body still huddled against the tunnel wall. He didn't have time to think about it. The train was picking up speed and he had to lengthen his stride to keep closing the distance to it.

The pain in his side flared again, threatening to stop him, bend him, break him. He refused to let it. He strained even harder, lifting his knees higher, pumping his legs beneath the tattered coat, ignoring the pain that was like fire in his ribs.

He was gaining on the car now. Slowly, but he was gaining.

Lunging, he reached out his hand toward the metal rail on the car's rear platform. Missed it, stumbled, and almost fell. Ran even harder, reached again, closed his hand over the rail, and squeezed it in a grip that matched its steel.

With a shout of pain that no one heard, he closed his other hand on the rail, lifted his feet, and dragged himself up onto the car's narrow back platform.

He lay there gasping, feeling the train gaining speed, aware of something hard beneath his right hip.

The rifle! Thank God he hadn't lost it in his wild dash for the train. The most important train he'd ever caught.

Rather, it would be if his luck held.

He rolled over so he could kneel on the lurching platform, then crouch, then slowly stand. He peered through the dirty back window into the lighted subway car.

His luck hadn't deserted him!

There was only one passenger in the rear car, a fiftyish woman slouched in one of the bench seats and reading a paperback book. She was wearing a gray blouse, dirty and wrinkled jeans, and her mouse-colored hair was lank and unkempt. Her ankles were crossed so her knees were separated in a posture that might have been obscene on a younger, more attractive woman. Her shoes were practical black lace-ups that were scuffed and badly worn. There was a faded red scarf or shawl over her shoulders that had fringe on it.

The woman's eyes appeared to be closed. At first the Night Sniper thought she might be asleep; then her right hand rose and went to her book, slowly turned a page, and returned to her side and was still. The rest of the woman hadn't moved.

Deep into whatever she was reading, the Night Sniper thought. Good.

He stood all the way up and opened the door.

At the motion and sudden rush of sound, the woman raised her gaze from the book and turned her head to look at him. He closed the door and met her bleary-eyed, baleful stare.

She knows something, everything. On a certain level, she knows.

He opened his coat and raised the rifle from its sling, bringing it to his shoulder. The woman's expression remained the same until an instant before he squeezed the trigger. There was a slight change in her eyes—perhaps they widened—and she opened her mouth to speak.

The train was traveling fast now, making a racket. The shot was barely audible over the clatter of steel on steel. When the bullet tore into the woman's heart, her body jerked and her book dropped to the floor. She slumped lower on the bench seat, as if settling down awkwardly for a nap.

The Night Sniper went to her and pulled her up so she was seated somewhat straighter. It was surprising how light she was. He retrieved her book from the floor, glancing at the cover. *Six Secrets for Sexual Success.* That didn't seem at all like the woman. He placed her fingers around the cover and propped the book in her dead hands. Her heart had stopped pumping immediately, so there wasn't much blood. He arranged her fringed red scarf so it tumbled down over her chest, concealing the glistening scarlet stain. With a deft, brushing motion of his fingertips, he closed her eyes.

Gripping a vertical bar for support, he moved back and surveyed what he'd done. The woman appeared much as she had when he entered the car. She might be sleeping or reading.

Or dead.

He glanced again at her book and found himself wondering, what were the six secrets?

The train rattled on through the dark tunnel toward its next stop. When it arrived, if the platform looked clear enough, the Sniper would get off and make his way up to the street. As sparse as subway passengers were these dangerous nights, it should take quite a while before someone discovered the woman slumped in her seat was dead and not reading or sleeping.

Whatever the situation at the train's next stop, the Sniper was sure that if he needed an alternate plan, one would come to him.

He was confident in a new way and with a new knowledge. It was going to be impossible for Repetto and his minions to bring him down. He understood that now, and the understanding was like a gift granted at birth and finally found. He couldn't fail and he wouldn't.

God or the devil was with him, and he didn't know or care which.

63

"He can't go far on foot," Birdy said. "He's gotta come up at the next stop or the one after."

He and Repetto were standing next to the unmarked Ford Victoria Birdy had just arrived in, parked well away from the subway stop where Dillon had burned. They could still hear the siren as the ambulance that had left with Dillon made its way through traffic. They both knew, after having seen and talked with Dillon, that there was no real rush. Nobody in Dillon's condition could have lived, or would want to live, much longer.

Three police cruisers were parked near the blackened area on the sidewalk where Dillon had lain, and techs from the crime scene unit were still busily measuring and photographing. Most of the cops were standing back. Two of them were smoking, one a cigarette, the other a cigar. They smoked for good reason. Burning tobacco created a different sort of smoke, with a different sort of odor that was definitely the lesser of two evils.

Repetto and Birdy were also keeping their distance because of the sweet scent of burnt flesh that hung in the air and became taste at the back of the tongue. The stench was still too cloying and evocative even at this distance. If Repetto had a cigar on him, he would have lit it.

"He comes to the surface, we'll get him," Birdy said confidently.

"He might branch off and take another tunnel," Repetto said. He knew Melbourne and some other NYPD brass types would be second-guessing him if the Night Sniper—Dante Vanya—escaped capture or death tonight.

If they'd kept secret that they had the Sniper's identity, he might have felt safe and returned to his apartment after his attempt to kill Amelia, and there encountered half the NYPD.

Repetto had understood his choice and made it. He'd opted to put out the killer's identity while they had him inside the cordon, rattled and on the run. They had his name and description now; they'd soon track him down. Someone who knew him might call the police. And if he did slip the police tonight, there was always the chance he might still return to his apartment without knowing the media had spread his identity all over the city.

Odds. Everything was about odds.

"Wherever our guy is," Birdy said, "I bet he's covering ground fast. Gonna make it hard for us."

Repetto pulled his cell phone from his pocket and pecked out the number for the Transit Bureau liaison, a lieutenant named Collingwood. He told Collingwood the situation.

"What he's doing, running around in those dark tunnels, is damned dangerous," Collingwood said in a grating voice.

"I wanna make it even more dangerous for him," Repetto said. "How trapped is he?"

"Where he is, there aren't many transfer points along the way," Collingwood rasped. "Until he gets to . . ." His voice trailed off as if he might be consulting a map. ". . . Lexington Avenue."

Repetto knew the stop, one of the major subway junctions in the city. If the Sniper shook himself loose there, he might slip away. "What trains travel along the tunnel he's in?" *Or at least entered.*

"He's following a route still used by the E and V lines."

"What I want is to flood stops along those lines with cops, along with intersecting lines at transfer points. And soon as possible I want the subway system shut down temporarily for a police action."

"I'll pass along the order for the troops to be deployed," Collingwood said, "but I think you oughta call Melbourne for authorization to shut down the line."

"Not the line," Repetto said, "the system. I don't want there to be any possibility the Sniper can get into another tunnel or somehow board a train traveling who knows where."

"The entire system? I dunno . . . Like I said, you better call Melbourne."

"I'll call him," Repetto said. "Then I'll see your ass is called on the carpet if you don't shut down the system."

"Hold on, now. The whole system can't be shut down just like that. What you're asking—"

Repetto broke the connection and punched out his number for Melbourne.

"Problem?" Birdy asked, while Repetto was pacing and waiting to get through.

"Goddamn disconnect," Repetto said.

"Phone, you mean?"

"Fuckin' bureaucracy!"

"Ah," Birdy said, understanding. He started to fidget, drumming his fingertips against each other, gazing up the block toward where Dillon had burned.

Still with the cell phone pressed to his ear, waiting for an answer, Repetto moved toward the car. "Let's drive," he said.

Birdy stopped fidgeting and stepped off the curb to walk around to the driver's side. "Where to?"

Repetto was already lowering his bulk into the car, so Birdy got in behind the wheel before expecting a reply.

"Melbourne?" Repetto said, as his call was answered. Then to Birdy, his hand over the tiny phone's flip mouthpiece: "Third and Lex."

Approximately two minutes after his conversation with Melbourne, Repetto's cell phone chirped.

"Collingwood," said a phlegmy voice, after Repetto had identified himself.

Repetto waited, knowing the lieutenant had been contacted by Deputy Chief Melbourne. He didn't want contrition out of Collingwood, only cooperation. And fast.

"Conductor on the V train called in a little while ago and said he felt resistance after seeing what looked like a bundle of rags near the tracks."

"He say exactly where?"

"Not far from the stop where Officer Dillon was burned."

Repetto felt his breathing pick up. Any aggravation he'd felt for Collingwood was suddenly gone. Minor. He knew what the bundle must have been. The two uniforms who'd gone into the tunnel after the Night Sniper might no longer be chasing him toward the next stop.

There'd be no one on the Sniper's heels now. He'd no longer be panicked—if he ever had been.

He'd be thinking.

"Shut down the system," Repetto said firmly, knowing Melbourne must have phoned this guy and reamed him out. He wouldn't be so quick to question an order next time.

"We're working on it," Collingwood said, not wanting to give up everything at once.

Repetto broke the connection and pointed out the windshield toward a van that was blocking traffic on the narrow street. "Go around that asshole."

Birdy touched off the siren, put a wheel up on the curb, and went.

* * *

Zoe took another sip of vodka and sat staring at the framed certificates on her office wall. The drapes were closed, the door locked. Private office. Right now it was private. Too warm, but she didn't notice. Her mind was set in one direction, and she hadn't had enough drinks for it to change course, or for the pressure that had become a headache behind her right eye to ease.

All the work she'd done, everything she'd lived for, given so much to accomplish, might be about to collapse in on her and crush her.

She felt crushed already.

Another sip. After putting down the glass, she used the tips of her forefingers to massage her temples. Her drinking was out of control and she knew it. Had been out of control for months. That's what explained the fling with—she knew his name now—Dante Vanya.

She looked away from the framed affirmations and validations of her scholastic and professional triumphs and stared at the simple memo on her desk. It was from Deputy Chief Melbourne and, in his jagged but readable handwriting, asked if it was consistent with what she knew about the Night Sniper that he might sometimes wear a red wig.

Zoe didn't think it likely, though possible. The Night Sniper, Vanya, her lover, wore a hairpiece as an instrument of ego, not as a disguise. She tried to imagine him with a bushy red wig askew on his head, standing nude at the foot of the bed, but she couldn't. If she were sober, she might have laughed at the carrot-top wild image, but right now nothing could strike her funny.

Because of her headache that was like a knife behind her eye. Because of that damned memo.

When she'd phoned and asked Melbourne why he'd asked his handwritten question, he told her about the strand of red hair found in the Sniper's suite at the Marimont Hotel. It hadn't been considered important at the time, and probably it wasn't. Which was why mention of it hadn't been included in the material sent to Zoe to analyze after the attempted murder of the mayor. The hair found by the diligent crime scene unit probably belonged to someone other than the suite's occupant, perhaps a maid or previous guest. Or maybe one of the investigating officers' shoes had picked it up from the hall carpet and tracked it into the suite. A hair, so light and transportable. A breeze might have even carried it in from outside.

But Zoe knew the red hair was important. The single red hair that had been magnified, cut and sampled, photographed, locked away in the evidence room. God, yes, it was important!

Or would be if it were ever matched with one of hers.

Hairs were distinctive and easily compared under microscopes. Hairs carried DNA. Hairs made dandy evidence. Hairs sent people to prison and to hell.

If Vanya were captured rather than killed, Zoe was sure he'd implicate her. There was no reason for him *not* to if he were found guilty, as he surely would be.

As he was.

She of all people knew.

Of course, he wouldn't be believed. Not at first.

Until someone recalled the red hair found in the suite at the Marimont Hotel. Or happened to question Weaver.

Weaver. Why had she confided in Weaver?

But Zoe knew Weaver wasn't the problem. Lies were the problem. Telling them and living them.

Tangled webs . . . lies . . . webs of red hair . . .

Her headache flared.

She reached again for the vodka.

64

It was working out for the Night Sniper. The platform at the Fifty-third and Third stop wasn't as crowded as usual when the train broke into the light and began to slow. And he was on the last car. Usually the train eased to a halt so the middle cars were more or less centered at the stop. The last car was accessible, but most passengers, especially if the platform wasn't packed with riders, simply entered the cars most convenient to them, the middle cars.

The Sniper remained in his seat and glanced at the dead woman with the book. When the train finally lurched to a complete stop, she was jostled and almost went sideways. But she remained upright. Even if passengers did enter the car, the Sniper would already have exited; by the time someone realized the woman was dead, he'd be long gone. Possibly she'd topple from her seat when the train accelerated, but it would take time and distance for anyone in the car to raise the alarm.

The car's doors hissed open.

The Sniper rose from his seat and moved quickly to the open door, then stepped out onto the platform.

The air was fresher there, and the surrounding wider space gave him an unexpected feeling of vulnerability.

He sneaked a quick glance around. Passengers were filing out of and into the cars ahead, but so far no one had decided to break from the pack and hurry toward the last car.

As he was about to walk away, satisfied he'd completed an important part of his escape, the Sniper froze as he noticed a tall, stolid figure in a rumpled brown suit.

Repetto!

Facing three-quarters away from him, but it was surely Repetto. And he was slowly turning around.

Most of the exiting passengers were on the platform, and the crowd ahead closed ranks as everyone slowed to board the cars. The figure was suddenly no longer visible.

But the Sniper knew it hadn't been his imagination. Repetto was here!

The Sniper's options presented themselves in fractions of seconds. He calculated the odds.

If he returned to his seat and stayed on board, Repetto was sure to spot him as the train rolled past, picking up speed.

The lesser risk might be to stay off the train and walk away from Repetto, toward a flight of steps leading to a side street exit. If he acted now, other exiting passengers might shield him from view.

He had to make up his mind.

He walked. As he headed for the steps, he listened for any commotion behind him and watched the faces of those walking in the opposite direction. Everyone appeared calm enough, displaying only the normal anxiety that was part of riding New York subways.

Feeling better, the Sniper continued to walk, careful not to listen to the interior voice shouting for him to run, to flee for safety. It was fight or flight. And this was hardly the time or place to fight.

Then he heard another voice. An announcement on the

public address system saying that beginning immediately, subway service would be temporarily suspended for a police action. The crowd groaned collectively, but they kept moving. They'd been through these things before and knew that service might resume within a few minutes. It wasn't yet time to change their plans, to consider returning to the surface for alternate transportation.

The Sniper hunched his shoulders. Now it was almost impossible not to break into a run. His back was alive with nerves and tense muscles, bracing for a bullet. A bullet from Repetto. He walked on. He was almost to the concrete steps that led to the surface and the concealing night.

The station was too warm and he was perspiring heavily. So much so that a few of the people walking past glanced at him curiously. One woman even hesitated and seemed to consider asking if he was all right. But when she noticed his ragged clothes, what he was, what he wasn't, she hurried on her way.

He made his legs move with great conscious effort, one step, the next, another . . . The rifle beneath his coat was bumping his right leg painfully, and it was all he could do not to let it alter the rhythm of his gait and draw attention.

Almost to the stairs.

Almost to the cool, safe night.

Passing faces . . . still the same . . . Repetto close behind . . .

Almost to the stairs.

Bobby was seated with his back against a steel support, facing the tracks so he wouldn't be noticeable. He'd come to the Fifty-third and Third stop because it was one of the busiest, and he was desolate and broke. Because of the Night Sniper, there were fewer and fewer places in the city that were crowded after dark. The Sniper was bad for business, all right, from Wall Street all the way down to people like Bobby, who begged a meager living in the streets.

His illicit panhandling in the subway stop had netted him six dollars and seventy cents. Not much, but something. After ditching the stolen cell phone and giving up on trying to get the police to believe him, Bobby had walked most of the way across town. He was exhausted.

He heard the announcement about the subway system standing down for a police action. It didn't matter much to him. There must have been some kind of emergency, a heart attack, a murder, some poor soul falling onto the tracks in front of an oncoming train. He rested the back of his head against cool steel and sighed. None of it seemed worth worrying about now, or even thinking about. He had no plans beyond the moment.

That was when he happened to glance down the platform and see the homeless man he'd been following earlier that evening. The man who didn't belong.

Bobby struggled to his feet and limped after him, his gaze fixed on the figure in the long tattered coat. The man wasn't exactly hurrying, but he was still walking faster than anyone else on the platform.

Suddenly Bobby wondered if the man was real. Or even if he was real, was it the same man? After all, this time he'd only seen him from behind.

"Hey!"

The shout had hurt Bobby's throat. He coughed and tried again. "Hey! Hey, bro!"

But the man hadn't heard him over the repetitious public address announcement about the subway system being temporarily shut down.

Or *had* he heard? He was walking faster now.

He was running.

Bobby began to run after him. The hurrying man wasn't going to escape. Not this time.

*   *   *

The Night Sniper heard the voice calling behind him. He couldn't be sure if it was meant for him.

Even as he made up his mind that he was close enough to the exit to make a run for it, he was sprinting. His right arm held the concealed rifle tight to his body, while his left swung to keep his balance and to intimidate or knock aside anyone blocking his way. He pushed past a man strolling and reading a paper, elbowed aside a woman walking with her head down and dragging a small suitcase on wheels.

He was going to make it. He was sure now he was going to make it!

At first he didn't notice the uniformed cop who came down the steps and was striding toward him.

When he did see him, there was no question in the Night Sniper's mind. No hesitation.

He smoothly swung the rifle out from beneath his coat, aimed, and fired at the blue uniform.

Repetto heard the shot and whirled toward its source. At the crack of the rifle, everyone on the platform had dropped low or run for cover, so there was nothing to obstruct his view of a uniformed cop lurching along and pointing toward a hunched, hurrying figure in ragged clothes, a long coat and worn baseball cap. The cop stumbled and fell. The hurrying, hunched figure turned, and Repetto saw the rifle swinging up from beneath the coat to point at him.

A bullet snapped past Repetto's ear as he struggled to un-holster his revolver. His hands, his fingers, felt clumsy and insensitive. He seemed to be in a different, slower time frame than the man with the rifle.

Another shot—not as loud.

The wounded cop was sitting up, firing his 9mm at the Sniper. The gun was bucking in his hand.

Suddenly realizing he was in a cross fire, the Sniper

leaped from the platform onto the tracks and sprinted toward the adjacent platform for trains running the opposite direction.

A play of light and press of wind, and Repetto realized a train was roaring in from that direction on momentum, trying to make its last stop as the system shut down.

He realized it was a break for the Sniper. If he made it to the opposite platform, he'd be on the other side of the incoming train and could make his getaway.

And he was going to make it.

Not only that, he was on a lower plane now and Repetto couldn't get a bead on him through the people lying and kneeling on the platform. Both he and the wounded cop had stopped shooting. There was no choice. Repetto had completely lost sight of the Sniper now.

The bastard was going to make it!

The Sniper knew he had it timed. As he bolted to cross in front of the oncoming train, he paused and turned to send a final bullet in the direction of Repetto, so he'd duck his head and not make a lucky shot with a handgun from that distance.

Simple risk management. How he'd survived for so long and would continue to survive and taunt his pursuers.

The rifle cracked. No chance of actually hitting Repetto, but that wasn't the purpose of the shot. The Sniper saw Repetto lower his handgun and duck, as if on cue.

No, *on cue.* It was the Sniper directing this scene.

Seeing Repetto, seeing the oncoming train, *seeing everything*, he spun back around, lowering the rifle, and took a few confident strides, knowing his timing was perfect.

"You! Hey, bro!"

The voice again. Not a cop. Not "Hey, bro!"

The Sniper turned his head and saw a ragged homeless man. A freak, an outcast, but someone vaguely and achingly familiar.

"Hey, bro! Brother!"

Brother? Who *was* he?

The man raised an arm, and at first the Sniper thought he might be aiming a gun at him. But the man's hand was empty. He simply stretched out his arm and spread his fingers wide, as if trying to reach across time and distance and touch him. As if trying to make any kind of human contact.

He did touch something.

The Sniper felt it in his heart, in his core.

Quickly he recovered from his surprise and regained his stride to cross in front of the oncoming train.

But he knew his timing wasn't so precise now.

Repetto saw the Sniper twist his torso to get off a quick shot in his direction. He ducked instinctively, then raised his head in time to see the Sniper almost freeze and stop running.

The moment froze with him. Then the Sniper lowered his rifle, tucked in his chin, and sprinted hard to cross in front of the train.

But he seemed to be the one in a different, slower time frame now.

The decelerating train struck him squarely and he halfway disappeared beneath it.

Steel wheels, and something else, screamed on the rails as the train dragged what was left of the Night Sniper past Repetto, past Bobby, and another hundred yards down the tracks.

Repetto strode faster and faster toward the front of the stopped train, stepping around or over people who were just beginning to sense the end of danger and starting to rise. The dead Sniper was acting as a vortex, drawing everyone to converge at the same point. Even the wounded cop had made it to his feet and was trudging in that direction.

Everyone was moving that way except for a raggedly dressed man limping slowly in the opposite direction, toward the exit to the street.

Repetto noticed him and dismissed him from his mind.

He no longer mattered.

65

The Night Sniper murders were ended.

The city began to breathe again at night.

Dante Vanya was the lead item in the news for weeks before receding to the inside pages of the *Times*. Then he dropped from mention to join fabled serial killers like the Night Spider and Son of Sam in the city's lore and history, the subject of scholars rather than of the NYPD.

Repetto returned to active retirement and a deepening relationship with Lora. They both became closer to Amelia. Almost losing her had jarred them into a different perspective and appreciation for a present that would too soon become the past.

A month after the Night Sniper's death, Meg moved in with Alex and began a tentative relationship that was a healing process for both of them. She'd thought it was her task to teach Alex how to live and trust again, and was learning every day that she needed his help as much as he needed hers. It was for both of them a sometimes troubled and painful relationship well worth the effort, because they both knew what could be on the other side of the pain. *A price for everything in life.* Meg believed it. She saw it every day in her job. She saw too many people who didn't believe it, who didn't live it, slowly drowning. The parallel world of the cop. She could live in it now. With Alex, she'd found understanding. They'd both found understanding.

As a reward for her diligence and initiative, Officer Nancy Weaver was promoted and honored in a public awards ceremony and assigned to the Detective Bureau's Special Investigation Division's Major Case Squad. Her future in the NYPD appeared bright enough to blind.

The mayor recovered fully from his gunshot wound, affected a slight limp even though he'd been shot in the chest, and basked in his new status as the most heroic figure in New York.

Bobby Mays, who was the first to suspect the Night Sniper and try to alert the police, became a local, then a national celebrity. As he granted interviews and became the subject of TV and radio talk shows, public sympathy for him grew. After his national appearance on the *Today Show,* a fund was established to finance his medical expenses. Public sympathy would guarantee him the help he needed. A chance.

On a warm fall evening, Repetto and Lora were dining at an outside table at an Upper West Side restaurant across from Central Park. They were on the way to the theater, so they were eating light, knowing there would be a snack later that night. Repetto had declined desert and was sipping decaffeinated coffee, while Lora was working on a latte.

"Isn't this where that young stock wizard and author was shot and killed?" she asked.

Repetto placed his cup in its saucer and glanced around. "My God, it is. Lee Nasad! I'd forgotten. Am I getting old, Lora?"

"Of course you are. We both are."

"Everybody is," Repetto said.

"Not Dante Vanya and his victims."

"Point taken," Repetto said, and raised his cup to sip.

"I called Zoe Brady yesterday to see if she wanted to meet for lunch. She put me off. She did mention she was re-signing from the department."

Repetto wasn't surprised. He watched a young couple across the street, both in sweatsuits and wearing bright white jogging shoes. The man was pushing one of those baby strollers that held two infants side by side.

"You didn't ask me why Zoe was quitting," Lora said.

"Uh-uh, I didn't. Why is she?"

"She said she's going into private practice. She's done enough public service and decided to earn more money. Thought she owed it to herself."

"Maybe she does."

"The way she was talking, my impression was we were never going to lunch together again."

"Clean break," Repetto said. "Good for people some-times."

Lora tilted back her oversize glass cup and took a sip of her latte. The remaining white froth on its surface left a filmy mustache above her upper lip. "She seems to have that atti-tude."

"Don't blame her," Repetto said.

"I shouldn't? Or you don't?"

"Huh?"

"Blame her."

"Zoe?"

"Jesus, Vin." Lora looked depressed. "Our conversations are deteriorating. We *are* getting old."

Repetto smiled at her. "Not you. You somehow cancel out time."

She didn't look any happier, but he knew she was pleased by the compliment. While she attempted to sip without leaving more foam on her lip, she stared across the table at him as if he were a puzzle she couldn't quite fathom.

"One thing about Zoe," she said, putting down the cup and daintily swiping the back of a finger across her lip, "she was good at her work. She really had the Night Sniper figured. His approximate age, the way he looked and thought, how he went about his murders, like they were moves in some kind of sick chess game."

Some chess game. "I'll give her that," Repetto said.

He hadn't reminded Lora, nor would he remind anyone, that a search of Dante Vanya's apartment hadn't turned up a red wig. Not even a red hair.

Some things you never knew for sure, or shouldn't know even if you could.

"That Detective Weaver, too," Lora said. "She's another one who knows her stuff."

"Uh-huh. She's a good cop."

"More than that. She understands how to deal with people. She'll be a high-ranking officer someday."

"Weaver will go far in the department," Repetto agreed. "She knows how to keep a secret. And how to play chess."

He raised a hand to signal the waiter. "Check."

Turn the page to read a preview of John Lutz's next thriller, starring ex-homicide detective Frank Quinn,

SERIAL

Coming from Pinnacle in August 2011!

I would I were alive again
To kiss the fingers of the rain,
To drink into my eyes the shine
Of every slanting silver line . . .

—EDNA ST. VINCENT MILLAY,
"Renascence"

I hear a sudden cry of pain!
There is a rabbit in a snare . . .

—JAMES STEPHENS,
"The Snare"

1

Millie Graff's feet were sore. She was a hostess at Mingles, a new and popular restaurant on West Forty-fifth Street near Times Square, and hadn't sat down for over five hours. After work, it was a three-block walk and a long concrete stairwell descent to a downtown subway platform. In the crowded subway, someone would probably step on her toes.

She didn't mind the work or the time at Mingles. Her paycheck was big enough that she'd soon be able to move out of her cramped Village apartment into something larger, maybe on the Upper West Side. Her job was secure, and there was still a chance she could land a spot in an off-Broadway chorus line.

Dance had been Millie's first love. It was what had brought her to New York City from the small town her folks had moved to in New Jersey. Dance and dreams.

She'd kept her weight down and was still built like a dancer, long-waisted, with small breasts and muscular legs, and an elegant turn of ankle that drew male glances.

In fact, as she jogged up the concrete steps to the entrance to her building, holding level a white foam takeaway container from a deli she'd stopped at on her way home, a middle-aged man walking past gave her a lingering look and a hopeful smile.

Not till you grow some hair on your head, Millie thought—rather cruelly, she realized with some regret, as she shouldered open the door to the vestibule.

She saw no one on the way up in the elevator, or in the hall. Pausing to dig her keys out of her purse, she realized again how weary she was. Just smiling for seven hours was enough to wear a person down.

After keying the locks, she turned the tarnished brass doorknob and entered.

She'd barely had time to register that something was wrong when the man who'd been waiting for her just inside the door stepped directly in front of her. It was almost as if he'd sprung up out of the floor.

Millie gasped. The foam container of chicken wings and brown rice dropped to the carpet and made a mess.

The man was so close that his face was out of focus and she couldn't make out his features. She thought at first he was simply shirtless, but in a startled instant realized he was completely nude. She could smell his sweaty male scent. Feel his body heat. She was looking up at him at an angle that made her think he was about six feet tall.

He smiled. That frightened the already-stunned Millie to the point where her throat constricted. She could hardly breathe.

"You know me," he said.

But of course she didn't. Not really.

"I have a gift for you," he told her, and she stood in shock as he slipped something—a necklace—over her head carefully, so as not to disturb her hairdo.

She was aware of his right hand moving quickly on the lower periphery of her vision. Saw an instantaneous glint of silver. *A blade! Something peculiar about it.*

He was thrilled by the confusion in her eyes. Her brain hadn't yet caught up with what was happening.

The blade would feel cold at first, before pain overwhelmed all other feeling.

He was standing now supporting her, a length of her intestines draped in his left hand like a warm snake.

He thought that was amazing. *Incredible!* The expression on Millie Graff's face made it obvious that she, too, was amazed. Her eyes bulged with wonder. He felt the throb of his erection.

Despite the seriousness of her injury, he knew she wasn't yet dead. He lowered her gently to the floor, resting her on her back so she wouldn't bleed so much. Carefully, he propped her head against the sofa so that when he used the ammonia fumes to jolt her back to consciousness, she'd be looking down again at what he'd done to her.

She'd know it was only the beginning.

2

"Why would you invite anyone sane to see this?" Quinn asked.

But he had a pretty good idea why.

New York Police Commissioner Harley Renz wouldn't be at a bloody crime scene like this unless he considered it vitally important. Renz was standing back, well away from the mess in the tiny living room. The air was fetid with the coppery stench of blood.

The commissioner had put on even more weight in the year since Quinn had seen him. His conservative blue suit was stretched at the seams, rendering its expensive tailoring meaningless. His pink jowls ballooned over the collar of his white silk shirt. More and more, his appearance reflected exactly what he was, a corpulent and corrupt politician with the fleshy facial features of a bloodhound. He looked like a creature of rapacious appetite, and he was one.

"Look at her," he said, his red-rimmed eyes fleshy triangles of compassion. "Jesus, just look at her!"

What he was demanding wasn't easy. The woman lay on her back on the bloodstained carpet, with her legs and arms spread as if she'd given up and welcomed what was being done to her so the horror could end. Quinn knew it had taken a long time to end. It looked as if the tendons in the crooks of her arms and behind both knees had been severed so she couldn't move other than to flop around, and her abdomen had been opened with some kind of knife. Small circular burns indicated a cigarette had been touched to her flesh. Shreds of flesh dangled from her corpse in a way that suggested it had been violated with a blade and then peeled from body and bone with a pair of pliers.

Quinn figured the butchery for an amateur job, not done by anyone with special medical knowledge. The killer's primary goal was to torture. He'd burned her and stripped away skin for no purpose other than pain.

He must have done this while she was still alive.

Pink bloodstained material, what appeared to be the victim's panties, was wadded in her mouth. The elastic waistband of the panties was looped around her neck and tightly knotted at the base of her skull.

Quinn looked over at Renz.

"Nift says she was alive and what was done to her took hours," Renz said. "The stomach was done first." His voice broke slightly. Not like him.

For the first time Quinn noticed the usually loquacious and obnoxious little medical examiner, Dr. Julius Nift. He was standing alongside a wall with a uniformed cop and a plainclothes detective with his badge dangling in its leather folder from a suit coat pocket. A crime scene tech wearing a white jumpsuit and gloves was over near the door. Everyone seemed to be standing as far away as possible from Renz.

"That's why there's so much blood," Nift said. "A stomach wound like that looks horrible, but the victim doesn't necessarily die right away. Whatever her condition, he somehow managed to keep her heart pumping for quite a while. There's a slight ammonia smell around her head, too. Could be he used ammonia like smelling salts, to jolt her around whenever she lost consciousness. So she'd feel everything."

Quinn could hear a slight hissing and realized it was his own breathing. Being here with the dead woman, where there had been so much agony, was like being in a catacomb with a saint. Then he understood why he'd made the comparison. Clutched tightly in the victim's pale right hand like a rosary was a silver letter *S* on a thin chain that was wrapped around her neck. Careful not to step in any of the darkening puddles of blood, Quinn leaned forward to more closely examine the necklace.

"Kinda crap you find in a Times Square souvenir shop." Renz said.

"That's where it might have come from," Quinn said. "It says 'New York' in tiny letters on the back."

"I noticed," Renz said, probably lying.

Quinn straightened up and looked around. The living room was tastefully decorated, with wicker furniture and a large wicker mask on one wall. On the opposite wall was a framed Degas ballerina print with MoMA printed on the matting. Not expensive furnishings, but not cheap. The apartment was cramped, and the block in this neighborhood in the East Village wasn't a good one.

Quinn wondered what made this a big case for Renz. Major money didn't seem to be involved. This woman appeared to have lived well but modestly. Politics might be at play here. Maybe the victim had been somebody's secret lover. Somebody important.

No. If that were true Renz would be using it for leverage. He seemed emotionally involved here. It wouldn't be because of the goriness of the crime. He'd seen plenty of gore in his long career. He—

Nift was saying, "You wouldn't know it to look at her now . . ."

Careful, Quinn thought, knowing how Nift was prone to make salacious remarks about dead female victims.

". . . but she was kind of athletic, especially for her age," Nift finished, avoiding an explosion from Renz.

"I wanna show you something else," Renz said, ignoring Nift. He led Quinn from the bedroom and into a small bathroom.

There was a claw-footed porcelain tub there, and a wash

basin without a vanity attached to the wall. Everything was tiled either gray or blue. White towels stained red with diluted blood were jumbled on the floor and in the tub. The tub, as well as the washbasin, had red stains that looked like patterns of paint applied by a madman.

"Bastard washed up in here after he killed her," Renz said, "But more than that." He pointed at the medicine chest mirror, on which someone, presumably the killer, had scrawled in blood the name *Philip Wharkin*.

"The killer?" Quinn asked.

"Maybe. The kind of asshole who's daring us to catch him. It's happened before. They're out there."

"Don't we know it."

Quinn moved closer to the mirror and leaned in to study the crudely printed red letters. "I don't think he's one of those. He was careful. This was written with a finger dabbed in blood, and it looks like he had on rubber gloves." He backed away from the mirror. "If nothing else, this is a passion crime. Maybe the victim had a thing with Philip Wharkin and it went seriously bad."

"That's how I figure it," Renz said. "If she did, we'll sure as hell find out."

Quinn could see Renz's jaw muscles flex even through the flab. This one was important to him, all right. Maybe, for some reason, his ill-gained position as commissioner depended on it.

They left the stifling bathroom and returned to the living room. The techs were still busy, having taken advantage of the extra space created when Renz and Quinn had left. Nift was down on one knee packing his black bag, finished with the body until it was transported to the morgue.

The corpse was unaffected by any of it. Its pale blue eyes, widened in horror, gazed off at some far horizon they would all at some time see. Quinn felt a chill race up his spine. Hours ago this bloody, discarded thing on the floor had been a vital and perhaps beautiful woman.

"How old do you estimate she was?" Quinn asked Nift.

It was Renz who answered. "Twenty-three. And it's not an estimate."

"You got a positive ID?" Quinn asked.

"Yeah," Renz said.

He leaned over the corpse and lifted it slightly off the carpet, turning it so Quinn could see the victim's back.

Her shoulders and the backs of both arms were covered with old burn scars. Quinn had similar scars on his right shoulder and upper arms.

"The killer didn't do that to her back," Renz said, returning the body to its original position.

Quinn looked again at the victim's features, trying to imagine them without the distortion of horror and the scarlet stains.

He felt the blood recede from his face. Then he began to tremble. He tried but couldn't stop the tremors.

"It's Millie Graff," Renz said.

3

After the body of Millie Graff had been removed, Quinn walked with Renz through a fine summer drizzle to a diner a few blocks away that was still open despite the late hour. They were in a back-corner booth and were the only customers. The old guy who'd come out from behind the counter to bring their coffee was now at the other end of the place, near the door and the cash register. He was hunched over as if he had a bent spine, reading a newspaper through glasses with heavy black frames.

Renz looked miserable, obviously loathing his role as bearer of bad news. Quinn was surprised to find himself feeling sorry for him. Though they held a mutual respect for each other's capabilities, the two men weren't exactly friends. Renz was an unabashed bureaucratic crawler fueled by ambition and unencumbered by any sort of empathy or decency. He'd stepped on plenty of necks to get where he was, and he still wasn't satisfied. Never would be. Quinn considered Renz to be an insatiable sociopath who would say anything, do anything, or use anyone in order to get what he wanted. Renz considered Quinn to be simply unrealistic.

"I haven't seen Millie in almost fifteen years," Quinn said.

"She healed up, grew up, and became a dancer," Renz said. "Saved her money so she could leave New Jersey and live here in New York. She was gonna break into theater." He sipped his coffee and made a face as if he'd imbibed poison. "I got all this from her neighbors. She worked in the Theater District, but was waiting tables in a restaurant." He shrugged. "Show biz."

"How long's she been in the city?" Quinn asked.

"Five months."

Quinn gazed out the window and thought back to when he'd first seen Millie Graff. She'd had metal braces on her teeth and was screaming with her mouth wide open and mashed against the closed window of a burning car.

He'd simply been driving along on Tenth Avenue in his private car, off duty, when traffic had come to a stop and he'd seen smoke up ahead. Quinn had gotten out of his car and jogged toward the smoke. When he got closer to the gathering mass of onlookers he saw that a small SUV was upside down, propped at an angle with its roof against the curb. It was on fire.

The vehicle was not only on fire. Its gas tank was leaking, and the resultant growing puddle of fuel was blazing. The crowd, sensing an explosion any second, was moving well back, occasionally surging forward slightly, pulled by curiosity and repelled by danger. The woman who'd been driving the SUV was upside down with her head at an awkward angle. Quinn figured her neck was broken.

The girl pressing her face against the window and screaming was eight-year-old Millie Graff. She'd apparently gotten her safety belt unbuckled and was trying to crawl out. But the door was jammed shut and the window remained closed. He saw the frantic girl make a motion as if she was trying to open the window, and then shake her head back and forth, desperately trying to tell someone looking on that the window was jammed.

Quinn moved toward the car and felt someone grip his

shirt sleeve. A short man with brown eyes popped wide was trying to hold him back. "It's gonna blow any moment!" he yelled at Quinn. "Smell that gas! You can't go over there!"

When Quinn drew his big police special revolver from its belt holster the man released him and moved back. That was when Quinn saw the blue uniform over by a shop window. A young PO standing with his back pressed against a wall. Quinn waved for him to come over and help. The man didn't move. A New York cop, frozen by fear.

Forgetting everything else, Quinn ran to the SUV and began pounding on the window with the butt of his revolver, holding the cylinder tight so it remained on an empty chamber and wouldn't allow the gun to fire accidentally. The girl inside pressed her hand against the glass and he motioned for her to move back.

She did, and a series of blows rendered with all his strength broke the glass. It didn't shatter much, but enough so that he could grip the shards and pull them out. He removed his shirt and used it so he wouldn't cut his hands as he tried to pry the rest of the window out.

The girl caught fire. She began screaming over and over, trying to beat out the flames with her bare hands. Quinn could see the flames spreading across the back of her blouse, reaching for her hair.

The sight gave him strength he didn't know he had, and what was left of the window popped from the frame.

He reached through the window, grabbed the girl's arm, and dragged her from the vehicle. Pain made him realize he was on fire, too. Both of them were burning.

That was when Quinn glanced beyond the girl, to the other side of the car. And through his pain and fear he saw a distorted miniature face and waving tiny hands in an infant seat. A screaming child. A baby.

Aware now of more flames in the street around him, more burning gasoline, he slung the wriggling young girl over his shoulder and ran with her across the street. He gave her to reaching arms. Hands slapped at him, and someone threw a shirt over him to smother the flames.

He saw the young cop still frozen against the wall. Quinn screamed around the lump in his throat: "There's a baby in there, other side, rear, in an infant seat!"

The man didn't move, only stared straight ahead.

Quinn shoved people away and ran back toward the burning SUV, ignoring the pleas for him to stay away. He was aware of sirens. Fire trucks down the street, a block away. *Too far away.* The flames inside the car were spreading. The vehicle was filling with smoke.

He glanced back and saw the young girl he'd dragged from the wreck huddled on the sidewalk, surrounded by people. A man was bending over her, maybe a doctor.

Quinn continued running toward the burning SUV.

The explosion knocked him backward. He remembered being airborne, then the back of his head hitting solid concrete.

Then nothing was solid and he was falling.

When he regained consciousness the next day in the hospital, he was told the girl he'd pulled from the SUV had second-degree burns on her upper back and arms, but she was alive. The driver of the vehicle, a teenage sister, was dead. So was the infant in the back seat, their little brother, ten months old.

Quinn had been proclaimed a hero, and the *Times* ran a photo of him posing with the family of the dead and their one remaining child—Millicent Graff.

The young officer who'd gone into shock and been unable to help Quinn, and perhaps rescue the infant, was fired from the NYPD for dereliction of duty.

The NYPD had sort of adopted Millie Graff. Renz had

used the charming child as a political prop, but that was okay because it was obvious that he also felt genuine affection for her.

And now—

"Quinn."

Renz, across the diner booth, was talking to Quinn.

"Sorry," Quinn said. "Lost my concentration for a minute."

"Where'd you go?" Renz asked, with a sad smile.

He knew where.

Quinn felt the beginnings of another kind of flame, deep in his gut, and knew what it meant. In a way, he welcomed it.

This killer had taken away forever something precious that fifteen years ago Quinn had saved. Now he had to be found. He *would* be found. Quinn wanted it even more than Renz might imagine.

This was personal.